MICHELLE

FAVORITA

TRANSLATED BY JEN CALLEJA

faber

First published in 2026
by Faber & Faber Ltd
The Bindery, 51 Hatton Garden
London ECIN 8HN

First published in German in 2024 as *Favorita* by park x ullstein

Typeset by Faber & Faber Ltd
Printed in the UK by CPI Group (UK) Ltd, Croydon CR0 4YY

A CIP record for this book
is available from the British Library

ISBN 978–0–571–39157–8

Printed and bound in the UK on FSC® certified paper in line with our continuing
commitment to ethical business practices, sustainability and the environment.
For further information see faber.co.uk/environmental-policy

Our authorised representative in the EU for product safety is
Easy Access System Europe, Mustamäe tee 50, 10621 Tallinn, Estonia
gpsr.requests@easproject.com

2 4 6 8 10 9 7 5 3 1

For my mother.

The dead are wrong if no one defends them after their death!
—Goliarda Sapienza
tr. Anne Milano Appel

I searched everywhere for the murderer's face, convinced he was in the stones or the walls, in the bath water or the palm of a hand, in the shadows behind the nuns' altarpiece.
—Johanne Lykke Holm
tr. Saskia Vogel

PART ONE

PART ONE

I

On the wall in my grandmother's kitchen there is a mortadella-coloured rotary telephone. It rings. I lift the receiver and say nothing into it.

An Italian woman speaks. She asks for my grandmother. I rub the receiver against my forehead, it feels cool; I sense the woman becoming impatient inside it, I clear my throat and say: My grandmother doesn't live here anymore, she doesn't live at all anymore.

The voice waits just long enough to come across as polite. Then she says: I'm sorry, I don't have much time. She asks if I might be my mother's daughter. She says my mother's first name, Magdalena, and a last name I don't recognise.

She is a doctor, apparently, my mother's doctor, a liver specialist to be precise, and has allegedly treated my mother for her illness. Cirrhosis, she says, so-called shrunken liver. But that's not why she died.

I'm sorry, she says, your mother has died.

She pauses, just long enough for me to picture a liver, pan-fried with parsley, and then she says: Listen, your mother died, and they say it's because of her liver, but I can assure you that it was not her liver. I personally saw her liver only last week, that is, I did an ultrasound, and it wasn't that bad.

Listen, she says again, it would be best for you to come here. But don't believe them when they say that it was her liver. I'm sorry, your mother was murdered.

She gives me the address and telephone number of a hospital in Naples and says: She didn't want to die. I've never seen someone fight so hard for their life.

I ask for her name, but the connection is already dead.

I nod to myself at the kitchen table.

Good, I say loudly, so that's settled.

For the first time, I feel glad that my grandmother is no longer here. Her greatest fear has come true. And mine? All these years, my mother had been a possibility, a task that I put off. Now I'm finally rid of her.

I try to conjure her face, fit the pieces together. The tar-black hair, backcombed. Thick rouge, false lashes. Saucer eyes, a huge red mouth. And then her teeth: long and prominent, proper horse teeth.

I can't.

I think of the day I last saw my mother. It was a long time ago. I remember it well.

I came home from school and could smell her immediately. Paused outside the apartment door. On the landing was a gigantic plush giraffe. It was unmistakably her coming through the door: the raw voice, the coughing laugh, the banging footsteps. I considered not going in, just turning around, walking the streets until it was all over, and she was gone again.

But I pushed down the handle and there she was. Leaning in the doorway to the kitchen, a burning cigarette between her fingers, talking to my grandmother. At first glance she looked less tall and scary than I remembered.

She let out a scream when she saw me.

Shoot me dead, she shouted, is that really my Filù? I wouldn't have recognised you if I saw you in the street! Do you remember, Mamma, when she didn't have a single hair on her head? You've turned into a right little bombshell!

She turned to my grandmother, who had protested, and said: Just kidding, she's a scarecrow, don't you feed her?

She reached out, grabbed my cheeks with two sets of claws, pinching and twisting my flesh, as if she was trying to tear it off.

It had been like that as long as I could remember; her visits were always tied to this terror and pain. Stuck in this vice, I couldn't resist when her face came towards me and kissed my twisted mouth.

She cried out in horror: had I been plucking my eyebrows?

I said: Of course not, I'm just a child.

She didn't listen and said I had already plucked too heavily: Come on, let me show you how it's done!

I ducked out of the way and my grandmother, who was smoking at the open window, said irritably: Let the child come in first. You're scaring her.

Magdalena, offended, let me be. She said I should be careful in any case and only remove the hairs that really bothered me: Because eyebrows don't grow back.

She pinched my grandmother's cheek and cried out: Unfortunately, I tore out all of mine because my mother never told me.

My grandmother slapped her hand so she would let go, her cheek was red. Magdalena turned back to me.

Yours are perfect anyway, she said, tracing my brows with her index finger: You have me to thank for that. How many times did I pray to the Madonna: don't let the little one grow up short and bald like her father.

My grandmother hissed: Stop shouting like that! Frau Müller is already looking out her window.

Magdalena laughed: We've got nothing to hide, right?

She went and stood beside my grandmother and waved wildly out into the street: Frau Müller, yoohoo!

My grandmother slammed the window: Are you crazy, she's the apartment warden now!

Awful woman, Magdalena said, and my grandmother shrugged. For once they were in agreement.

Magdalena shook her head: Do you remember when she smashed the swallow's nest under the roof with a broomstick? The baby birds lying dead on the pavement. They didn't even have feathers yet.

She does that every year, I said.

Magdalena threw open the window again and shouted: Hey, sourpuss, yes, I mean you! You better make sure I don't shove you off the roof with the broom. Murderer!

She laughed, leaned far out the window, whistled: Where are you all? Frau Schneider? Doesn't anyone want to say hello to me? Ciao, Signora!

My grandmother dragged her away from the window.

Frau Schneider lived in the apartment below us, she was also Italian, also married to a Swiss man, also a widow. She would sometimes come up for a coffee, and if we bumped into her in the street we would stop and ask how things were going.

Magdalena sat down and murmured: It's not a crime to want to say hello to Frau Schneider. She was always nice to me.

Then she reached out her hand, clamped my chin between her fingers, drew my face close to hers. We scrutinised one another, right down to our pores. I smelled her perfume and the smoke on her fingers, looked at the smudged mascara in the creases of delicate skin under her eyes. Eyebrows lined blue, the cleft between them; frown lines. Capillaries over her nostrils, pearls of sweat beneath them; lipstick bleeding into the furrows and dried out. There was something unsettling about her eyes, they swam and trembled until she abruptly released me and shouted: Mamma, she's so horribly pale! Did she . . . did she *get* something?

I froze. I had actually got something that morning and had been deeply disturbed by it. I hadn't told anyone, my underwear full of bloody toilet paper and my back full of cramps. I was horrified that it might be exposed, feeling panicked at having to talk to Magdalena about it. And deeply impressed that she had seen it in me, just like that.

My grandmother said: What? Of course not, she's just a child.

I had to flee, mumbling something about having plans. Magdalena wanted to accompany me.

7

A party, she cried out, I'll come with you. Where are you youngsters going out tonight? Maybe I'll still know some folks – wait, I have to get changed, and what about you, what are you going to wear?

I answered coolly, choosing my words carefully, as if she were slow on the uptake: We're not going out. We're hanging out in the street and chatting; it won't be interesting for you.

Everything's interesting to me, she exclaimed, you're so fucking grown up, look at you, I can't believe it.

She looked as though she were about to burst into tears, and I really didn't want to see that.

I snuck out. Out on the street I heard her barking from the window, laughing after me as I ran. When I got home the giraffe was gone. All the windows were open, a draught flowed through the apartment, and my grandmother was sweeping, erasing all trace of her. She was very upset. I wasn't allowed to ask her anything about it.

Your mother is crazy, was all she would say, your mother is dangerous, I want her to leave us alone, you hear me, it's better for everyone.

We never saw her again.

*

I expected her to return, just like I'd returned. Every evening when I got back from the hospice where my grandmother was lying like a naked baby bird, I anticipated finding her in the kitchen. I opened the three locks in the apartment door with my heart hammering, braced for her finger-pliers. I feared this meeting and prayed for a miracle. My grandmother didn't want Magdalena informed; absolutely no one should know about her condition. When she could still speak, I caught her cheerfully lying down the telephone to Frau Schneider that she would be home soon and a visit wouldn't be necessary, and anyway, I was here.

So how was Magdalena supposed to know, wherever she was? She didn't come to the funeral either. A neighbour hugged me and said, as if consolingly: She never belonged to us.

When my grandmother died, trying to contact Magdalena suddenly felt like the natural thing to do. She was the only family I had left, after all. I'd always found my grandmother's fear excessive. It seemed to come from the same source as her fear of hell and the evil eye – I didn't believe in it. Magdalena was crazy, but dangerous? We kept our worlds separate; I moved confidently and independently around mine. It was unimaginable that Magdalena and her frequently invoked underworld could in any way harm me.

My grandmother would absolutely have been against it; she repeated as long as she was able: You'll soon go back to your own, wonderful life.

I didn't disagree with her and kept it a secret that I had given up my room in the city immediately after I'd got news of her diagnosis. While she forbade me over the telephone from worrying and told me not to make a fuss, I was already packing my things. Looking back, it seems as if I'd been waiting for it, for a trigger, a justification, in order to mess everything up. Nothing was keeping me in this city. I'd done it all for her. The wonderful life that she'd wished for me – I didn't tell her that I'd terminated it, painlessly handed in my notice like I did at all the underpaid jobs she'd imagined to be dream careers. I could have spent a long time explaining to her that times have changed: that interns receive neither pay nor praise, that uni pays you with credits, and I earned my rent working night shifts at bars. She didn't want to hear that studying wasn't enough to secure a career and a bag full of money these days.

My granddaughter, she beamed, the first in the family to go to university!

I wasn't allowed to complain.

She was glad when I had to move to the city for university after I'd finished school. My guilty conscience at leaving her alone was brushed away with a wave of her hand. I think that my studying proved to her that she had successfully shielded me from Magdalena's influence. For my part, in the city I felt relief that Magdalena didn't know my address. And yet I was dogged by a constant unease that she might suddenly appear at the most inopportune moment to expose me. That she might descend upon my precarious pretence of a life and rampage through it like a thunderstorm.

When I was growing up, I had studied myself in the mirror,

obsessively searching for her features. What did I get from her? Braces saved me from her teeth, my grandmother had spent a fortune on them. I monitored my gestures, my voice, my actions, my body, my thoughts. Would I go mad like she did? At the tiniest suspicion of a similarity, I trained it out of myself. I would shape myself, like the braces had formed my teeth, so I wouldn't take after her. But time passed, and Magdalena slipped away from me the more I tried to remember her. How could I compare myself to her if I no longer had any idea what she was like?

The images faded until she was only pithy anecdotes. Magdalena became a phantom, the cheek-wrenching bogeyman of my childhood. And every supposed memory summoned forth made her weaker, more counterfeit, more make-believe. The border between true and false memories, those that were mine and those of my grandmother, between photos and stories, became permeable. It was soothing, thoughts of her became easier. She no longer had this oppressive presence, this hazy sensation of fear and pain and shame. She remained stuck in time, like someone who'd died, while we moved onwards and made and remade her according to our own tastes.

After my grandmother's death, I planned to look for Magdalena, but it never came to pass. How could it? She had disappeared. In reality, she might have been long dead, who knew. I didn't bother trying to find her. Yet the possibility of the search remained a pain in my neck, I put it off, I'll do it later, maybe.

Well, now I've been released.

What had the woman on the telephone said? It's best if you come here. She was murdered.

I put on a pot of coffee. Slide empty bottles out from under the kitchen table, shake them, put them back. Dig in the kitchen cupboards: amaretto or advocaat. I clamp the receiver under my chin and dial the number. It really is an Italian hospital. I ask after my mother, Magdalena, and her unfamiliar surname. A voice says: One *attimino* please, I'll have a look.

I hear the tapping of a keyboard. Then the voice draws in a breath, clears its throat, and says: Signora Unfamiliarname passed away last night here at the hospital.

How? I ask.

It says here that she succumbed after a long illness, cirrhosis. One moment—

I hear other, animated voices in the background.

Then the voice comes back on the line: Excuse me, who is it that wants to know?

Her daughter.

The voice cries out: Daughter! Really? Madonna.

And hangs up.

The coffee boils over. I remain seated, watching. If my grandmother was here, she would now be shouting: Ma! Ma! Magdalena!

That's how we'd kept her memory alive, in our own way. A joke. In impossible situations, we invoked her like a saint. If one of us was being especially forgetful or scatterbrained, the other would pretend she was being just as deranged, just as crazy as my mother, and would ask while laughing: Yes, Magdalena?

*

Ever since I was a child, my grandmother had forbidden me to go into her bedroom alone. I kept my word, even after her death. It ought to remain forever as she had left it. While she was still dying, I had promised myself I'd do things differently: she would not be forgotten, not one bit. The memory of her had to remain freshly preserved: I wouldn't touch the room, or let any air into it, it must stay tightly sealed. But when I came home from the hospital the day she died, an awful hex had already been set: the apartment suddenly seemed decayed, messy, fusty. My grandmother died and everything that she'd owned lost its lustre. On her body her clothes had radiated elegance; now it became clear to me, the glow had come from her. She brightened every room with her presence; even a serving fork appeared graceful in her deft hands.

So, after my childhood home had transformed into a collection of rubbish, I went to her wardrobe. I rummaged desperately through her things in the hope of finding a spark, some evidence of her. Yet in the forbidden drawers it smelled of mothballs. Her billowing silk scarves were made of polyester, the gold of her clip-on earrings was plastic, chipped. Overcome by guilt, I closed her chest of drawers, and behind me, her bedroom door.

I'm now opening it for the first time since that day.

The bureau has a strong scent. Maybe it's polish, glue, stamps or old paper. On the shelf there is a lonely bottle of nail varnish. Jungle Green. It was expensive, my last birthday present to her. I'd sent it in the post with a guilty conscience and with the promise of visiting no later than Christmas. Now I'm turning the cap and slowly painting my nails. I have to wait for them to dry. Then I fold down the desk.

I find children's drawings, postcards, a wish list (*Dear Nonna, for Christmas I would like: money*) and several boxes of matches. She'd collected them, pocketed them during her coach trips for retirees, free souvenirs. I turn them one by one between my fingers; this is what remains of a life. Empty matchboxes advertising a beer garden.

Only then do I pull out the shoebox of photos.

Fingerprints, bygone faces.

A rainy autumn day at the port of an Italian coastal town. A woman propels a pushchair over wet cobbles. She poses: stands on tiptoes, pushes out her chest, draws up her eyebrows. My young grandmother, Lavinia. Two boys on mopeds yell out to her. She always holds her chin up high, she is a *lady*. Her fingers are swollen and chapped from working, but she's proud. She's wearing a pink suit, a fluttering foulard, clip-on earrings, open sandals, just to run an errand to the bakery. Mesmerising bunion.

A different picture, maybe taken the same day, on the beach.

Foamy sea, dark-damp sand, bent leg in nylon stockings. Magdalena had taken off her shoes, here too: a jaunty orb below her big toe. She sits in her stockings in the sand, next to her squats a curious toddler. She's writing my name in the sand. FILA. Short for Filippa, after my father. My grandmother wouldn't hear a single word about him; she gave me the name of her day off: Domenica, MIMMA for short.

The third photo has fascinated me for as long as I can remember: a black and white portrait of a child. The child's wearing a pinafore, its short dark hair is slicked down on its head, piercing look to the camera. *Maddalena's first day at school* is on the reverse, in Italian, in my grandmother's curly handwriting. The child looks very serious. This was when she had newly arrived in Switzerland; this was before her name changed, became Swissified. When she looked at this picture, my grandmother always said, she didn't have an easy life, your mother.

She was an illegitimate child, this was *the shame*, as my grandmother referred to it. Her father, my grandfather, a Swiss man on holiday in Italy. After he'd returned home, my grandmother found out that she was pregnant. They wrote letters to one another; he promised: *Wait, I'll come for you.*

After six years she was sick of waiting, she packed her bag and the child and travelled to him.

There's only one photo of him in the box. Prickled with sepia, taken from behind, he's standing on the bank and fishing. He was a drinker, choleric – Magdalena got that from him, my grandmother said.

I have my sticking-out ears from him.

He died shortly before my birth, shrunken liver.

That's actually all I know about him. I also don't know my father, apart from the way my grandmother said his name: *Filippo*. As if her tongue was rotting off. With her voice lowered, as if he could hear her.

She reproached herself for having neglected Magdalena; that she had turned out the way she did because there was something missing when she was a child. She blamed herself for having forced Magdalena out of the house and into Filippo's arms.

I set her aside far too much – those were her words.

And she told me: In Italy I always carried Maddalena when we had to walk a long way. Here I had other worries. A new place, a foreign language. We had to eat. Suddenly it wasn't just the two of us, there were all my in-laws to look after. I took care of everything and everyone.

She shook her head: Holy piggy bank, that man never had any money! Don't ask how much money he had, ask how many debts! I wasn't used to that – I'd always earned very little, but I'd never had debts, I saved. On payday I waited all night at the window, in the morning he'd come home, blotto, having polished off all his wages! I started taking in work at home. He would swear, throw the basket of freshly ironed laundry down the stairs: *My wife doesn't work!*

Sometimes I had to pick him up from the pub because he

couldn't walk anymore, I felt so ashamed.

Yes, she said pensively, when she looked at Maddalena's photo, I definitely set her aside far too often.

Magdalena is dead, I say it out loud.

Why doesn't it affect me more?

I examine my feet. Stare at the photo on the beach until it dissolves. Try to put myself in the shoes of these figures, in this moment. That was me, why can't I remember?

I would like to feel something. I stroke the photo of Magdalena as a young woman, my mother. Nothing. Nothing happens. No overwhelm, no wash of emotions. I'm mildly moved, like a stick floating in a well.

*

I'm woken by the telephone ringing.

A man is on the line, from the hospital, slimy voice: Signorina.

He calls me by the unfamiliar surname. I say: That's not my name.

He remains as nice as pie: Of course, Signorina, I do beg your pardon. You must know that we cared deeply for your mother, she was known to us here. Her death is a terrible misfortune. Unfortunately she was a heavy drinker, and that is what took her to her grave, well, practically: she's in the cold storage, with a ruined liver, shrunken liver, so-called—

I interrupt him: I'm leaving immediately. I'm coming to say goodbye to my mother.

II

The train clatters over the rails. In the hazy windows, the sun sets over the outskirts of Milan. Washing flaps tantalisingly from balconies, practically offering itself up to the filth and particles of piss jumping from our train like fleas. Milano always makes me feel so sentimental.

The first stop on every trip to Italy: a disturbing sense of return. *As if I were coming home.* All it takes is the train announcements, the names of the towns – throbbing heart and hot eyes. Touched to the most embarrassing degree.

My grandmother didn't want to hear about it: Roots, roots, there are no roots!

She had severed herself from them and let them wither at a secret location, where I would never find them.

Every year we travelled to Italy, but never to where she was from, where Maddalena was born.

I don't want to, was all she would say, there's nothing there, I don't like it anymore.

She claimed that there would be no one to visit, no friends, no relatives. Her older brother emigrated to the US while she was pregnant with Maddalena – on account of the shame, she would say. Her own mother had died when she was still young, while giving birth to a brother who lived for a few days and then died as well. It had been her dying wish that Lavinia would grow up in the city with her grandmother, while her older brother stayed with their father in the country. My grandmother told me that he had to walk miles to work, barefoot, sometimes through snow.

I liked that she grew up with her grandmother, just like I did. When I asked what her nonna was like, she would only say: She was a bigot, always with the priest. And on the night before La Befana, she put lumps of coal in my stocking.

Bigots, she said, are women who pack parcels for poor people while gossiping about them.

But Nonna sent her to school, in shoes. And when Lavinia brought the shame upon her, she remained living with her, and when the shame arrived, the grandmother looked after the child while Lavinia went to work.

If Nonna hadn't been there, she said, I wouldn't have known what to do.

I was gasping for these stories, these sad fairy tales about separated siblings, half-orphans; bigots and broomstick-riding witches. The images of poverty seemed ghoulishly romantic: cave-like rooms with smouldering coal fires; walking shoeless through the mountains. And best of all: this was my family story, it was about me; it told me something about myself.

It became even more exciting whenever Magdalena was around: she would contradict everything.

Nonsense, she would shout, when my grandmother talked about her mother: She didn't die in childbirth – she fell while collecting water! She was heavily pregnant and had to carry heavy buckets, she broke her neck. I'm sure of it, Uncle told me.

This uncle, my grandmother's brother, hadn't, according to Magdalena, moved away because of the shame, but on account of the poverty.

He crossed the ocean with an empty suitcase, she explained with her wine glass raised, and he said to himself: When I arrive, I want a car and a wife and a plate of spaghetti. And he got it all, didn't he? He's now a rich man, your brother. Anyway, when he came to visit he followed me into the shower. I was thirteen, and I screamed and made a scene, so he wouldn't dare look at me ever again. Are you listening, Fila, that's how you do it!

My grandmother acted as if she hadn't heard and just nodded absent-mindedly. She didn't take Magdalena's stories seriously: Alcohol makes you confused, she used to say, with alcoholics you never know what's real and what's not.

My grandmother didn't want to talk about Italy; she gave me Dante and Boccaccio in German translation.

The culture's interesting, she would say, the art, the food, nothing else.

She never said: We're going home.

We went on holiday. For a week, that was enough for her. In places accustomed to tourism. *Turisti di merda. Shitty tourists.*

We went in autumn, that's what we could afford. Sat on a deserted beach, squinting and imagining what it looked like in summer. I played in the empty changing rooms, stroked the horses on the stationary carousel. My grandmother couldn't swim, we walked in the foam at the edge, no more than ankle-deep.

Just like my roots. Shallow, washed up.

Whenever I would say that I'd like to see the place where she grew up, the house where she received coal for La Befana, she brushed it away with a wave of her hand. Before didn't interest her. That's what it was like before, and it can't be changed today.

So, what was it like? I cried out.

You can't imagine. Before, the world was different, different to how it is today, completely.

But how?

And her, exasperated: Everything was good, everyone was happy.

Why did you go to Switzerland then?

Come, not go! To get married. Because your grandfather was Swiss, that's why. That was the whole reason. What more can I say?

She held the Before far away from me like an infectious disease, as if the story alone would rub off on me, taint me.

She would only say: There's nothing to tell, it's boring. Like you when you keep asking me questions like this, don't you have anything else to talk about?

They were the opposite of boring, these terrible stories. And I wanted to hear them, again and again, in all their detail: Will you finally tell me about the shame, isn't that why you left?

Occasionally, she would give in and begin to tell me:

It was because of the name. We had to get married to have a name. I had a name, but it wasn't valid, only the father's name was valid. We weren't married, meaning my daughter wasn't his daughter. That's why she was an NN. *Non nominato*, born out of wedlock. There were a lot of NN children back then. They'd even write it on the report card: NN. *The shame*; it marked you for life. Without a name you were no one. And Magdalena was already big, she would be starting school soon. So we came for the marriage. And Magdalena got her report card with a name, and I signed it. But her teacher sent it back. He needed the father's signature. He said mine wasn't valid. Imagine!

And what was he like, my grandfather?

Good.

But Magdalena said—

He had an illness. When he drank, he wasn't himself.

Like her?

Yes.

And my father?

He doesn't exist.

I knew from Magdalena that my father had saved her from her father. Seventeen, black hair, she climbed into a yellow convertible and let herself be kidnapped by Filippo. My grandfather pulled over the bookshelves in anger. Magdalena didn't care anymore – she drove to the toe of the boot, where she learned the dialect and became a servant to Filippo's family.

My grandmother looked at me in astonishment: That's what she told you?

I nodded, she made a face: Magdalena married Filippo out of spite. Because her father didn't want her to shack up with an Italian. She took his name to be rid of her father's. She was crazy. But she also didn't stand a chance. From her sick father to this *primitive* man. And his relatives, strict Catholics, bigots . . . She didn't stand a chance.

I nodded again as if I understood it all: I'll never get married, Nonna.

It's all right, she smiled, we'll see. I didn't want to either. When I saw what kind of sickness your grandfather had. But being a single mother didn't make a family back then. And the neighbours said: Cohabiting isn't permitted. And I, a foreigner – the immigration police could have picked me up if someone made a complaint. I didn't want to go back to my grandmother. So we got married, chop-chop. Like every woman, I hoped it would get better, but it got worse and worse.

I hung on to every word, until she thought better of it and broke off the story: And I stayed, and now I'm here. Now we're done, it's over. Let's eat.

And when I protested, she would turn her back on me and wildly stir the bubbling sugo: That's enough, I don't want to burden you.

23

Ah, that's exactly what I wanted: to be burdened! It felt as if I might fly away at any moment, dissolve, as if my fragmentary, weightless existence wasn't real.

I tried to make her understand that without knowledge of my past I couldn't develop, that I needed to be rooted in the world in order to grow.

She would get angry. I was only being nosey and didn't need anything, I had no idea what was good for me, her past was at any rate not mine, and that of my mother definitely not, would I kindly focus on my own life, etc.

I felt ashamed. She was right: I wasn't there, it was nothing to do with me. I ought to in fact be glad of this and respect her decision: she had snipped her connection to her past. The only witnesses to the sealing of the wound were the bunions and the burned-down matches – my inheritance. And yet I sensed that there was more.

It still seems to me as if this past, their pasts, had somehow passed into me, as if they had rubbed off on me.

*

To me, every Italian trip is a quest and a time machine. Eras and towns blend together; clues, traces, memories, I see them everywhere. Because the true location is missing, all Italian locations become sacred excavation sites of my family history – and everyone turns into a potential relative.

I get off the train in Milano, take in the scene on the platform. Women say goodbye in front of the beeping train doors, others look around searchingly; some walk unaffected to the exit. The guard blows his whistle, a woman in high heels hastily approaches, he waves her through. I stand alone and watch them. Hairstyles, faces, gestures, gaits: Lavinia and Magdalena. When I close my eyes, I hear them: those are their voices. They could be their sisters, their aunts, cousins – or mine! I want to follow these women like a stray dog; my nose twitches after the smells from my childhood they leave wafting in their wake on the platform: bleach and ladyfingers.

This is why my ridiculous heart is attached to fascist train stations. Smitten, I wander through the halls and feel so deliriously in kinship with every barista. He transforms my lofty feelings into an invitation for lasciviousness – and, moved by every acknowledgement of my Italian existence, I convert it into a feeling of belonging. I sit in front of him at the bar until my connecting train arrives. He jokes around, I laugh. Glad to have deceived him, with my looks, my remarks, my demeanour. I dazzle myself, do not recognise myself: as soon as I speak Italian, my body is transformed, my voice is higher, my laugh silky, my arms fly around – who am I?

I adapt like a chameleon. On the surface.

I counterfeited the language for myself. Lavinia and Magdalena spoke Italian, but seldom with one another and not with me.

When I was small, my grandmother sang me songs from her childhood, prayers and ring-a-ring-o' roses. I rode on her knee to songs about evil men who slip into houses and steal children – that was the moment when she would part her knees and I would fall laughing into the gap.

On holiday we watched Italian television and she translated Donald Duck, who's called Paperino here. He splashed frantically in water, quacking my first Italian word: *Aiuto*.

Help, said my grandmother, the most important word. If you're in danger, scream it as loud as you can, understand?

I laughed and shouted aiuto, aiuto, like the spluttering, drowning Paperino in the well.

My grandmother spoke Italian with Frau Schneider when she came over to smoke secretly. I eavesdropped on their sounds and insisted I could understand everything: she needed a break from her husband, that much was clear.

One time, Frau Schneider's brother came to visit from Italy. He poked my grandmother in the side and laughed: What's up? Have you forgotten where you come from? Why aren't you speaking in dialect?

She waved it away, but didn't say much after that day.

When I was older and asked her to speak Italian with me, she stopped after two sentences: I can't do it anymore, she said, I've forgotten it all.

She hadn't wanted to be a chameleon. She had her own unruly

German, with a strong accent and resolutely Italian syntax. She found Swiss German abhorrent, in moments of meanness she teased me for it. She mimicked me, laughing: The way you speak, what an ugly language.

On arrival in Switzerland she had sworn to herself: I'll never speak like the people here, never in my whole life.

She very much enjoyed performing this story: how on her first morning in Switzerland she heard her neighbours hanging laundry in the yard. – I thought to myself, I can't be hearing right! My goodness. It horrified me! Is that them talking? Krkrkrkkk.

She gripped her throat: It hurt me here, and here! It was dreadful. And then there was the silence. The whole village was so quiet. No children, no cars, even a moped was rare. Let me tell you, when you come from a town in the south – I thought, I'm going to die here. I can't carry on living here. The first thing I thought was: go.

But she stayed. And because her husband prided himself on being against so-called foreign infiltration, and therefore forbade Italian within *his four walls*, this is how Lavinia invented her own language. This is how she spoke to Magdalena too. Until arguments broke out in any case, then Magdalena would explode into incomprehensible cursing, and Lavinia would hiss in Italian: You don't speak like that here, not inside *my four walls*. Aren't you ashamed of that vulgar dialect?

And Magdalena would scream: You're worse than Pappi!

My grandmother asserted that she had already cleanly cast off her dialect when she was still a young girl. She took great pride in that. Magdalena having mastered various southern Italian dialects over time through her men – swearing, at least – provoked her. Sometimes I think that Magdalena married men exclusively for this purpose.

I want nothing more than a dialect, the grubbier the better. Instead, I have superficial, school Italian over which I place Lavinia's melody. This is how I cheat my way through fleeting exchanges. Most people can't place the sound, but they swallow it. It's only when the conversation becomes more complex, when I try to tell the barista about my origins, that I swerve off course. Withered brain roots end in nothing – I'm unmasked: *turista di merda*.

Luckily my train's being called, a couchette heading south. I stumble towards the exit, wave to the barista, whisper inaudibly: Ciao, cousin.

*

In the couchette, appearances are still deceiving. We're sitting stiffly on the small bunk beds, trying not to touch one another. There are five of us, the round of introductions has taken place: two crooks travelling to a horse race; a teacher nearing retirement; a sailor on shore leave. I mutter something about visiting family. Why not?

The sailor resembles Roberto Benigni in *Coffee and Cigarettes*,

28

and behaves like him too. He can't sit still for even thirty seconds. He drums his knees with his fingers, finally jumps up, staggers into the corridor, smokes hastily, falls back into the compartment, the cigarette butt stuck to his shoe. He rummages in his bag, pulls out a packet of tissues, manages in his nervousness to pull them all out in one go, making them fly around the room. His head jerks like a pigeon, he jolts out of the gap in the door, keeps watch for the conductor, calls for him in a low voice: Ò, Signore, ò!

We need sheets, he repeats as if his life depended on it, sheets.

It's still early, though. The criminals are playing cards on their bunk, laying them down in the free spot between them. I'm sharing my bunk with the teacher and the wriggly sailor. He bends over, kicks the old lady's bag on the floor, awkwardly sets it back up, frantically grabs the rolling paraphernalia from the sticky floor: throat sweets, wet wipes, toothpaste, a rosary.

That's all we need, I think, a bigot.

The bigot puts the bag on her lap and folds her hands over it. The sailor contorts his torso once again towards the opposite seat, interested in the game the others are playing. He puffs so heavily that the cards flutter upwards.

Ò! the grifters shout angrily.

Thankfully, the conductor arrives with the bedding. The sailor takes the pile and insists on making all our beds. He shakes the pillows and blankets out of their plastic packaging onto his seat and pulls down – without asking – the topmost bed. He rubs at his brow, the bed hit him while hurtling downwards. Then he throws all the bedding in the air, a pillow falls onto the floor. The teacher and the criminals draw threatening breaths.

I quickly say: I'll have that one. No problem.

I won't need it anyway, seeing as I'll sleep with my head on my bag. They can bet the teacher's money at the races; mine, however, they won't be having. My grandmother drummed that into me from an early age: never trust strangers.

*

Whenever I ride the night train, I think of Magdalena, our last trip together. At that point, she was already holding herself at arm's length from our life. That is, until she would appear again out of nowhere and act like nothing had happened.

It was the start of the autumn holidays, the train was still in the station; we were stowing our luggage in the compartment when she appeared outside our window. My grandmother reflexively closed the curtains. I held my breath. We could hear Magdalena screeching at the conductor: Stop! Ow, you shut the fucking door in my face, I'll wring your damned neck. Stop! I'm warning you, you better wait or— Thank you, Signore, thank you so much, and my suitcase? Very gracious of you, very kind, what's your name, sweetheart?

There was already a knocking on the compartment door. My grandmother raised her chin and put her face in order.

Next to the conductor stood Magdalena, wearing sunglasses

and a headscarf in spite of it being a night train.

She belong to you?

Magdalena didn't wait for an answer, she tottered into the compartment, fell down into the seat next to me, pressed my head into her lap, and tightly pinched my cheek.

Surprise!

She smelled of smoke, of being unwashed.

I'm coming too, she said, tugging on my cheek flesh, well, what do you think of that?

The conductor squirmed: She doesn't have a ticket.

My grandmother paid the conductor and asked him for an extra sheet. He nodded, backing out of the compartment, carefully closing the doors.

My grandmother slid the bolt and rounded on Magdalena, speaking in a low voice: What's that all about, have you converted? Take that headscarf off this instant.

Magdalena did what she was asked with a shrug of her shoulders. Out from under the sunglasses and the fabric, bruises appeared. My grandmother closed her eyes. Then she gripped Magdalena by the wrist: How did you find us?

Frau Schneider told me—

Does *he* know where you are?

She shook her head, rummaged around in her handbag, lit a cigarette.

I touched her chin with my fingers and asked: Does it hurt?

She exhaled the smoke, half coughing. I feel a whole lot better seeing you.

31

The weather was bad on that trip, it rained, we sat in the apartment and froze. Even though Magdalena was constantly complaining and claiming that she was about to pack up her stuff and take off, I hoped she would stay. For the first few days we held our breath as we observed her, moving and speaking only with extreme caution, but nothing happened. She didn't explode. It seemed like she was making an effort, or rather, she seemed cheerful. I started to relax. While Lavinia cooked, we watched television, Magdalena on the sofa, me on the carpet, she tapped her toes against my back.

Remember, Magdalena said, when we all lived together?

My grandmother pretended she hadn't heard. I watched the television and wiggled my head as if by coincidence.

My grandmother swore a broken curse; her superstition prevented her from swearing properly. She had forgotten to buy parsley.

Mimma, can you go get some?

Magdalena pulled me up: We'll go together.

It had stopped raining, there was a market in the village. I enjoyed walking with her, alone. Magdalena spoke with the market sellers as if they knew her, she chatted and laughed with them. They wanted to know if I was her daughter, and she said: Of course, look at her!

I reminded her about the parsley, and she called out: E già! Prezzemolo!

She had shouted so loudly that people turned their heads to look at us. Magdalena flashed her teeth: Funny word, isn't it? Prezzemolo.

Then she pointed at a boy my age who was walking past, pulled my hand up in the air, waved it wildly and shouted: Ciao, Prezzemolo!

I shut my eyes, horrified; she laughed until she could only cough.

On the way home, she said: That was fun, now I need a coffee. You coming?

In the bar, there were only men. One of them stroked my hair and bought me a Coke, I liked him. Magdalena pinched my cheek, laughing: She's already becoming my competition!

My face grew hot. I smiled into the void, while she flirted with him, they were getting on well. When I'd finished my Coke and the ice had melted, I picked up the shopping and stood up. Magdalena stayed seated and shuffled closer to him. He gave her a little plastic bag, while stroking her fingers.

Go on ahead, Magdalena said to me, I'll be right there.

What's that, I asked, and she laughed: Prezzemolo.

That night, I woke up because Magdalena was shrieking. She was squirming in the bed. My grandmother grabbed me: What's happened? What did you do?

I tore myself free and hid in the wardrobe. Pressed my head between my knees so I didn't have to hear them screaming, one senseless with pain, the other full of anger and fear. At some point the paramedics came, heaving Magdalena onto a stretcher. My grandmother apologised for her daughter, who was struggling and spitting, grabbing at the medics, pulling their hair.

They wanted to know what she'd taken. Lavinia threw open the wardrobe, shook me, I'd never seen her like that before.

I don't know, I wasn't there!

I ran out of the house and to the sea. It was raining, the wind slapped my hair in my face, I prayed to the Madonna: Don't let her die, not yet.

The next day we picked her up from the hospital. She was jolly and sprucing herself up; that evening she went out with one of the paramedics.

She didn't come back, not even the day we were leaving; we went home without her.

*

The bigot rolls over beside me, we have the topmost bunk. The other beds are empty. The crooks are traversing the train, and the sailor is standing in the corridor smoking. Oppressive heat in the compartment, we've been at a standstill here for a while. A fly buzzes against the windowpane. I'm infinitely tired.

As a child, I was often trapped in a tortuous game of make-believe while half asleep: the three of us are standing on a cliff, my grandmother, my mother and me. I have to push one of them, I have to choose. If I refuse or sacrifice myself, all three of us will be shoved to our death.

At least I don't have to decide anymore. Not that it had ever been difficult.

I roll over on my bunk towards the window and stick my finger through the open gap like a prisoner. There are voices, men's laughter, another stopped train. It sighs deeply.

I close my eyes – the feeling of falling. My eyelids jump back open, like on a dumb doll. Since childhood I've been pursued by a recurring dream: I'm falling down a well shaft, and when I hit the bottom, I awake with a start.

The fly becomes louder, pesky, the train hasn't moved. I grip my throat, feel my heartbeat. Unsettling sound. That can't be the fly. I burst out laughing when I realise: it's the bigot. She's snoring, no, she's roaring; a miracle that she doesn't wake herself up.

Roll over, I whisper, roll over onto your side.

It doesn't occur to her, she becomes ever more wild, whistles and gurgles. Her face is in shadow, I can only see her stomach inflating and falling, swollen fingers linked over it. There's nothing human left; the teacher has become a huge white maggot that is transforming beside me, noisily undergoing its repulsive metamorphosis into a carrion-eating moth—

Finally, her breathing stops, several beats of silence. I hold my breath with her until she grunts. I stare at her, full of revulsion. If only she would just stop breathing altogether.

I'm too well brought up to hurl a pillow at her head, and I fear that she'd just carry on snoring. Someone would have to shake her, but I can't even bring myself to clear my throat. Bloody manners! I'd smother her with her own pillow if I wasn't so fucking nice.

The train gives a slight jolt and slowly starts moving again. The snoring takes on the rhythm of the juddering train. Through the wall I hear children whining in the compartment next to ours, and the sound of a mother calmly *ssssh*ushing.

I feel for the bag underneath my head and pull something out of it. An envelope addressed to me. Inside it is a Polaroid photo. Magdalena is wearing a white cowboy hat. She's become older. Each of her arms around a guy, she smiles into the camera. A bar in the background. According to the date on the bottom edge, the picture was taken less than a year ago.

Fila, Filissima,

Your letter! Wonderful, as the Americans would say. Today I want to tell you something that you'll find interesting. On the day you were born, my bedroom was where your bedroom is now. Back then I slept with my head against the doors, and I screamed so much the neighbours called the police. Imagine! Mami was the first to hold you. She still had real black hair back then.

I was born in Italy! With plenty of marsala between contractions. You see, that was our Mami! Unfortunately I've got the same miserable character as she has. Seven husbands can confirm. I'm divorcing the last one, but he doesn't want to. I say: sur le prochain!

That you haven't informed me of the status of my Mami did hurt. She said herself during our very last phone call literally: Just stay in Napoli. It wasn't that she didn't love me anymore. She didn't want me to see her like that.

Love-love-love. Pride-pride-pride.

Well, her and Pappi dictated these words.

Pappi was a philanthropist and a humanist!

Mami was grumbling after her death until I went to her grave.

She always had the thickest skull – la coccia dura!

Juchallah we reconcile ourselves to these circumstances! I'm fine with it. Juchallah!

PS: Mami became an angel! She brushed past me once in flight. I could really feel her feathers. Che requiem sunt in pace. Amen.

The letter was lying in the mailbox at my grandmother's a few weeks ago. Unfranked, unstamped, without a sender. As if she had come by sometime and secretly put it in there. Did she want to prove that she really had been at the grave? I didn't believe a word of it. So she must have sent somebody. I started to check the locks; my grandmother had three. *Never trust strangers.*

I immediately hid the letter. She was crazy, what she had written was crazy. I'd never sent her a letter – how could I, without an address? I didn't even know her last name. She was always changing it, she went deeper underground with each new man.

And the way she talked about being in contact with my grandmother! She had repeated on her deathbed that she didn't know where Magdalena was and that I shouldn't look for her. She didn't want her to come to the funeral.

Miserable character!

37

Her senseless words made me angry. Lie-lie-lie. I didn't want anything to do with her jumbled stories, her false aspersions. Now I read them over and over, her last words to me, and try to straighten them out, interpret them, understand them. The more I consider them, the more disturbing they become.

Philanthropist and humanist!

When her father died of his shrunken liver, Magdalena returned. She left my father Filippo and his family on the tip of the boot and, with me in her belly, followed the same route Lavinia had taken with her. Only she was coming from, not to, a marriage. Lavinia took her in, for a while the three of us lived together; I was too young to remember. My grandmother said that it was the apartment that had become too small. Magdalena lived with boyfriends, who she would sometimes marry, take their names, disappear. And when that fell apart, she would come back for a brief stint, and the walls would move in closer until plates flew against them.

Love-love-love. Pride-pride-pride.

I stare at the photo until my vision blurs. What can't I see? It's there in the darkness. It was there. It's still there.

*

The maggot keeps snoring. I sit up, climb down the ladder,

wrench open the compartment door: Wake up and breathe, will you, while you still can.

I bum a cigarette off the pacing sailor, swan off through the train. Ghosts climb out the tip of the cig, dance around whispering to me, are reflected in the panes of glass: it's me. Outside is a roaring black, within me a storm; I throw open a window, stick my head out so a power mast will knock my head off. A man pulls me back, I scream at him, totter to the toilet and throw up onto the tracks.

I pull down my trousers, stuff them with toilet paper, regard my bloody fingers, wipe them down my trousers, let them think what they want. I sink to my knees, lay my head against the shaking wall. This is how I fall into the well shaft, look up and see the light and fall, I'm sitting in the bucket, the chain rattles until I hit the bottom.

I pull myself up on the washbasin, the wet cigarette inside it. The mirror is almost blind from dirt, doodles, death masks. Lavinia. Magdalena.

They both had short eyelashes, as if cut with scissors, and deep, dark eye sockets. If they were tired, their eyelids drooped, that's what happens to me too.

Fila. Mimma. I hear their voices, one in each ear.

What does that even mean, a miserable character?

I rub the crumbly soap between my fingers and try to rinse them under the meagre trickle of water. Catch myself in the mirror, smile at myself.

On shaky legs I sway back, falling into the walls, against windows, the ghosts. I climb up to my bed, the bigot has rolled onto her side, is a human again, not a monster, wheezes deeply.

Outside, the sun is coming up.

III

The city in the south is acting all innocent, but the early morning heat is a foretaste of its true colours.

I cross the station plaza and sit in front of a bar. On the table there are some remains, a carefully ashed column. The waiter comes, wipes it away with the palm of his hand: Are you alone?

I nod.

Shame, he says with a suggestive grin that he holds steadily until I surrender a tired laugh. His tone immediately becomes curt. Then you'll have to order more if you want to keep sitting here.

Even if I get really drunk?

He once again wipes the table impatiently. I sigh: But it's too early, you know, I have to be strict with myself. When I'm not doing well and I want to keep drinking right from the moment I wake up, when the thought of a hefty gulp is the only thing that can get me out of bed, then I must deny myself. It runs in the family, drinking, it's in my genes, I cannot allow myself to. My mother bit the dust because of drink, just like her father before her. I have to be careful that I don't fall into the bottle and crack open my head, you understand.

The waiter aggressively bats his eyelashes.

I order three coffees, line them up in front of me and look

at them. Faces form in the foam, shrieking spirits, witches. I drink them all quickly. The tiredness, a pressure on my eyeballs, begins to flicker.

Fila, a whisper in one ear. Mimma, in the other.

What do you want from me? What am I doing here? I'm not seeking an answer; the answer is clear, the answer has happened. Magdalena's death is the answer to her life. What was the question again?

They laugh, ringing and banging. Soon they start screaming.

It's inevitable: Magdalena and Lavinia are like chemicals that explode when they come into contact with one another. Magdalena is poisonous, dangerous of her own accord, mercury fulminate. Lavinia is the flamelet that warms me, who at the mere sight of her mercurial daughter overheats to the point of combustion.

Together they sink into a world they won't let me enter, where they drink and smoke and come into their own, become loud, laugh, gesticulate – they became *cannone*, cannons. During these hours, certainties and truths shift. Magdalena vilified my grandmother in front of me in a way only she could; she was jealous of our relationship and wanted me to see her mother the way she did. She accused Lavinia of awful things, and her eyes would become so wild that I believed the allegations. I no longer recognised my grandmother, she made me afraid too. It had to do with the Before, which was none of my business, which I didn't understand. I hated being left out; Magdalena took my grandmother away from me – even more so when they were amicable. Then Magdalena would burst with pride telling me how beautiful Lavinia had been as a young mother, how popular, how happy, everyone was chasing after her. Mamma, she shouted, remember!

My grandmother laughed while thinking of their shared memory, and I saw them before me: a young Lavinia with a small Maddalena on her hip, always together, a happy mother–daughter unit. My insides crumpled: I wanted them to fall out, for her to finally clear off. I was glad when she left us in peace, when I had my warm, soft grandmother back.

Ò, calls a voice, what do you want here then, you hypocrite, ò?

I turn around. On the table behind me an old woman sits bent over her handbag, her hands buried within it.

Ò, she says, have you got a lighter? I had two in here and now I can't find either of them.

She's wearing a tiger-print dress; her few curls of sparse guinea pig hair squiggle around her head. Glamorous sunglasses, plastic pearl earrings. Bling flashes on her splayed fingers as she pushes back a whorl of hair.

She looks left and right, whispers desperately: I want to smoke now.

I well up.

You remind me of my grandmother, I say, my eyes wet.

She murmurs: I had two and now I can't find either of them.

*

The waiter is blocking the sun.

You have to order more, he says, if you want to keep sitting here.

I look up: Did my tragic family history not move you even a little bit?

He slowly shakes his head at me. I stack up the coffee cups, push them towards him: Bring me whatever you want.

He leaves the cups where they are, deliberately backs away so I can get a good look at him. He is lanky and slight with small ears. Hair combed back and fixed down with pomade. I like that style a lot on younger men, but he is over halfway through his life. His eye tics, it twitches, and suddenly I feel a pinch in my stomach: maybe it's him. Maybe he was the one who had Magdalena . . . At any rate . . .

I stare at him. At any rate, it could be him as much as it could be anyone else.

His hands tremble slightly as he sets down a small white cake with a glacé cherry on top, next to the ghost coffee cup tower.

What's that?

Virgin's Breast.

Pardon?

A breast of Saint Agatha.

Bring me the other one.

The waiter looks around and offers me a cigarette.

Thanks, I say, I shouldn't smoke either, weak lungs on top of everything, most likely from my father's side.

The waiter looks at me strangely. He pulls out a chair and

sinks into it. He speaks slowly, so the dialect doesn't make his tongue gallop and I will understand him.

Do you know who Agatha was?

I shake my head.

Agatha was a radiant virgin. A powerful man wanted to marry her, but she was a virgin for Jesus and didn't want him. The man couldn't allow this: because she turned him down, he locked her in a whorehouse. After a month he came back to rescue her, but she still didn't want him. As punishment, he had her breasts cut off. During the night, Saint Peter appeared to heal her wounds with balm. She turned him down too. When the powerful man saw this, he threw Agatha into the fire.

The waiter puts a cigarette on the table for me, I stick it behind my ear.

He goes back to the bar.

Wait, I call after him, what happened to the man?

He was trampled to death by a horse.

Now there are two snow-white breasts with cherry nipples in front of me. I stab a slightly dirty spoon into one. The sacred breasts are sweet. I eat them greedily.

The square fills with life. Men come to work. They spread sheets out on the pavement, arrange trainers and bags. Others roll up in small carts from which they offer batteries, torches, radio alarm clocks. Fresh catch, straight from the port. Cars are

45

jamming, honking, there's a bang from somewhere.

My senses are heightened from insomnia.

In front of the café, a man appears with a guitar: O sole mio.

I vigorously shake my head. That's going too far, a cliché of the kind that disgusts even me. But it's already too late: emotion crawls down my back, claws at my throat, fills my eyes. After the song the singer doffs his hat, shuffles towards me, I give him the change reserved for the waiter, sink into the soft tar of self-loathing.

I hear laughter, rub my eyes. At the table behind me there's a group of young people. Perfectly groomed, necks like morning dew, hair parted with a knife, bathed in cologne. Gold crosses hang from their throats, their tracksuits are freshly starched. They're laughing at me; at the way I'm sweating and how I've obviously completely given up on myself. *Turista di merda.*

I get up and leave without paying. Turn a corner and run. Wildly sidestepping – this tiredness that turns every bag into a dog, every sack of rubbish in the gutter into a panther ready to pounce.

*

There's a market here, cobbles slippery underfoot. Smells hit my nostrils – what got into this prezzemolo for it to smell so perverse? The fruits scream for attention, singing competitively with their colours and scents. Indecent. Overripe melons, delirious peaches, drunken pears and tantalising figs; grapes, grapes, they shine and shimmer, ringing bright and clear like cymbals.

I push my way through the crowd until I become one with it, surrendering and floating, merging into it. But it doesn't work; the mass repels me, I'm a singular foreign body. I should be like Magdalena, she fits here like a fist in an eye socket: aggressive, vulgar, devious, loud, extreme, as if she were missing all filters and controls. I try to keep up with she who lived here, who walked here, try to evoke her in me, to have her speak through me. It's not working. I've carved myself into her opposite – they're eating me alive here. The chameleon has failed, my cover blown, I shine beneath the spotlight of otherness. So I walk stiffly straight ahead, repelling the bodies burrowing around me like magnets with opposing polarities, like water droplets off a wax jacket. My glaring repulsiveness makes me stumble.

I want to fit in, buy something, grapes, may I try them, my grandmother says you always have to try them.

The market women shake their heads suspiciously. Displeased, they act as if they don't understand my Italian, as if I were talking in a very far-flung foreign language. Whatever I examine is unsold, laughed at, ridiculed: the answer to every question is scornful spitting. They open their mouths to continue their screaming, luring calls through the gaps between their teeth – not for me. My attempt at fitting in here is presumptuous; my full, expensively adjusted set of teeth is already giving me away.

Metre-long beans, prickly cucumbers, squirming chillies: I flee through the enemy territory of never-ending stalls. Colourful dustiness, right and left. School smocks, synthetic clothes, old biscuits, kitchen utensils, perfumes, and mussels in their bubbly baths; like snails, they stretch out their feelers. Fish men shoo flies from the glittering bodies with plastic bags. Polyester crackles; sweat hisses when it meets static, evaporates.

And then, out of nowhere, a gap: a ramshackle stand. Just a table with some junk on it: Marlboro Red, stained notebooks, lighters.

A plump boy belongs to the stand, pale with an inky smudge of black hair. He pecks at the elbow of a yeast dough woman. She's welling up all whitish from within a plastic chair. On her lap sits a massive baby, ancient face. White and round and framed with lace, the child looks directly inside me. I shudder. My grandmother had often warned me: the evil eye!

The woman reaches out a hand towards me, wailing. I shake my head, mumbling, I already gave too much to the Sole Mio.

I want to keep going, but I'm petrified: the moon child's curse hits me like a blow to the neck. My guilty conscience presses my head down towards the ground. A momentary stillness settles over the noise and everyone and everything seems to stop.

Someone is wiggling me by the ankles, I turn around angrily. I curse, the child begins to whimper, the woman screams excitedly. The packs of cigarettes bounce on the table, lighters skip across the slick cobblestones. Oranges tumble out of their crates, roll and burst, people throw their hands up to the sky and dance. The boy has crawled under the table, I yell at him: Stop shaking. His eyes widen. The moon child does not waver, holding its piercing gaze on me while the woman, its throne, is shaken about in her chair; she curses heaven and hell.

After a while, it stops. My bones and the church bells hum, the murmur swells back up. Men crawl out from underneath their stands, brush the dirt from their trousers with their hands, run their hands through their hair. One of them pats me on the shoulder, talks at me, I don't understand, can't hear, a whistling in my ears. He crosses himself and kisses his fingers, pointing towards the sky. I look up, underwear quivers on a washing line. The boy collects up the cigarette packs. The woman in the chair laughs toothlessly at me.

I turn around, walk faster, men grab my arms, mumbling: Were you frightened? It was just a little earthquake, a greeting from the volcano—

Their faces are too close, sour breath; I look straight ahead, pretend not to notice, they laugh.

And finally, finally, I hear Magdalena's voice: Don't let anyone touch you if you don't want them to. Say no, no matter who it is, strangers or friends. Scream it loudly and say Sir – that's important, never be casual.

49

She gave me this speech when I was small; to this day, I've never listened to her. I was ashamed to scream, never wanted to sound like her: *No! You pig, let me go, Sir!*

I do what I always do in these situations: I listen to my grandmother.

Don't bother with the men, she says, look at them and move on. Chin up and smile, but not too much, with sealed lips, and most importantly: don't stop. Smile and keep going, always keep going.

*

A military vehicle clatters past. I finally stop and look around. The men who were following me have disappeared. The streets are wide here, the houses are palaces. Tall palm trees wave at me.

In front of the museum, two soldiers are standing guard. They're wearing funny seven-dwarfs hats, which take away from the threat of their boots and weapons. I give them a nod and walk in between them.

On entering, there is suddenly silence. Cool and dry as a grave. Every step I take is accompanied by Roman statues. The heat falls away from me along with the otherness, I can breathe again. This is my air, this is how I like it, in a mausoleum of holy art. I greet the sons of gods with cheeky winks, their strong thighs; among swollen loin muscles, toe-sized penises relax. The marble sparkles where he's chipped; arm stumps, rusty wire. Proudly lustrous buttocks.

I am doped by tiredness, my blood is pulsing in my fingers. I cool them on the marble chest of a noble Roman. And something miraculous happens. He breathes. His ribcage rises and falls beneath my fingertips, completely real, his eyelids flutter. He turns his eyes slightly, between his lasciviously parted lips the tip of his tongue twinkles. I stand on tiptoes so I can kiss him. My chapped, open lips meet his smooth, perfect ones, I close my eyes. Fall into the well.

I tear myself away and stride through the lined-up busts of powerful marble-white men. Alabaster cheeks and sugar mouths, pensive creased foreheads and nibbled earlobes. Important faces that say: It was a struggle, but it was worth it; I am still here. My legacy is set in stone.

Psst, hisses one of them with a curly beard, psst, over here!

His marble eyes shine: Well, where are you from? Do you like it here? We've seen better times, that's for sure. The monuments are falling into ruin, our reputation is crumbling, men are letting themselves go, like animals. But don't be fooled – our greatness, our pride, still slumbers within them.

He raises his voice and it thunders through the hall: For we Romans invented this world! We are the cradle of civilisation – what's so funny?

I twirl his beard: The Romans? They just copied what the Greeks did before them.

Outraged murmuring begins to swell. The generals object,

the philosophers grumble, and the rich smack their lips in embarrassment.

And what about the Egyptians, I continue to prod, what about the Mesopotamians, heard of them?

Curly Beard is the first to pull himself together. He breaks into throaty laughter.

You're just jealous, he sneers, because you have no history. You will go as you came: furtively, accidentally, pointlessly. No one will notice when you're gone. You're nothing, like your mother, you will rot, you will be forgotten in no time at all—

I nod. Yeah, and? Look at yourselves, your ridiculous attempts to force us to remember you. Because you can't stand transience, you do everything to ensure that your rigid faces last throughout time – and for what? I'll chip off your noses! I can clearly feel your empty eyes pestering my arse. The way your skin is becoming mottled with excitement because of the same old daydreams in which your arms grow back, sinewy fingers that can finally dig into Proserpine's marble-soft buttocks . . .

Curly Beard puckers his lips: Come over here, little one, I'll make you immortal.

No!

Now I really do scream. He starts to dart his tongue in and out like a snake. Then they all start moaning, begging me, beckoning me, insulting me.

I unlock my jaw: Leave me alone, Sirs, you old perverts!

Then they say no more.

Pleased with myself, I raise my chin, banish them to the corner of my eye, smile and keep going, always keep going.

Until someone blocks my path, forcing me to stop. I kneel at her feet and marvel at the beautifully wrought sandals, her long toes; read the text on the plinth: Agrippina . . . first Roman empress . . . Terrible legend . . .

I look her in the face. Sublimely pinched lips. The terrible legend is a bitterly exhausted mother. Only her breasts are those of a teenager, two firm tartlets under the sheer fabric of her dress.

I tap her toenail. It doesn't seem to bother her. She stares, permanently tired, into nothingness, kneading her hands.

Incredible, I murmur, that you, an empress, were portrayed in this way. Even the most obscure common or garden philosopher among those guys over there has more triumph in their expression than you do. You look as though you've given up, become haggard and withdrawn into yourself.

The foot twitches, she swishes her cloak: I am Agrippina, the murderer. She who dines with death, who serves up poison, who lost her mind and ultimately her life to dress her son in power. I made them drop like flies, left and right. All of it to make my son great, to make him the greatest emperor of all time. And when he was finally great . . .

I glance at the text: He had you killed?

I would do it all again, she says. I am his mother, I know what is best for him.

I mutter: Looks like it.

She makes a face: You will understand when you have children.

53

I shake my head: My mother never looked like that. But she didn't sacrifice anything for me either.

That is not possible, Agrippina says, then she wasn't a mother.

I raise my voice: Don't lecture me about motherliness! At least she wasn't killed by her own kid.

Are you sure?

Agrippina breaks into laughter, a wicked, screeching laugh.

You are to blame, and your grandmother is to blame, you are both bigots. You both knew that she was in danger, and what did you do about it? You pushed her out, you expelled her, again and again you sent her to her death.

You're crazy, I shout, no wonder your son had you assassinated!

You are right, she howls, you ought to go and look at the depictions of the Virgin Mary if you want to see something beautiful, all the saints are beautiful!

The snaky curls on her head squirm and flick their tongues, she laughs an awful murderer's laugh, I run away.

I stand agitated in the picture gallery. It's oppressively warm in here. At the end of the hall, curtains stir at open windows. They billow their yellowness into the room, like a ship pulling into the harbour with straining sails. They swallow the street noise; outside is far away, maybe even completely gone, I can only hear my footsteps. Walking past the gore in opulent gilt frames: spears in muscular bodies, lasciviously dying faces. All saints are beautiful, but they aren't moving.

54

Agrippina's laughter resounds in my ears. And what if she's right? What if we could have saved her?

Then there's always revenge, says a quiet voice.

I turn in a circle, there's no one here, I'm alone. It is the young woman on the wall, I'm pretty sure, who just spoke. She seems kind of busy right now: with a long sword, she's sabring off the head of a bearded man. Bull-necked, this man, arms like hams. She reluctantly holds him by the hair while cutting through his windpipe, looking repulsed. The blood sprays. She's almost through. The man gurgles. I wonder why he isn't fighting back. He looks a lot stronger.

A cackle comes from the darkness. There's an old woman, wizened, who almost shreds her apron between her fingers in excitement.

Harder, she whispers, faster!

The wall text says that the young woman is a Jewish widow of considerable charm: she is called Judith, and the old woman is her maidservant. Together they tricked the General Holofernes, who had attacked their town and robbed, raped and murdered her sisters. Using her beauty, Judith slipped into the enemy camp and bewitched the general. She got him drunk – and was soon taking his head for a stroll.

I study her expression. It's not possible: carrying out such a violent, demanding murder with such a calm face. Her earrings don't quiver; only a small crease between her brows, where the entirety of her loathing is concentrated. The beauty of saints, miraculously beautiful. I feel dizzy.

I reel through the room, fall onto a wooden bench. Lie on my back so I don't have to see her anymore. Can't close my eyes, everything is spinning. This is how the painting on the ceiling is placed on the globes of my eyes, a system of coordinates. It tingles, and a maelstrom forms, pulling me up, I levitate; I rise onto the red clouds. Whirl in the draught of beating robes, sky-blue tunics, the golden hiss of cymbals; silken angel fingers on the furrows of my brow, soothing whispers. Honeyed breath flows into my ears, spreads throughout my knotted brain and strokes the place behind my sore eyes. Cloudy cottonness envelops me like a cocoon.

*

I'm wearing Judith's earrings and I'm drawing a sword – I'm on the search for the man who cut off Magdalena's breasts. There he is, standing at the well; I bewitch him while trying to con-ceal the weapon. Holofernes gives a thunderous laugh: You're not of considerable charm!

I bob and weave, but can't deceive him, he sees right through me immediately. I fling the sword – it glances off him, just a small, superficial nick. He becomes angry, he is so terribly strong. He takes the sword and cuts off my head. I know: he is my father. I can still hear him crying: Promise me that you'll miss me.

I climb out of the well and smell sulphur. It's raining, a freight train thunders over the bridge standing high above a steaming river. I climb down the slippery slope, try to keep my head straight so it doesn't fall off. With both my hands on my ears, I reach the hot spring. It stinks and steams and drips. Sticking out from the rock are moss-covered plastic pipes, out of which water splashes into stone basins. Bloated figures with long hair sit in them decomposing. They're all crab red and have heavy eyelids. They lean back their heads and allow the spurts to hail down onto their skulls.

Yoohoo, Fila!

Mimma, we're over here!

I hear them laughing: What's that? I quickly wrap a scarf around my throat so I don't shock them. The fog is thick, I step into nothing, rush towards the calls. Steam rises up: they're sitting happily in the sulphur hole waving me over.

Welcome to Hades, Magdalena shouts, take your spot in the hotpot of the dead!

She barks, and Lavinia pokes her in the side, giggling. Their naked bodies embarrass me, I try not to look. In spite of everything, they're wearing rollers in their hair. My grandmother reaches out her hand: Mimma, get in.

I'm worried about my head, the wound, it doesn't seem very sterile to me.

Magdalena snarls: You think you're better than us.

Coward, Lavinia shouts, in with you! It's pure balm, a fountain of youth. Look at us!

She appears to have her rosy luxuriance again, glowing skin. Magdalena's bruises have also faded.

I climb unsteadily into the tub. The water is wonderfully hot.

I try to take my grandmother's hands but Magdalena shoves me so I slip and end up floating on my back. They tug softly at my hands and feet, make my body glide through the water and position my head under the jet filling the tub up with sulphur juice. It drips into my eyes, I have to close them. Incomprehensible murmuring, the patter of the jet is very loud underwater.

And the way it smacks, stinking, right onto my skull finally unfurls a deep sense of relaxation in me.

Until they begin to thrash about, kicking me with their bunions, and it sloshes over my face. I sit up spluttering.

Stop fighting, I shout, it's in the past, and we're all together, what more do you want?

Then I notice that my head is no longer attached to my torso. I see my headless body stand up and walk around, watch it slip, see it attempt to climb out of the basin. And I watch Lavinia and Magdalena, they're grabbing one another by the throat and pushing each other's heads underwater.

What are you doing? I shout, Stop it!

They don't listen to me, carry on, spluttering: We're baptising each other!

I remain lying in the lukewarm water of half-asleep. They have trampled me into a certainty that, as soon as I try to grasp it, escapes back into the steam.

Waking up is like fighting my way out of hot sweet jelly. I barely get out and remain stuck to everything, to gravity. I push myself up from the wooden bench, run my hands over my face. Two tourists are standing in front of the painting of Judith, taking a selfie and giggling. The pictures have grown still; through the open windows, the evening traffic rushes and beeps. The light has changed. It nuzzles submissively against my skin, brushing gilding onto the little hairs on my arms. I feel sick. The curtains are beckoning. Magdalena is waiting.

IV

The hospital is an unrendered concrete structure with watch-towers, like a prison. The entrance hall is empty, the receptionist ignores me. I walk past him and turn down the first corridor that I come to. My heart thumps in my throat, I raise my chin. The walls are green like my nail polish. The smell makes me feel nauseous. It reminds me of my grandmother, her time in the hospice. She didn't want to eat anymore and fed me instead: You must be hungry!

While I chewed, she praised the good cake and the nurses who treated her like she was a queen. For dessert, I gobbled get-well-soon chocolates, which Frau Schneider and the other neighbourhood ladies sent her.

I feel light-headed, I lean against the jungle-green wall, close my eyes until I hear steps and a friendly voice. The doctor has silky wavy hair and eyelashes like butterfly wings. Her inflated lips intimidate me. Thankfully her coat is a little crumpled, which gives me some courage.

I say: My mother died here.

Her whitened teeth show that she understands me.

She says she's called Maria. She's very sorry about my mother, she wants to help me find her. As if I were a child in a supermarket that had lost their mother while daydreaming in the sweetie aisle. As if she were about to proclaim on my behalf: Magdalena, please come to the tills, your daughter is looking for you.

I must have made a funny face, Maria grips my shoulder. I convulse with tears, I can't hold them back, they break out of me. Maria pulls me to her chest as if it were the most natural thing in the world. She smells like my grandmother, like bleach and jasmine, her coat crackles. I hug her back, reach into the soft hair, scrunch it. She strokes my head. It leaves me shaken. I really do want to pull myself together, but the more I resist, the more the crying surges.

I'm sorry, I try to say, it was a long journey, I don't know this town, the earthquake, I've already been to Hades—

Maria nods as if she understands.

I'll take you to the office, she says, not to worry, we'll find your mother.

Actually she says *Mamma*.

A stick of candy floss begins to twirl within me: what if I misunderstood what was said on the telephone? What if Magdalena isn't dead at all, but rather lying somewhere here in the hospital, with a non-functioning liver? I see her before me, secretly smoking out the window and bribing the nurses to smuggle in some wine for her: It's the blood of bloody Jesus, I hear her say. Damn it, Maria! It's there to wash my sins away. Can't you see how much I need it?

Maybe she needs a liver transplant. That would make sense:

she'd have me summoned for that. I become angry again, but I'm smiling. Tastes good, the candy floss. Sweet. Magdalena would heal from a piece of my liver. I could live with her here, she would lead me around in the foreign language, the dialect. We'd argue a lot of course. Does she still have all her teeth?

I remember the doctor on the telephone. *Ammazzata*, she had said. Murdered.

The candy floss stick falls stiffly into the dust.

*

It smells different in the office. Cloying, like it's putrid, the faint scent of polish and a subtle trace of cigarette smoke. In the centre of the room is a massive wooden desk, on it an old computer, behind it a man being a doctor. He stands up and takes off his coat, folding it in such a way that I cannot read his name tag. He comes towards me with his hand outstretched: Signorina!

He takes my hand in his paw and pats it a few times. Then he beats his hand on his chest and introduces himself: Dottore.

He puts his hand on my shoulder and pushes me into a chair. His arm slithers over Maria's shoulder and he whispers something into her ear. Her eyes widen, she looks at me, then at the floor. He presses a file into her hand, and she disappears.

He sits, sighs: Signorina.

Then he rolls his chair out from behind the desk until he stops beside me. He puts his hand on my knee and says: It pains my heart.

My knee jerks upwards, he takes back his hand and frowns: Your mother was a remarkable woman. It is such a pity that she had to go so soon – even if it is not surprising. When the liver's that far gone, nothing can be done.

Really, I say.

Drinking, he sighs, lifting his hand as if in helplessness, is a grave sin. We can help some people, but your mother – you know how thick her skull was.

My heart skips a beat: *la coccia dura* – Magdalena's letter.

The doctor looks at me pityingly: Still, what bad luck!

She shouldn't have done it, he states sorrowfully, drinking herself to death. Why, why? But God's ways are unfathomable, he has now called her to him. May she rest in peace. Amen.

A whistling starts in my ears, I say loudly: I've come to say goodbye, can I see her please?

Of course, he says, no problem. Sister Maria is preparing the paperwork, after that she'll take you to her. She'll be right back, let's wait a moment.

We sit in silence. Blood pulses against my eardrum. My eyes travel around the room until they settle on a cage hanging on the wall. The Madonna behind bars. She's holding her head to one side, so that she can just about see through them. She has her arms crossed. Her gaze exudes total disinterest.

The doctor spins in his chair with abandon: Are you planning on staying for long?

I don't know, I say truthfully.

If you're planning on eating seafood you should get a vaccination. Hepatitis is going round. Especially from mussels.

Is that so, I say.

Do you know how many people have died of it this year? The risk of getting sick here in the city is high, with all the people and rats and filth. The conditions in this country are shameful. When you think that we were once the masters of the world. But you can protect yourself. I can give you the injection.

I don't know if I should laugh or not.

He looks at me expectantly.

I say: Now, while we're waiting?

No, no, he shakes his head. I don't have the vaccine here. Ran out a long time ago. The whole city has been cleared out. But I hear that there's some in the Vatican City. You could head over there, pick up the stuff, and I could inject you. I'm an expert, trained in tropical medicine. I have a hospital in Tanzania, he says, I'm travelling back there soon. You ought to try and source the stuff quickly if you still want to catch me, in any case. Until then I would impose a strict ban on mussels. Especially blue mussels. Do you like pizza frutti di mare?

Not really.

What about impepata di cozze?

Yes, I do.

You see, he says triumphantly, that's the most dangerous.

He looks at his watch: If you go now you could still make it today.

Thanks, I say, I'll wait, I'm here for my mother.

Of course, he nods, of course. I just wanted to warn you, hepatitis isn't to be trifled with.

The hair comes to mind. Magdalena lost her hair. I must have been very small, my memory is dim. What I see: the way the bin in the bathroom is overflowing with hair. The way wet hair swayed like seagrass in the bath and puffed up drying in the sink. It got caught in cobwebs and hung from the ceiling, wafting gently back and forth. Tufts of it scurried through the living room like black mice. Hair in food, on our clothes, between our toes, everywhere.

Magdalena used a hairbrush, showed me the bristles full of hair. Look, she said, running her fingers through her hair, look. She let the hair sail to the floor, gripped my two little braided pigtails and said: If I plaited all my hair, it'd only be as thick as one of yours.

I want thin pigtails too, I say.

My grandmother said we had to get the illness out of the house. We opened the windows and shook the bin of hair into the wind, it fell in clumps and whirled through the air. My grandmother washed the bath out with bleach.

She drummed it into me not to use my mother's toothbrush, because the illness was contagious. Magdalena said that she had got the illness when I was born because I had been so difficult and she'd lost a lot of blood. They'd given her blood at the hospital, contaminated, it contained the illness and now it was in her.

In the letter she said that I was born at home.

Lie-lie-lie.

Later there was an argument at school because a girl went around saying that my mother had given her father hepatitis.

The doctor rolls his chair to the cabinet, leans forward, pulls open a drawer without getting up, and rummages around in it without looking. He rolls back with a small, brown apothecary bottle, which he sets down in front of me: For the time being, I'd absolutely recommend this oil, you need it for every trip. When I go to my hospital in Tanzania – you can visit me there if you like?

He blinks at me awaiting an answer. When I don't respond, he draws the corners of his mouth down and stretches his neck like a turtle in order to express his slightly offended apathy. He twists off the top of the little bottle and picks up where he left off: No matter where I go, I always have this in my luggage. I brought it back from South America many years ago. It works just as good here as in China and everywhere else. You rub it over your entire body. Critters don't like the smell and you won't be bitten. If you are, you rub the oil over the bite or sting, and it helps to prevent itching. It makes sure that no eggs are incubated under your skin. It also prevents worms in your feet, it protects against everything! Come on, let me give you a sample.

He pours some oil into his empty hand, rubs it in a circular motion, and a repulsive, foul smell fills the room. That's what it is, the unidentifiable room smell! He takes my hand in his and rubs the stinking oil into my skin.

It's as if I'm petrified. While he clamps my fingers one by one between his own and firmly strokes them, I feel the dying hands of my grandmother. They were no longer how I knew them, strong and rough and chapped. They were soft from the oil I massaged them with daily, to memorise her knuckles and nails forever.

She whispered: I don't want to die yet.

What had the doctor said about Magdalena on the telephone?
I've never seen someone fight so hard for their life.

Someone's knocking at the door.

Ah, the doctor lets go of my hand, visibly relieved: That'll be our Maria.

He gestures to encourage me to stand up. He pushes me to the door, shoves me out.

Arrivederci, he snarls, and don't forget: Come any time for a vaccination. Maria will explain everything.

He shuts the door, turns the key from the inside. Now I'm standing alone with Maria in the corridor. Involuntarily I imagine removing my shirt so she can give me an injection.

She's carrying a large plastic container, a kind of compost bin. She hands it over without looking at me.

Heavy, I say, what is it?

Two and a half kilos, Maria says to the floor.

She turns on her heel and disappears.

I turn over the container and read the label on the underside.

Magdalena Unfamiliarname.

67

It seems to me that the urn is still warm.

*

Disoriented, I wander through the city. Magdalena feels heavy in my hands. I consider putting her down, to keep going, to evaporate.

I put her down on a bench and sit next to her. A rose seller creeps up from behind, waggles the flowers, presses their soft heads against the nape of my neck.

I say no, she remains persistent. Her face is young, but she's missing some teeth. She talks at me with a singsong voice.

Magdalena had sold roses as a young girl, she told me that once. I take in the girl, she resembles her, perhaps she is her, a ghost?

I grip her wrist: Who are you?

She blinks: Why didn't you ask me when I could still answer?

I give her all my money, she gives me all the flowers. She wants more, I don't have any more; after a while she shuffles off. I lay the crinkling wrapped roses on the urn.

Here, I say, they're quite old. The girl ripped me off. But I felt sorry for her, and I wanted to buy you a place in heaven.

Magdalena keeps schtum.

*

I sit on a hill and look out. The sulphur-yellow sky lies heavily on the sea, the water acquiesces, reflecting it back wanly. The port lies in fog, anxious hoots from incoming ships. The disappearance of the sun takes place unnoticed, a quiet red glow on the horizon, as if a drop of blood had fallen in milk. Who knows if it will ever return. The volcano puffs little clouds from its crater, the city inhales the smoke like a Marlboro Red. I lie flat on the warm earth and feel the seismic thrills. Impatient murmurs.

The smoke is so dense, it hides the boats sinking on the horizon, being sunk. The people on the boats, their waving arms; the wind wipes away their cries, wretched accomplice.

When the volcano's had enough, it explodes. I'm waiting for it. When it happens, I'll hurl the compost bin into the wind. My mother's ashes will mix with the ash of the volcano; that would suit her: an eruptive, roaring finale. Some will be carried out to sea by a covetous wind and will melt on the glittering surface of the water. But most of it will vanish in a collective blizzard. Treacherously silent, the ashes will sink and smother everything. Or will softly cover over the dirt and violence and bigotry. And soon vines will grow over it – for the wind and the rain, and later perhaps, much, much later, for the new life that will come crawling out of the sea.

*

I went once with my grandmother to Pompeii. We walked over two-thousand-year-old streets with tyre-sized paving stones, setting foot in what remained of the houses, dwellings and shops. After the volcano erupted, the ash lay so high that not a single chimney could be seen, and the powder became as hard as stone.

That's how people would later come to walk across the roofs of the city without noticing that a forgotten world lay beneath them. It was found by accident, millennia later, while digging up the land.

I remember a house that was remarkable because it had an intact roof. I slipped inside it alone, it was dim. People clustered together and strained their necks so they could see the ceiling. They pointed upwards with their fingers and laughed. There were some drawings, obscene, but I couldn't see them clearly, because grown-ups were always blocking my view. I went in all the rooms, looked at the beds, they were short and made of stone. How was anyone supposed to sleep on them?

An elegant man came up to me and said: They would put sacks full of straw on them, as mattresses, that was normal back then. Nowadays a lot of people think that a bed like that was punishment for easy girls. But their clients had it just as hard.

He went to the bed and sat down on it.

It's interesting, is it not, he said, that the brothel is the only thing standing after the catastrophe?

A tall woman stuck her head around the door, was shocked at the sight of me and shouted in a shrill voice: Showing your daughter something like that! You ought to be ashamed, the child is far too young to see this!

The man shrugged, stood up and left the room. I was disappointed that he didn't play along. He might have also profited from impersonating my father.

We didn't go to the museum where the plaster impressions of

the dead are. It cost extra. And my grandmother had the same idea as the woman in the brothel: I was too young.

I saw them anyway, the dead. Through the bars that separated the expensive museum realm from the ancient street. I secretly peered through them and saw children looking at plaster casts of dead children. They lay balled up in the arms of their mothers, who lay protectively over them. Only one child was alone, bending his small white body over a small box.

There were also impressions of animals: a wretched, curled-up dog, they had all been suffocated by ash or struck dead by collapsing houses. With time, the bodies had decayed and left behind voids in the hardened ash. During the excavation, a resourceful scientist had poured plaster of Paris into them. Then he prised out radiant white figures, negatives of death.

*

It grows dark, the lights of the city flare up. The quake has stopped, the volcano doesn't intend to waste itself this evening.

I make my eyes as sharp as a pair of binoculars: the milky, tinted horizon is empty. A freighter sailed into the port a while ago and is resting in the basin. Magdalena liked the sea. Seawater heals every wound, she always said. I take the urn that's sitting next to me and put it on my lap. I grip the plastic with both hands and try to conjure up a beautiful memory.

The cowboy hat. Puffy, watery eyes. Her face swims. I can't remember how she spoke, I only hear screeching. I have no idea what a death negative of her body would look like. Maybe if someone poured plaster inside me, into the void that she left within me. Maybe if I empty something into the urn, nail polish. It would creep around the hollow space of her ashes. I'd wait until the polish had dried, shake the ashes into the sea, and in the urn would be a small, gleaming statue: a Magdalena in jungle green to hang from my neck.

I unscrew the lid of the urn and reach into it with a shudder. Finely ground dust gives me goose flesh, like chalk on a blackboard: powdered sugar and flour, magnesium in sports lessons, combed beach sand in the summer. But Magdalena's ashes aren't anything like that. They're coarser, with bits, like flotsam on an autumnal sea. I let it run through my fingers: pumice, rounded shards, sepia limestone, softened wood.

An image flies up before me: my mother and I on a stormy beach, our fingertips tracing lines in wet sand, our names.

I gently fondle the ash-sand, close my eyes, dig, try to remember more.

Instead my fingers hook a piece of paper. I fish it out, blow away the dust, which drifts down towards the sea. The note is folded twice. The pencil writing looks like Doctor Maria, silky waves.

Peace Alley (Street of Women)

I close the urn again. Look down at the blinking city.

V

That is how I end up on the Street of Women.

The area seems uninhabited, the houses are dark. Smashed windows, some are boarded up, others have shredded curtains. Electricity cables weave heavy nets between the rows of houses. On the walls are names with hearts or insults. A rat scurries across the pulped newspapers on the cobblestones.

As soon as I see people, I slip into a doorway. The street lights have been shot out, I wrap myself in the gloom. I have a good view of the small piazza. It's like a stage bathed in the dim light of two lanterns. There's an old woman with a vendor's tray full of cigarettes. She is standing under the street sign, the name on the slip of paper. Vico della Pace. Peace Alley. I squeeze the urn, murmuring: Welcome home.

There is life in the alley off the piazza. A Madonna shrine on the wall lights a row of small doors that lead directly from the alley into rooms; I imagine they're caves. Women sit out in front of them in net stockings, cracking open sunflower seeds. Some of them stick their heads out of the windows in the doors, chatting with the others.

One of the women reminds me of Magdalena. Less because of how she looks and more because of her manner, how she moves; the raw, demanding voice. She has a loud laugh that makes her bright blue dress quiver over her stomach. She throws back her head, sashays her body; swings and sways up and down the piazza, borrows a cig from the cigarette vendor while the other women in the alley remain where they are, not moving from their doorways. She, on the other hand, seems free, as if the square belongs to her. She approaches other women, nudges them. She makes them stretch out on their chairs and photographs them.

When men arrive on the piazza, she greets them. Lays her hand on their arm, feels their muscles, strokes the back of their head, giggles in their ear. She points to the alley, to this and that, the men kiss her cheek. Some of the women are impatient, they shriek at the passers-by and laugh filthily when they flinch. Others duck when approached and close the door on the men. They negotiate through the window and then bring them inside.

And the men smirk and grope; curse, grab, wrench shoulders, hair, wrists.

A moped comes speeding in, honking; everyone scatters, disappearing into the shadows of the broken lamps. The moped cuts straight through the piazza and races towards me, past me. The cigarette woman shuts her box, shuffles in my direction. She shouts: But who is it? Who's coming?

I duck into the darkness. The woman squeezes her eyes shut and listens. When nothing happens, she opens up her shop again, and the women open the doors in the alley, the men return.

I stand there for a fascinated eternity. Watch until I imagine that I know the women. I fabricate biographies for them: what they studied, who has children and how many, how long they've been on Peace Alley. What they thought of Magdalena.

One of them looks like Maria from the hospital. An angel in golden trainers. She leans against the wall of the house, swinging her hips, fiddling with the earphones in her ears. Then she speaks to a boy who has been hanging around the corner for a while, looking unsure. He immediately pulls out his wallet. She is a head taller than him, winds her arms around his neck, leans down towards him, whispers something in his ear. He gulps, splutters; she laughs and draws him into her cave. When she re-emerges a little later, she claps her hands together and walks with long strides across the piazza to the Magdalena-woman, they chat.

I really want to be her friend.

That I've ended up here doesn't surprise me. I just hope my grandmother's not watching.

*

The day the newspaper arrived. That day Magdalena finally broke away from us for good. At that point, she no longer belonged to us. On that day she became a stranger.

I see them before me like in an old film: Lavinia and Magdalena, each ready to fight on their side of the wobbly kitchen table, where the local paper is lying between them. On the front page Magdalena, baring her teeth proudly in front of her establishment.

Lavinia gasps for air: Are you crazy? – lights a cigarette – Have you completely lost your senses?

Magdalena gets into position. She too clamps a cigarette between her lips, bends towards her mother, so she can light it. Lavinia drops the matches and lowers her voice: Is this *Filippo*'s doing?
     Magdalena becomes angry: You're paranoid.
     Lavinia mutters: I'll kill him. I'll kill the both of you.

Magdalena picks up the newspaper and fans it around: You could be happy for me! An opportunity presented itself and I took it. You should be proud of me. You brought me up that way, drummed it into me, that I shouldn't be dependent on a man, should earn a living independently. And you're right! But I'm realistic; the world isn't my oyster. I don't have an education, not even a school leaver's certificate. And I can't spend my whole life standing at a counter serving liver sausage like you do. Or die inside like Pappi. I inherited his sickness, and when I'm not doing well I drink even more. I admire you for your righteous life, but it would destroy me. I'm like your brother: I want more, to dare to do something, to achieve something, my own house with a swimming pool.

Look at me, I'm an entrepreneur! I've got contacts, great contacts, just in this scene. What's so bad about it? It's the oldest profession in the world. It's recession-proof. It's a wonderful thing. Who says it's not wonderful? Bigots say that! You don't want to be a bigot, do you? This work is merciful, that's what it says in the Bible. Mamma, for heaven's sake – your face! I don't even do it myself. I give the girls work and safety, I take care of them, they've got it good at my place. They don't have to freeze out on the street and get into strangers' cars. Do you know how many girls disappear that way? How many perverts are out there just waiting? They've got it better at mine than anywhere else. Because I'm a woman. I know what I'm talking about.

Up to that point Lavinia had kept silent. Opened her mouth again and again, but not a sound came out. Finally she says, and her voice only shakes a little: You bring shame on the family. I never want to see you again.

Before Magdalena closes the door behind her, she says: As soon as I have my own place, Filippa will come live with me. Do you hear that, Filuccia, I'll come for you, I promise.

And then my grandmother finally starts screaming: That is not her name! You're just like your father! Irresponsible! Empty promises!

Magdalena remains standing on the doormat as if she were considering whether it had been an offer to stay. Lavinia could see it, she too seems to hesitate. And I knew that this was my moment. Only I could reconcile them. But I don't and that's how I make up my mind forever. Their faces both display the same resolve to not give in, to stay tough. *La coccia dura.*

Magdalena slams the door.

*

My grandmother could never forgive Magdalena for opening a brothel.

In our neighbourhood, she would repeat over and over again, in the newspaper, with her photo and name! My name! I can't leave the house anymore, I'll never leave the house again.

She drew the curtains and was granted sole custody of me. Now whenever Magdalena came to visit, she was immediately dragged into the apartment so that none of the neighbours could see *what she looked like*. Magdalena took no notice.

Then I'll smoke with the windows closed, was all she'd say, lighting up, it's not like you didn't used to fill the apartment with smoke. Especially with Frau Schneider!

She showed me her teeth: When I used to come into the kitchen as a kid and those two were sitting together gossiping, I couldn't see my hand in front of my face because of the smoke.

My grandmother objected, Magdalena drowned her out: That was my childhood.

She wanted to see me close up, to touch me, she demanded that I should tell her something.

I didn't know what. No matter what I said, she wasn't interested, she would interrupt me and not even notice: Mamma, I've just remembered, I saw so-and-so out in front of the building—

She never listened, her gaze wavered, I couldn't get through to her. Her movements were erratic, I would duck, she would get angry. If I refused her, either by keeping silent or hiding, she would get rough. She would pinch me and laugh, pull my hair. Time and time again she would threaten to take me with her, and my grandmother would shriek: You're not allowed, I'll call the police!

To which Magdalena would reply, laughing scornfully: Call them then, I know them all personally.

Over time, the visits came less often. Magdalena's moods became more and more extreme, she swung from affection to revulsion in seconds. My grandmother said that it was the sickness, the alcohol. Magdalena had drunk for as long as I could remember, but she wasn't always like this, there was something else. She was shaken up.

Her establishment, as she called it, had to close down. My grandmother withheld from me all information about it; I don't know what happened, if it had something to do with the fact that she was disappearing more and more. She moved to Italy, sent a postcard, port city with volcano. I'm back home, she wrote, I wish that you would come and visit me. No address. Over the years postcards came from different cities, other countries, always just a few gushing lines: Like a dream, you've got to see it. During one of her last visits she told us that she was running a dog grooming salon in Paris. She did, as it happens, have a small poodle with her, it was constantly yelping, and she yelped back. I watched my grandmother: she jumped at every bark, like I did.

We only spoke of her in hushed voices. Magdalena had brought shame on the family.

It often came up, this word, in the discussions they had with one another. Lavinia used it as a hiss, so that the neighbours behind the thin walls couldn't hear it, and as an argument killer, as if there were no response. But it had a strange effect on Magdalena – it made her angry, joyful, combative. She said it with irony, *shame*; saying it didn't bother her, whereas it burned Lavinia's tongue.

Shame: it had something to do with the neighbours, with whispering and drawn curtains, and in many ways with fathers. On account of the shame of her getting pregnant out of wedlock, Lavinia's father didn't speak to her again. Responsible for this shame was Magdalena's father, my grandfather. And he himself was *the shame* because he was a drunk. My father Filippo was the reason for Magdalena's shame. Ever since she married him, she had heaped shame on herself: her behaviour, her dialect, the bruises; shame-shame-shame.

This was probably why it didn't impress Magdalena, because she had so much of it. She was lavish with it, shrieking out the shame and hammering her fists against the wall so that the neighbours would flinch in shock, like the quivering lap dog that barked anxiously. She was born *the shame*, she didn't know anything else. And she wanted Lavinia to free herself from the fear and own her shame, as she used to say: then no one can have anything over you.

She performed monologues on the subject, which I followed through the keyhole. The smoke would cloud their faces, but I saw Magdalena's great jaw, which spat out sentences like these:

I would like to remind you that you were also *the shame* once upon a time. Your family threw you out in the name of shame, and now you're doing the same to me? I'm not judging you, I just want you to understand. You shouldn't be ashamed of anything, and I'm not ashamed either. The shame is an invention to keep us small, Mamma, and it only works when we submit to it. Who fucking cares what people say, they're bored, they're stupid, that's why they talk about that stuff. Why do you care? We're smart, we're beautiful, we know it. That's what they don't like. But the ones who judge the loudest are the ones who come to see me the most often. That's how it is, Mamma, like you've always said: a world full of bigots!

Lavinia seldom responded to these barrages, she would only watch Magdalena with concern.

One time I asked her when we were alone once more whether it could possibly be true that she had once been *the shame* too.

She boxed my ears and shouted: Never say that again.

Then she defended herself: I'm a normal woman. I was young back then – and I was in love. I don't know, it just happened. Back then, we didn't talk; everything was shameful back then. I can't explain it, it was so different to how it is today, like day and night. If two people went out with each other just once, they were already engaged. You had to be married to have a kiss. A girlfriend of mine was slapped by her future father-in-law because he saw the way she smiled at her boyfriend. You can't even imagine. Watch old films – they're shown in the afternoon nowadays they're so innocent! That's what my world was like. No one had told me where babies come from. My father didn't tell me anything, but he also didn't look at me afterwards either.

They were bound by the shame, it stuck them together like tar. And yet Lavinia didn't want to see Magdalena anymore. Until the very end she was afraid, of her and for her.

*

All of this goes through my mind as I stand in this alley staring at the piazza. My whole life I considered my grandmother para-noid and anxious, irrationally influenced by night-time TV shows. But actually, I was afraid of Magdalena too; I was afraid of her and didn't want to know what she was up to.

I once more attempt to conjure her up, to see her dancing by the light of the street lamps, hear her piercing voice. Had she really stood here and felt men's biceps, whistled admiringly and patted their bald heads? Had she encouraged the other women, cheered them on, kept an eye on them – or, in her words, taken care of them?

She should have taken better care of herself.

I screw the note up in my fist. My gaze follows a man entering the square who gives Magdalena-Lookalike in the blue dress a kiss on her hand. I feel sick to my stomach: maybe it's him. Maybe he's the one who… I stare at him. Does he look like a murderer? Sure, just as much as anyone else. And if – even if I knew I'd found him – what could I do? Report him? Here's my proof: a compost tub full of ash and an unrecorded phone call from a doctor without a name. Or should I seduce him and drag him into my cave, saw off his head, like Judith did with Holofernes?

Maria from the hospital wanted me to come here. She had a plan: the note is the proof, it's my key to solving the riddle. I have to speak to the women. The one in the blue dress and that one that looks like Maria – in my fantasy they were friends with Magdalena. They could tell me something about her.

I scan the square, they've disappeared.

And now, finally, Magdalena appears before me after all, but not dancing in the light of the lanterns, not laughing. Just her lifeless face on the stretcher, dried blood, blue-black marks. A thumping fear courses through me. And a bony hand grasps my shoulder.

*

Are you new?

A glowing face in the darkness of the alley. Quivering moustache, a little breathless, the pointed cap of the military. The rest of the body is also in uniform.

The soldier twitches his lips into a smile; he's missing a piece of incisor, his eyes are deeply, darkly rimmed.

My heart is still beating in my throat, I try to swallow it down; it gives the impression that I'm a bigot because he asks: Or are you from the church?

Of course, I snort.

He plucks at the old roses I'm still holding tightly in my fist: Are you going to give me one of those?

No.

You won't be able to sell these.

I don't want to sell them.

How come, did your boyfriend give them to you?

No.

Did he stand you up?

Leave me alone.

Fine, he says, how much?

More than you can afford.

I'm a soldier, he says.

I can see that.

He screws up his eyes: I feel like I know you somehow.

Then he straightens up impatiently: Don't you want to? You're new, I can recommend you to my friends, we're all young and good-looking.

Don't exaggerate.

He wrinkles his nose: Are you sure?

Thanks, I say, maybe some other time.

I take a few steps to the side and lean against a wall. He does the same, but keeps a bit of distance. He looks at me with curiosity.

You're not from here, are you?

I shrug.

Not many of them are from here actually, but I don't recognise your accent. Why are you standing over here and not over there with the others?

I'm not with them.

He raises his eyebrows: Then you better watch out, they don't like competition.

Understood.

I'm serious, they'll scratch out your eyes with their sharp fingernails. Happened before.

But I'm not competition.

A nun after all? Are you trying to convert them?

He raises his hands: Calm down, I don't mean any harm. Obviously no one has told you, so allow me to: you shouldn't hang around here. If Favorita finds out that someone's been sniffing about, she'll make short work of you.

You know your way around, don't you? You must be here a lot.

Ha, he puffs.

If you're that good-looking, I say, why do you have to pay poor women to wank you off?

So you are a woman of the church, go to hell. Poor women!

85

He doesn't say anything for a while, and then he says: I work a lot, I don't have time for a girlfriend. Women are so demanding and complicated, you need to endure lengthy rituals in order to get them. I'm a man, what am I supposed to do? So how about you name your price?

He moves closer to me, I push him away: Get lost, I'm not one of them.

He grimaces disparagingly.

Right. And I think that's exactly what you are. You're being coy. But that doesn't work around here.

He bites his lip and says, finally: Are you hungry? We could grab something to eat first.

The memory of food hits me in the stomach like a punch. But with him? He doesn't look particularly dangerous. And what are my alternatives? I gave all my money to the rose seller.

Let's not then, he says grumpily, examining me: You shouldn't start doing it, you know. It's a sin.

I have to laugh out loud. He makes a throwaway gesture and mumbles an insult.

Excuse me?

You can't loiter here on your own, he says, it's dangerous.

You're repeating yourself.

Come on – he grabs me by the waist.

Let me go, I shout.

Stupid cow – he puts his hand up as if I'm holding a gun, and whispers angrily: I'm not going to do anything to you.

86

I'm just trying to help you.

I don't need any help.

Fine, he says, I'm going. Are you sure you don't want to eat anything?

I don't respond, he shrugs his shoulders: They're going to mash your brains with their stilettos.

He turns around and disappears into the dark. I hear a quiet call: Absolutely sure?

Knock it off!

Then I call him back, he stops, I step out from the shadows and rush over to him.

Do you know her? I show him the photo of Magdalena with the cowboy hat.

Favorita?

My heart gives a jolt.

Where did you get that? he asks, stunned.

I clear my throat to fight down my beating heart and put away the photo.

Is that who I need to watch out for?

He looks at me closely, I avoid his gaze, try to laugh: I'm not from the police if that's what you're thinking.

He snorts: You don't look like you are. What do you want with Favorita?

She offered me a job, I say quickly.

He breathes his suspicion straight into my face.

I took the photo when we met, I lie. It was a while ago, besides roses I sold snapshots from Polaroid cameras back then.

She thought I should keep the photo to remember her by, if I'd like to return to take up her offer. She wrote down the address for me, here.

I smooth down the note for him. The soldier examines it and then shrugs again. Did he really swallow it?

I haven't seen her today, he says, she's probably in the office. I can show you the back of the building, but you have to go in there alone. I don't want her thinking that I'm meeting girls behind her back.

I nod, it bubbles out of me: I already went there, round the back, she's gone out, Favorita that is. The other women intimidated me, that's why I wanted to wait here, but now you've infected me with all your rabbiting on about food.

He laughs: I knew it. But then I get mate's rates after.

That's for me to decide, I say, baring my teeth like Magdalena in the bar.

You can discuss that with Favorita, she has the last word. Now let's get out of here before word gets out that I'm buying.

He grabs my arm, the one that's holding the urn. While trying to hide it from him, the flowers fall all over the ground.

What is that you're schlepping about?

I step over the flowers and mutter something inaudible.

Two and a half kilos of mother, Magdalena, and now Favorita: the woman who has the last word, who makes short work of people.

*

We go to a snack bar, and I eat with determination. The soldier acts amused: What are you, a rubbish chute?

I order more, even more. He acts like he's getting impatient: You'll owe me, he repeats.

During all of this, I see that he actually doesn't want to. It's as if the role is gradually becoming more uncomfortable. He rubs his heavily ringed eyes, looks at his watch, looks out the window. He's making me nervous too: my plan's not working. I had imagined getting him drunk, steaming drunk – I'm good at that, I can hold my drink. I was going to play a little game with him, like Judith did with Holofernes.

But this soldier doesn't drink, not a drop. He sniffs the bottle I've slid towards him repeatedly with disapproval. To make matters worse, the food is making me awfully sleepy.

Order me a coffee, I say, then we'll go.

Fine, he says, swallowing a yawn, but that's enough. I can barely contain myself.

I don't believe a word of it. He goes to the bar, I stand up, he looks back, I smile. He finds me strange, and that's what I am: I leave my mother behind. What am I supposed to do – take her home, bury her, if possible with a priest present reciting a hypocritical poem?

This boy knew her, possibly better than I did. He calls her Favorita. He should be the one to take care of her. Without the mother-dust, I am finally free.

I move through the room as if in slow motion, towards a door

with a piece of paper stuck to it: WC, written in pencil. I close
the door behind me, breathe through my mouth, analyse the
wet floor, the dirty sink – no window.

Then I walk with long strides back, past the bar, towards the
exit. The neon light dazzles me, the soldier in the corner of
my eye, he's watching me, I run, my shoulder shoves the door,
pushes it open, my body slips out into the exhaust-filled
evening air.

A bird flies towards me and hits me with a dull thud on the
back of the head.

Then I fall into the well.

VI

Around me there's noise, screeching, fluttering. Magdalena's scent brushes me like a wing. I see the flowers in time lapse: rose petals floating, swirling in a wild dance; I close my eyes and open them again, the petals glide by me slowly, as if underwater.

The flowers hit my head rhythmically, screams in the distance, like at home when we're all together. I smell Magdalena again. Why is she so angry? Leave me alone, Mamma, go away, you stupid cow.

Suddenly I'm awake.

The woman in the blue dress is standing over me with Maria, the fake Maria from the piazza. Their faces are contorted, they're hitting me with their fists and shrill curses.

Stop, I shout, please stop.

You've messed with the wrong people, they yell, there's no room here for flower girls—

I try to protect my face, my eyes dart around, the soldier has disappeared.

When we're finished with you, your mother won't recognise you—

Then it occurs to me, and I yell: My mother is Favorita!

It works. Flowers keep flapping against my head, but the woman in blue drops her fists.

What did she say?

The flowers continue to thrash against me: Lies, she's lying!

No, I shout through the cursing, Magdalena – Favorita is my mother.

Lie-lie-lie, the fake Maria shouts, whipping the thorny stems in my face.

The woman in blue pulls her back: Stop it.

Then she turns to me: Why are you here?

I don't know how I could ever have compared her to Magdalena. I see a bulldog panting down at me through the haze over my eyes. I blink. There's a ringing in my ears. The blue Molossian hound nudges me and regains a human face: Come on then, what do you want?

To talk to you, I say weakly, about my mother.

Where is she? the blue one asks, but fake Maria interrupts her: Look at her lying, she's a liar. When Favorita gets her hands on you, she'll wring your neck, you hear me!

The woman in blue looks at me strangely: She's not lying.

The fake Maria snorts. Close up, she doesn't look like the flawless doctor Maria. Her lips are peeling, leaving pink sores and dried bloody crusts. Cheeks speckled with acne scars. And if her lashes had once been butterflies, someone has dunked them in liquid pitch.

She is even more beautiful than the real Maria.

Just look at her – the blue one points at me: One hundred per cent Favorita.

Her?

Blue shakes her head: How can you not see it? That's got to be her daughter, the one who lives with her grandmother – where?

In Switzerland, I reply.

It's her.

Fake Maria crumples her forehead: How do you know that?

Favorita told me.

She never told me anything.

Why should she tell you anything?

And how do we know she's not lying?

I can prove it, I say quickly, I've got a photo with me, and a letter she wrote to me, and—

What?

The urn! I left it in the bar with the soldier, I say.

That walking pair of balls, Fake Maria shouts, the next time I see him, I'm going to cut a bit of him off. Wants to be a regular, but hooks up with a flower girl right under my nose—

Blue shakes my shoulder: What are you talking about?

The ashes, I shout, I wanted to get rid of them when I was about to run off, and then you came—

Blue shoves Fake Maria: Sorella, go to the bar right now and see if you can find anything.

She watches her go, then she grips me hard by the chin: Now

you're going to tell me everything. From the beginning.

She's dead, I say, and see that Blue isn't surprised.

Who gave you the ashes?

The hospital. They called and said that she's dead. That some-one killed her.

They said that?

Well, one of them said that, the others said it was her liver.

Liver?

Shrunken liver, yes.

Blue sinks into silence.

Fake Maria stumbles out of the bar and the waiter slams the door in her face. She gives him the middle finger and laughs at us: I've got it!

*

They stare spellbound at the plastic box.

Fake Maria narrows her eyes: How do you even know it's her?

I sigh.

So, you've got no idea. You've let yourself be lied to and then you're spreading it around – didn't I say she was a fraud?

I lift up the urn and show them the name on the base.

That doesn't prove anything, Fake Maria claims. Have you looked inside it?

Yes, I say, there're ashes inside it. And a note that says Vico della Pace.

What in hell's name! Blue exclaims.

Someone at the hospital wanted me to find you. So you could tell me what happened.

They would know better than we do, Fake Maria mumbles.

She clumsily opens the lid and a little ash spills onto the ground.

Pig God, she shouts, that could be anything! That's just sand, dirty city beach sand. She laughs shrilly: That's not Favorita, they've done you over.

But Blue keeps staring at what spilled out.

Pick that up, she orders, and Fake Maria starts picking the ash out from between the cracks in the cobbles with her fingernails.

I'm sorry, Blue says to me, but why did you bring her here?

I didn't know—

It was a shit idea, she interrupts me. Are you really that naive? Do you want to follow in her footsteps?

She looks around and says: This is no place to chat – help her up.

Fake Maria pulls at my wrist like she's about to rip it off. I quickly sit up.

Did anyone else see you? Blue asks.

Only the soldier, I think.

Did you tell him who you are?

I shake my head.

Did he take a close look at the urn?

I don't think so.

The two of them exchange a look.

We need to get her away quickly before she starts to stink, Fake Maria says.

What?

Before anyone recognises you and rumours spread.

Blue extends her hand towards me: Come on, stand up, we're getting out of here.

I stand before her and stick out my chin: Do I really look like her? Favorita?

Not even a little, Blue lies, and Fake Maria says: Barely at all.

*

This is how they lead me away. Flanked like a criminal, one stuck to each elbow, pulling me forwards. We run through the labyrinth of dark passageways. I close my eyes and let myself be towed along, my little feet tapping away all by themselves.

We sit on the steps of a church. It's squeezed in between two houses, small and inconspicuous, if it weren't for the bollards with skulls and crossbones perched on top of them. The life-size skulls are polished, as if they had been rubbed by countless fingers. I raise my eyes to the church entrance. There too, between the angels carved in stone, the gap-toothed grins of skulls over crossed bones.

The two women light cigarettes without offering me one. They introduce themselves as Crocifissa and Genuflessa. I don't know if I should laugh or not.

She-Who-Is-Crucified and She-Who-Kneels, Fake Maria

explains, do you understand? They're ancient names perfumed with incense that inspire reverence among the men here and make their wives pray to us.

Blue, Crocifissa, shows me her palms, as if proving her innocence to me. Her fingers are red and swollen, like my grandmother's hands.

We're saints, Fake Maria declares solemnly, then bursts out laughing: Saints!

Someone told me about Saint Agatha today—

She interrupts me: Agatha is a cow. She thinks she's better than everyone else, like that arrogant guy Jesus. We are true saints: we embrace the lepers and don't make a song and dance about it.

She points the burning end of her cigarette at me: And what's your name, daughter of Favorita? Come on, think of something.

Crocifissa pulls out a bottle from her handbag and unscrews the cap. She takes a sip, then pours a lake into her palm and dips the fingertips of her other hand into it, flicking it in my face. It burns.

She pinches my chin and studies my face: We baptise you . . . Dolcetta.

It that a saint too?

They can't stop coughing with laughter.

Call me Sorella, Fake Maria says, sticking her cigarette between my lips.

She runs her fingers tenderly over the scratches on my forehead.

You really messed her up, Crocifissa says, digging in her bag. Don't we have anything to patch her up with?

Sorella cups my face in her hands, framing it: Madoo, such a pretty face. Would Favorita have been this cute without those teeth of hers?

She gently presses her fingertips on my eyelids: You'd be fierce competition for me if you ever decided you want to go on the job.

Don't say stuff like that, Crocifissa shouts.

Sorella laughs: Why not? What do you think she's after if she's not here to take over her mother's business? Maybe she even wants to become the next Capo.

There is a malicious glimmer in her eyes. She presses her hand over my mouth and says: Either way, we absolutely cannot leave her alone with Lorenzo, he'll fall in love with her immediately – but that's my customer, understand? Hands off Lorenzo.

Crocifissa soaks a handkerchief in schnapps, holds out the bottle to me.

I don't know anyone called Lorenzo, I mumble, removing Sorella's fingers from my face and taking a sip from the bottle.

Now it burns inside and outside. Sorella dabs my nose with the hanky, presses a little too hard and says: Look how innocent she's acting. To think I wanted to smash the bottle over your head.

The cigarette makes me feel heavy. I lie my head against Crocifissa's soft shoulder and murmur: It's strange what we remember. I hadn't seen Magdalena for so long, her face has disappeared.

But since you've been around, I feel like I can smell her.

Crocifissa clears her throat.

I sit up: What?

Sorella points her finger at her: She stole her dress.

Crocifissa jumps up: And what about you? Do you think we haven't noticed you limping around? Squeezing your flippers into Favorita's little golden shoes!

That dress is ten sizes too small for you, Sorella snaps back. It was already too tight for Favorita if we're being honest.

It didn't suit her at all. She didn't have the tits or the arse for it.

Now don't look so shocked, Dolcetta, that's how we operate here. We thought she had moved on.

Moved on where?

Somewhere. Another city, I don't know.

Why?

Why! That's how we are, we move around.

Magdalena's postcards come to mind, all the different cities.

Crocifissa nods: Some come back, some don't. That's life.

The two of them exchange a look.

I grab Sorella's arm: What do you know?

Us? Nothing.

Sorella looks to Crocifissa for help. She takes my hands. Bambola . . . I'm sorry. We didn't see anything.

She fixes her eyes on Sorella until she murmurs, I don't know, I wasn't even there that night.

I need you to tell me who did it.

What do you mean who, it was her liver, Sorella says dryly.

You know, Crocifissa says carefully, she really did have a thing with her liver. Because of the drinking, she was getting treatment. She went to the hospital a few times – for a detox, as she put it.

Sorella laughs: She was very proud of her detox. And whenever she came back, she got drunk. She always claimed: *The doctor told me to drink a lot.*

Crocifissa nods: We didn't know it was that bad.

I get up: You're no better than the disgusting doctor, than everyone in that lying hospital. You're all lying to my face. Lie-lie-lie!

Sorella shrugs: Sometimes a lie is better than the truth.

I howl with rage: So you admit it?

It's for your own protection.

I don't want any—

Crocifissa sighs: Even if we wanted to, we couldn't help you, Amore.

Why not?

Crocifissa throws up her hands: Because, because—

Sorella murmurs: Maybe she has a right to know?

Crocifissa yells: What? We don't know anything! Nobody knows anything, nobody saw anything. You know how it works.

Sorella shakes her head. Then she says: Have you seen the Coach since?

She takes a punch to the upper arm, then rubs at the spot angrily: What?

I look from one to the other: What coach?

Nobody, Crocifissa gives a fake laugh and presses the bottle to my lips, forget about it, take another sip.

He was Favorita's husband, Sorella says, the Coach.

Crocifissa smacks her forehead.

I want you to take me to him.

No, you don't want that, Crocifissa says firmly, you want the opposite of that. We're going to church now, and tomorrow morning you'll get on a train and take your poor mother home. You were never here.

She takes my arm intending to pull me up.

NO! Yet another scream. My face is glowing, it feels good: My sweetness and brava, it's worth nothing! I am Favorita's child; I have her cells. I want to become like her, loud and dangerous. I'll smash all your faces in!

Crocifissa sighs, pulling me up: If you must. But we're still going to church.

What the hell are you going to do there, Sorella grumbles, light a candle?

That's exactly what we're going to do.

*

It's dim inside the church. Incense smoke drifts into my face. I look at my companions to see if they cross themselves. I don't want to embarrass myself: I don't know how to do it properly. The holy water basin is empty, dirty residue on the stone. Crocifissa in her Marian blue dress walks past it without so much as a glance, Sorella follows after her.

They stride through the incredible marble arches as if it's the most natural thing in the world, without taking in all the lathe work, the gold, or the royal blue cloak of the Madonna in the huge fresco, not even out of politeness.

I always think about my grandmother in churches. She wasn't devout, she didn't cross herself. We never went to church back home, only in Italy. And we only went there to be hit around the head with the pageantry and to light candles for the dead: her mother, her grandmother. It had to be in front of the Madonna. Under no circumstances a bleeding Jesus, Sebastian or some canonised priest; she found these suffering men repulsive. She didn't want anything to do with the church, *church is bigoted*.

And yet, she used to say, I cannot deny Maria.

This made an impression on me, even if I didn't understand it: *I cannot deny Maria*.

So I head towards the altar for Maria, but Crocifissa hisses me back.

What are you doing over there, she calls in a hushed voice, come here right now.

She slaps the empty air as if I were a small child being summoned for a telling-off. When I reach her, she puts an arm around me tightly and draws me towards some stairs that lead down into darkness.

The saints aren't going to run away, she says. First we're going down into the cellar.

Sorella remains at the top of the stairs: I'll wait here.

Oh no you won't, Crocifissa commands, we have to enter as a united front and demand some respect. They've been acting up for too long.

Who? I ask.

The plague dead, Sorella whispers.

What?

You've got no idea, Crocifissa mewls, be quiet. And best to keep your mouth completely shut down there, otherwise a soul might fly in and possess you.

Sorella rolls her eyes.

And so, we climb down into the underworld.

*

A hall with high vaulted ceilings and rounded arches opens up before us. There is no gold or pomp here, just whitewashed walls from which the plaster is crumbling. We throw long, prancing shadows. The only light comes from the centre of the room, where four flickering torches joined by iron chains form a square. On the floor beneath, inside a flower pot, sits a real skull, laughing.

Welcome to the plague cellar.

Crocifissa's voice resounds as we keep walking, following her through the archways and corridors with reverberating steps. In the walls are boxy recesses, inside which are more bones and skulls. A few of these niches carved into the stone are tiled on the inside in bright bathroom colours. Some are plain, with only a damaged skull in them; others have shelves full of stacked-up bones, on top of which, on an embroidered doily, a skull is enthroned.

The walls make it like a dovecote or a morbid display case. Here, the skulls reside in their doll's house apartments, neatly beside and stacked atop one another. Every room tiled a different colour; some have dried-flower visitors, others snuggle in woollen coverlets, asleep on a pillow. Some are missing the top of their skull, others their lower jaw. They don't seem to mind; they appear quite content.

There are shrines with family-sized tables in front of them loaded up with flowers and images of holy saints; photographs and portraits of multiple generations; candles and statues with a garland of rosary. Lying on them are yellowed death notices, but also invitations to christenings, weddings, confirmations. Tacky Christmas cards and scratch cards, dried potted plants, football cards and stuffed animals.

Crocifissa slaps a cigarette from Sorella's hand, which she had stolen from an altar. Then they pause. A long room sprawls out before us like a kind of vegetable patch: a row of identical graves, covered with sandy earth, a dried rose stretched out on each of them. At the furthest end small crosses stick up, at their feet grave candles flicker. Far above the graves, rusty hooks stick out from the walls.

Sorella follows my gaze: They hung the dead from them. From the back of their necks. To dry out, like washing or sausages.

She strokes her cold fingers over the nape of my neck, I shake them off.

Don't believe me? Look, up there, the hatchway. During the plague they threw the bodies down it, they piled up here. And the undaunted sisters, the nuns, took them in. In spite of the deadly pestilence they carried them around, sought out a free hook. And then prayed, of course, so that the souls of the damned could find salvation all the same. Once they were dry, they were taken down and dismembered. That's how they ended up in new piles, sorted according to different kinds of bone. Here are all the thighbones, here are all the little finger bones, here are all the shinbones. Why was that, Crocifissa?

Maybe they were bored. Be that as it may, the bones are still here and at your service. You can pick one out.

Sorella shakes her head: Leave Dolcetta out of the game, she doesn't want to.

What don't I want?

Crocifissa prays to them. As if they were her very own personal saints, responsible for all her very own personal desires.

Bah, Crocifissa scoffs, you don't understand. Anyway, I'm not doing it for Dolcetta, I'm doing it for Favorita, she needs this now.

Sorella raises an eyebrow: She would laugh at you if she was here with us.

Crocifissa grabs my wrist, pulls me along with her: And if she is, she needs it all the more.

Crocifissa climbs over a pile of old skulls, stoops and wheezes: You need your own, who only looks after you.

She lifts up a skull, considers it from all sides, then waves me over so I can take a look at it.

Its jaw is missing and all of its front teeth; eyes and nose yawning hollows; a meandering crack runs across the forehead.

This one's good, Crocifissa says, I think it suits you both, what do you think?

I nod.

With the skull in hand, we go back past the hooks into a narrow windowless corridor, where Crocifissa finds a small, lonely niche. She brushes away a few bones with her palm and triumphantly places the skull inside.

It seems a bit sparse, she says, but not to worry, I'll make it look nice. A few tiles, a pretty curtain—

Maybe a television, Sorella suggests. She's a real social climber.

We giggle. Crocifissa hisses: You shut your mouths right now, otherwise she'll never help you.

She moves her face very close to the skull and places both her hands on its bald head. She starts whispering. Sorella sighs.

Rosaria says you should stop getting on my nerves immediately, Crocifissa reports.

Who's Rosaria?

Crocifissa punishes us with a furious look, as if we had just made her look foolish in front of her skull. Then she once again eavesdrops at its half jaw.

Rosaria says she died of the plague.

Sorella rolls her eyes: Of course she did.

Crocifissa ignores her: Rosaria, can you help us? Favorita, the mother of this clawed kitty here, recently began her journey to the realm of the dead.

I clear my throat.

She sends a *Shh* in my direction, and back to the skull: She has – possibly – been violently murdered. Can you accompany Favorita on her journey down the river to the underworld to help provide some peace for her stormy soul?

Then she gets a little bottle out and begins rubbing the skull's forehead with oil.

She murmurs: Above all, help this innocent creature, our sweet Dolcetta, reach salvation.

I feel sick. The smell of the oil is pungent. I can't help but think of the doctor, his oily fingers gripping Magdalena's skin; how he shoved her into the oven. I close my eyes, imagine Magdalena drifting down a dark river. The river is a tube slide, her body swings around the corners, but the river never stops.

Crocifissa gives me a nudge: Dolcetta, say thank you to Rosaria.

I curtsy in front of the skull: My grandmother always said that Magdalena wouldn't make it to heaven. Now she will after all, thank you.

Sorella snorts: Your grandmother was right, people like us don't get into heaven. We'd just get bored there anyway.

Crocifissa places the skull carefully in the niche.

Then she says, wait, there's one more thing.

We follow her to another shrine where a few dried flowers are lying in front of a skull. Crocifissa removes it, the flowers fall to the floor. With her flat palm she hits the skull against its cracked forehead.

Idiot, she shouts, good-for-nothing dust catcher. I've been taking care of you for years and what do you give me in return? I get down on my knees and beg and pray for my daughter to grow – and what happens? Nothing. Tomorrow's her third birthday, and she's a fucking doodlebug. Make her grow right now, or I'll smash you to a pulp.

She throws the skull against the wall, a couple of pieces crumble off. She breathes heavily and puts it back in its place. She looks at it, overcome by hatred, grabs it and hurls it into the corner. She screams: And keep us safe, I said! And what did you do? Just because I didn't visit you for a couple of days? I've had it with you.

She sinks to the floor, panting.

Sorella turns around and says: Come on, let's go light some candles.

*

Back in the church, they leave me on my own. I stand in front of the shrine to Maria and reach into the tin holding the tapers. What am I doing here?

A peculiar smirk contorts my face. The skulls! They've crept inside me.

Candle flames heat my cheeks. Images flicker in the gleaming glow.

The bones in the cellar. The women. The scuffle. The soldier.

The hospital, doctor's hands and Maria's lips.

The beards at the museum, and Judith. The men at the market, the moon child.

The waiter, Agatha, the breasts.

The train journey, the kitchen, the phone call.

Magdalena. Lavinia.

The skulls.

I'd like to lie down with them. Go to sleep. But I'm not tired. I want to run out to the women and get smashed with them; hit the ground over and over until I can't get up again. Am I even awake? In any case I have grown: I stand like a giant over my own body and look down on myself. What are you doing, little girl? What are you going to do?

As I light the match and then the candle wick, I try to hear Lavinia's voice: *I cannot deny Maria.*

I copy her movements, the match burns out. I feel nothing. I can't think of them, neither of them. What should I say: Ciao, Nonna, I'm good, how are you? Don't worry?

Or: Hey, Mami, how's it going? I got you a skull and a candle, so things will be better for you soon.

The Madonna smiles at me encouragingly. But I only hear bubbling magma, hellfire, and my own skull voice: *I want retribution, not salvation.*

*

Outside on the steps we light cigarettes. As I try to give Cro-cifissa back the lighter, she shakes her head: You know what, I think it belonged to Favorita. Keep it. She didn't leave you much else.

She considers her neckline and says: I can give you the dress later, don't have anything else right now.

Sorella slips off her shoes and shunts them over to me with her naked toes.

You can have these too, she says.

Thanks, I say, but I never saw my mother wearing trainers.

Sorella nods: She used to say that she was born in heels, like her mother. But recently she only wore these.

She was in pain, Crocifissa adds, because of her bunions.

The thought that Magdalena had aged. Tying the shoelaces with slightly shaking fingers. The sight of these worn-out gold trainers affects me more than anything else.

They're too big for me, I lie. You can keep them.

They're all out of shape, Sorella says, wiggling her feet back into them, you're not missing anything.

On the lighter is the image of a stoned cartoon cat in front of a rainbow. The little cat is sticking out its tongue with both its middle fingers in the air. A message is emblazoned over the image in glowing bubble writing, it's exploding in white clouds and black stars: GO TO HELL.

*

Astride motorbikes we blaze through the alleyways of the night. Tear through deep-fried air from the panzerotto stands, past the military tanks and pointy-capped soldiers; the blinking lights of the caged Madonnas swipe across my eyes like fireflies.

We're on our way to a party, the whole town's going to be there. It's too far by foot, so we get a lift with a couple of adolescents on souped-up bikes.

That's my cousin, Sorella says to my biker, she's here visiting, and if you touch her, I'll kill you.

He laughs and revs the engine. I put one arm around his middle, and with the other I hold the urn tightly. We reach a boulevard where cars are lined up honking; a long and winding tin snake with red glowing eyes, we pass it by.

We've left the others far behind us. I've given up trying to remember the route I would run back along after successfully escaping, and I've stopped trying to mentally compose the words I would use to insult my attacker before kneeing him between the legs – I wouldn't have a chance. The question of whether my new friends have just sold me or whether the boy I'm embracing has single-handedly stolen me, I let flutter away on the wind.

I let go of everything and give myself over to the airstream, the smell of diesel and charcoal smoke, it's like we're flying.

The alleys get narrower, he shifts down the gears, we putter at walking pace through swarms of people, the smoke is getting thicker. We dodge a dog fight: men flogging the animals with their wads of cash, yelling. I hold the urn tightly to my chest, but my heart is wide open. My face is glowing, a distant music pumps over our heads. I look back and see the other motorbikes behind me: Sorella, Crocifissa. I can't stop smirking, the bass takes over my pulse, I take my hand from the boy's stomach, throw it into the air and dance around on the saddle. The boy hoots, the whole town hoots, Crocifissa yells: FAVORITA! The boys on the street howl after her, bellow the name up to the rooftops. The ashes shiver to the beat of the cobblestones.

At the end of the street the world opens up. A square full of people, deafening music; drink stands, barbecue grills. I jump off the motorbike, he drives straight off.

Bambola, Crocifissa shouts, her rider has stopped courteously, she's only now climbing down from the saddle: Come on, I'll buy you a skewer.

The houses hemming the square are ruins from the war. Lettering that reads *Banca Nazionale* is chipped, half the building has been bombed away. On the façades, behind which there's sometimes a living room and sometimes only air, giants and monsters are painted. On the occupied balconies little girls dance. On the edge of the piazza fathers teach their children how to ride a motorbike; the youngest do their doughnuts on three wheels: candy-coloured princesses with an army of little cavaliers trailing behind.

Sorella is already standing by the grill, where a delectable boy with slicked-back hair is turning what look like twisted sausages.

What's that?

Brain.

He grins. A crucifix bounces on his bare chest. I want to eat him.

He picks up one of the sizzling coiled brains with his fingers and skewers it on a wooden stick.

Limone?

He squeezes the juice from a wedge, licks his fingers without taking his eyes off me.

I groan, Sorella pulls me away.

Just like your mother, Crocifissa says, shaking her head.

What! I shout, gobbling down the brain, the best thing I've ever eaten, and chuck the stick into the crowd.

You know, Sorella says, I just can't take men seriously. I have no respect for them. Thankfully they're so basic. I stick their head between my legs and say something devastating. And they're over the moon.

I have to laugh and look over at the boys, trying not to imagine her.

And you, she says, without taking her eyes off me, you're really only interested in guys?

What, I shout, why?

Sorella shrugs her shoulders: Your mother was that way at least. She was crazy for men. They could do the worst things to her, and she would still see the good in them. She's probably in the process of seducing the devil himself.

Crocifissa nods: She treated men like sons.

My grandmother was the opposite, I scream against the loud music, men didn't interest her. After the death of her husband she'd had enough for a lifetime. She always used to say: Serving one man is enough for me!

A very clever woman, Crocifissa says, passing me a plastic cup, I hope you take after her.

I don't know, I say, smiling at the boy on the grill, I could happily eat a few of them a day. And on top of that, for money?

Sorella snatches at my hands: Sure, do it! Join the business!

Crocifissa stops dancing: Are you crazy? She has a good life.

I spit out an ice cube: Me? I've got nothing. What do you know about my life?

She presses her hand over my mouth: Shut your trap.

Sorella cries out: Croci, she's Favorita's daughter! What could she have passed down to her if not that? And anyway, it's only natural that she wants to learn more about her mother's life.

Croci presses her fingers even more tightly over my mouth: Favorita would turn in her grave.

I bite down until she lets go, and say: She doesn't have a grave.

I almost don't feel the blow. My right ear whistles, through my left I hear: Your mother gifted you a normal life. Your inheritance is to get far away from what she did.

I knock back my drink and smirk: Did you swallow her last will and testament?

*

We dance wildly and aggressively. Bodies wet with sweat, pumped up by bass and booze; one mass, one movement, everything obeying an invisible power. Strobe cuts: the surging people vanish into nothing and reappear in flashes. Thumping in my throat, a feeling like having a fever: strange intimacy and uncanny strangers. Faces disintegrate, torn open mouths, wet teeth—

The mass gnaws on brain skewers and dances till its feet are bloody. They give brain to the dogs with half their ears missing, they give brain to the babies and the flirtatious tricyclists. We dance in the middle of it all.

My armoured shell has been shed, I trample over it and soak the booming present into all my pores. Is this the way Magdalena experienced the world, did she move like this? Am I transforming into her right now? Pleasure flows through me, joy tingles in my fingertips.

My life fits together, in this smoke and screaming my thoughts become clear: it feels good, I understand. Of course she lived here, this was her world. I've found everything: the meaning, Magdalena, myself.

Without looking I wrap my arms around the body behind me, let myself be hotly kissed on the nape of my neck, give myself to the maelstrom, dive in. Sink down into the gullet of ecstasy.

*

As the sun comes up we crest the hill, stand on its cusp and look at the sea.

We raise our cups to the yoghurt-hued sky: To Favorita!

I shunt in afterwards: The worst mother in the world!

Hey, Crocifissa grunts, I don't want to hear any of that. You were always taken care of. Who's to say that good mothers have to bring their children up themselves? Important women, revolutionaries, had their children brought up by others – because they had to travel or flee, because they were in prison or busy making the world a better place. That doesn't mean they didn't love their kids.

My mother wasn't a revolutionary, was she?

Crocifissa waves it away, spluttering: That's not the point.

I toast the sea: To Favorita, a woman I didn't know.

Porco dio, Crocifissa cries, I have to go. It's birthday day after all!

I stagger over to her, fall into an embrace: Auguri!

Not her birthday, Sorella laughs, her daughter's.

I birthed her, didn't I, so it's my birthday too.

I hang off Sorella: We're staying here and having a snooze, aren't we?

Certainly not, Crocifissa says, you're coming with me. If I can't sleep, no one can sleep. We're off to a kid's birthday party.

VII

Four rattling bus journeys later, we finally reach the outskirts.

While we bounce on our seats over potholes, Sorella explains where they live:

It was once an old salami factory, technically uninhabitable. But there were a lot of us, and we needed somewhere to live. So we moved into the factory. That was a few years ago. We built everything ourselves, you'll see, it's one big work of art. It might look a bit dingy from the outside, but it's really clean and cosy inside the living quarters.

The bus stops right outside the factory. It looks like a fortress; only a watchtower juts out above the high wall. On it is a telescope welded together from rusty barrels and pointing at the moon, pale in the morning sky. On the tower wall is a sundial with no numbers, instead it has letters that form the word: REVOLUTION. On the outer wall is a huge mural of two women lying on top of one another kissing, their legs entwined.

Welcome to the moon, Crocifissa says.

Sorella opens the huge iron gate while Crocifissa sticks her fingers in one of the countless mailboxes of different sizes haphazardly stacked on top of one another. Through the bars I can see the yard, the walls are decorated here too. A woman is sitting in front of a guard hut, yawning, over her shoulder hangs a rifle. She nods to us as we enter. Inside the vast factory a door flies open, a horde of children run out and into us. They have us surrounded.

Hello aunties, they shout.

Hello my beauties, Crocifissa says.

The little ones show the gaps in their teeth, they jump and scream, yank on our fingers. A boy presses himself between my legs, stands in the middle of us: I'm Iku.

From a window, someone hisses him away.

We're mistrustful people, Crocifissa says, and Sorella explains: We have to be careful. There are evictions every day in other squats in the city.

If they even so much as show their faces, Crocifissa says grimly, we're armed.

You bet, Sorella says. We have a rocket—

Crocifissa interrupts her: Stop telling the whole world about it. After all, she's Favorita's daughter, we don't know . . .

What?

What side you're on.

I protest and she waves it away: Just don't say anything to anyone here. We're all paranoid.

Sorella wants to show me the factory, while Crocifissa takes two children by the hand and goes to prepare the party. I stop in front of a painting on the wall of the building: a rocket flying to the moon.

A child has followed us, asks me for a cigarette. I don't have any. Sorella hits him on the back of the head with the flat of her hand.

That's me, the child says, pointing at a little green Martian inside the rocket.

Really, I say, and how was it out in space?

It was totally silent, the child says. But it was a Sunday.

And that's why you came back?

Yeah, the child says. It was boring.

And it's better here?

The child lifts his shoulders up to his ears.

We're going again soon, he says, maybe you can come too.

To the moon?

The child runs off.

We enter the factory through a dark reverberating hall. Drips fall from the ceiling, which slumps as if it will collapse at any moment. Rivulets run along the bottom of the walls; it stinks of sewage. A couple of children are sailing paper boats. The walls are covered in drawings of birds flapping inside cages.

Sorella takes me into the former slaughterhouse.

Careful, she pulls me away from the wall, the hooks are still sharp.

Whole pigs are hanging in here. Painted life-size, they dangle upside down from the hooks. The rail where the living pigs were hung before being taken into the next room to be dismembered is still on the ceiling. But the painted pigs break free at the door and float with angel's wings towards the sky.

119

Just like us, Sorella says, following my gaze. In the end we're going to fly away from here.

We climb upstairs to the living quarters. Giant plaster snails stick to the walls, they crawl in bright colours right up to the ceiling.

Snails always have their home with them, Sorella says, like us. We're not from here and not from there. We're always on the move, always fleeing – like witches, that's why they fear us. They used to burn us as witches, did you know that?

Before I can answer, three young women approach, push past us with their melon bellies; sheepish smiles.

Sorella says: Here, every pregnancy takes a tooth.

We reach the hall on the upper floor. Small low houses have been built here, they barely reach over my head. Shoeboxes with no lids, instead, they have windows and doors. Protruding from the top are ducts, which wriggle like plump veins along the ceiling of the hall to fetch fresh air from smashed windows. We walk between the little houses through a small passageway. The windows are covered; a child lifts the curtain, there's no windowpane, he shouts out: Ciao!

The passageway leads to a kind of inner courtyard in the hall. Children are sprawled in garden chairs between clothes horses. Above them pigeons are sleeping in the rafters.

Sorella knocks on a window frame, and Crocifissa shouts out:

Sit down in front of the little house, I haven't tidied, we'll head to the terrace in a minute.

Sorella tips a child out of their chair and falls into it.

From within we hear the tired voice of an older woman, a squeaking little voice and Crocifissa, who is singing a song and making lots of popping kisses.

More and more children come into the yard, they're abuzz, they want to party. Up they pull Sorella, who had been lolling in the garden chair with her eyes closed, and drag her giggling to the terrace. Outside four women are busy with a folding table; they portion out different flavours of crisps into large foil containers. Rattling music rings from a loudspeaker, the boy named Iku dances and shouts: Look, look at me dancing.

A toothless woman with layers of skirts smiles to me and points at the door.

They're coming, she says, they're coming.

Crocifissa appears in the dark of the door, small girls tiptoe behind her like a row of ducklings wearing princess dresses, they're holding hands. They're heavily made up: round red cheeks, lipstick and blue-eyeshadowed eyes. Crocifissa lifts up the smallest of the girls and shouts: This is my daughter. It's our birthday today. I gave birth to her three years ago.

Auguri, I shout.

She puts the girl on the table, a little foot lands in the crisps. Even the thickly applied rouge can't conceal her translucent skin. The girl begins to dance. Crocifissa cries.

Sorella grabs my arm and pulls me into the darkness.

*

Up on the roof, we sit in the shadow of the watchtower.

Sorella says: I'm happy for her, but it breaks my heart when I see her with her daughter. I become a small child again, whose own mother never did anything nice like this. I told Crocifissa that once. She's called me *my sweet little girl* ever since. She's a good mother.

We fall into silence and look out over the landscape. There's a broad road leading into the city. There are car dealerships on both sides: huge fields of lacquered beetles shining in the sun. Among them a red wind puppet throws its arms in the air.

The sound of the birthday party floats up to us: music, rejoicing, shrill children's voices, crying.

A woman with a machine gun walks past, Sorella waves, the woman sticks out her tongue.

All quiet?

As always.

Sorella, I say, after the woman has disappeared around the corner, why do you live in a fortress?

She opens her arms wide: Look around you. What do you see?

I close my eyes.

Pig ghosts. Kids' art. Hand-sewn curtains. Barbed wire . . .

She smiles: You're only just realising.

No men?

Boys are allowed if they behave accordingly. They can decide to put aside their masculinity, then they're allowed to stay. Some of them do, but not all of them. You saw Iku, he'll most likely go. We try to pass on what's best for the cause. We need allies on the outside too.

I nod as if I understand.

I'd prefer it without walls and cannons too. But if we want to survive, we have to fortify and defend ourselves.

I don't say anything, she gets angry: You think we're overdoing it? Didn't you see what was going on out there? The uniforms: the police, the soldiers?

Those funny hats? I shout. I thought they just stood in front of tourist attractions because of terrorism?

Fila, they're fascists! They are the terror. They see us as a natural resource that they can exploit and destroy, like the planet. They take every last thing from us and force us to the rubbish dump.

I mutter: But it's really nice here.

Precisely, she exclaims, we transformed a cesspool into an oasis. Because we didn't have anywhere else to go, we built our own world in this inhospitable terrain – from the rubbish that others threw away. And it's blooming!

Sorella jumps up and walks back and forth: In their eyes, we're no longer worthless, now we're a threat, because we show them how wrong they are. The way we live here, autonomously, doesn't fit into their image of things. They want to see us out on the street, dehumanised by misery. For them it's about politics, for us it's about existing. We have our freedom here, do you even know what that is? If you experience it even once, you won't want to live without it. But that means that we have to be on guard constantly, have to keep them far from our walls and keep the fortress locked up. This is how we're free, in eternal resistance. And if they penetrate the walls, then we'll fly.

Flee, where?

No, fly. The moon will grant us asylum.

I laugh: What's with the story about the moon?

We have to live somewhere! And there isn't a place for us in this city, in this country, in the whole cursed world. It's cheap on the moon. But the homesickness is intense.

I can't tell whether she's being serious.

Why the moon?

It belongs to everyone, the moon is free. There's no right to property up there. On the moon we can live together in peace. The children have written rules for the moon world, did you see, down there, on the path? They are their wishes for how they want to live. The writing leads the way to the launch pad.

There really is a rocket?

Are you surprised? Just look around you! We managed to build a home in a stinking salami factory – in the middle of a war. Because it is a war. That's what Otrere says too.

Who?

Otrere. She encouraged us to arm ourselves, to get our fortress ready to defend ourselves from the war. I was a pacifist before all this, I didn't want anything to do with weapons. War makes more war, etc. But Otrere is right. In tough situations we have to tell ourselves: I am a fighter! It changes everything. They pursued our mothers and grandmothers and their mothers before them – of course they're afraid of our vengeance. If they want to hold their position, they have to be oppressing us constantly. If they attack us and we don't fight, they'll bulldoze this place. One day we'll turn the tables on them. They'll exploit and kill us, as long as we don't defend ourselves. We'll be able to educate the new generation, but the older ones . . . The violent only understand violence. Did you hear about the rebels who dismembered a man? He wanted to let their children starve – they sold his flesh. Mothers are the most remarkable warriors, Otrere says.

One day, during the founding period, she was standing in the yard telling the children about the Amazons. She'd trespassed without an invitation, so we had to beat her up. She fought well. And we found her ideas convincing. She was the one who suggested building a rocket. We told her: Listen, pal, we're already working day and night to build our homes!

But Otrere said that we would need more than just the essentials. We shouldn't want to just survive, but also to dream. She was right. Now we have a present and a future. We're ready for anything.

And where's Otrere now?

She disappeared once the rocket was finished. Probably to a new group she's training to become fighters. I'm sure we'll see her again. At the revolution at the very latest.

You believe in a revolution?

You don't?

Sorella pulls me up: Come on, I want to show you something.

We climb up the fire escape to the top of the watchtower, where the telescope is. It's comprised of three barrels welded together with some kind of binoculars at the end where you put your eyes.

Look through it, Sorella commands.

I obey.

Do you see anything?

I nod. There's the moon with its craters, across it is some writing: *The Archive of Murdered Women*. Sorella stands close to me, I can sense her warmth, her scent.

Click, a picture covers the moon. A black and white photo of a young woman, she's laughing.

Sorella's breath brushes my ear.

That's Sisina, I hear her say. She was famous in Otrere's youth. She died in her village, shortly after the Second World War, aged nineteen. She was on her way to collect water from the spring when she was killed.

Hmm.

What?

My great-grandmother also died young while collecting water. At least that's what my mother claimed. That she was pregnant and she fell—

Sisina had her throat slit.

I sniff, embarrassed.

Sorella continues: Her fiancé was arrested and released. He was celebrated as a hero, he even had books written about him. Otrere said that's why she became a fighter. For Sisina.

Click. A new image appears, this time in colour. A woman our age, she winks at the camera.

That's Fiammetta, Crocifissa's niece. She lived with her boyfriend in the city and was studying, Crocifissa was very proud of her. She died three years ago, the boyfriend strangled her. His relatives raised money for him, he's been free for ages.

Click. A woman, maybe fifty, a snapshot, a little blurry, she's smoking, concentrating.

That's Francesca, she taught many of our children. Her ex threw her out of a window. He said it was an accident. He was drunk, which helped him. He lives in her apartment now.

I detach my eyes from the telescope.

Do you want more?

She runs her finger over the slides lined up on the side of the telescope, which is actually a peep show.

I came up with the design. We initially wanted to build a real telescope so we could look at the moon, but we couldn't chase down all the parts. At the same time, we've been thinking for a long while about creating the archive.

Sorella wipes the glass of the eyepiece with her sleeve and clicks further:

There are new ones daily. At the beginning there are the ones we knew, those who were close to us. We don't have photos of all of them, but we try to collect their names, their stories, try not to forget them.

I have a picture of Magdalena, I say, Favorita.

She nods.

*

We sit along the edge of the tower rooftop, swinging our legs. In my hand, the photo: cowboy hat at the bar.

Was she part of this?

Favorita? Sorella shakes her head.

Why not?

She doesn't respond. I feel a stab of realisation run through me: You didn't want her here.

Sorella looks at me: You know what she was like.

No, I say, I don't know.

She was . . . not a team player.

She was too much for you.

Fila, she wasn't . . . How can I say this? We couldn't trust her.

Why not?

I . . .

You thought she was against you?

No, I don't know. She wasn't on any side, I think.

Why didn't you ask her?

Fila, you don't understand, she wasn't in any state . . .

Because she was crazy.

What does crazy even mean?

Unpredictable. Quick-tempered, egocentric, spiteful? A drunk?

Well—

I understand perfectly well, she would have been a risk. A burden. So you left her on her own.

Sorella doesn't say anything. My heart's thumping: Did you know that she wanted to leave her husband? She wrote to me and told me. You thought that she couldn't fight. But the doctor told me—

What?

I look at the photo, Magdalena's teeth.

Nothing.

I've never seen someone fight so hard for their life.

Sorella lights a cigarette, blows out smoke: I'm sorry, Fila.

I'm sorry too.

It's not your fault.

No. Yes. I don't know. She was all alone. I know she wasn't a pleasant person. Not someone you wanted to have around. It's her fault, I think, she should have made more of an effort. To be nicer. Uh, I don't know. Maybe if I'd come looking for her . . .

It's not your fault, Sorella repeats.

It was easier, you know. Without her. Not looking for her was easier for me.

Yeah, Sorella says, I understand.

I shake my head: She was my mother, I love her.

You don't have to—

No, you don't understand. She needed so much love. She demanded it, desperately, aggressively, but somehow my love didn't arrive, or not quickly enough – as if she were a desert, and my cautious drops of love evaporated immediately on the dried-out ground. It was never enough, it made her furious. Once, when I saw how badly she was doing, when the fear for her tightened around me, I yelled: Stop it! Why do you keep saying that no one loves you, I love you!

It didn't help. She sobbed: What am I supposed to do with that? You're my daughter, you have to love me.

No one made me as angry as she did, helplessly angry. It wasn't my love she needed. She always felt wrong, misunderstood, as if everyone was against her. She hit out before anyone could get close, attack as pre-emptive self-defence. I was scared of her, of her outbursts. When she was around, I was so tense and I couldn't wait for her to leave. And when she was gone, I missed her. Then I would remember the good times: that's how it could have been. If I had been more patient, stronger, more loving; she was so vulnerable, fragile. My guilty conscience was always gnawing at me – but she was so horrible! The most exhausting person I've ever encountered. She was impossible.

I turn the photo in my fingers, the words reverberate in my head afterwards. Impossible. Our relationship was impossible – and this realisation was liberating. But was it true? Or was this an excuse too, an evasion, an assertion that had been repeated so often that I believed it?

Sorella watches me attentively while I sit in silence. I clear my throat, continue:

I had to find a way to live without becoming crushed by her. I mean, it wasn't her that was crushing me, she wasn't there of course, it was more the thought of her. The fear. The guilt.

Sorella looks at me searchingly. I say what has suddenly become clear to me, what I have never expressed before: I was always afraid that she would die. And I always felt guilty because I couldn't prevent it from happening.

My face twists into a grimace, I breathe deeply and smile.

So I told myself, as long as I don't hear anything from her, she's OK. We're better without one another. But that was for me. It was better *for me*. That's what I thought. And then I hear about her, about her death, and I'm relieved. It's over. Finally. The fear falls away. But just like whenever she was gone, I begin to miss her, and—

I can't keep talking. Sorella swims in front of my eyes, as she says: And this time it's forever.

The sky grows black, falls like a curtain, Sorella catches me.

A while later I come to, release myself from her embrace. Sorella gives me a cigarette: You shouldn't smoke so much.

I take a deep drag: I don't smoke at all.

Sorella laughs: No skin off my nose what you tell your grandmother, you smoke like a barbecue.

And you?

I'm without sin. The pope absolved me.

Cin cin!

It was her husband, I say, wasn't it, this Coach?

Sorella doesn't look at me, she looks out over the shining roofs of the cars, watches the wind puppet dancing.

Why are you covering for him? I thought you were warriors.

She flicks the cigarette from the roof and fixes her gaze on the puppet energetically casting out its limbs.

I grow angry: You're afraid of him because he's dangerous, that I understand. But he can't just get away with it. I have to do something!

Sorella exhales deeply: What?

Go to the police.

Sorella laughs cruelly: Of course, the police. And what are you going to tell them? They did a good job: there's no longer a corpse. You show up there with the urn and say it was the Coach. They'll laugh at you.

You're laughing at me!

Dolcetta, didn't you listen to me? Why do you think the archive is getting fuller every day? Men murder us because no one stops them. Because they know that often they won't even get punished. And even when they do, they'd rather accept punishment than be left by us, than lose control over us. But the Coach is a man with powerful friends. They'll let him go, even if they catch him in the act of stabbing someone. For someone like that they'd turn everything upside down, they'd tamper with the knife they took out of his hand. And suddenly your fingerprints are on it. Do you understand, there are no police. Not for us, and not for men like the Coach.

What does that mean?

She shakes her head in disbelief: Are you stupid? Your mother wasn't some bourgeois woman. She was one of us. Whether and how we die, they don't care, they're not interested, not in the slightest. How many of us disappear every day? What do you think? And do you reckon that someone goes looking? Some are found dead by chance, others stay missing. People don't give a shit about that. They think it's part of our job: Ah, a murdered prostitute! Probably a client that wanted to feel really powerful for once in his life. Who can only get it up if he nearly kills a woman – or finishes the job. What's that pretty term? Lust murder, lush. Yep, that's what we're here for, social buffers. So loser men can vent, so the streets are safer for everyone else. Do you think that when one of us dies, someone looks for the perpetrator? The blame lies with us, we're the perpetrators. There, where we end up, we've earned all of it.

What do you think happened to Favorita in the hospital? They were all there: police, paramedics, quacks. Believe me, they know exactly what happened, but they don't see us as people. They saw your mother and said: Not worth the effort. Into the oven with her.

Rain is falling from somewhere. Droplets on my face.

I recall what my grandmother said: She never had a chance.

I'm sorry, Fila. That's our life, it was Favorita's life too. Crocifissa's right: Your mother kept you out, and she wouldn't have wanted you to get involved now.

Be quiet, I say, I'll stab the Coach's eyes out. What's he going to do, kill me too?

Sorella grips my shoulder: Forget it, girl.

I shake her off angrily: Girl? You're barely older than I am.

She has a crooked smile: I'm a hundred and twenty years old.

I watch a murmuration of starlings, how it meanders across the sky, and say: She was completely alone when she died. She didn't want to die, you know.

I know.

What do you think I should do?

You can't do anything. What happened, happened. I think that Favorita would have wanted you to go home and live your life.

You sound like my grandmother.

They both wanted you to be happy. You can choose to take it easy, do you understand? After all, Favorita was really ill.

You think that I should believe that she died of her illness?

I move along the edge of the roof, look out over the yard, the field of cars, the broad road.

It would be a comfort to believe in the illness, in a natural death. It would be her own fault. And there's no evidence to the contrary. The only person who told me anything different was a nameless voice on the telephone. If I try and remember it, it seems like a dream. Maybe I misunderstood the word *ammazzata*. Maybe it was a different word that I didn't know, and I translated it incorrectly? I mean, why would the people at the hospital lie? It doesn't make sense.

No, Sorella says, it's senseless.

Well then, I invented it. I was overtired and heard voices in my head.

Sorella looks at me steadfastly, I tear myself from her gaze, speak into the abyss:

On the other hand you're telling me that this Coach is dangerous—

Others are dangerous too.

You think it was someone else? A client?

Sorella picks her fingernails.

But how come you lot here didn't hear anything about it? You would have heard something like that, there would have been screams, and if the ambulance came—

I wasn't there.

You weren't there, I know. But someone or other must have been there!

Sorella takes my hands in hers and pulls me up: What do you want to do?

I want to believe that it was her liver. That she drank herself to death. Or . . .

Or what?

Or plunder your weapon cabinet and shoot the Coach and every man in the whole city.

Sorella nods: Ambitious.

I want to fight, I say, with you.

She gives me a strange look. The entwined women in the wall mural spring to mind.

I pounce.

*

135

I'm woken by drum rolls. Raspberry sky and shimmering amoebas; starlings deploy their evening parade. Sorella is hurriedly getting dressed – get up, she shouts, they're coming!

Who's that drumming? I murmur.

They're here, she shrieks, they're clearing us out! I can't believe it, now of all times. Fuck, this is going to be a bloodbath. Get down!

I get up and look out to the yard. A fleet of black police cars and army vehicles are streaming through the torn-down gate and spreading like a pool of pitch.

Sorella, I shout against the din, it's not drumming, it's the tanks.

She looks fixedly at the sky, listening: I have to go to the rocket right now. They've already started it up, can you hear it?

Through the pounding and rattling a loudspeaker booms from the hulk of metal below: This building is contaminated. It must be cleared out immediately. Complete evacuation for reasons of safety.

Sorella swears, wipes her eyes: Lying arseholes.

Give yourselves up peacefully and you will not be harmed. You have twenty minutes. When that time has run out we will storm the factory.

Sorella grabs the back of my neck: I have to get to the rocket.

I'm coming with you!

Don't be afraid, they won't do anything to you.

In response: a shot whistles by. And another and another.

I think that spares us the discussion, I shout.

Sorella pulls me to the ground.

Some of the rifles sound like frantic woodpeckers. Others like fireworks. The rocket-propelled grenade strikes with a hiss. We cough from the smoke.

Brainless idiots, Sorella scolds in the direction of the guard tower, just shooting down on them like that, we would have still had time! How the hell are we going to get down now?

We crawl across the terrace and see a few women taking cover behind the tower and shooting into the yard. The recoil shudders through their bodies. Police and soldiers fall on their backs like beetles. Through the doors, a cannon is rolled onto the roof. We cover our ears. Below, a car goes up in flames. The women rejoice. The first bullets fly back, towards us. Projectiles hit the tower, a rhythmic chiming.

We lie on the ground holding hands. I protect myself with my steel-hard eyelids. In the darkness the shots whistle around us, hammering down.

Sorella lets go of my hand and I open my eyes: If we want to get out of here alive, we have to go.

She nods towards the open door that leads inside the building: Now or never.

We jump up and run inside, between the little cardboard houses, beating our way through curtains and damp washing, startled pigeons.

Retreat to the rocket! The call rings through the halls, retreat to the rocket!

Where's Crocifissa?

Sorella pants: She made it, and we're going to make it too, everything's going to be OK.

A group of women and children run into us in the stairwell: They've blocked the way! We have to go through the slaughterhouse!

Have any of you seen Crocifissa?

They shake their heads and stream past us.

Sorella stays where she is and looks out of the window.

Why aren't we going with the others? I shout. What are you doing, come on!

She shakes her head: The way through the slaughterhouse is too far.

But they—

They don't stand a chance. Can't you hear? The rocket's starting at any moment.

Through the muffled gunfire there's a glimmer of a hum growing ever louder, making the windowpanes shudder.

Sorella's voice is strangely calm: They have us surrounded, we can't get past them.

What are we going to do?

She smiles: There's two of us, we're quick. We're going to jump. And run, faster than you ever have before. The rocket is behind a rampart, we'll be protected from fire there. We just have to make it over there.

She rattles the window, it's sticking. Then she tears a yellow plaster snail from the wall and uses it to smash the window. A blue snail swiftly follows. She climbs out onto the ledge and jumps. I go after her.

Running through a hail of bullets wakes me up. Jumping over the moon laws of the children.

Gelato every day.
My own room.
We decide when we're sleepy.
No police.

And there it is: the rocket. Red and mighty against the burning sky. Projectiles dart past us, but we fly on; I can't feel my feet, only my arms, beating through the air and dragging me on. We've almost made it. Women and children are climbing the rocket, they rush up the ladder. We reach the rampart, the projectiles hit the concrete behind us, we've reached safety. I laugh, hug Sorella. She expels an awful sound, like a wounded animal.

The rocket starts to release vapour. Smoke shoots out under high pressure, fogging up the ground and crawling up the ladder. A metallic announcement rattles over the place: Checks complete. Ignition sequence ready. Extinguishing water system ready. Otrere IV ready to launch. T minus 10 . . . 9 . . . 8 . . .

We're too late, Sorella yells in despair, we've come too late!

Then she tears free from me and runs towards the rolling, roaring fog, which almost immediately swallows her.

4 – the rocket emits flames, 2 – it trembles and finally rises. Three pillars of flame force it high into the sky.

I go up in fiery smoke.

PART TWO

You wake up because you're coughing.

You open your eyes. They dart around.

You're in a car, on the back seat. You feel the vibrations of the engine. The uneven road. The damp seat fabric itches your cheek, it smells of old smoke. You feel sick.

There's a milky filter over your eyes. You blink, try and focus. An almost empty, misty bottle of water trembles on the dusty mat in the footwell. Little drops roll out their drawings on the plastic from the inside. You follow their tracks; the soft drone grows to an acceleration buzz. Then, braking, your body is gently pushed forwards, you see the male hand gripping the stick, second gear. An emblem on his sleeve, slender fingers.

You push yourself up on your elbows, half sit up. The shining field of vehicles in a used-car dealership. You wipe your nose on the back of your hand.

You stop at a red light. Your right arm aims for the door but it doesn't listen to you, it moves snakily, doesn't belong to you. You use the left, angry with the other one, it's fallen asleep. You might have guessed: the door is locked.

You watch the driver in the rearview mirror. He's still acting as if he hasn't noticed you're awake. You can only see his crumpled forehead, now and then he raises his eyebrows. He stretches his back, your eyes meet, you quickly close your eyes. You can also tell from his collar: he's wearing that military uniform.

He seems familiar to you: that restless brow. You try to remember. His fingers swirl in the glove compartment for a lighter, he lights a cigarette. You inhale the fresh smoke. Need to cough. Consider whether he would give you one.

Your head hurts, take down your hair. Strands fall over your face, shimmering images. Memories weakly oscillate. You smell your fingers. Wonder where your shoes are. You push your bare feet under the front seat, where they butt up against something hard. You discreetly pull it out with your toes. The driver acts as if he hasn't noticed anything.

He rolls down his window. Warm exhaust fumes clap you around the face, the sound of tyres rolling over cobblestones flutters in your ears. You lay your head against the headrest, murmurations of starlings in the sky, breathing formation. The city flies past you.

You come to a standstill. Evening rush hour. He flicks the cigarette in the street, spits after it. It glimmers in the gutter among withered leaves, a scooter overtakes and whirls it all up. The soldier rolls up the window. You're right next to the museum. Two soldiers are chatting outside the entrance. Sunburned tourists stand indecisively on the pavement, gazing emptily over the clogged road, right up to you, but they don't see you. It's like in your dreams: even if you shouted for help, no one would come.

Aiuto.

The white Panda in front of you. You try to make eye contact with the young woman in her rearview. She's alone, she's laughing along with the radio, her ponytail shakes. You can hear the radio presenter waffling.

You clear your throat. Tragic attempt at masking the sound of the door handle. You haven't tried the left one yet. The soldier in the rearview shaking his head at you. He suddenly hits the accelerator, swerves right, your head slams against the window. He mounts the kerb past the columns, honking, the woman in the Panda smooths down her eyebrows with the tip of her finger. You leave her behind, jolt down off the kerb, onto the clear lane towards the motorway.

You feel the cold pane, there, where a mark has been left from where you hit it. Then you lean your pounding forehead against it. You can no longer see the rearview mirror, instead you see his left ear. You search under the seat with your toes for the object, which the swerving has shunted back. The soldier doesn't notice. He's too busy careening.

Soon you're out of the city. The gun vibrates under your soles. You feel the cold barrel, the rough surface of the grip. You raise your chin, grip the seatbelt and try to fasten it. The buckle is broken, the belt whooshes back in place. The soldier stays in the fast lane.

A lorry nears, drives level with you on your right. It indicates

145

and pushes into your lane. A wall rises up next to you, comes dan-gerously close. The soldier swears, honks, lurches into the crash barrier—

VIII

I wash my hands at the rest stop. The blood behaves itself and graciously comes off my skin. Thin pinkish red rushes down the plughole. I clench and flex my fingers beneath the jet, they are numb. The water in the filthy basin becomes clearer, soon it's colourless. I leave it running.

After a while I notice that I'm no longer alone. Someone has entered, is watching me from behind, his gaze prickles the back of my neck.

The stranger turns away as I step up to him, without turning off the water, in order to burn him with my eyes. He flees backwards into a cubicle, closing the door behind him, and I hear him not moving. Now I feel that the water is cold. I run the thumbnail of my right hand under all the nails on my left and vice versa. Dark red clots swirl into the hole.

Outside, the sky is royal blue. Petrol and piss and the rushing sound of the motorway. The asphalt under my bare feet is warm.

I walk past a parked truck towards a brightly lit bar. Boxes of wine on offer and taralli crackers by the bucketful in the entrance. The cashier eyes me suspiciously, bruised as I am, while the barista polishes the steam-spewing machine with a cloth.

The soldier is standing alone at the bar. He's the guy from the Street of Women. Who recognised Favorita in the photo, who I ate with in the snack bar. Two tiny cups of espresso in front of him. He slides one over to me.

Panino? – I nod.

Then back on the road? – He nods.

The bouncing of the car makes me sleepy. I'm now sitting in the front, we've left the motorway and are driving on the night-black road, heading north.

I feel strangely peaceful inside. As if a switch had been flipped. All my life I've been trained to guard against a situation like this. Take nothing from strangers. Keep your knees together. No need to shout. Conduct yourself like a lady. Dress respectably. Wear shoes you can run in. Don't leave your drink unattended. Stay sober. Trust no one. Only walk on well-lit streets. Appear confident, never seem afraid. Pretend you're making a phone call. Hold your keys in your fist. And as soon as you get home, slide the bolt and draw the curtains, so no one can see you're alone, understand? Don't let anybody in.

I was one of the seven little goats trained not to let the wolf in. As a child I went to a self-defence class for girls once a week, where we learnt to kick evil men between the legs. I've never found myself in that situation. I went with photographers who promised me a career. Met up with men from the internet by myself. Got drunk with friends, who suddenly groped me. I let it all happen. And when they undressed me, I quietly scolded myself: I should have seen this coming.

My grandmother warned me how wicked men could be: Don't fall for their tricks.

It was my fault.

I would never have dreamt of ramming one of them in the balls with my knee. I pitied these men.

Like the soldier sitting beside me staring at the road. He looks so tired. What does he think is happening here? Why did he take me with him?

The images flash up again: Sorella, the flames—

I don't want to know. It's over. I want peace, and the soldier is quiet. He can do whatever he likes with me. I look at his slender fingers on the steering wheel, his twitching legs, his wild saucer eyes. I'm not scared of him.

I don't even know your name, I say after a while. It sounds foolish.

He scrutinises me with a sideways look. That's how he looked at Magdalena's photo, with a small deep crease between his eyebrows. Can he see who I am? He said that he knew Favorita. Did she tell him about me? Why would she have? During a cosy hour perhaps, beside one another in bed? I shake my head, shake the image away, no. And even if she did, she would have told him about Filippa, Fila, Filù.

I'm Mimma, I say, we haven't introduced ourselves.

Lorenzo, is all he says.

A tense silence spreads between us. I try to estimate his age. His limbs are youthfully lanky, but his skin is sallow, deep dark circles under his eyes. He evades my gaze.

So, you're a fascist?

And you, a communist?

I have to laugh, he gets angry, uptight: I'll throw you into a ditch if you're a communist.

I look out the window and say nothing.

Maybe I should be scared, but I feel nothing.

Other people would be grateful, he grumbles finally, I rescued you.

Rescued? You attacked us!

Us? Do you want to belong to them?

Why shouldn't I?

They want to corrupt you. They're communists, they steal children, they're murderers.

Says the soldier who shoots at women and children!

He laughs bitterly: Women? They're not women. And they fired first.

They were defending themselves.

I didn't shoot, he says, not at anyone.

You saint, I sneer, Padre Pio himself, let me see your stigmata.

I got you out of there, doesn't that mean anything?

And why did you?

He doesn't say anything else, and looks nervously into the rear-view mirror.

What's up with you, I jeer, can you see the spectre of communism?

I'm a deserter.

I turn my head, the road behind us is empty.

Are we being followed?

He keeps looking forward: I don't think so.

But people are looking for you – and if they find you? What's the punishment for desertion? Hang you from a lamp post?

He shrugs: I felt sorry for you.

You should feel sorry for yourself.

It was my fault that you ended up in that place. I shouldn't have left you alone with them. I felt responsible when I saw you lying there.

His words grow quiet, as if the volume has been turned down. The numbing heat of the rocket rolls over me. I feel the blast wave, Sorella's hand being pulled from mine.

Did he see her lying there too? What did he see?

I close my eyes. The hum of the engine becomes a cloud of flies buzzing around me.

I murmur: I hope they find us and shoot us down.

*

When I wake up, I see the sea. It's so bright.

You were snoring, Lorenzo says, turning off the engine.

Was not, I mumble, subtly wiping drool from my mouth.

He jumps out of the car and stretches. Then he disappears

behind the car and opens the boot. We're on a coastal road with a steep drop. A rockface rises up behind us, no houses. Below us are fallow fields leading to a wild beach. It would be easy to make someone disappear here.

Lorenzo opens my door. He's changed his clothes, the uniform's gone.

Are you coming?

I don't have any shoes.

He turns around wordlessly. I hear him rummaging in the boot. He comes back with a pair of shoes I recognise.

Here, he says, holding out the golden trainers.

My voice is raw: Where did you get those?

They were lying there where I found you.

I yank the shoes out of his hands. Check them for flecks of blood, scraps of flesh – nothing. Are these all that's left of Sorella? Did the rocket pulverise her? She can't have made it, I definitely watched her—

Lorenzo, I say in my head, when you found me, was I alone? You could have taken Sorella too, if she had been lying there, couldn't you?

I can't ask, I don't want to know. Maybe she survived and was able to flee, barefoot—

I try the shoes on. They fit me perfectly. Just the bunion void that stays empty: it still needs filling.

I've got your weird box too, Lorenzo says. It's in the back in case you want it.

The urn! I X-ray him with my eyes. What does he know? He

looks back almost as if he is embarrassed.

He tries to give me his hand. I don't take it.

Girl, he says, I'm only trying to help you. The car is high, you could fall.

I'm older than you and don't need your help.

When my feet meet the road, I feel the pain jump in my bones like thistles. I don't let him see. It smells of salt and sickly sweetness. The sea is dazzling.

Where are we?

At the Ships.

Lorenzo points down towards the beach. Four long white structures lie like beached whales in the scrub-covered sand. Curious buildings that really do look like war ships. They have countless portholes along their sides, which give them the appearance of toxic caterpillars.

Lorenzo grins: Even the communist likes them, eh?

Why shouldn't I?

It was a fascist holiday camp.

Really! I exclaim. My grandmother spent her summers in holiday camps like these, when she was a child.

And were they bad?

I consider the question briefly and then say: She didn't talk that much about it. When I spoke to her about it, she would say: *I can't say that Mussolini was all bad. He gave me a lot, he made sure my childhood was nice too.* They were very poor, but thanks to him, as she said, she spent a month at the beach every summer.

Lorenzo nods: Nice.

But it's weird, I say, because she couldn't swim at all. What did they do at the beach all that time?

He doesn't say anything, as if he hadn't heard me. It feels strange that I told him that. I've never told anyone any of that before. It feels like an ingratiation, forced bonding through confession: I can tell him this, he doesn't judge her. Do I?

I remember coming home from the football pitch and saying that the older kids wouldn't let me play with them. My grandmother got upset: Those foreigners trying to give orders.

And she ordered me: Now go down there and play harder than ever!

I laughed: But Nonna, you're a foreigner!

And she retorted, in her strong accent: But they're different. The Italians behaved quite differently to them.

I thought to myself that she ought to watch less television.

I kill the prickly grass with Magdalena's golden shoes; a putrid smell rises from the earth.

Lorenzo, were your parents fascists?

I don't have any parents.

So that's why you're like this. Bad childhood!

Fuck you. If anyone's to blame then it's my teacher. She was a proper communist, like all teachers. We were always writing essays: What was Mussolini's greatest mistake? I would say: What was Lenin's greatest mistake? Why aren't we talking about that?

154

Look, I say, the Ships have faces: three eyes and a mouth. They look happy.

Lorenzo doesn't respond. I stop and screw up my eyes. Make the Ships blur, try to see children running between them. Doors fly open, screaming down the stairs. Soles throw up the sand, jump into the sea. One of the kids could be Lavinia. Barefoot, black hair, tanned. She looks at me expressionlessly. Maybe they also wore uniforms and weren't allowed to run, only form neat rows, march and salute. And a picture of il Duce was hanging in every dormitory. My grandmother never told me this, but I've read about it: how children received toys from the fascist youth organisation, and for this they would need to include il Duce in their evening prayers. *Loyalty until death.*

I open my eyes and see the ruins. Lorenzo walks ahead of me and doesn't look back. I slip across the dunes, trudge around a bloated dead dog. Lorenzo gives me a black neckerchief, which I tie around my mouth and nose. He does the same with his jumper. We reach the Ships in silence.

The doors are locked. Through the windows we look into empty rooms, former dining halls, perhaps. We sit on the bottom steps of one of the Ships' staircases. Watch the foaming sea. The stench penetrates my damp fabric mask.

Shame, Lorenzo says in a muffled voice, what's happened to this place.

What happened to the water?

155

Everyone knows about it, no one says anything. The cowards would rather die of cancer than say anything, change anything. We need someone who will take charge, understand? Someone that can take on everything, who clears up, mucks out.

I shake my head. A strong leader, or Duce, perhaps?

Why not?

Before I can answer, he stands up and trots towards the water. He collects stones from the ground and throws them into the foamy waves. When he comes back, he coughs and swears. Without looking at me, he walks past, stamps through the dunes in the direction of the road: Where are you going?

Into the past.

*

The coast road snakes up against the rock. Lorenzo drives slowly, swerving around rockfall debris and potholes. The urn gently scoots back and forth in my lap.

I look behind us, check if anyone's following.

Don't worry, he says. We'll reach a village in a few kilometres, I can drop you off there.

Thanks.

But not if you're going to start up again with that communist rubbish, in which case I'll drop you right here in the wind.

And what will you do?

Sit tight. The Coach will help me, he's got a plan.

There's suddenly a rushing in my ears: Who?

156

He doesn't respond, lights a cigarette.

I hug the urn tightly: Favorita's husband?

He seems surprised: You know him?

I clear my throat: Not personally. You?

He's like a father to me.

His voice reaches me as if through cotton wool. A high-pitched whistle sings in my ears; movements are slowed. I want to press my hands over my face, shield my eyes from the light, but I smile in what I think is a detached way.

I have to go to ground for a while, I hear him say. Fortunately the Coach has some influence, even in the military. He says he will fix it, calm the waves and stuff.

Waves, waves, waves in my stomach, in my head. I try box breathing, calm the waves.

Have you, I hear myself say, told the Coach about me?

Lorenzo looks at me intently, I breathe a box around his head.

No, is all he'll say, his eyes back on the road.

The whistling in my ears quietens, I feel my fingernails in the heels of my hands.

The Society has a hunting lodge in central Italy, he says, I'll drive there.

Which society?

He doesn't say anything.

I look out the window, breathe the box bigger and bigger until it envelops and carries the entire car.

Lorenzo rolls down the window, his movements are once again erratic and birdlike. Warm wind splashes me in the face; he says: You used up all the air with your wheezing.

I laugh. There is a flurry of emotions within me that makes me strangely cheerful. He must have known Magdalena well if he's so tight with her husband. Then he hardly could have gone to bed with her, thank God. Maybe he can tell me more about her.

I look at him from the side. *Like a father*, he'd said. That would make him almost like my stepbrother, right?

I grin: A hunting lodge, eh?

He nods: I grew up in the area, it's quite nice there.

And this Coach will be there too?

He looks at me with an impenetrable expression and then says: Sooner or later. Why?

I'm coming with you, I say, and sense the weight of the urn in my lap. The gun lies soft and muffled in the ashes.

I've never been hunting before.

*

Shortly after passing a sign for a town and stopping at a cross-roads in an industrial quarter, Lorenzo begins cursing: I hate this place.

He spits out the window: See over there? That's a clothes factory. That's why there's only . . . filthy communists. And none of them pay tax.

Now listen, I say, but he interrupts me:

Look at them, how comfortable they are. And of course, it's our lives that the state plunders.

He angrily shakes his lighter, which will only spark and not light.

The elites are mugging us off, understand? What we work hard for, they take back in taxes. Do you know how much tax I have to pay? I can't work enough to pay my taxes! And the politicians, criminals, serve them. The elites – and the foreigners. Did you ever see any of them pay tax? No, they stick their money in their own pockets and send it home, you get me? I've got nothing against helping people, some are really poor, and helping others is right and good. But we can't help everyone, we have to help ourselves. We have to come first, otherwise we'll soon be gone.

Who?

He drags deeply on the cigarette, which isn't burning properly.

Us of course! Italians. Why are you laughing? Dyed-in-the-wool communist, you can't fool me.

My grandfather was like you.

Italian?

He was Swiss. He met my grandmother on holiday in Italy. By the time he travelled back home, she was pregnant. *The shame.* Her family, the whole town wouldn't speak to her anymore. People would stop talking when she walked into a shop. She lived in silence. And when she moved to Switzerland to escape the silence, she married this man, who thought like you do. He was ashamed of her. Because she was one of the foreigners he was always cursing. He forbade her to speak Italian with her child. He brought her back to silence.

Lorenzo listens attentively. I wonder if he understands. So I double down.

Don't you see, I say, the same thing is happening right now. My grandfather would spit on you, and now you're spitting on others. Everyone's looking for a good life – some travel in, others out. What's the difference between the millions who move out of Italy and those who come here?

They're different, he mutters.

That's what my grandmother used to say too.

A wave of shame crashes over me. What am I doing? Feeding a fascist my family history – and for what? To warm his cold heart? To move him to tears that will clear his view? In fact, I'm putting my grandmother in an unusually bad light – and questions burst like stinking bubbles: had the fact that she grew up under fascism played a role in the attraction between her and my grandfather, an ardent right-winger?

You see, I hear Magdalena laughing, she wasn't a saint either.

I realise now that I didn't know either of them.

Do you like music?

Lorenzo looks at me in a friendly way. I nod, shrugging.

Then choose something, will you, he snaps, throwing a sticky case into my lap.

I flick through self-burned CDs covered in scrawled writing, all the great cantautori.

I hold one up: Are you even allowed to listen to stuff like this?

He mumbles: What do you think? The 68ers were revolutionaries too, we've got some things in common.

Soon a piano clatters out the speakers. Rino Gaetano's voice plays around our hair, riding the airstream. Lorenzo nods along in appreciation, properly lights a cigarette and mumbles along. I hold my hand out the window and let it swim in the headwind.

Il cielo è sempre più blu. The sky is always bluer.

IX

We speed through the forest in the dark. The car jolts over roots
and potholes; the headlights jump up the tree trunks and fall back
down onto the road. Families of boars scuttle across our path:
hoglets like rabbits, the mother's eyes glow green in the lights.

There's a bang, we swerve, come to a stop.

What was that?

Lorenzo looks at me as if I had betrayed him.

You ran over something, I assume.

He loads a rifle and gets out of the car. I stay put, staring
vacantly out of the windscreen. My heart is pecking. Moths
and mosquitoes dance in the beam of the headlights, some of
them fly into the glass, soft rapping sounds. I shout. No answer.
I climb out.

Lorenzo is standing in front of a dark mountain of fur. Dust
whirls up from it, twirling in the headlights. I lay my hand on
the flank. Cold. Crusted over hair, congealed blood.

We didn't kill it then, I say. Look, maggots. Is it a bull?

A gnu, he says.

Do they have them here, in the forest?

No, he says, sometimes. Get in, I'll take care of it in the
morning.

Lorenzo reverses and drives around the gnu. He's driving very slowly now, carefully, as if he can sense a shot animal behind every turn. In fact, I'm imagining that the headlights are catching further corpses between the trees.

Lorenzo doesn't bat an eye.

The steepest bend's coming up, is all he says, hold on.

The engine howls, and Lorenzo cranks it. As we shoot out the top, the road is tarmacked, and a striking villa appears on the right. Torches burn on both sides of the gate, illuminating a heap of something at the fence: leopard print dancing in the firelight.

Duck down, Lorenzo commands.

He seems tense, murmuring as if to himself: No one's supposed to be here.

He drives past the villa and further uphill. The headlights brush against vines, groves, rocks, they get lost in corners and crevices, until the road straightens out and the light catches a few roofs. Lorenzo brakes. We slowly roll towards the houses. When the slope noticeably flattens out, he stops. Now I can see that the houses are in ruins. The headlights illuminate collapsed roofs, broken windows, billowing scraps of curtain. It's completely silent. No lights burn inside. I hear my breathing. Lorenzo stares fixedly past me out of the window into the darkness.

Where are we, I ask, what is that?

My voice sounds hollow: Why have you stopped driving?

There's just this road, he says, there's nothing else.

What are we doing here?

Be quiet, he says, not turning his head away from my window, as if he were trying to make out something outside.

I bite my lip and look through the windscreen as something lights up between the houses, a sparkle. I climb out. My shadow is large and mighty as it strolls off ahead of me, I throw my hands in the air, make them run up the façade of the house, up the stairs that lead to nowhere. A mean wind sweeps through the open doorways. I look back, Lorenzo is still sitting in the car.

The light of the headlamps grows weaker the further I walk. One house is completely overgrown with thorns. Trees grow from others, out of the windows and the uncovered roofs. Through an open door I see a kitchen. A footstool covered in bits of plaster. A wobbly table, on which still lie playing cards and matches, a full ashtray. As if the people had just stood up, walked out and never come back.

I walk up to the end of the street, where the houses stop, and the path runs into a thicket. Here there's a car, a new laundry whirligig. This last house seems oddly intact: the door is freshly painted, Marian blue. Against the wall there's a row of dishes with half-eaten cat food. Above the door frame a glass sphere embedded in the wall shimmers, at its centre is a Madonna statue. I step closer. On the door frame there are drawings, scrawled in chalk, but clearly identifiable: small rockets, they're flying to the Madonna in the moon.

A cat rubs itself against my legs. I instinctively raise my eyes to the window – there's someone's head! It ducks away.

I quickly go back, force myself to look straight ahead, not turn around. A wind roars up. Howls through the broken windows, whips the branches against the remaining roof beams, slams doors. It stays dark, the light of the car doesn't appear. I set off running. Shadows jump out of my way, hissing.

Lorenzo is sitting motionlessly in the car, with the headlights off. I drop down next to him, he doesn't move. I follow his gaze. Now, where my eyes have become accustomed to the dark, I see the hills and groves in the moonlight. Between them, the walls of the villa glow.

*

On the way back, I don't say a word. I close my eyes and let myself be shaken by the hard jolts of the unpaved road. Lorenzo explains that the village has been uninhabited for a long time, ever since the earthquake.

It's built on crumbling ground, he says. In the next quake the rock will break off and the village will tumble into the depths. The villagers were resettled, they were glad to end up in modern houses. There wasn't any running water up there. They always had to make their way through the forest, to the spring.

Back near the villa, he turns the car through the gate. Gravel crunches under the tyres. The headlights roam over Roman columns, two round trees, a fountain with putti. There are animal carcasses in the yard too.

Pigs, Lorenzo mutters, degenerates.

He stops and turns off the engine. The lights go out. We can hear the cicadas, the clicking of the cooling car. Then he opens the door, indicates for me to wait and jumps out. I see his silhouette in the flickering light of the torches as he works at the well. Then he rushes to the gate, stretches up and puts out one torch and then the other with a wet cloth. Now we're in gloom. Lorenzo disappears around the corner of the house. I wait a while, and then I open my door, slide off my seat and spring onto the ground.

An intense smell is coming from the dead animals. I run the sole of my trainer over the bony leg of a giraffe, against the direction of the fur. Its belly is full of black, bloody holes. Suddenly, there's a sound – the fountain comes on. Light on the veranda. I crouch down next to the giraffe and hold my breath. Its cloudy eyes, eyelashes with flies. Nothing happens. I remember the plush giraffe, Magdalena's last visit. I thought she had brought it for me, but she shrieked: That's my giraffe, I take it everywhere with me!

I touch the dead giraffe's neck, its ears, the mossy horns. Its tongue hangs out black between its teeth. I feel sick.

Lights come on in the villa and suddenly there are quick steps across the gravel.

Lorenzo, who does something like this?

You wanted to come here, he says gruffly, I did tell you it's a hunting lodge.

But the animals—

They release them here for the hunt, he says, as if that explained everything. They got bored of boar and deer. Come on!

In the entrance hall, there are traces of a raucous party. The stone floor is sticky, broken glass. Blood-red pools of wine, trampled cigarettes, torn-down curtains. I go to close the heavy front door, but Lorenzo says: Leave it open. It needs airing out in here.

I hesitate, he laughs: Are you afraid of wild animals? They've shot them all. They don't do things by halves, they just don't clear up after themselves. But we'll take care of that tomorrow.

On either side of the entrance hall, marble staircases lead upstairs. Lorenzo grips my wrist and pulls me under the stairs into a dark corridor, leaves me standing there, his steps move away. I close my eyes and breathe in deeply. It smells like centuries-old dust. I'm suddenly unbelievably tired.

A light switches on, illuminating a large kitchen. Lorenzo shoos a few flies from an oven dish with dried-out contents, sniffs it and scrapes the leftovers into a bin. He lets water run into the sink and stacks pans up in it.

A good soak, he murmurs, soak everything first.

The smell of fermenting melon makes me woozy, along with Lorenzo, who is busy clambering around between beer crates, wine boxes and kitchen waste.

Can't we do that tomorrow?

He roves around and stares at me as if he had forgotten that I was there.

I follow him down the servants' corridor. Lorenzo opens doors, glances in quickly, closes them again. Pantry, broom cupboard, cellar stairs, laundry room.

Don't worry, he says, as if confirming it for himself, no one's here.

At the end of the corridor there's a narrow wooden staircase. Lorenzo opens the door beside the stairs, puts on the light: a bedroom. High ceiling, vaulted. Red stone floor, open fireplace.

Here, he says, everything you need should be here.

I remain standing in the doorway: What do we do now?

We wait.

What for?

Instructions. I'll know more tomorrow. Good night.

He pushes me into the room, takes a step back and closes the door behind me.

For a while, we both just stand there. Then I say good night too, and his steps retreat from the door.

I take off the shoes, cool stone. Smells like old smoke; ash in the fireplace, blackened logs. In the corner there's a stained armchair. An old bed is by the window, made from dark ornate wood, pink woollen blanket. Opposite is a wardrobe with a cloudy mirror.

Ghosts live in those, I hear my grandmother say. Don't look into it, otherwise they'll pull you over to the other side – or even worse: they'll crawl inside you.

I put the urn on the mantelpiece.

Inside the wardrobe hangs a single white nightshirt. Made of thick linen, T-shaped, antique. I get undressed and put on the shirt. It doesn't smell that bad.

A door leads through to the bathroom. I run cold water into the bidet, put my swollen feet into it. Dunk my hands, rub my face. I stand before the mirror, dripping: scratched, battered, very pale girl. What are you doing here? She smiles at me. Fall backwards onto the bed. On the ceiling, a mould stain has spread. It's the shape of a martini glass with a snake winding out of it. I close my eyes and fall into the well like a stone. The trees in the driveway are pomegranates. From the forest, a tiger roars.

*

When I wake up, the sun is shining right in my face. The heat has undressed me, I'm lying naked on top of the pink blanket. I don't know where I am straight away. Dazed, I take in the room: the outlines are sharper, the snake in the glass – I remember, and wrap myself in the blanket. From far away I hear a fly buzzing. A soft languor stays on my eyelids and makes my thoughts sticky; I feel strangely carefree.

The morning is dazzling, the sky is freshly washed. There's a vegetable garden in front of my window, behind it a tender green hill and right up top, on a rocky outcrop, there are a few houses: the small village from last night. I try to make out the house with the Madonna, the drawings of the moon rockets. It seems like it was all a dream. Did I really see a head in the window? My eyesight's too poor to see the houses clearly. Peculiar birds dart across the sky, rapidly flapping their wings, before clamping them tightly against their bodies—

I quickly slip into the nightshirt. Look in the mirror: in the daylight it looks like a dress. I stuff my old things under the bed; I don't want to remember anything.

As I step out of the room, a flower falls out of the keyhole. I pick it up. The corridor is empty. I take a few steps towards the kitchen, my bare feet slap against the stone floor, no one's here either. The scraps are gone, dirty dishes are piled in the sink; on the floor there's a row of pans half filled with water. I have to laugh: I recall Lorenzo, overtired, murmuring to himself: soak, soak.

There's a pot of coffee on the stove, lukewarm. On the large marble table there's an opened box of plum cakes. I take a little shrink-wrapped cake from it, squeeze it gently, make the plastic pop. The smell – it still has an effect on me: plum cakes are the embodiment of absolute, fleeting comfort. The greasy-smooth surface, peeling away the soft paper case . . . I feel warm.

It might be my most wonderful memory: a holiday apartment

by the sea, Magdalena sticking small candles in the yellow cakes for my grandmother's birthday.

I cram the little cake into my mouth, put another in my shirt pocket and take a cup of coffee with me.

From the kitchen, a windowless passageway leads past the pantry and a barred cellar door, from where a musty breath rises up the stairs. Then it opens into the old drawing room, now also a dining room. It smells like old smoke. On the ceiling there are chandeliers, paintings, wine-guzzling putti. There's a fireplace here too, with a mighty gold-framed mirror above it. A table in the centre. Sideboards on both sides with neatly lined up empty wine bottles, full ashtrays. On the table are vases full of withered flowers, burned-down candles. I set a fallen chair back on its legs.

Double doors lead into the garden: a patch of lawn with a long wooden table, protected by tightly packed trees and high hedges. I step outside and squint in the sun, it has to be midday. By the head of the table there's an opening in the vegetation: spread out behind it is a sloping meadow that gives way to the forest. A lonely swing seat. I put down my cup and run across the meadow with my arms open wide. It ends at some semicircular stone steps that lead down to a large gate. Behind it, dark, rustling forest. The gate is locked with a heavy iron chain. A noise, I spin around: the swing is creaking, moving in the wind. I feel like I'm being watched and go back to the house. Sit on the stone bench against the outside wall of the house and look through the window into my room. The covers are on the floor, where I left them. The flower comes to mind, on the floor by my door. I jump up from the bench, my eyes scan the garden. Someone must work here regularly: the beds freshly weeded, dug up, plants tied up ... there! So that's where the flowers grow, where they bloom, aubergine blossom.

I walk around the house to the driveway. The carcasses have disappeared. A cold hand is placed on the back of my neck.

Do you always sleep that long?

Do you ever sleep?

Lorenzo doesn't answer, the rings underneath his eyes look even darker today.

Where are the animals?

He shrugs: That's what happens when you sleep the whole day.

We went to bed late.

I could never sleep that long.

Fine, you're hardworking, I'm lazy. Are you in a rush?

The Coach has given me instructions.

My heart bucks, I gulp it down.

The house has to be prepared for the next meeting. If you want to stay, you have to work. Tidying, cleaning, can you do that?

I roll my eyes. Lorenzo takes a deep breath, as if the conversation is draining him: You're free to go whenever you like. But be careful in the forest, there are boars. They can slash you open if they get the urge.

I laugh, not believing him, but he remains serious: And if you meet anyone on the way, don't tell them that you're a communist.

I'm not a—

Don't shriek like that. I'm going to drive into town today and can take you with me. After that it'll be tricky. When the Society gets here, there's no going back.

Understood, I say.

I imagine I'm standing here with the Coach. I point the gun at his chest and shoot. The Coach slowly sinks to the ground, wheezing. A dark pool spreads across the stone slabs.

Aren't you drinking your coffee?

Lorenzo snaps his fingers in my face.

What is this, I say irritably, what are you scolding me for?

We've got things to do, he says, they might even arrive this evening.

The Coach?

The Society.

Do you have any milk?

Are you crazy?

Do I have to drink it black? So early in the morning?

Early in the morning, porca miseria.

Lorenzo walks cursing into the house.

I take the calming little cake out of my pocket and begin to eat it. Close my eyes, Magdalena laughing, my grandmother blowing out the candles. The coffee is bitter, I don't drink it.

After a while Lorenzo comes back: There isn't any milk. Only children drink milk.

Thanks for checking.

I drink the coffee down in one gulp and shake my whole body.

Brava, he says.

This word trickles tepidly down my throat. *Brava*, from an Italian man – a sunbeam tickles the walls of my bare, cold chamber of belonging.

I feel a bit nauseous.

By the way, I call out, it just came back to me: last night I had a strange dream. I woke up because someone was tickling my feet. I thought it was you. But when I put the light on no one was there.

Oh, says Lorenzo, that was probably Sisina.

Who?

The beautiful Sisina.

Is that your girlfriend?

He laughs: Are you jealous? I'm glad, but she's not my girlfriend.

So, who is she?

Are you scared of ghosts?

Of course I am.

Lorenzo clears his throat.

Are you telling me this place is haunted? Why are you only just telling me this now!

They're only stories, he says, playing it down. Tales from the countryside. The things people talk about during long winters so they don't die of boredom.

Explain! No, wait. Do I want to know? Tell me!

Right, well. Sisina does exist. She was the most beautiful girl as far as the eye could see. She worked here in the villa as a maid. The Conte, the owner at the time, killed her.

My eye twitches involuntarily. Lorenzo acts like he hasn't noticed. Does he know about Magdalena's death? Is he testing to see if I know?

I try to sound naive: Oh, killed. Why?

She had a relationship with him.

Yeah, and?

They say that she was pregnant and he didn't want the kid. How do I know? It was like that back then.

Back when?

Just after the war. Sisina went to him and said: I'm having your baby; I want them to have a good life and to have your name.

Ha, I say, my grandmother said the same to my grandfather. She had to marry him so my mother would have a name.

Lorenzo nods: People say that the Conte paid two crooks to have her killed. They waylaid her in the forest on the way to the well.

Wait, I say, it sounds familiar.

Could be, it's a famous case. Preoccupies people to this day, her killer was never caught. Her fiancé, a young farmer, spent two years in prison. Then he was freed because he was inno-cent of course. It was the Conte, he had bought himself an alibi. Rich Swiss people like you always get off.

I'm not rich.

Shame.

I suddenly feel like I'm being watched again, look inconspicuously over my shoulder.

Lorenzo grows impatient: It would be nice if you could do some work too. People are coming soon. We have to get the house ready.

I clap my hands together: Come on then!

He throws a look at my nightshirt: Don't you want to get changed first?

I shake my head: the shirt suits me.

*

Lorenzo hands me a mop and a broom.

Scopare, I say, I'll do that happily.

He looks so dumbfounded that I have to laugh. I swing the bucket, throwing up dust: Scopaaare.

Lorenzo breaks into hysterical laughter.

What, I say, what, what is it?

Scopare – he can't control himself – what made you think of that?

Well, scopare, I say, just sweeping.

He laughs until he cries: Scopare means, no come on—

What is it!

Fucking. Scopare means fucking.

What?

I feel myself going red. It's not that I'm embarrassed, it just happens of its own accord.

No, I shout, what are you talking about? It means sweeping, my grandmother always said it, scopare. You can stop laughing now!

Maybe people said that a hundred years ago, but today it absolutely means, well, I won't say it again. You really talk like a grandmother, do you know that?

How was I supposed to know that! How was she supposed to know that, she emigrated a hundred years ago. No wonder, what with you prudish guys, my God, calm yourself. You're going to break your ribs.

I have to laugh too, at the way he's standing with tears pouring down his face and clutching his side. Then I get sad. Lavinia had not only left her city and Italy, but also her language. She always said that she watched Italian television to stay up to date language-wise. It clearly hadn't been enough.

I suddenly see myself through her eyes: what am I doing here? Crying tears of laughter with a soldier – who calls the murderer of my mother his father? I think about the gun in the ashes. I can't let my goal out of sight: I must stay cold, hard.

We climb the servants' staircase next to my room. On the upper floor, a corridor with doors on both sides. Lorenzo opens them all. I have to clean the rooms and put fresh covers on the beds. And not look so gloomy. He wants to cheer me up; he points to the room at the end of the corridor and says: That's where it's most haunted.

Who, who says that?

People who were here. Some only hear furniture being

moved around, and people on the stairs and slamming doors in the night. Others are woken because their feet are being tickled.

That's not funny.

He laughs: Believe me, you're not the first one that's happened to. But that's harmless, compared to others. One guy said he was lying in bed and had a face next to him the whole night.

You're lying.

Or some guy, he was sleeping in the room opposite, he suddenly felt some pressure against his body. As if someone was caressing him, touching his legs, his feet. He was paralysed for hours. Something had lain on him until the morning, so heavy that he couldn't get up.

Stop it.

She was seen here in the corridor too. She runs along the carpet and goes around the corner, the white veil drifting behind her.

Lorenzo pulls down a door handle: In this room she jumped on the bed. You don't have to be afraid of her, she's a cheerful girl.

Have you ever seen her?

Sisina? I don't believe in ghosts.

Me neither, I lie, carrying the cleaning supplies straight into the haunted room.

*

I spend the whole day fucking the rooms and wiping them with a mop. The floors are made of rough stone slabs. A thorough clean is difficult because the dust holes up in the cracks and scars in the stone. Despite this, the rooms look better than they did before. I open all the windows and let fresh air in. Something happened in these rooms, I can tell. But what? I take off the bed covers and throw the washing down the stairs. I check the wardrobes, dressers, bathroom cabinets. Everything's empty, save a few woollen blankets. Most of the rooms are as bare as mine. As if someone – Lorenzo – had pre-tidied, eliminated all traces. Only here and there a dried bunch of olive branches, ears of corn; a couple of petrified mussels on the windowsill.

I crawl under the beds and see the old bedsteads, rusty springs. Lorenzo keeps coming in to check on me. Each time, he brings something as an excuse, polish, fresh sheets. He doesn't want me to discover something.

What are you doing? I ask him.

The same as you, he says.

Where?

Upstairs.

In the tower?

Yes.

Can I see?

No.

Why not?

He leaves and closes the door behind him.

Strange that an old villa like this is so empty. It has an odd atmosphere. I wonder if it's just because of Sisina. Something to do with the awful crime casting its shadow. A pleasant shiver creeps up my back, the hair on my arms stands on end.

I turn in a circle, the nightshirt billows out. I pretend I'm Sisina doing her work as a housemaid. If she still jumps on the bed and is cheerful, she must have had some good times here. I imagine her bouncing on the mattress for fun – or did she do it with her lover, the Conte?

I haven't done it for a long time, and try it. Just gently, on my knees, because the bed twists, then a bit harder. I jump on my feet and higher and higher, hit my head on the ceiling, squeal. I want to see if I can empathise with her: why does she do it, as a ghost?

I fall to my knees. Heat rises to my face. Lorenzo is standing in the doorway grinning.

Come on, he says, smirking, I've cooked.

*

The pot is still bubbling away on the hob. Lorenzo is gruffly busying himself, mood like an April day. I leave him be and wander through the ground floor. Behind the drawing room with the painted ceiling, a small corridor leads to a dripping toilet. Directly beside it is another door – locked – and a window in the wall. Through the fly screen, I see four wooden church pews, an altar; the ceiling is decorated with golden stars. The small chapel doesn't seem to be in use, it's functioning as a storeroom. On the pews and all along the walls are stacks of boxes.

The chapel gives off a dark power that doesn't fit with the rest of the house. Next to the image of Maria above the altar is the portrait of a young woman. Black hair, in profile, she's smiling. She seems familiar.

Lorenzo calls. Soup. He doesn't want to eat outside, but when I take the pot and carry it into the garden he follows me. The soup is thick with grains and beans, cooked with vegetables and cheese. It's surprisingly good. Lorenzo eats quickly, burning his mouth, his face contorts in the dazzling sun.

Hey, I say, the picture in the chapel, is that Sisina?

He mutters something in confirmation, lights a cigarette.

My heart thumps, I try not to let him notice. The photo in the chapel – I think it's the same as the picture in Sorella's telescope, The Archive of Murdered Women. The girl from after the war, *killed while fetching water*. It had burned into my memory: like my great-grandmother, who died while fetching water, according to Magdalena. What was it that Sorella said: It's what made Otrere a fighter. What was her name? Was it Sisina?

Lorenzo, I say, why is the chapel closed? Can I get into it?

What do you want to do in there, he grumbles, pray?

Maybe.

Out of service, he says, that's where all the things for the hunt are kept. Gear, traps, stuff like that. You don't need to go sniffing around in there. Aren't you going to eat up?

I quickly shove the spoon in my mouth and chew.

I have to go, he says, putting out the cigarette, so you really want to stay?

I nod automatically: When will you be back?

He stands up without a word and climbs up the steps to the house. He leaves his plate.

I stay sitting until I hear the engine start and the tyres rolling over the gravel. Then I jump up and start pacing like a tiger in a cage. A turmoil yanks at my insides. It's digging, I have the urge to run. But where to? These questions tug me back and forth. If this Sisina is the same as Otrere's then . . . What? Then she has something to do with Sorella? Then everything's connected somehow, with Magdalena, with my search for her. But how?

I remain standing and listen carefully. Grumbling sky. Yes, it's clear: I've set out to solve my mother's murder. It can't be a coincidence that I've ended up here, at the place of another unsolved crime. They belong together, and it's my task to solve this puzzle. Isn't it?

A wind comes up. Whispering trees.

Or am I making a mistake? Am I crazy and fantasising an excuse not to do the only sensible thing: leave immediately?

I burst out laughing, eerily unrestrained laughter: of course I'm crazy, my plan is to shoot the Coach!

Magdalena, I say out loud, what should I do?

*

I march and hop and stagger along the road. Where to? To the abyss. The valley drops steeply below me. Rocky ridge like a Stone Age knife. Fields, wide expanses, olive clusters; cypress trees like tin soldiers. A bird of prey circles. I stand here and let the wind decide my fate. It's very sentimental. It braids my hair and giggles in my ear. Wind, what should I do?

I stride down in the direction of the trees. What was it Lorenzo said? Sisina was killed in the forest, she was fetching water from the spring. Bugs buzz around and follow me, mosquitoes and horseflies, filthy wasps; I walk in a humming cloud. Flies nosedive into my hair, my eyebrows, my eyes – as if their dark quality magically draws them in. My grandmother murmurs in my head: Chin up and smile, with lips closed, smile and keep walking, always keep walking. Like Sisina – where was she ambushed?

The forest fizzles and crackles. The wind blows all around me, stirring up leaves, murmuring nervously. Out from the trunk of a tree the face of an owl grows. Cat-like little screech owl. Bird of death. I crouch and stare into the face. It looks back evilly; I'm trying to understand. A red and yellow fly keeps me company, all the rest have vanished in cowardice. Sisina hisses from all around. The wind grows stronger, it wants to intim-idate me. I push through the trees, twigs pull on my dress.

Drops start to fall. Where do ghosts hide when it rains?

On 6 July 1946
on the Day of the Holy Virgin
here died
barbarically killed
19-year-old
Sisina of Stefano

A stone cross at the edge of the road: I've found her. The plinth is exposed, as if by a landslide. Dead leaves all around; a bulbous vase of dried flowers and a dried-out pot plant. I lift it up, underneath are two fat woodlice. Nice, I think, life.

An oval ceramic tile with a photo on it has been embedded in the stone: happy young girl. The picture is the same as the one in the chapel, the same as the one in the telescope at the salami factory, I'm now sure of it. Only this one has cracked in the middle; a rift splits the porcelain face.

So this is where she lay. Blood running warmly over her face, from her throat and into her ears. She can still feel the ground living beneath her, the woodlice, the forest. Above her the tops of trees sway in the wind, gleaming summer sky. Eyelids wipe eyeballs in slow motion, the cicadas become quieter and quieter. Ants hurry across her hands.

Sisina looks as if she knew what was going to happen to her.

As if she acknowledges it gently as her fate: barbarically killed. Who is Stefano? I look around. Did she see her murderer? She smiles soothingly: there wasn't a struggle; she was surprised. Sisina died quietly, full of grace, almost relaxed. The opposite of Magdalena, who fought like a bull. For Sisina it only lasted a second, she was not afraid. All that she felt was astonishment, a thought: Really? Is this what you're willing to do?

In the photograph glued to the stone she has already forgiven her murderer.

In her face there is no fear and no pain. She is redeemed and smiling about the senselessness of life.

NO, hisses the suddenly furious wind.

Sisina? Are you here?

Sisina smiles, she already seems familiar to me. I'm alone, as alone as she is. We're similar, we would have a good time together. The plastic flowers on the plinth quiver lightly. Who brought them to you? No response, I know. The dead don't speak. Even my mother, the loudest of them all, was silenced. But she doesn't get a memorial on the edge of a forest, she doesn't get a pretty picture. You're right, that won't bring justice either.

Sisina, I whisper, I'm against violence, but I have a gun.

*

I hear the car driving up and don't move. I lie in the foliage of limbo; I have no one left in the world. Sisina rustles around me like a little mouse. Thrilled, because I will solve her case and avenge her, like Magdalena. I will do it, I promise. I'm not afraid, not of dying. Falling into the well one last time, now I know what awaits me below: my grandmother, on a sunny, blissful beach. Warm white pebbles. Bunion toyed with by clear water.

The car stops. I sit up. Lorenzo opens the door from the inside. He's alone, no Coach in sight. My relief falls to the ground. Here among dead leaves lies a weathered image of a saint. I pick it up. Let him think I robbed Sisina, but I know that we're bonded, sistered, kindred. We have business with each other. This picture is a trace, a piece of the puzzle, a key to the cursed in-between world. I run my fingers over Saint Agatha, she becomes earthy.

I climb in wordlessly. Boxes are piled up on the back seat, I sit next to Lorenzo. He hits the accelerator. At the bend another car comes jolting towards us; the boxes clatter about as he brakes sharply.

Pig God!

The green off-road vehicle shows no sign of stopping, Lorenzo curses while putting the car in reverse, and manoeuvres us into a ditch. The other car brakes and stops level with us. The car window rolls down, and the face of a woman appears. I don't trust my eyes. Sisina? She's older, with short grey hair and a camouflage parka. I blink. She gives us the finger and says she hopes we die. Then she races off, spraying mud.

Lorenzo starts the engine. I watch the car go. I've seen it before, up in the ghost village, in front of the house with the drawings of the moon rockets.

My hands flutter, the saintly image rustles: Who was that?

A witch.

There is a hostile silence until we roll into the driveway of the villa.

Lorenzo leaves me to bring the shopping from the boot into the house: food for a hundred parties. He carries the boxes into the chapel. As I go to take one from the back seat, he shoves me gruffly to the side.

I'm hungry, he says, make yourself useful, cook something. I've got some things I still need to do.

In the kitchen I find a bloody creature nestled in a casserole dish. I sprinkle a handful of salt over it and put it in the oven.

*

Lorenzo sullenly prods at his plate.

Do you like it?

I can't eat that, he says angrily. What's so funny?

In my head a memory replays. The three of us are sitting at the table. As always happened when Magdalena said she'd be visiting, my grandmother had cooked a lavish meal.

Her fluttering, servile manner makes Magdalena go berserk, her constant jumping up and gesticulating: Here's the salt, have a bit more lemon juice, are you sitting comfortably?

Magdalena snaps: Will you sit down, calm yourself, you're running around like a startled hen, you're making me nervous.

As soon as we begin, she shouts her grace: Mamma! What the hell is this? Have you still not learned how to cook?

And she goes for her, trying to drag me into her cruelty: Does she still spoon out fermented milk and say it's *just like* yoghurt? That's what I had growing up, can you imagine? Poor Mamma, trying to palm me off with sour milk, that's how poor we were. Crespelle of water and flour, that's how she nourished me. Meat was only for Pappi, we were allowed to watch him. But what with this shoe sole that she's served us, I have to say I was lucky. Mamma, really, I can't eat this.

Once she speared a cutlet on her fork and waved it around as if to prove her point. It flew in a high arc and hit the wall. I held my breath. My grandmother didn't react. After a while, Magdalena picked it up off the floor and put it back on her plate. She sawed away at it and said: You need new knives, this one's blunt as anything.

And my grandmother burst out laughing.

Lorenzo stares at me mistrustfully. I feel sorry for him with those dark circles, so young and so many worries.

Hey, I say, you asked me to cook.

And here was me thinking you were Italian, he mutters.

What's that got to do with it? Do you think that all Italian girls come into the world cooking with glee?

He shrugs.

My grandmother couldn't cook either.

I don't believe you.

She never learned. Her grandmother never let her near the stove. She was to become a lady, and a lady doesn't cook.

And you were supposed to become a lady too?

Sure. I had to study above all else. The kitchen wasn't for me, only a desk. My grandmother wanted to stay at school longer. She always used to say: I was a *cannone* at school! She was the best, she could have definitely gone to university. But she didn't have any money; she had to be happy so long as she had shoes on her feet. So she went to work in an office, it wasn't bad; it was new, chic. All the bustling young ladies with heels and foulards, she was one of them. When she came to Switzerland, she didn't think about giving that up. It would not have occurred to her: a husband who would forbid her from working. And on top of that, a law that required written permission from the husband to allow her to work. Imagine! It made her happy that at least I had the opportunities that she had left for. I should accomplish what she was denied: studying and becoming something great.

And, what have you become?

Ha! Well...

So you haven't made anything of yourself.

You probably like that, don't you?

Why? You can't keep house, you can't even fuck the floor properly.

Haha.

You'll never find someone to marry you if you carry on like that.

189

I snort: Do you know what my grandmother used to say? *The bride who laughs will soon cry*. I was not raised to get married.

But to—?

The goal was independence. I should never be at the beck and call of someone else, like she was.

I draw patterns on the plate with my fork and say: I feel bad because I gave it all up. It's all the same to me. The things I used to do, studying, aspiring for something – it all lost its meaning when she died.

Lorenzo's moustache hair quivers. Then he shoves his fork in his mouth and chews: That may be, but this is a crime. You deserve to be punished for this.

And so it came to be that this soldier spent the rest of the day trying to teach me how to manage a household. Him: nervous, stiff and sullen; me: amused, impatient and increasingly interested. Not so much in the tasks. But his scent, his swift hands. When I see men's fingers, I can't help but imagine how they will enter me. I must get that from Magdalena.

That evening we stand embarrassed in front of my bedroom. I remember the flower from this morning.

What flower?

You didn't put a flower in my keyhole?

You'd like that, wouldn't you?

No, really, there was one!

And why would I do that?

Who did then?

Who indeed.

He kisses me suddenly on the cheek and runs up the stairs. I hear him nearly tripping over. Swearing. I close the door behind me. He laughed, for the first time he laughed. I shake my head, satisfied: lost, confused boy. Let's see if we can drive the fash out of him! He's on the right path, deserted. Now he just has to experience a few nice things.

*

I position myself in front of the fireplace and wait to see whether Magdalena will say anything about my romance. I always used to imagine how she would comment on my acquaintances, how she would act in front of them, kiss them exuberantly, intimidate them. I would never have admitted it, but I enjoyed these imaginary scenes. I once brought a boyfriend home to my grandmother. She was so cold towards him – and to me, when I asked her about him – that I shielded her from that part of my life from that moment on. Instead, I fantasise, with the familiar shudder of fear, about how Magdalena would appear and pull off some kind of southern Italian mother drama; or at least what I would imagine one to be. Crying, ripping out hair, rowdy hugs, oaths of love and death threats: If you break my daughter's heart, if you so much as harm a single hair on her head—

And I would shout: Magda, are you crazy, stay out of it, it's just a casual love affair!

At which point she would dramatically hold her breath, approach him dangerously slowly and whisper: You don't want to marry my daughter? Are you the stupidest person in the world? What's your problem?

But it wasn't like that, and she remains silent. Nothing moves inside the urn.

*

I look at myself in the mirror while brushing my teeth, make Magdalena appear by raising my left eyebrow. When I think back on it now, I would say that she was no taller than I am. And yet she was this striking character, voluminous; her being took up an incredible amount of space. Her piercing voice, sweeping gestures, suits crackling with electricity, teased mane, cloud of perfume . . . She was a knockout, a force of nature. Not a classical beauty with her bad overbite and her shrill laugh. My grandmother found her *vulgar*. Lavinia was the complete opposite: a lady who made sure that her knees were always closed. Anything to do with sexuality was held hidden there and hushed. She chastised my endeavours in this direction with majestic disregard.

I raise my chin, try to recognise her within me. She always stood as straight as a candle, whereas Magdalena swayed, staggered, stumbled. Lavinia wanted me to be drawn up by a thread from my skull, like her. She did gymnastics, for her face too, ate a banana every morning at five thirty. She was fit as a fiddle, as she used to say, her body was twenty years younger than she was, as the doctor assured her. Months later, she was in a coffin.

I twist a strand of hair around my finger, release it, it stays straight. Lavinia and Magdalena, they were totally different, the only thing they shared was how they did their hair. With nightly curlers, hard, spiky things, which they slept on like a bed of nails. Aside from that, neither of them had their eyebrows anymore, but they did have impressive breasts. And me? Not I. I have thick brows and straight hair and in the evenings I have more wrinkles than my grandmother ever had. She only used Nivea from a tin. I take her last one, I dunk my finger into it and realise: there is something that we all have in common. We apply face cream like warpaint.

Now I feel like I'm not alone. I turn around and try to avoid the gaze in the mirror. I'm sure that I would see someone standing behind me.

*

I don't sleep. I wait for Sisina. With every crack in the beams, every rustle at the window, every pause of the cicadas I hold my breath. My blood thumps in my throat. The moon is red.

To calm myself, I think about Lorenzo. What's up with him, is he shy? Since our arrival he hasn't made any advances, any moves, hasn't staked out a claim. That's fine with me; I don't feel particularly drawn to him. But it would do him some good, stiff and tense as he is. Maybe he likes this power that he has over me; I'm at his mercy. He probably knows just as well as I do that the dynamic would be reversed as soon as he was lying sweaty on my collarbone. Or he despises the communist that he takes me for, and is thinking of nothing but how he will destroy me. Maybe he doesn't know himself what he wants from me.

The cicadas rasp like cheese graters.

And the Coach ... when will he arrive and what will I do when I'm standing in front of him? What has Lorenzo told him about me? An idea worms its way frostily up the back of my neck: what if the Coach has sent Lorenzo to get me out of the way? Because he knows what I suspect ... what I'm planning to do? But Lorenzo doesn't know that I have his gun. Although he must have surely noticed that it's disappeared from his car. Why hasn't he asked me about it?

I throw back the covers and jump out of bed, shake the urn. It rattles, the gun's still there. Good, I nod repeatedly, and lie back down in bed. My knees tingle like crazy, the drunken moon is laughing at me.

I will lure the Coach into the forest and shoot him there. It will be easier than I thought. Or, if he's sleeping here, I could surprise him then. Boom. Lorenzo would have to scrub the walls afterwards. That would get him worked up all over again.

When I've carried it out, I'll finally do what I've always wanted to do: I'll travel to my grandmother's town to find my roots. Fantasised a thousand times, they're like images from a film:

me arriving on the piazza. The old folks squinting in disbelief in their plastic chairs: Lavinia?

I laugh, they embrace me and shout: Lavinia's granddaughter has come home!

And we sit together, drinking, and they tell me my story.

If the town still exists. Perhaps it's been abandoned like the ghost village, where the wind creeps through open doors. Where plates and bottles of oil stand on dusty sideboards and there are playing cards on the table as if the players had only got up and left a moment before. Maybe everything fell to pieces behind her when Lavinia left; she never looked back.

Yes, she would say, in real life the story is buried, and the old are dead.

Not all of them, Magdalena objects, one still lives in the ghost village: Fila, you saw them.

Suddenly, my entire body begins to itch with tension. Did I lock up? I look over at the door: the key is rattling as if moved by a ghost hand! I crawl under the covers, pull them over my head. Don't come, leave me alone – Nonna, protect me. The restless dead are frightening.

Before my squeezed-shut eyes, Magdalena is wheeled by on a gurney. Her face beaten unrecognisable, her arms hanging lifelessly. And I see Sisina lying in the forest, blustering treetops, she sits up . . . She walks through the grove, snails crawl across her skin. The wind flows through the large cut at her throat, it tickles.

Please, stay outside, I beg you both. I will leave you both in peace, forgive my curiosity, my empty promises—

The night song, the cicada creaking has slowed.

*

Sisina doesn't come. There is only the moon, embalmed, and a screech owl in the tree. Instead, a blast of wind opens my window, and I climb out of it. Hurry through the moonlight into the ghost village, the gravel shimmers, and the little leaves of the olive grove cackle at me. One house has a tree growing through its broken roof and its upper windows are illuminated. I climb the stairs, knock on the door. Inside there's laughter, cigarette smoke.

Magdalena and Sisina in black and white. They're sitting on the floor playing cards among the debris. Magdalena is wearing sunglasses, lipstick; in spite of that, you can still see the bruises. Sisina is wearing a red scarf around her neck.

Magdalena waves me over without looking up, she pats the floor next to her: Come on, play with us. What's your bet?

What are you playing? I ask.

Sisina says something incomprehensible and plucks at her cards, deep in concentration.

What are the rules?

Magdalena shouts: Ma dai, if you don't know it then you can't play it, we're in the middle of a game.

Sisina scratches with irritation at her neck.

Magdalena pushes me: Your nonna is in the kitchen. Go on, go to her, but don't tell her anything about this.

She points at her face.

Sisina snorts: She isn't stupid, she's known about it all for a long time.

Both of them laugh, exposing bloody teeth.

In the kitchen next to the tree, my grandmother is standing at the oven, dropping a large bone into a bubbling sugo. Red sprays up the wall, something laughs. I scan the kitchen's dirty nooks.

Lavinia is standing with her back to me, but I can see how angry she is.

What are you doing here? she thunders. This is the past! You cannot enter, you will always be a stranger here. You'll only make your fingers grubby and scratch open our badly healed scars.

Don't be afraid, I say meekly, don't worry. I still know the first word: *aiuto*. If the Coach comes, I'll scream.

It won't do you any good, a voice from behind me says while prodding me in the back. I fall, past the tree, into the well. No sound comes through my throat.

When I wake, my heart is thumping so loudly it's as if someone is knocking at the door. Of course! Now she's coming. I watch breathlessly as the door handle moves slowly downwards. I hold my breath. Go away, I whisper, please, stop it.

Scratches at the door, I raise my voice: Go away, I don't want to see you, I'm sorry, please leave me alone.

Mimma, are you awake? It's me, Lorenzo.

He seems so harmless with his dark circles, I want to hug him.

Sorry, he says, astonished, I didn't think you would be asleep already.

He seems awkward, shy. I bark at him: What do you want?

I forgot to mention it before, he says, I found something. Maybe it'll interest you?

I open the door a little wider, he holds a little book out towards me. At the same time, his eyes fall on the urn on the mantelpiece, and then meet mine. He quickly looks down at the floor, takes a step backwards, stumbles and murmurs: Well then, good night.

He rushes up the stairs. I want to call after him: Come back! I can't sleep alone. I'm scared.

Instead, I quickly shut the door and turn the key.

*

An old, simple school exercise book, bulging. Well-worn, torn at the edges, the cover separating from the rest of it. There's a comic strip on the cover: *The Whale Hunt*. The pictures show a wild sea, a great ship and a frothy whale, harpoons. Beneath this is a small box: This book belongs to . . . Someone had filled in the empty lines with a fine nib: *Daily Journal, Lessons, first year girls' class, school year 1946.*

1946! The year Sisina died.

In one of the images a sailor is blowing into a long funnel: *Whale in sight!*

I delicately peel the cover from the first page. A lesson plan. Monday to Saturday: *The first half hour of every day is a review of order, cleanliness and moral conversation – How the good girl helps those who are suffering.*

This is followed by lessons in religion (*telling the girls about the Lord God and the miracles of Jesus*), dictation, reading and writing, moral and civil education (*how every virgin must fulfil her duty with serenity*), recitation, mathematics, science and hygiene, calligraphy, history and geography.

I run my fingertips over the wavy, yellowed paper of the exercise book. The gossamer-thin paper sticks together. My pulse is throbbing in my neck as I slowly pull it apart in the middle. Sisina is smiling at me.

The book is full of newspaper clippings about the murder of Sisina. Much of it is underlined in fountain pen, exclamation marks in the margins and comments in teacherly handwriting: *Don't believe it. Lies.*

I carefully peel more pages apart. There are pictures of the villa, of the memorial stone by the road in the forest. Photos of Sisina's family. A sketched map of the area: the village on the overcrop that is now deserted; the road to the villa and the surrounding hamlet; a few houses and stables. An arrow points towards a building on the edge of the forest: *Sisina's house.*

The road continues through the forest, the well is sketched, halfway along there's a red cross: the scene of the crime. Slowly and with some effort I turn the pages and look at the pictures, black and white photos from the time. Names beneath them, designations. Sisina's sisters in court, gesticulating. They resemble her closely, only they look more serious. Sisina's parents: her mother in mourning, with an absent look. Her father a leathery little man with a flat cap, his shoulders drawn up to his ears. It looks as if he's grinning, practically toothless. A man behind bars: Sisina's fiancé, Vito. His father can be seen in a few of the pictures, a long, gaunt man with a face like a screech owl. Witnesses; soldiers; journalists. Crowds of people: protests for Vito's release.

I flick back to the picture of Vito in prison. He's holding on to the bars tightly with both hands, his body behind them is out of focus, as if he were moving, he's screaming. His face is distorted with despair and powerlessness.

I close my eyes, a memory swims up: Magdalena, screaming, clinging to my grandmother. We're visiting, visiting the cell, there's a single bed and a washbasin, a free-standing toilet, I suddenly remember it very clearly. I got a can of pop from a friendly policeman, but Magdalena is screaming. She's not happy to see me, she wails and shakes her mother: I have to get out! Get me out of here!

I hear her shrieking still when we're standing back in the corridor and the policeman has shut the cell door in front of us.

He's no longer friendly. Magdalena has to stay inside.

I sit up in bed, look at myself in the mirror. Between my eye-brows are two perpendicular shadows, Magdalena's frown lines. The night song of the cicadas outside the window. The cracking of the beams. I smile at myself. Spooky. I close the book.

A shudder runs over my legs. Something touched my feet, like a cat rubbing its oily fur against my soles, a sadness wells up inside me. I hold my breath. The invisible cat wanders over the mattress, and I can sense the weight of her paws beside me. I'm sure that she's sniffing the book. Rubbing her head against it, purring, a corner bends. Suddenly the weight is gone. It's jumped off the bed.

I remain still for a while and keep holding my breath. Then I start to read.

GIRL SLASHED TO DEATH IN FOREST

Yesterday, Sunday, 19-year-old Sisina A——, daughter of Stefano, engaged to Vito M——, was killed in the so-called Witches' Forest. The body was found just 200 metres from her house.

The small village community of L—— had gathered in front of the church that afternoon. The church became famous in the last year of the war because its statue of the Madonna is said to have started to bleed during a mass for fallen soldiers. In her honour, the holiday of Madonna del Sangue was declared, and celebrated for the first time yesterday.

Those congregated were still waiting for the statue to be carried out and for the procession to begin when the terrible news rang out: 'They've slit open Sisina!' The community then made its way to the scene of the crime.

No further details are known about what led to the crime. The parish priest said of the victim: 'She was a good girl. Beautiful, a little spirited perhaps, but with a heart of gold.'

WHO WAS THE BEAUTIFUL SISINA?

The name of the girl who was brutally murdered on the last Lord's Day is Sisina A——. But in her village, everyone just called her 'the beautiful Sisina'. It has been a great shock. Why did she have to die?

The daughter of an honest farming family was on her way to the spring to fetch water for the next day's bread. She was overpowered by a stranger and dragged into a bush, where she was raped and her throat cut. She was due to be married in a few weeks. Her bereaved fiancé is a young war veteran who returned from a concentration camp in Germany less than a year ago.

'As if he hadn't been through enough terrible things already,' complain the women in the village square. 'Such a sweet boy, quiet, prudent – completely different from his Sisina. But they liked each other, that's all that matters.'

The couple seems to have been popular in the village: 'It was a joy to see them together, a wonderful sight to behold. His kind face looking down at her admiringly, his fingers toying with her wild curls. They liked to tease each other, that was obvious.'

Sisina's temperament challenged the reserved Vito, and not only because it is known that she had already been engaged twice in her youth. 'Everyone liked her. Wherever she went, she brought good cheer: she helped where she could and exuded a cheerfulness that was contagious.' – 'Her gaze was like a spotlight that shone generously on everyone, and she had a friendly word for everyone who crossed her path.' – 'She was very capable, no work was too hard for her. It's a catastrophe. Who will help Vito's old parents now?'

The landowners, who Sisina helped as a maid, were unavailable for comment. The Swiss aristocratic family C——, consisting of the widowed Contessa and her adult son, own not only the villa, but also the surrounding hamlet and the tract of land that Sisina's family leases for their small farm. Sisina was last seen alive in front of the house next door, also owned by the C—— family. She called on her friend Livia to ask if she would come with her to the spring. This Livia replied that she had already fetched water that morning. So Sisina went off on her own.

A few hours later, the girl was found decapitated. Was it a coincidence that she was the one who fell into the hands of a brutal monster? Or did the beautiful Sisina have a dark secret? Certain voices testify that her generous smile had already led to some misunderstandings. Did it then lead to her downfall?

AUTOPSY: BEAUTIFUL SISINA NOT A VIRGIN

The autopsy on the 'beautiful Sisina' was carried out yesterday in the chapel of Villa C——. The body had a large cut across its throat. The department of forensic medicine also found various wounds in the chest area; these injuries are said to have occurred after the throat had been slit. The cause of death was exsanguination due to a perforation of the carotid artery. The blood seeped into the respiratory tract, leading to suffocation.

The dead girl was wearing an artificial silk vest trimmed with lace, a matching petticoat and a brassiere. A brightly patterned dress with a tight waist and flared skirt. A wool jacket with wooden buttons. Each item was swimming in blood. Her shoes were found clean some distance from the body. At the time of the crime, she must have been barefoot.

The body was not wearing any knickers. The victim's little sister testifies, however, that she saw her sister putting on a pair of knickers that morning. She described them as sun yellow and frilly. A burlap cloth, the kind that good peasant women tie around their heads to carry heavy jugs, is also missing.

The report states that the dead girl's heart would have been calm at the time of death. This suggests that the underwear was removed consensually. The hymen is torn, but it had been for some time. There is no evidence of sexual intercourse immediately before the crime. There were also no signs of a struggle. No one heard her scream, which throws up the theory that the encounter in the forest had been arranged in advance.

UGLY MAN ON THE RUN

There has been some interesting news in the case of the Madonna del Sangue murder: a widow saw an unknown man cycling past on a bicycle on the day in question. The young stranger had a 'grim, twisted face with wild eyes' and rode 'as if the devil were after him'. The woman had told her sister how ugly this man was. 'I immediately suspected him, hideous as he was.'

WHERE ARE THE SUN YELLOW KNICKERS?

In the case of the murdered girl from L——, there is still no trace of a perpetrator. While the village community patiently faces a double interrogation by the police and the press, the gates of the Villa C—— remain closed. This is all the more shocking as rumours have been circulating that a man from the neighbouring village who owns a small car had to drive a guest in a mad rush from the villa to the train station in town on the afternoon in question. It is not known which train he took.

Nothing more has been said about the guest in question. 'Strangers are constantly coming and going at the villa,' a source who wishes to remain anonymous reports. 'Since the war, the gentlemen have spent more time here than in their palazzo in town. They live it up, party all night long. Don't ask me what they have to celebrate.'

Meanwhile, the area is still being combed for the missing evidence: the victim's underwear and an apparently very sharp knife. Both appear to have vanished into thin air.

An explosive discovery: investigators found a knife buried near the crime scene. It has, however, been established that the knife is not the murder weapon. Is this a false trail? It has got the locals talking: 'It certainly didn't grow from the manure of us simple farmers,' one of them told us, nodding almost imperceptibly towards Villa C——. 'Only the upper classes are that cunning...'

REPORTS ON THE MURDER OF THE GIRL

The whole country is reporting on the poor peasant girl who was gruesomely killed during a procession of the Madonna. 'The beautiful Sisina' had intended to fetch water from the spring, but she never made it there. What happened on that tragic day? We have travelled to the distant hills, where the hearts of the peasant population are deeply wounded.

At the crime scene in the forest, the investigation is in full swing. Onlookers crowd the roadside to catch a glimpse. The victim's father, who found the body, is there to accurately explain the course of events to investigators and the press. He bends back a few branches on the embankment. There is an opening in the undergrowth: a kind of drainage channel for rainwater leading sharply downwards. The murder must have taken place in this dry ditch at the centre of the so-called Witches' Forest.

The father points out dark splashes of dried blood, still clearly visible. A policeman confirms that this must be where the crime took place, just a few metres from the road. From there, the body was dragged down the slope in the direction of the Tigress's Stream. The drag marks are likewise easy to make out. Her father says: 'I rushed down screaming, barefoot. After a hundred metres, I saw her colourful dress among the branches.'

Halfway up this path, behind the trunk of an old evergreen holm oak, the victim's sandals were arranged neatly, and the dry jug had been placed upside down. Two sweet wrappers were also found, bearing the names 'Seventh Heaven' and 'Perugia Chocolate House'.

The investigators and the victim's father now climb carefully down the steep slope. They go to the place where the body was found. The father lies down on the ground to recreate the position of the body. It was lying on its right side, with branches hanging in its hair. It was lying directly under a blackberry bush. 'The thorns didn't affect her beauty,' assures the retired village policeman. As one of the first people to arrive at the crime scene, he instructed the family not to move the body.

The father says that he, his sons-in-law and Sisina's fiancé kept watch at the site all night. The body could not be removed before the police arrived the following morning. It is now laid out in the chapel of Villa C——. The funeral will take place tomorrow, its urgency is due to the heat.

FIRST CLUES IN THE GIRL'S MURDER

The police have finally made a discovery in the case of the murdered farmer's daughter. Footprints were found near the Tigress's Stream. They are the soles of American soldiers' boots, around size 40. Although the ground was very damp, the tracks clearly indicate a hurried, agile step.

Meanwhile, the victim has been buried at the small local cemetery. As her wedding was imminent, the girl was buried in her wedding dress. She wore a scarf around her neck and her wedding ring on her finger.

According to eyewitnesses, the fiancé appeared remarkably composed, almost detached. Someone even claims to have heard him say to the deceased's brother-in-law after the service: 'And now, a nice, cold beer!'

The village teacher found more appropriate words: 'It's a tragedy. The wedding dress had been hanging in her wardrobe for months, and every day the girl stood in front of it and dreamed about the best day of her life. Now she's wearing it in her coffin, poor thing. The wedding should have taken place long ago. Sisina's family had postponed it until the autumn because they didn't want to give their daughter away before the harvest. She was so hardworking, after all. A great loss for both families.'

DID SISINA HAVE TO DIE BECAUSE OF LINEN?

The investigators in the Madonna del Sangue murder case are still groping about in the dark. But the victim's fiancé has offered explosive new information. 'I know who it was,' he announced in the church square. And he continued: 'If I see the linen seller, I'll kill him.' Choice words from the young war veteran, who up to this point has appeared rather anxious. Is grief driving him mad? Or is there some truth in the accusation? Who is this linen seller?

A travelling salesman from Yugoslavia came to Sisina's house a few days before the murder to present household linen for the upcoming wedding. She had already bought a set in town, which she showed him. He said that it was bad quality and that he would exchange them for a good price. When Sisina refused, he became angry. He is said to have shouted: 'By the Holy Madonna, you will never marry!' The man has not been seen in the village since.

The lead investigator states that the linen seller is tall and strong. He has ruled out the possibility that the footprints found at the scene (size 40) could be his.

Meanwhile, fear among the local population is increasing noticeably. The boys in particular no longer leave the house, except to work in the fields. The victim's fiancé has friends escort him when he is out on the street. He was seen barricading his front door and bricking up the bottom window. It is said that he only sleeps with the light on and in the same room as his parents.

BREAKING NEWS: FIANCÉ DETAINED

The police have arrested Vito M——. He is suspected of murdering his fiancée Sisina A—— in the so-called Madonna del Sangue crime. The incriminating factors were washed-out bloodstains on his left trouser leg and his jealous behaviour.

FLIRTING WITH TROUBLE

The relationship between the accused Vito M—— and his fiancée, known as 'the beautiful Sisina', was evidently anything but harmonious. People close to him say that the girl was very agitated leading up to her death. 'She was afraid of acquaintances greeting her when she was out and about because her fiancé had become so jealous.'

Statements of this type made the lead investigator sit up and take notice: 'The fiancé had come into my sights,' he announced at the press conference, 'so I wasn't surprised when we found a pair of bloody trousers during a search of his house.' From the traces, it can already be determined that it is human blood of group A that has been treated with a little water. Vito and Sisina both belong to this blood group.

The investigator is relieved: 'The fact that we were able to catch the culprit so quickly and put him behind bars is a well-deserved consolation for the victim's family.'

Meanwhile, the village community of L—— expresses its dismay: Vito M—— is a 'normal, likeable boy'. There is a lot of speculation about the reasons that could have driven him to commit this act. Some say that his girlfriend's popularity was not easy for him to bear. As a quiet man, he found it difficult to deal with her impulsive, open nature: 'It bothered him that she paid so little attention to him.' Was the act a desperate attempt to bring his fiancée to her senses?

A source close to the community reports an anonymous letter that Vito is said to have received a few months ago. 'Take care, watch your woman, she's trying to deceive you.' The source says that the accused then forbade his fiancée from working in Villa C—— or with her brother-in-law at the charcoal kiln in the forest. When Vito heard at a party that Sisina was offering to help her brother-in-law anyway, he asked another girl to dance, whereupon Sisina also danced with another boy. 'Vito was deeply hurt and wouldn't see her for weeks afterwards.'

A local woman who works as a fortune teller advised the girl during this period of separation. She says that Sisina was very upset. 'I attested to her fiancé's strong jealousy.' But did he have good reason to be jealous? A family friend threw cold water on the theory: 'It would certainly have been noticed if Sisina had not behaved honestly. After all, everyone's eyes were glued to her.'

The accused, meanwhile, has been generously providing information. He receives us in his cell and confirms both the receipt of the anonymous letter and the relationship crises. 'It's true that our engagement was broken off twice.' The separations were both instigated by him and clearly took a toll on Sisina. 'She couldn't eat or sleep without me. When we crossed paths once near the spring, she showed me the dark circles underneath her eyes and how her dress was hanging off her. She begged me to take her back. I stood firm and set my conditions. She had to start showing me respect.'

The defendant continues, saying that his fiancée's family also acknowledged her mistakes. Her mother and sisters reprimanded Sisina on several occasions. 'How am I supposed to react when I find out that my fiancée has been seen in the forest with her ex? She made it worse by claiming that they had met by chance and only exchanged a few words. But I knew that they had talked for a long time and laughed loudly together.' The last straw was a visit to her married sister, the charcoal burner's wife, which she made without his permission.

And yet he still wanted to marry her? The defendant gives a resolute nod of the head: 'Everything was ready: I had already bought a kilo of wedding sweets. Sisina promised that she would do better and had proved her loyalty to me. I had no reason to doubt it.'

He does not want to hear anything about the blood on his trousers. 'If it's there, it's probably from a burst boil.'

SCAPEGOAT, BEWARE

The events in the Sisina murder case have recently escalated. The village priest has now commented on the fiancé's arrest: 'Poor lad!'

Many locals harbour similar feelings. The police chief's accusations were 'pulled out of thin air,' say friends of the accused. Particularly explosive: the size 40 footprints, which until recently were the only evidence, cannot be linked to Vito, who wears a size 42. It is highly unlikely that he could have squeezed himself into shoes that were far too small for him in order to commit the crime. Additionally, the tracks disappear near the charcoal kilns – Vito's house is in the opposite direction. He would have had to make a very big detour.

In fact, there are some indications that the inspector, who is still inexperienced in his position, wants to close the high-profile case as quickly as possible. Blinded by the spotlight, he has resorted to the simplest motive: jealousy. After all, it is known that men buzzed around Sisina like flies.

The policeman is barking up the wrong tree and taking his chances out on the branches. In doing so, he is neglecting all other leads: the noble C—— family remains unchecked. During the interrogations with the villagers,

summertime has caused some confusion: since most farmers do not change their clocks and continue to orient themselves according to the sun, contradictory time statements have slowed down the investigation process even further – this does not always seem to be entirely by accident.

One thing is clear: by arresting Vito M——, the inspector is driving a wedge into the once united rural community. Many people support the accused and are gifting his parents cigarettes and fruit: 'For your brave boy.' On the other side, there are those who do not want to wait for the judgment: they have already declared Vito guilty.

Tragically, the latter includes the family of the murder victim, who have callously turned away from their once beloved soon-to-be son-in-law. Sisina's friend

and neighbour Livia L——
has also fanned the flames
of the scapegoat theory by
expanding on her original
statement: 'When we came
back from mass on the day
of the Madonna del Sangue,
Vito asked Sisina if she would
go to the spring after lunch.'
When asked by the press why
she was only mentioning this
now, she replied that it had
only just occurred to her. In
addition, she had 'no idea'
why her friend had asked her
if she would come with her to
fetch water. 'She knew that I
would not come, I had already
told her at the morning mass.'
Truly inconsistent and suspicious behaviour!

After all, the scandalous
circumstances have outraged
even the legal elite. On the
same day of Vito M——'s
arrest, three top lawyers
announced that they would
defend him pro bono. They
report that Vito M—— sur-
vived the first night in prison
well and showed exempla-
ry willingness to cooperate.
Their client is 'concerned and
exerting every effort'.

VITO TELLS ALL

The accused in the 'Sisina'
murder case is still in custody.
From his cell he reports his
experiences on the day of the
crime. He speaks very calmly,
allowing his good character
to shine through.

'That morning before mass,
I waited in front of my fiancée's
house. I was used to her taking
her time, so I spent a long time
chatting with my future moth-
er-in-law, who invited me to
lunch. She was making soap
and wanted to give me some
for my mother. When Sisi-
na came out, she gave a twirl
to show me her new dress. I

teased her a little because she had kept me waiting.

'At lunchtime, I took her home from church. We agreed to meet for the procession in the late afternoon. Although my soon-to-be parents-in-law insisted on me eating with them, I went home: my mother had cooked. After eating, I lay down on my bed. It was a holiday, after all, and I had got up before sunrise to feed the cattle. I slept soundly until the church bells woke me up. I complained to my mother: Why didn't you wake me? There wasn't enough time to pick up my Sisina.

'I took a shortcut and reached the church in time. I saw women crying. Poor Vito, they sobbed, haven't you heard? They found your fiancée. I screamed three times: No! No! No! Then I took someone's bike and rode to the crime scene. I hugged my Sisina until someone dragged me away. I would never have let her go.'

The young man in the dark cell needs a moment to regain his composure. Then he says, in a choked voice: 'Everything was covered in blood. I must have got the stains then.'

The alleged burden of proof evaporates based on this statement: the murderer must have been covered in blood after the crime. Two tiny drops on a pair of trousers are therefore not proof of guilt, but of the opposite: innocence.

THE MOTHER'S SECRET

The case of the murdered village beauty is becoming more mysterious by the minute. The rumour mill is humming away: many people agree that Sisina was killed because she was caught with a lover. When viewed in this light, the mother's statement, which has so far received too little attention, appears particularly mysterious. It's understandable: the mother's pain inspires respectful distance. But now the evidence indicating that an innocent man is in custody is piling up. It is time to turn over the more sensitive stones.

Shortly after the crime, the victim's mother recounted to us the last time she saw her daughter alive. According to her, Sisina left the house after lunch. The mother saw her calling for her friend, who did not want to accompany her. The jug in her hand and a shawl over her shoulders, she set off alone. The well is 390 metres from the house; when Sisina did not return after more than an hour, her mother became worried and decided to look for her. She walked along the road through the woods known as the Witches' Forest.

'The ditch drew me to it as if by magic,' her mother explains. 'I looked left and right and then into the bushes: there I saw a large pool of blood and a few smaller spatters. But I said to myself: no, no. I picked up some branches and covered the blood with them. I couldn't go further down; it was as if an invisible hand was holding me back. So I went back to the main road and continued to the spring. I became worried when I didn't see the jug. On the way home, I forgot about the blood.'

Let us interrupt the story here for a moment. Why does the mother go looking for her daughter in the first place? We are talking about broad daylight – what is she so afraid of? The woman explains that she was afraid that her daughter would meet someone in the forest and 'lose herself'. When she saw the blood, she felt her suspicions were confirmed: 'I didn't want anyone to see it and think the same thing I did.' Namely? 'That Sisina had lost herself.' The mother thus indicates that she thought the pool of blood came from her daughter's deflowering. But why does she associate such a large amount of blood with this act? And how could she have 'forgotten' it afterwards?

When she gets home, she wakes her husband but does not tell him anything about the blood. The sisters and brother-in-law are also roused from their beds. So the whole family sets out to search for Sisina.

The father says the body was still warm. The former village policeman, who arrived a little later, says it was already cold and the blood had congealed. He didn't even get dirty when he carried her back to the crime scene.

These discrepancies are striking. Taken with the mother's more than strange behaviour, they raise important questions. And a shadow falls over the victim's family, of all people.

WAS THE BEAUTIFUL SISINA EXPECTING?

In the Madonna del Sangue murder, there is speculation from all sides about the 'blood miracle': how did the telltale drops (some claim they were in the shape of a question mark) end up on Vito's trousers? The defendant provides a previously unheard explanation in a new statement.

When asked about the final big argument that the notorious couple had in public, Vito M—— let slip something that he would probably have preferred to keep secret . . .

A few days before the murder, the victim's sisters accompanied the couple into town to make the final wedding preparations. According to her sister Virginia, Vito M—— went off by himself for a while to choose the ring. 'He came back with cigarettes, two pairs of socks and the wedding ring.' When it turned out that it was made of tin and not gold, Sisina joked about her fiancé's thriftiness.

A terrible argument broke out. Her sister Alessia reports that Sisina was lying in bed crying the next morning: 'She wasn't well in the days before her death.' The doctor was called, who examined Sisina because she was severely emaciated and exhausted.

The defendant confirms: 'When I heard that the doctor was with my fiancée, I was very worried – in any case because of the secret. Sisina had recently confessed to me that she was afraid she was pregnant. So after work I went to her with a basket of fresh ricotta. She greeted me with the words: "Do you know what the doctor said? I should try to argue less with my lover."'

Was the reason for Sisina's discomfort not the argument, but the fear of a secret pregnancy? Alessia denies it: 'Nonsense, she bled all over the bed.'

Vito M—— could have got the stains on his trousers during this visit. It is understandable that he kept quiet about this possibility: men simply don't speak about menstrual blood, let alone a late period.

IRON SILENCE

In the 'Beautiful Sisina' murder case, something seems to have happened behind the scenes that has left people in the area speechless. There is now a yawning silence towards the police and the press. The only responses still being given are: 'I don't know' and 'I wasn't there'. A police officer responsible for interviewing witnesses says: 'These people wouldn't talk even if you threatened them with death.' Those voices who mere weeks ago named 'he who is highborn', the Contessa's son, as a possible perpetrator have fallen silent. Instead, shady characters, such as the victim's girlfriend, whose statements are being used to incriminate the accused, are speaking out more and more. What is the reason for this sudden change of heart? Does the new, conspicuously expensive coat that Livia L—— has recently been wearing, according to eyewitnesses, have something to do with it?

THE MADONNA DEL SANGUE MURDER TRIAL

The courthouse is almost impossible to enter on this humid morning, so large is the crowd gathered in front of it. Workers, office girls, students, they are all convinced of the defendant's innocence: 'He just doesn't look like a murderer.' They want to show their solidarity – or simply find out first-hand the news of what is probably the most famous murder case of the post-war period.

It is almost exactly a year since the young Sisina A—— was found lifeless in the forest. She was on her way to the well, but she never arrived. There is great hope that the secret of her murder will be revealed during the trial. Everyone eagerly awaits the first day's witnesses: the accused himself and the victim's family will be questioned.

The socialist lawmaker S—— will lead the defence. He describes the trial as a witch hunt: 'A heroic war veteran and hard working farmer must pay for the ignorance of a local policeman? These are not the values of our country. I stand against it.' The crowd at the entrance cheers him on. 'Viva Vito,' they shout, 'he is innocent.'

In the courtroom, the accused stands in the so-called tiger cage next to the judge's lectern. He has a fresh haircut and is wearing a white shirt. The accusations against him are read out: bloodstains on his trousers and contradictory attempts at an explanation; baseless accusations against a travelling salesman known as the 'linen seller'; pathological jealousy and quarrelsomeness in relation to his fiancée; the unswerving journey to the crime scene without having been informed of its location; denial that he had an appointment with his fiancée at the spring; his weak alibi, caused by inconsistencies in his parents' testimony; his conspicuous behaviour at the victim's funeral; an extreme display of fear after the crime.

The interrogation begins. The accused is asked about the footprints of American boot soles found at the crime scene. He denies having received shoes from the Americans when he was released from the German prison camp. He radiates an impressive calmness, always speaking of 'my poor Sisina'. 'She was always a good girl to me,' he emphasises, 'I was never jealous; I was fond of her. And of course, if someone is fond of someone . . .' A few tears in the courtroom.

'If I had doubted her honesty, I would have left her. But I found her intact.' He explains that he had 'possessed' his fiancée several times in the two months before the crime. About ten times: twice in the field and on other occasions in the doorway of Sisina's parents' house. At midnight when saying goodbye, while her mother was in the kitchen.

This story triggers a sudden crisis in the victim's mother. The woman springs up from the bench and screams: 'I'll scratch your eyes out!' The judge calls for calm and summons her to the witness stand. Mariapia R—— is dressed all in black, holding a rosary between her fingers. For an uneducated country woman, she shows surprisingly little fear of the gentlemen of the court. She immediately expresses her dislike of the accused: she feels mocked. 'I want to say something to the accused. The expert [the medical report, author's note] has already said that Sisina was not all right [deflowered, author's note]. And now Vito says that he was the first [first sexual partner, author's note]. Fine, but what is the use of telling everyone cheerfully how, where and when?'

The mother is asked about the day of the crime and her search for her daughter. She was calling quietly through the forest because she suspected that Sisina was somewhere with her fiancé. The defence asks: 'In the first interrogation she said "with someone or other"?' The woman waves the question away and continues to explain how she found the pool of blood in the ditch. How did she know where to look? Mariapia answers: 'If my daughter wanted to "lose" herself, that would be the best place.' She tells the court how she covered the bloody puddle with leaves. Why? 'I didn't want anyone else to see and understand what I had just understood.' [That Sisina had been deflowered, author's note.]

The defence lawyer speaks up: 'Excuse me, are you a woman?' Mariapia says yes. Then surely she must know that the loss of virginity may produce a few drops of blood, but not a pool. 'Did your daughter ever tell you that she was afraid of being in a delicate condition?' [Pregnant, author's note] – 'Never!' The victim's mother bursts into tears. The crowd murmurs snidely. The defence lawyer notes that it is strange that the mother did not faint.

The victim's father is called. The little man seems practically chatty and plays excitedly with the buttons on his jacket. He explains how he trusted his ex-nearly-son-in-law unconditionally and was a vocal defender of him at the beginning. That only changed when the bloodstains appeared. When asked how he found out about them, he answers: 'From the newspaper.' A voice calls out from the audience: 'Stefanino, since when can you read?' The whole room laughs.

The father is followed by the sisters. One seems haughty, the other extremely confused. Virginia gets caught up in a discrepancy because she says that her mother woke her up from her siesta. But her husband said it was Alessia. Who woke whom? Only one thing is certain: the family are talking themselves into a hole.

This brings the first day of the trial to an end. Vito M——'s supporters are still chanting outside the court. They will not stop until they hear word of an acquittal.

THE EVIL STEPSISTER – GOT AWAY AGAIN?

The second day of the controversial trial against Vito M—— is already over. The proceedings have been adjourned indefinitely and will probably be moved to another court.

What happened? First up for questioning was the woman who had informed Vito of Sisina's death. 'I was standing in front of the church when I saw him arrive. I said: Don't you know? They slit your lady's throat.' She is certain that she did not tell the defendant where it happened. And yet he rode straight to the crime scene.

Livia L——, the victim's friend, also makes an incriminating statement. When the girl takes the stand, the courtroom descends into uproar. Many people do not take care to make their remarks quietly. The reason: a few months ago she gave birth to an illegitimate child. Even under oath she keeps the secret hidden behind a sphinx-like smile: 'The baby's babbo? There isn't one.'

The presiding judge reprimands her sharply: 'There is nothing to laugh about, this is a serious matter!' When asked her age, she says she is nineteen, but she is in fact twenty-one. The defence lawyer notes that the girl is mentally unstable. He recommends that her statements be given no importance. In spite of this, the girl is questioned further.

L—— describes how, on the morning of the day in question, she went to mass with Vito, Sisina and her sisters. As they passed the cemetery, Vito said: 'Look, the gravedigger has dug up a fresh field. I bet the carrots are a sight from down there. Who do you think he'll bury first of us lot?' The audience objects loudly. As does the defence lawyer: why is she only saying this now, did someone tell her to say it? 'What do you want from me?' L—— shouts. 'It was such a long time ago.' The prosecutor asks if she slapped Vito because of the comment? The witness says she does not remember. 'He must have just been messing around.'

The third witness to appear is Filomena – known as the 'evil stepsister': her mother Mariapia brought her into the family from her first marriage. Incidentally, she is not legally married to Stefano. Poor Filomena takes the stand to excited murmurs from the crowd. According to rumours, she confessed to the murder long ago because she found Sisina in the forest with her husband, the charcoal burner. The same charcoal burner with whom the accused did not want his fiancée working. This was because he had received an anonymous letter advising him to stop sending Sisina to his brother-in-law. The stepsister confirms that she knew about the letter in question. Sisina told her about it after Filomena asked why she was no longer helping them.

The accused states that the letter had nothing to do with his decision to forbid her to go. He simply did not want his future wife to work. The presiding judge then exclaims: 'Is it somehow forbidden for a bride to continue working?'

The atmosphere in the courtroom is fiery. The talk of a possible romance between the in-laws has stoked emotions further: the crowd now displays open hostility towards Sisina's family. The public prosecutor finally asks that her relatives be given increased police protection on the way to the train station; they were attacked several times that morning alone. The defence lawyer expresses doubt regarding the necessity of this measure – the audience applauds enthusiastically. The presiding judge rings his bell, the defence lawyer becomes verbally abusive. All hell breaks loose. The courtroom is cleared. The senior public prosecutor suggests that the trial be adjourned due to bias. The defendant bursts into tears. The onlookers outside the court are also disappointed and upset. An anonymous witness says he would not be surprised 'if a few stones are let fly today'.

ATTACK ON THE COURT

The security forces at the courthouse managed to thwart an assassination attempt today. The motivation was most likely yesterday's decision to postpone the trial against Vito M——. The court confirmed receipt of an anonymous letter, the writer of which claimed to be Sisina's murderer. He threatened to commit further murders if Vito was not released immediately. The court did not wish to comment further on the matter.

The victim's family in the Madonna del Sangue murder have been much discussed in the course of the aborted trial. No other party has been the target of as many rumours, theories and claims. The father's abrupt manner irritated the public and aroused much suspicion, especially since the family members cannot agree where 'Babbo' was at the time of the crime. Was he under the fig tree, with the cows or in bed? The mother has stoked the fire with her strange stories and is derisively referred to as the 'mother of mysteries'. Is there any truth in what people are saying: 'Who knows what goes on behind closed doors . . .'? Who are these country folk and what do they have to say for themselves? While everyone is busy talking about them, we visited them at home – to talk to them.

In the dark kitchen of the small tenant farm, it becomes obvious that the flower of the family has been snatched away. None of the three sisters sitting around the table has the murdered Sisina's beauty. The two older ones are already married, their husbands are sitting by the stove smoking. The father is wearing boots, he is on his way out to the stable. The cows never clock off for the day. The mother wrings her hands, impatient to begin. She says: 'Vito was like a son to us. This uncertainty as to his guilt is driving us to despair.'

Is that why they went to see the witch? The youngest sister, Alessia, blushes: 'It wasn't like everyone says, the newspapers are full of lies! We didn't bribe her and we certainly didn't threaten her.' What happened then? Alessia admits that she and her sisters visited a fortune teller who goes by the name of 'Yeast': 'She read our cards, but they were unclear. On the one hand, they showed that Vito was guilty, on the other hand, they ruled it out. We brought coal as payment. She was supposed to get more if she could show us the murderer. But we never asked her to name Vito or anyone else as the murderer.'

The father says, while standing in the doorway: 'Shortly after my daughter's death, I was running errands up in the village. I was standing at the bar drinking a glass of milk when I heard certain people accusing Vito. I said loudly: If Vito is a murderer, may I be struck in the head by a hoof.' Then he excuses himself: 'The cows are calling.'

'We didn't suspect him,' says the mother, 'we were stunned when he was arrested.' What changed? After all, they are the ones who took their son-in-law to court. Will they now drop the charges? 'The evidence convinced us,' explains the middle sister Virginia. 'First of all, there was the blood on his trousers.' They hadn't wanted to see it before, says her husband. 'We couldn't see it, we should have noticed it earlier.'

Their neighbour Livia told them that Vito and Sisina had arranged to meet at the spring after lunch. 'But that's not all.' The men by the stove exchange a glance. They speak of a disturbing event the night after the murder. 'We stayed with Sisina in the forest; she was not to be moved until the police arrived from town. We took turns keeping watch over her body, and when I roused Vito, he woke with a start and shouted: *No! No! No! What have I done?*' The charcoal burner, the eldest sister's husband, nods. Sisina had helped him with the work in the charcoal kiln until Vito had forbidden her from doing so. Why? Did the flame of passion between the in-laws flare up over the glowing coals in the lonely hours in the forest? The sister gets angry, her husband shakes his head: 'But we were never alone. My brother was always there, often with others.'

'Vito acted terribly jealous,' the little sister Alessia interjects. She was the closest to the deceased. 'He was constantly making accusations against Sisina. She was always nervous that she would do something wrong.' In Alessia's opinion, Vito was just looking for an excuse to leave his fiancée. 'I kept telling her: he couldn't pull that kind of act with me.' He pestered her with doubts and allegations about her fidelity and painted a terrible picture of their future together. 'He claimed that his friends were saying bad things about her, but it was him: he called her a slut.' For Sisina's little sister, it was clear: he wanted to humiliate her, to wear her down.

'Do you know the story of the ring?' A few days before the murder, the fiancé, Sistina and her sisters drove into town to buy the wedding ring. Most of the things for the wedding had already been organised by the family. 'He really didn't contribute anything to the preparations,' Virginia exclaims, 'he said he had to save money for the gold ring.' 'And then he comes skipping over with that cheap thing!' Alessia shouts. 'He said she wasn't worth it . . .'

The mother apologises and leaves the kitchen. 'She still can't believe it,' explains Virginia. She is the most serious of the sisters. She had also noticed

Vito's relationship fatigue: 'I told Sisina that she shouldn't provoke him any further. He is such an authoritarian. I was afraid of how far he would go.'

The parents enter the dark kitchen together again. They remain standing by the door. The mother clears her throat: 'I also told her to behave. We didn't want to lose Vito.' Could it be that the fiancé had just become impatient because he would have liked to have married sooner? The mother shakes her head vigorously: 'He was even the one to suggest postponing the wedding.' The father shuffles in with his boots and mutters: 'He also claims that he wanted to cover the costs of transporting the body and the funeral. That's not true. He never offered to do that. Not to me, anyway.'

Vito has shown no visible grief during this entire period. 'And above all, no sympathy for the family,' adds the mother. 'He just went out drinking with his friends.' The father says, 'He turned away. He, who practically used to live here, has only come by once after Sisina's death.' The mother adds: 'And then only to warn us about the police, about their questions. He told us not to make things messy.'

It's getting late. Virginia lights a lamp. The stepsister and her husband, the charcoal burner, set off for their house in the forest. Crickets chirp on the country road. An owl hoots. And the house of the mysterious family melts into the darkness of the night.

MURDER TRIAL RESUMES

The courtroom is packed to bursting. Nine months after the postponement of the trial for the Madonna del Sangue murder, the defendant Vito M—— is back before the court. It has been almost two years since his fiancée, known as 'Beautiful Sisina', was found dead. He has been in prison for almost that long. Since then, the number of people convinced of his innocence has grown. Many in the public gallery have travelled from elsewhere to support the defendant.

The jurors are introduced: an actor, a butcher, an orthopaedist, a salesman, an engineer, a clerk. The defendant must convince them, and he turns to them first: 'I am not only innocent. I want justice for my poor fiancée, more than all of you put together.' The victim's mother sniffles loudly, the father seems annoyed, audibly asking the journalists whether he has to be there every day.

The accused is questioned about his weak alibi – which, incidentally, all the witnesses share: they were all asleep at the time of the crime. Vito explains: 'We country people work day and night. We use the holy days to get a few hours of sleep, drink vermouth and see our fiancées.'

Instead, he had to see his Sisina's body in the bushes. 'I stumbled, fell to my knees beside her, stroked her cheeks and her hair, she was covered in dirt.'

At this point the victim's father shouts: 'He never touched the body! I was there, I saw it, he didn't touch her!' The father is asked to sit back down so that Vito can continue: 'I immediately thought of a pervert. Only a pervert could do something like that.'

Then he turns to the father of his dead fiancée: 'I want to tell you something about your daughter. They say I made her ill. All I can say is: Sisina was the Cinderella of the family.' He once again addresses the public: 'My ex-almost-father-in-law made her work without a break, even on Sundays, in the mined fields. I accused him of it often, to which he replied: Be quiet so I don't kill you.'

The first day of the trial ends with this unpleasant scene. Sisina's family is driven home and will be picked up again the next morning. The father remarks: 'If they want us here, they should make more of an effort.' One thing is clear: this behaviour will not increase their popularity by any means.

NOW THE WITCHES ARE TALKING

The second day of the trial of the mysterious 'Causa Sisina' introduces some interesting personnel: two fortune tellers. Both were visited by the young village beauty – shortly before she died a brutal death.

One of them is an inconspicuous middle-aged woman from the village of L——. She read Sisina's cards about a year before the murder. At this meeting, the girl said to her: 'Look how thin I am, I'm all skin and bones.' When asked why Sisina had sought her advice, the woman replied: 'For a bit of fun.' The presiding judge draws the fortune teller's attention to her earlier statement. According to her, Sisina said: 'I think my fiancé doesn't love me anymore. Read the cards for me.' The woman claims not to remember. Strange that clairvoyants apparently only see the future and not the past.

The other specimen is a professional clairvoyant from town. 'Yeast', as she calls herself, is a real character who lives in her own world, in a common-law marriage with a younger man. Sisina ventured into these realms – just a month before the crime. According to 'Yeast', the girl wanted to know two things. 'What does a married man I know quite well think of me?' And: 'How will I die?' The fortune teller could only give a vague answer to the first question, and to the second, that she would soon die a violent death.

As we know from reliable sources, the plaintiff family also visited this 'Yeast'. They promised her gold and coal if she would testify that Vito was the culprit. The fact that the enchantress did not mention this ugly attempt at bribery in court today shows her good character.

THE MOST TERRIBLE WITNESS

The murder trial against Vito M—— has been simmering away, but today one particular splash made the whole pot boil over: a witness who, at first glance, did not seem like the type to cause any trouble. Chiara T——, thirty-three years old, known by everyone in the village as 'the little teacher'.

She reveals fresh information. In the summer of 1945, the little teacher rang the bell at Villa C——. She intended to pick up costumes for a school party. As no one opened the door, she went straight in. And who did she find in the stately drawing room? Stretched out on a sofa, in the arms of an officer: Sisina! And then what happened? 'I apologised. The officer brought out a book and pretended to have been reading. Sisina fled into the garden.' Vito had not yet returned from his time in captivity during the war.

The last time the little teacher had seen Sisina was two weeks before the crime. She was out with Vito and asked him: 'When are we finally going to eat these sweets, then?'

The little teacher goes on to report how she went to the crime scene on the day of the murder. The victim's little sister was standing in the street and shouting: 'You coward, you scoundrel! Just because you didn't want her anymore, you didn't have to slaughter her like cattle. My poor dear sister! Who will tell poor Vito now!' The teacher swears that Mrs So-and-so heard it too.

As the crowd murmurs, the aforementioned Alessia appears in the witness stand. She states that she did not see the teacher that day. She wasn't long at the crime scene, before leaving with her mother and sister Virginia.

But that's not all: an old woman and a man claim to have heard Alessia screaming at the scene: 'Poor Sisina! You stayed away from the dinner table for fifteen days. And today, when you finally came back, look what happened to you!' When asked about these words, Alessia shakes her head. She doesn't remember any of it.

Meanwhile, Mrs So-and-so has been spotted in the room. She is supposed to testify to what the little teacher claims to have heard from Alessia. The teacher jumps up and shouts: 'It wasn't Mrs So-and-so, it was someone else.' She mentions other names that she saw at the crime scene. A few of them are present and shake their heads. 'The little teacher wasn't there,' they say in unison. No one saw her that day. Chiara T—— is given a warning by the presiding judge.

Now, the highlight: the Contessa makes an appearance. Despite her age, the lady of the manor, Signora C——, still has the grace of a ballerina. Rumour has it that she once danced on the greatest stages. The heels of her crocodile shoes echo through the courtroom, a hunting scene is depicted on her printed silk dress.

Of course she knew Sisina, the lady nods, she knows all her tenants. 'She was very sweet, a little coquettish . . .' She runs her perfectly manicured hands through her hair and moves with girlish vanity. But Sisina didn't work for them, her sister Virginia did. It was only when her sister was ill that Sisina came to help them out.

Naturally, the conversation turns to the officer. The lady confirms that she sometimes hosts high-ranking military officers as guests. During the time that Chiara T—— spoke of, however, there was only one at the villa. He had extended his stay for a party that the little teacher had organised for him. 'The young lady often asked me for help with her little performances. We were not particularly close.' She doubts that Sisina was at the villa that day. 'Even if she had come to bring a basket of eggs or some milk, she would not have entered the drawing room. She would not have been able to and was not permitted to. It must have been another girl.'

At this, the little teacher raises her hand like a particularly eager student in class. She can no longer contain herself and bursts out: 'It wasn't a performance, it was a poetry recital that I organised in honour of the lieutenant. I was confused before because I had organised several parties for him.' The lady responds, slightly irritated: 'In any case, it could not have been that day.' 'But Signora,' cries the little teacher, 'don't you remember? The party in honour of the special command! I saw Sisina in the drawing room, on the knee of a corporal. I'm telling the truth!'

The presiding judge intervenes: 'No, stop talking. Keep quiet or I'll throw you in the lock-up.' He turns to the Signora: 'Is your son also an officer?' – 'Yes.' – 'When Sisina died, where was your son?' – 'He was with me in Rome, for a property negotiation.' So the villa was deserted in the days around the holy day in question? The Signora says no: an employee was living in one of the rooms. However, he was away on the day of the crime. He learned of the murder that evening and the next day expressed condolences on behalf of his employers. The Signora is then dismissed and the presiding judge turns his attention to the little teacher: 'You are confusing times and places, getting caught up in contradictions – especially in relation to the Contessa! You have made a very bad impression on the court. Be gone and do not show your face here again.' His words boom through the courtroom like a thunderstorm. This is the end of the third, most revealing day of the trial.

WHY VITO IS GUILTY

The end of the murder trial is approaching, and the voices in favour of the defendant Vito M—— roar from every corner. But there are many indications that the young man is not the revered saint some claim him to be.

Let us start with the blood on his trousers. The defendant has made several contradictory statements on this subject. At one point he claims to have known nothing about it, then he knows exactly where it came from: the spattered branches at the crime scene; from touching the corpse; even from the deflowering – the circumstances of which are now known only too well by everyone. But science rejects all these possibilities.

The blood cannot have come from an accident at work either, since the item of clothing in question are the Sunday trousers that Vito M—— had already worn to morning mass that day. In the afternoon he asked his mother to iron the trousers again before he left for the procession – even though he was already running late. Why did the trousers have to be ironed twice? The answer is obvious: he stained them with blood during the crime and quickly washed them off in the Tigress's Stream.

In terms of a motive, only Vito has one. In his dealings with his fiancée he showed his dark side, he was possessive and suspicious. A deliberate act of violence cannot be ruled out. The timing is perfect: a hot holiday, with all the men asleep for the entire afternoon.

These reasons suggest that the jury should find the accused guilty. Will they dare to do this against the will of his horde of admirers?

IN THE WITCHES' FOREST

Court takes place today in the hills of L——. In the trial

against Vito M——, suspected of murdering his fiancée Sisina, it is hoped that an inspection of the crime scene will give further clarity to the situation. In the early hours of the morning, a caravan with the accused, the presiding judge, lawyers and jurors sets off to arrive at the crime scene around midday. Locals call this place 'The Witches' Forest' or 'Purgatory'.

A local farmer, leaning against his cart, explains the origins of the remarkable name: 'Many bad things have been done in this place. It is our way of saying that if someone does something to another, there will be some *sweeping*, you know what I mean. When asked what 'bad things' means, he answers: 'You know, rape, stabbings, assault of all kinds. Many people in the area avoid this place. That's why it's the perfect place for doing certain things.' Like premarital unions? The farmer laughs, a little embarrassed: 'Of course, but that's harmless. They held real orgies here, black masses . . .' When asked who did this, the farmer declines to go into further detail. Nor does he want to say whether these kinds of events took place during the war. However, he rules out a ritual murder in the Sisina case.

As expected, a crowd of onlookers and press has gathered at this notorious place. Some were obviously unaware of the off-track terrain that provides the setting for the tale they have all been sharing breathlessly for months. One young lady from the papers in particular is struggling on her high heels. She slips into the ditch – exactly where the victim, 'the beautiful Sisina', was killed almost two years ago.

Stuck in an awkward position, 'Miss Puss-in-Boots' is mortified and calls out for help . . . which the village youths gladly provide.

Meanwhile, the presiding judge has ventured into the hollow armed with ski poles and suspiciously tests the walls with their pointy ends. Distances are measured half-heartedly, questions are asked. Everything has already been examined several times over. Today it is only a matter of getting one's 'own impression', especially crucial for the jury.

The heat is clearly affecting the men of the court: their jackets hang sweatily over their shoulders. Those who can, undo all the buttons on their shirts. One of them groans: 'Now where is this well? My throat is so dry.' A country woman rushes over with a bulbous bottle wrapped in straw. She pours the men wine to much jubilation.

The onlookers want to cheer their hero most of all: Vito in his natural habitat. The young man from the village shows the jury the front door of his nearly parents-in-law – the notorious meeting place with his fiancée: 'This is where I *possessed* her.' The people celebrate the brief return of their martyr with socialist chants and shouts of 'Viva'. At times, scenes of a grotesque nature take place: the defence lawyer is forcibly dragged into the crowd and kissed. They have obviously confused him with the defendant. When the police car transporting Vito back to prison leaves, it is adorned with flowers.

It remains to be seen whether the case has progressed even one centimetre today. The longer this trial goes on, the more it seems to be deteriorating into pure public entertainment. Perhaps the young journalist has learned one thing at least: the murderer was probably not wearing high-heeled ankle boots.

BRAWL IN COURT

Sparks fly once again at the Madonna del Sangue trial. Today's session was brought to a halt after less than an hour. The courtroom had to be cleared by the police. What happened?

A witness who wanted to watch the trial 'out of interest' says: 'I've been following this witch hunt against poor Vito for weeks. Today was the first time I managed to make it into the courtroom. I was waiting outside the door from four in the morning! And I wasn't even the first in line. But it was a great spectacle, it was worth it. This defence attorney is a real humdinger.'

The argument began as a dispute between the lawyers. The prosecutor accused the defence lawyer of organising a fundraiser for the defendant, causing the crowd to burst into spontaneous applause.

This was the last straw for the presiding judge. He ordered the courtroom to be vacated: 'Out! Get the public out! Out, out, out!' Carabinieri, plainclothes police and the military pushed the furious crowd out the courthouse, while the judge shouted: 'Shame! Shame on the Italian people!'

Anyone wishing to experience what will probably be the last day of the trial in person tomorrow will most likely have to forego sleep tonight. The steps in front of the court are already occupied.

The trial against the 'people's hero' Vito M——is coming to a close. The bookies are taking bets: Guilty or acquitted?

In the next few hours, the jury will give its verdict. The prosecution and defence have made their closing arguments. We were in court and recorded all speeches in full. This way, the public can read both sides' reasons and form their own opinion.

CLOSING REMARKS FOR THE PROSECUTION

'It all began in a house where three girls flourished. Young, beautiful, hardworking – consequently desired and courted by the youth of the entire vicinity. This naturally fed the envy of the neighbouring houses, blessed with less attractive specimens. When the crime occurred, the entire community felt pain and horror. But as always, death is quickly forgotten . . .

'I would like to remind you of the real tragedy: Sisina. Not the man who wanted to get rid of his future wife. He is not a tragic hero. He is a murderer. He has shown his true colours several times. Recall him saying that she, his fiancée, did not deserve a gold ring! Sisina is left with only the gaping cut across her throat, like an eternal scream: It was him! Only Vito could do this to me!

'Don't be fooled by his composure. Inside this cage is a creature who lives outside the realms of normality. He denies all guilt and blames everyone else: It wasn't me, but the linen seller; not me, but my brother-in-law; not me, but Sisina's ex;

not me, but – brace yourselves – her babbo. He blames her father, gentlemen!

'That really is a cold-blooded theory – too awful to be true. So the fear Vito displayed after the murder was quite natural. He said he was afraid that the same thing that happened to his fiancée would happen to him. Of course it would, if he was throwing around false accusations! His fear also came from his own soul. Something was tormenting him: the shadow of poor Sisina.

'There are always possible incentives for murder between two lovers. One thing is clear: the girl was attacked from behind, without seeing the attacker – by someone she knew. She did not scream and the crime scene and victim showed no signs of struggle or violence. In fact, impressions of two people sitting

were found. Who could this girl have been sitting barefoot in the woods with if not her legitimate fiancé?

'For this reason, we must answer one question here: was Sisina promiscuous? I do not know if she was beautiful. But I do know that she was a simple girl: in love, serious, good. Even the accused confirms that he was only able to convince her into a sexual union after much persuasion and that he found her physically intact.

'Physically intact! Whenever these words are spoken, people in the room start smiling. They are sceptics who arouse a great bitterness within me. Such suspicion of a dead girl who cannot defend herself. Yes, she gave herself up, but out of fear!

'And we have conclusive proof: the drops of blood on his trousers. Three witnesses have testified that they touched the body without getting dirty, because the blood had dried before the body was found. All present also deny that Vito even touched the body. But he claims: "I got stained by her, I had to wash my hands. Some women gave me water." But these women deny this and say: He did not wash any blood from his hands.

'Another treacherous lie: Vito denies that he ever sat with his fiancée in the hollow where she was killed. In fact, this small forest near the spring was a regular meeting place for the couple. They had obviously arranged to meet that day too. Why else would the girl have called out loudly for her friend so that the whole family could hear, even though she knew that she wouldn't come with her?

'Vito often accompanied his fiancée to fetch water.

When they met there for the first time after the break in their relationship, it was likely not by chance. But he continues to claim: "We never met in the forest because the risk of being discovered was too great." At the same time, he claims that he had possessed his fiancée in the open field and outside her front door!

'The fact that Sisina was not wearing her knickers shows that she had already prepared for the act of love. The much-discussed question of whether or not she was wearing them on the morning of the crime is therefore irrelevant: if she had put them on, then only Vito could have taken them off. If she had not put them on, it was only because she was planning to meet Vito, who would have taken them off anyway. No, Sisina was not a forest nymph. She was a decent girl from a decent home.

'Look at this family: they are anxious and full of pain. If there had ever been any doubt about the defendant's guilt, the family would have withdrawn their charges. Although the parents are not married, they are good, moral people. Sisina and her behaviour were obviously the exception. But you all know how these things go. And so close to the wedding...

'Her mother was unable to prevent it, despite all her efforts. Her primal intuition even made her suspicious to others. I must admit, initially I was also confused by her strange handling of the pool of blood: can a mature woman and mother of several children really believe that a puddle like that was virginal blood? I had it explained to me by a medical specialist who is writing his dissertation on defloration. Indeed, the blood sacrifice of the first time is usually only a few drops. In rare cases, however, there can be heavy bleeding. So we no longer need to be surprised by the mother's reaction.

'Perhaps a few other female characters also require an explanation. Thousands of letters have been received at court accusing Sisina's stepsister of catching her husband, the charcoal burner, with the victim. Why not? Farmers' wives always carry a knife in their pockets. But this is not the act of a jealous woman. A woman would not have fled quietly. She would have stood on the street and screamed, telling everyone her reasons. Of course, a woman would also never have stolen the victim's underwear.

'The logical conclusion from all this is: Vito is the guilty party. His behaviour in the weeks before the murder was already an indicator. Not that he planned the crime in detail, but rather a seed grew in him that ultimately led to the crime: he wanted to get rid of her.

'But why? Why did he decide to get rid of his fiancée? Quite simply: he didn't like her sexually. This is proven by all those episodes that were designed to weary the fiancée and cause her to call off the wedding. If he left her, he would have had the whole village against him. He saw no other way out. During his time in the German prisoner of war camp, he experienced such horror that human life no longer meant much to him. So on the day she gave herself to him, Sisina unwittingly signed her own death warrant.

'The accused shows no signs of an unbalanced psyche. So far, there has been no evidence of serious violence before the crime. It is to his advantage that he has no previous convictions and that he never tried to throw mud at the memory of the dead girl.

'Vito, look at me. You will soon be free: your peace of mind will begin with the conviction. But do not think that Sisina is praying for you in heaven. She would do that if you had killed her because you loved her too much. But you have sacrificed her out of boredom and convenience. For that, she cannot forgive you.'

CLOSING REMARKS FOR THE DEFENCE

'First of all, I would like to stress that we are honest men. Reporting to fulfil a duty. A duty towards the family of the deceased – but even more so towards the society that has been aggrieved by this crime.

'That is why I must ask you all: Vito, a murderer? He who left mass meek and pious, where he paid homage to the Madonna in prayer, should suddenly have felt bloodlust? Why?

'Nobody knows what happened. Why do we not trust Vito's word? Anyone who refuses to have trust is refusing justice.

'Let us take a close look at whose words we trust in this trial. Let us begin with Livia L——. A coarse girl who whispers one thing to me and another to the inspector. We believe her, this innocent little dove! And yet she brought a sprog home to her family and no one knows where it came from. Let's listen to her! Very well. But the teacher? Better not, because the word of a noble lady in crocodile shoes is of course sacred. Like the secret surrounding this whole trial...

'I can assure you of one thing: there is something and someone behind Livia L——. This matter has nothing to do with Vito. This goes higher up.

'But the inspector doesn't want to see that. He continues to conduct his puppet show and eagerly searches for evidence. He wants to find blood, blood! So he runs in circles and finds what? Ah! Little flecks! Two teeny, tiny droplets!

'Gentlemen, this whole trial is made of papier-mâché. Let's be honest: if Vito had been the murderer, he would have been covered in blood and most likely wouldn't have just rinsed his trousers with water. Yes, if he had the character that the prosecution claims, he would have killed his Sisina long ago. When she was dancing with other men or walking with her ex. He didn't do it then, so why would he have done it this day?

'They accuse him of arguing too much with poor Sisina. Come off it: arguing as a motive? That's the seasoning of a relationship! If arguing were a crime, I'd have to go to prison every week.

'Let's talk about jealousy. The favourite topic of the inspector, who has obviously never read a book. Otherwise, he would know that jealousy is a burning tension that doesn't permit the lover to leave the couple. The jealous lover can only live in the lap of his beloved. Art, history and culture all testify to this truth. The jealous man walks stooped; he is compelled to be tethered to his beloved. Would a jealous man leave his union and break off the engagement? Twice?

'A truly jealous man does not let his fiancée get away so easily: he watches her, quietly and secretly. Did Vito do that? No, even if he sees her dancing with someone else, he does not hesitate to confront her.

'Gentlemen: that is the stuff that love is made of. Of course, he must consider what kind of woman he wants to marry. Of course, he must pause for thought when she acts in certain ways. But he is sincere, he is direct. He goes to her and says: "You have done an ugly thing, don't do that anymore. You know that you disgust me when you do that." And what does she do? She lies down in bed and cries.

'And he is supposed to be the murderer? Look at him, he cried when he saw his fiancée lying dead and that cannot be faked! That is an invincible argument! In his behaviour lies the definitive proof of a truth that no one can deny.

'One more thing makes this whole trial unnecessary: Vito wanted to marry Sisina. If it had been up to him, they would have been married long ago. But thanks to the selfishness of the farmers, who value their stomachs more than love, the wedding was postponed: the family did not want to give their hardworking daughter away before the harvest.

'This brings us to a love that is much greater and more important than that of the engaged couple: the love between two families. Its loss is the fault of the inspector. As soon as he appeared on the scene, Sisina's family turned away, their love dissolved like a cloud in the wind. I am sure that in her grave Sisina is sharing my thoughts: the destruction of family love is worse than the killing of the flesh.

'The behaviour of Sisina's mother and her strange statements ultimately point to only one thing: a serious secret lurks in this family's house. I cannot get a memory from my apprenticeship out of my mind. A man was convicted of murdering an eighteen-year-old girl. The evidence against him was far stronger than that against our Vito. I will never forget his cry after the verdict: "But I am innocent!" This voice has been pounding in my heart ever since. Because after ten years of torture in prison, the voice of a dying man was heard, the voice of the real culprit: it was the girl's father.

'A great lawyer once said: It would be better for all life sentences to be overturned, for all criminals to roam the streets of the country, than for a single innocent person to be sacrificed to assumptions and suspicion.

'Remember that, gentlemen of the jury. Now I am trembling in anticipation of your verdict.

'Vito! They have humiliated you, stripped you and dragged you through the mud, violated you in spirit and in body. But you remain resolute, you stand unmoved on the cliff in the storm. An inner voice gives you strength: it is the voice of your Sisina. Your calm is proof of the union of your souls which no one can ever destroy. Vito, rise up! The hour of the resurrection has come.'

ACQUITTED!

The cheering in the hall is deafening. The news spreads like wildfire: Vito M——, accused of murdering his fiancée Sisina A——, is acquitted by the jury. Thunderous applause interrupts the presiding judge in the middle of his sentence. It takes several minutes before he can continue. He clarifies: 'Acquittal due to lack of evidence.'

The presiding judge emphasises that there is a lot to suggest Vito's guilt. 'There are many serious clues that have legal relevance. But the bond of causality is missing, and doubt remains. So we have no choice but to acquit him.' The public breaks into euphoria again. The president does not seem satisfied. It is strange, he notes, how the people and the press have sided with the accused and painted a distorted picture of Sisina through shameful rumours. Outside the courtroom, the victim's little sister says: 'What can I say? I hoped for justice for my sister.

Instead she was buried under a pile of manure and slurry.' As one of the plaintiffs, her disappointment with the verdict is evident. The supporters of the acquitted man won't let this dim their elation. On the steps of the courthouse they spontaneously erupt in celebration of their martyr.

THE RETURN OF THE HERO

The day after Vito M——'s acquittal, a dozen rented buses are waiting outside the prison. Hundreds have come from all over the country to accompany their hero home. Home is a hamlet in practically untouched hills, surrounded by forest and fields.

The convoy stops in the neighbouring village around midday. There, a festival awaits the acquitted man. The houses are decorated with lanterns. Long tables with food and wine are set up in the church square. The crowd chants his name until he appears on a friend's balcony. He waves, smiles, thanks them all.

When he gets into the car, it cannot drive off: the crowd has surrounded it. People want autographs, want to touch him, kiss him. They run alongside the car, applauding the whole way – at the end of the village there is a triumphal arch. A girl hands him a huge bouquet of sunflowers: 'From the Association of Women's Solidarity.' Vito replies: 'I'll put them on my poor Sisina's grave.'

The older women sigh: 'How could they have convicted him, with that handsome face. The face of a good boy!' A girl rides her bike in front of the car. She reaches Vito's parents' house before him and goes up to his mother:

'Give me your son. I've always believed in his innocence and I'll marry him immediately.'

That evening there is a big celebration in Vito's home village of L——. Congratulatory telegrams from all over the country are read out on a stage. Girls collect money for the trial costs. The celebration will last until late into the night. The journalists then get into their cars and drive back to their cities. The forsaken son has returned. This tranquil spot of earth can finally find peace.

X

The sun is coming up. I put down the book and breathe out.

The house seems threatening today. It creaks, the snake coils itself inside the martini glass and darts its tongue in and out. Did I hear footsteps? It sounds like they're keeping a beat, like a dance. Snakeskin soles. And what was that? A thwack, like army boots being hit against one another. What if they're all still here? The Signora, the officers. Perhaps they never left, and I'm moving around among them like an intruder.

I shake my head: the haunting is over, I'm going to pull myself together. This book full of newspaper articles has moved me somehow. It speaks of the real world; there's nothing spooky in it. Sisina sounds exactly as I'd imagined her: funny, feisty. And her boyfriend sounds like an arsehole. I feel light-headed. Keeping my eyes on the ceiling, I say to Magdalena's ashes: Good thing we were spared that.

I get up, pull off the nightshirt and get into my old clothes. Tuck the urn under my arm. As I open the bedroom door, a flower glows on the stone floor. What does this strange guy want with his floral offerings? The flowers for Vito pop into my head. His car adorned with flowers, fat bouquets for the hero. I step over the flower as if it were poisoned.

The empty driveway confirms my fear: the car's gone. Lorenzo has flown off, but he was meant to drive me into town, *in a mad rush*! Like the guest who, on the day of Sisina's murder, was rushed from the villa and taken to town. Who could it have been, a soldier? There wasn't anything more about it. And where is this train station anyway?

The map unfolds inside my head: here's the villa, the hamlet with its surrounding farmyards, there's the forest, the road through it that leads to the well. The scene of the crime, where the memorial stone is today, and behind it the embankment down to the Tigress's Stream. The village L——, today a ghost village, its church, the graveyard. I can see it before me: Sisina's route, alive and dead. I'm standing in the middle of it. But how I'm supposed to get out, I don't know. I can't remember the route that we took; the night-time journey through the forest was long and serpentine. I have to wait for Lorenzo, he'll be back soon. If I'm lucky, he'll still be by himself. But even if the Coach is with him, it won't change anything: I'm going home.

I pace around the house, waiting, I feel the flagstones in the corridor against my bare feet, the same ones that Sisina must have walked over. As if the wear and tear was a kind of Braille, as if I could suck the secrets out of the cracks through my naked soles. I search in the cupboards, in the cellar, in the chapel. They cut her open here, rummaged around inside her in the name of their virgin fetish. Before she was laid out, bloodless in her wedding dress. The farmer's daughter lying alone and cold in the manor house. But why? Signora Serpent standing in the doorway, holding back crocodile shoe tears and rumpling her nose: *coquettish*.

I lie down on the sofa in the drawing room and press my face into the cushion. Maybe it still smells of Sisina and of the soldier?

The ashes rustle inside the urn: Why does this little farm girl concern you? You were interested in me once. You've become bored of me so quickly? I've tried everything to get you to notice me. You're no better than those hypocritical patriarchs: getting off on the last gurgles of a very fresh bride. There's nothing more poetical than the death of a beautiful woman . . . And what about me?

Magda, I say breathlessly, you're driving me crazy even when you're dead. It's your fault I'm here, have you forgotten? You want to know why I'm so interested in Sisina? Because she reminds me of you. They eliminated you both and blasphemed over your dead bodies. Your death was covered up, I can't find out anything about it. But Sisina's murder was written about: copiously, brutally, cruelly and fraudulently. I'm seeking a truth between the lines that concerns both of you. I see her autopsy report and think that they have used it to kill and disgrace her, all over again. They bring shame on her – yet it is they who act dishonourably; they are the shame. The language used by the journalists, by the lawyers, but the people too; the way they talk about Sisina, the one who was silenced, the way they control her: this is violence. And me, the way I read it and the little hairs stand up on my arms from excitement – why? I'm taking part in this rape. As if we all want to *possess* her, like Vito had *possessed* her.

It disgusts me, but I want to know what's in your autopsy report. What were you wearing when you died – the cowboy hat? What were your injuries? Does it matter? Yes: did you suffer? For how long? I think that it would soothe me to know about your final moments. As if I could comprehend, empathise, sympathise, so you wouldn't be alone anymore.

That's it. I want to stand by you both.

But that's not possible, so I follow the violence: I want revenge.

You and Sisina, neither of you had justice. I think that it's connected somehow, we're all connected somehow. There are so many parallels! People also didn't speak, or lied, about Sisina, they were afraid. *I don't know, I wasn't there.*

Or Vito forbade Sisina from working, just like your father forbade your mother. Or: Sisina died while collecting water, like your grandmother – what was it again? A bold thesis is building in my head: What if she was Sisina? Rubbish, you're right. Embarrassing desire for everything to be about me. It doesn't matter now anyway: we're just waiting for Lorenzo, and then we'll go home. Sit tight in the meantime, I'm going for a walk.

I stroll through the garden, fall down in the grass, the clouds like lurid rips. I lay an arm across my eyes, Sisina's face appears, smiling, silent. The swing seat creaks. I break out in a sweat: why were you dressed so warmly, Sisina, woollen jumper, skirt and dress, on a hot day in July? What were you trying to hide, from whose gaze did you want to protect yourself?

The wind comes up, an agitated wind. It makes the gate to the little forest squeak as if someone were trying to prise it open. I sit up, no one's there. I squint. The gate is open. A cicada starts laughing. Dried-out blades of grass prickle me. I'm not wearing any underwear or shoes.

*

In feverish expectation of an appearance I march along Sisina's routes; I measure her steps with my own. I hear her whispering everywhere, her breath brushes against me, she tugs at me. I'm searching for her, haunting her, burrowing into the forest for her secrets, spreading out the unending possibilities of her life before me and calling out to her to answer me: What really happened?

The sky comes down heavily onto the ground, I tilt back my head and let my eyes get washed out. Mist circles my feet, it is quiet, just the dripping on the leaves. I wait for Sisina to come and meet me. Do ghosts like rain?

Through the foliated haze, a clearing suddenly appears through the trees, in it is the well of my dreams: the great draw well into which I fall until I crash and wake. Strange, I've never seen a well like this before; how can it be that I've been dreaming of it since I was a child? I approach it, convinced that it will disappear at any moment, a mirage. But it remains, and I stand before it: a circle made of stones piled atop one another. The shaft is deep and empty, just like me. I sit on the edge of it and wait.

The fog draws in from all sides and swallows the landscape. Only the tops of the trees stand black against the sky like a cutout. On a peculiar right-angled branch sits a dove. It's looking at me. It sees that I'm observing it. We nervously twitch our beaks.

It coos: While I was still alive, my fiancé accused me of not being faithful. He developed such a passionate hatred for me that even on my deathbed he did not hear my protestations of innocence, his suspicions and disgust were too loud. Only after my death could he forgive me, and ultimately he also died within the true faith. Yet since then, he's been trapped for eternity between coldness and darkness.

I jerk my head: Why do you care about that deadbeat? You're the victim here.

The little dove pants with its tongue: Don't you want to help me?

I flap my wings in excitement: Of course I'll help you, Sisina. What can I do?

She coos: Reconcile us with each other here in this world, so that we may attain our salvation.

How can I do that?

We'll come to you tonight. Then you will give the verdict on which of us is right and place our hands on one another in reconciliation. Then we'll say the Ave Maria and ascend.

I will never do that!

Why not?

Because I don't want you to go back to him! He hasn't earned your concern. Forget him, damn him. You were a cheerful, loved girl and he's an insecure loser. Instead of being happy with you, enjoying life with you, he saw your strength and your radiance as a threat. He wanted to control you, to lock you up, to break you. He made you sick with his jealousy, with his claims of ownership, don't you remember? Maybe he even killed you – did he?

Sisina jerks her head vaguely, I flutter excitedly: Either way – I hate him. The way he treated you! And you want to help him?

Sisina blinks: A soul that goes into eternity harbouring even the slightest resentment cannot be saved. If you want to help me, come tonight.

The dove flaps its wings and flies off.

*

The warm air smells like spiced broth after the rain. Back in the garden, I try to pin the sun to the sky. Unperturbed, it sinks into the forest. As the sun sets the fear creeps out from the trees and climbs from the wet grass up into my ankles. All of a sudden, a bird gives a long, drawn-out, penetrating cry, I see the screech owl plunge from the tower window. It hunts over my head and disappears into the forest. The draught ruffles my parting.

Sisina, I whisper, are you angry with me?

I lock my bedroom door, pull out the key and throw it onto

the mantelpiece. In the bathroom, I splash cold water on my face, avoiding the mirror. Then I see the marks. Red dabs, on the edge of the sink. Look up to see if it's dripping from the ceiling. In the mirror, whether I . . . ? Nothing. I tap my little finger in it, the fluid seems fresh. No peculiar smell. The tip of my tongue touches the tip of my finger: salty, soapy, metallic.

In one motion I pull the shower curtain aside. I let out a laugh, of course the bathtub is empty. I climb in and blanch myself until my skin is crab red and my brain is boiled. The bathroom is full of vapour, the mirror is fogged up: I'm invisible. In the basin there are still reddish drops. I scrutinise my steamy finger, pull at softened skin. It's intact. It's not my blood.

The vapour towers up and crawls inside me. I'm tired and afraid, I want to lie on the dusty floor and wake up at home. I'm not like Magdalena. Through injustice and bad luck, she became stronger, louder, immense. Leave me alone, you ghosts, I can't help you, it was a lie. You're scaring me, I'm weak. Leave me in peace, what do you want from me? I live in better times, I know how to behave, it will be different for me. I'm leaving.

*

Once dressed, I sit on the bed and wait for Lorenzo. Outside it is night. A mosquito buzzes, lurking. Like Vito, I'm waiting with a light, the key turned twice. Did she haunt him with her throat spurting? Did she laugh at him, wail, whisper nasty things in his ear? Or was what he said true, and he was actually afraid of the murderer, someone else?

A threatening thought creeps up my spine and grips me coldly at the back of the neck. What if the ghost wandering around here isn't Sisina at all? Not a funny, joyful girl-ghost who jumps on mattresses? But rather it's her murderer? He, the perpetrator, has real cause to be uneasy: a malicious ghost that doesn't like the fact that I'm on his trail! My heart suddenly starts beating like crazy. I pull the covers over my head and breathe inside the cave.

Sounds come from outside. Rhythmic beating, like chopping wood. A boar? No animal makes precise movements like that. It sounds like an axe, wielded by a human. Under the covers I murmur fragments of Italian guardian angel prayers that have stayed with me since my earliest childhood.

Angelodidio-seiilmiocustode – – – dallapietà-Amen.

My grandmother is sitting on my bed speaking to me. Her voice, heavy and warm, cocoons me in honey.

Amen, I murmur, sighing.

My body begins to relax, before it's once more shaken by a dry sob. She will stay with me until I've gone back to sleep, until I know that I can close my eyes.

She strokes my head and says: When I was a child, I called to my mother in heaven whenever I was afraid. She protected me, and she will protect you too, you don't have to be frightened, she's always with you.

And Magdalena?

I have this question in my head, but I don't say anything, I keep my eyes closed, so she doesn't see what I see: Magdalena in a dark alleyway. Magdalena will abduct me. Magdalena in a pool of blood.

How many nights of my childhood did I wake bathed in sweat, how many times did I hear and say the angel's prayer – how can it be that I no longer know it?

I hold my breath, listen to the sound outside, my blood roars in my ears. Ghosts versus ghosts, I think, my dead will protect me. They position themselves in front of me, shadowy: my grandmother, her mother?

Nonna, I whisper, please don't let them in.

My mouth begins to hum, to sing: *Ninna Nanna oh*. It rises out of me hoarsely, the archaic melody of this bedtime lament; that's not Italian, it's dialect! I can't recall the words, they come of their own volition, appearing with deeply submerged images. The wolf and the lamb in the moonlit meadow, the wolf eats the lamb – I'm singing with my grandmother's voice: *What do you do when the wolf comes for you?*

After what feels like an eternity, the beating stops. I re-emerge breathlessly into the uncanny brightness of the lit-up room. Where the devil is Lorenzo? He was always so tired, looked like he hadn't slept in years. Did he doze off at the wheel and is now lying in a ditch? All the men in Sisina's life got up in the middle of the night to work, the farmers and the charcoal burners. Was that the reason for the murder: rage from exhaustion?

I keep being startled, listening to hear whether a car is approaching. Images swim up: Lorenzo shot through with bullets – or do they still hang deserters from lamp posts? Lorenzo covered in blood through the smashed windscreen. Or alive and trapped in the crushed car. In the morning I'll set off to look for him. I have to ask him where he got the notebook from.

It must have belonged to the teacher, Chiara T——. There's a picture of her, above the article that describes her as the most awful witness. Underneath the photo it says: 'The Little Teacher and Journalists'. In it, she's standing among a group of men who are gathered around a newspaper in amusement. She's at least a head shorter than all of them; a light-coloured perm and little double chin. Her brow furrowed, she's looking up at a young man who is in the process of saying something filthy to the reader of the newspaper. Everyone's laughing apart from her. She has the look of a woman who feels superior while knowing that she is being swept under the carpet. No one is paying any attention to her. And that's not all: on this newspaper page she has to share the space with the very woman who embarrassed her in front of everyone. 'The Contessa and Journalists.' In this second photo, the elegant Signora, grandezza in Italian fabrics, is handing out wrapped gifts. The men are smoking and joshing, they're enjoying conversing and joking with an important lady.

I take a good look at her, the Signora, her alert eyes, which seem to be saying emphatically: 'This salami is the best you have ever tasted! The whole family thanks you for your discretion, we don't like being in the headlines.' Is she an Agrippina, ready to walk over corpses to save her son and his reputation? In the background, intimidated policemen smile. Did they also receive gifts?

What a perfidious juxtaposition: while the rich Signora effortlessly gathered dashing military men around her, the teacher jumped through hoops to impress these men (or just one of them?) with cultural events. She obviously doted on men in uniform. And what thanks did she get? Instead of overpowering her with their strong arms, slinging her head first over their broad backs and tying her to the bed, they pined after young Sisina. The eager Chiara T—— doesn't even get a look-in. She will always be the little teacher. That's tough – but is it enough for murder? No, appearing in court is her revenge. She can finally tell the truth: Sisina is a perverted witch who teased those soldiers with her devilish magic. But instead of satisfaction, Chiara gets a knife in the back. From the noble Signora, of all people, who gathered all the wonderful lieutenants under her magnificent roof.

Was it this humiliation that prompted the teacher to create the notebook? The appalling injustice of standing like an idiot in front of these men in court with their powerful words, their assurances that they would not throw mud on Sisina's memory while wringing their filthy hands towards heaven. And her? What had she done wrong?

Instead of spending her evenings writing down what she had taught the girls about Jesus and suffering and the importance of clean clothes, Chiara T—— trawled through newspapers. National, local – she cut out every article about Sisina and neatly pasted it into the notebook. She archived the media's portrayal of a femicide and its setting, which was also her home. But why? Was she looking for the murderer? Or had it much more to do with the people who had mocked and belittled her throughout her whole life?

I leaf through the book, the photos. Sisina's mother is also deeply mired in shame. In court she wears a black veil and keeps her eyes lowered. She clutches a handkerchief, her teeth clenched. She sits surrounded by young people engaged in lively conversation. She does not seem to notice the commotion, she seems absent, in another world.

The teacher has put a note under the picture: *Mariapia is lying*.

Her obsession with virginity seems absurd, but she is not alone on that front. Her fears come true: supposed experts look between her daughter's legs, tinker and ponder and triumphantly announce: Not a virgin! The hymen is torn! They reinforce one another's claims and false beliefs about the mythical hymen.

Mariapia's mortified covering of the pool of blood could not prevent the public digging around in her daughter's body. What did she do wrong? One daughter is dead, and on the stand her remaining daughters are embarrassing themselves. Alessia, who can't control herself. Who starts screaming at the crime scene and must be quickly carried home. Private matters ought to be private.

Why did Sisina stay away from family dinners? Because she was ill? Or banished? Why? Is there something to the rumour about pregnancy? The bed was covered in blood, the sister says. An abortion? Maybe that's what the mother thought of when she saw the pool of blood?

The child couldn't be Vito's, or so the mother thought – after all, she broke down in court when she found out that Vito and Sisina had already done *it*. Besides, that wouldn't have been a big issue: the two would have been married soon. So who could she have suspected?

The sisters resemble the dead woman, especially Alessia when she smiles. The older, married ones look more serious. Virginia is standing next to her husband in front of their parents' house. Either he's standing on a step or he's two whole heads taller than her. Wasn't there a favourable story about Vito, how he could look down on *his Sisina*?

The giant looks into the distance with a pinched face, possibly being blinded by the sun. Virginia has linked her arm through his and is looking sternly at the camera. He is handsome compared to his charcoal burner brother-in-law, the husband of half-sister Filomena. The latter seems so naive with his cabbage leaf ears, helpless with his toothless smile. The caption underneath is wicked: *Sisina's forbidden love?*

I cannot work out what Sisina's father is thinking. In the only picture of him he looks old, tough and wily. The accusations against him seem made up. Or are they? The teacher notes: *Small man, small feet.*

And the man with the feet that are too big? The possessive fiancé you wouldn't wish on your worst enemy? Murderer or not, the celebration of his heroism is bizarre nonsense. His lawyer doesn't only defend him, but all male possessiveness. This top-class defence lawyer who has been at Vito's side from the very beginning, as if he was sent from heaven. Who fuels his own popularity by mocking the victim and slandering her family. Supported by thousands who flock to the courthouses and chant for an acquittal: Vito is innocent!

How is he innocent? Because Sisina had provoked him, as some people say? Or because it really wasn't him?

An entire photo report is dedicated to his return after his acquittal. Aerial shots of the church square: an exuberant crowd. Open mouths, waving arms, a hysterical commotion. In the middle of this is the car that Vito is supposed to be brought home in. When he gets out, he finds himself surrounded by excited young women. They call out to him, want to see him, touch him, give him gifts and flowers and little notes. Those who come up to him put their hands on his back and shoulders. Vito smiles. *I will put the flowers on my poor Sisina's grave.* The Solidarity Women shudder with jealousy. How can they ever compete with a dead saint?

The question hovering over Sisina is: why did she become so legendary? How many girls and women are killed and quickly forgotten by the public – what is different about Sisina? Or is it not about her at all? Is it more about him?

Vito, a small glass of schnapps in his hand, toasts a young woman and her father.

Hearty congratulations also go to Vito's tall, birdlike father, who absently raises a limp hand. He radiates a fascinating calm that at times seems pleasant, at others authoritarian, then dismissive; sometimes all of the above. In one picture he can be seen with the teacher; they're shaking hands while staring daggers at one another.

The teacher – didn't she claim to have heard Sisina tell Vito that she wanted to eat sweets with him? And weren't sweet wrappers and the imprints of two people sitting down found at the crime scene?

Sisina and Vito are chilling barefoot in their hiding place in the hollow, sucking wedding sweets. The jug is still empty beside her; a short break before the endless housework continues. And then? Something happens, a knife is pulled out. Sisina flees up the slope, slips, falls just before the opening leading to the road. She is killed and dragged back down again. The large pool of blood remains.

In the next picture, Vito is sitting at the dining table, an older woman is proudly serving him a large portion of something. At the end of the table is a young man: black moustache, gaze piercing the camera, hands hidden behind his back. Impatience is written all over his face. He looks like an angry bodyguard who wants to put this circus behind him. The teacher has drawn an arrow pointing towards him with the reproof: *shoe size???*

I look at him closely. That could have been it: a brotherly favour. The moustachioed friend with small feet and American boots lures Sisina into the bushes under the pretence of a surprise from Vito.

Don't take anything from strangers.

Here, he says, dangling a necklace in front of her eyes, a gift from your fiancé. As an apology for the business with the ring.

Sisina turns around to allow him to put the jewellery around her neck. What did the newspaper say? *The dead girl's heart was calm.*

Vito has the same smile in every picture. Turned up from below, head meekly bowed, a little bashful. Was it him? Does it matter?

I hear myself breathing.

It's so quiet.

I'm most interested in Livia. The last person to see Sisina alive. As her friend, she witnessed Sisina's suffering in her relationship with Vito. She is one of the few people who still proclaimed his guilt long after he became popular. But it's actually something else that fascinates me. Her illegitimate child.

Of course, she reminds me of my grandmother. The social ostracism she experienced, the collective punishment of SHAME. I know so little about the young Lavinia and her life before she came to Switzerland that I read Livia's story vicariously as hers. I study the photos, her face, her body, and imagine similarities. I want to see the connection!

Livia is sitting on a bench in court, next to Alessia, Sisina's sister. It looks as if they're waiting, possibly outside the courtroom, until they are called in to testify. Livia has folded her arms over her chest, a frown line between her brows, she's staring at the ground. Anger is clear on her face, and defiance. The slim-cut suit underlines her spider-like elegance. Next to her, Alessia looks almost coarse, sloppy in her worn-out summer dress. Her crossed legs indicate impatience. Alessia seems to be concentrating, her lower jaw jutting out, perhaps she is listening to someone. She almost seems indifferent, while Livia exudes a deep sadness.

Did the two of them argue? Are they friends? Are they fighting together or against each other? For what?

A year after the murder, Livia has a child and a new coat, both of unknown origin. She also shares new statements that incriminate Vito. The coat's fabric looks expensive. As valuable as keeping quiet about the child's father? What else do the newspapers say between the lines? Livia gives false statements to cover up for the real murderer, her lover, who, coincidentally, is the same man with whom Sisina is said to have had an affair: il Conte in my villa.

Does that sound like a voluntary exchange: a coat for a life of shame? And if this Conte is actually the child's father and Sisina's murderer, wouldn't Livia be keeping quiet more out of fear?

Why is there always talk of consensual relationships? Isn't it much more likely that the landowner simply took what he wanted? Sisina wasn't well in the time before the murder, she seemed disturbed and frightened, ill.

The fact that the body was laid out in their own chapel and the memorial stone erected suggests that the noble family was involved. They felt guilty. Or the opposite: they wanted everyone to remember who was in charge when they walked through the hamlet. Perhaps il Conte was known for having a weakness for young farmers' daughters. But at least until Sisina, no one dared to say anything.

I prefer to imagine that Livia became pregnant at a lavish party. That she fell in love. Not with il Conte, no, perhaps with his Swiss cousin who was visiting the villa. I imagine him as blond, with protruding ears: he looks like the picture of my grandfather.

Lavinia and Livia are superimposed onto each other like templates: unmarried mothers with children without names or fathers. I fill in the gaps in Livia's story with my fantasies about the young Lavinia. I know that she went to a party with a friend in another city. That's where she met him, the Swiss man.

The sparse stories combined in my child head with images from fairy tales: a dazzling ball, a flaxen-haired prince, a kiss – she had to be back in the cave with the bigot by midnight.

I remember how Magdalena laughed at me when I told her once about her beginnings at that ball. She claimed that Lavinia had remained in that other city and that she and my future grandfather had lived there for a while together:

Your grandmother has always been an independent woman, Filissima, she never let anyone tell her what to do.

I imagine Livia to be just as proud and stubborn as Lavinia. Even more pig-headed, in fact, because she didn't want the guy in her life. She chose the independence that comes with loneliness, with exclusion from the community. Maybe she found it repugnant after everything that happened with Sisina.

When I look at Livia, I start to understand my grandmother. Her caution, her seemingly irrational fears. She was Livia: a single mother and worker, who showed that she could do anything. And was punished all the more for it. The strict rules and ideas that she imposed on Magdalena and, later, on me were meant to protect us from the shame and exclusion that she had experienced.

I see Magdalena before me, on my grandmother's balcony, gesticulating with her cigarette: Shame! The corset that conditions the slave. It is passed on from generation to generation: the mother puts it on her daughter, teaches her to serve her husband and family. Every attempt at liberation is suppressed and defended against—

She gave this speech for me. And for the neighbours. She stood at the railing and lectured into the courtyard until my grandmother discovered us and pulled us into the apartment hissing, as Magdalena called out laughing: Anyone who does not absolutely submit is under attack and will ultimately be expelled!

Perhaps this is what connects them: not the murders, but the resistance. The struggle against a life of shame. Maybe that's the real story of my mother and grandmother, of Sisina and Livia – could it become mine too? Is that where we meet, through our roots, our origins? Maybe I'm not looking for a murderer at all, and I'm actually digging for myself.

*

I'm already standing on the country road in front of a house. I hear myself calling until a head appears at the window: the face of a young Lavinia.

Livia, will you come to the well with me?
Ma va! I've already been.
Please, I don't want to go on my own.
You'll survive. See you later!

I'm walking inside a humming cloud. I carry the empty jug

on my hip like a child. Mosquitoes bite my ankles, my hands, my neck. At the bend, I put the jug down and wrap my scarf around my head. The sudden feeling of being followed. I snort a fly from my lip and keep trotting along. Chin up and smile, but not too much, my lips firmly closed so that no creatures get the idea of jumping onto my tongue. Even more important: don't stop moving. Smile and keep going, always keep going.

The rule applies to men and bugs alike.

An owl calls my name. I stop and listen. A fly lands on my eye-lashes. I blink it away and make the call of the dove. The owl answers. I spin around, the path is clear. The buzzing of flies.

Where are you? I call and cough – a fly has hissed down my gullet.

The gentle call of the owl breaks into a snicker. There is a crack, and on the embankment my friend's face appears, as round as the moon.

Did I scare you? she coos.

Ma va. Swallowed a fly.

Livia skids down the embankment like an avalanche.

Very elegant, I cough, batting leaves off her Sunday dress.

She slaps me on the back: Not everyone can be the prettiest.

I push her away: You are much prettier!

Livia pretends to be outraged: If I were, I would have been waving from the balcony of the villa long ago.

He invited you to the party, didn't he?

Me? He asked you—

Because I just happened to be there. He expressly said that

I should bring you with me. I heard his heart pounding, and when he said your name it stopped—

We burst into laughter.

What are you talking about, he never pays any attention to me—

He is completely forlorn, his love is as big as his ears.

Yes, with you, because you are so beautiful—

Nonsense, you are beautiful—

My father said he would smash both my legs if I set foot in the villa again.

I grin: Then you will have to let your Swiss man carry you around, for better or for worse.

Imagine if Vito found out that you're going dancing—

Ugh, him. If it were up to him, I wouldn't be allowed to do anything. He's jealous of every little bug.

Livia laughs: Did I tell you what he said to me in church earlier?

She changes her voice: Try explaining to your friend that she can't make me look like an idiot.

I shake my head: Well, we have to go now, for that reason alone.

You're the best. It'll be wonderful.

And what if your father beats you up?

So what. Let a little time go by and I'll feel even better than I did before. How's your admirer?

I smile: Which one?

Ma va!

Seriously, if Vito keeps behaving like this, I wonder what

things will be like after the wedding. What does he want, to lock me up?

Don't you want him anymore?

Yes, yes.

But?

We swore to one another that we would never fall for a man.

That we would go away together—

We'll pack our things in the darkness of the new moon and disappear into the forest. Run until the forest ends, keep running, until we reach the city—

You'll become a maid and I'll become a typist.

Hey, are you crazy, I want to work in an office!

All the better, then we'll both go. In high heels and knotted scarves.

Mmm.

Imagine if you really did leave Vito. He would go berserk.

I'll tell you what he would do: cry his eyes out.

Your father would be happy.

My mother would kill me.

Or Vito would.

Ma va, he just says that. Didn't you want to stay at home?

Livia has a good stretch: They're lying there like stones, I sneaked out. I needed to be on my own. Do nothing, think nothing.

And has it worked?

Of course not, I'm overwhelmed by weighty thoughts. Have you ever noticed that boys always talk about *possession*? I *possessed* her.

I giggle.

No, listen to me. Men say that, *possess*, while us girls whisper about one other: She *lost* herself. What does that tell us?

That we're going to hell.

She laughs.

So are you coming with me to the spring?

Let me think about it. No.

If we walk really slowly, we'll even miss the procession.

Tempting. My father would strangle me.

Mine too.

Are you happy you're moving out soon?

Am I! It'll be a new life.

Livia puts her hands in my hair and braids it, she sings: Tomorrow, my child, your life will be over, you will be a slave.

I wriggle free, laughing: Nothing could be worse than my parents. Do you know what my mother said to Vito? *Couldn't you find anything better as a war hero?*

Livia tilts her head to the side: Really? And what did he say?

That his German blonde was too tall for him.

No!

Then he laughed like an idiot, so I slapped him.

She grins: You have to stop hitting your future husband.

Ma va, didn't you just clout him in front of everyone?

I couldn't help it!

You see, that's how I feel every day.

Livia snorts: And your mother?

Well then, Auguri, she said, and poured the dirty cleaning water out of the window.

Auguri, Livia repeats, then kisses me on the cheek. The bride who laughs will soon cry.

I push her away, giggling: Get out of here! Run home quickly and be a good girl.

She curtsies: Quiet and good, you know me. Go lose yourself properly. Will we see each other later at church? Is Vito coming too?

Of course.

Are you going to make another scene?

Maybe.

You two. At your wedding I will dance like a madwoman. The floor will be slippery with the blood of my chafed feet.

I want to see that.

And if you decide to run away after all, let me know, then I will dance with your Vito until he screams.

And bleeds.

You grind up male hearts like mincemeat.

Not me.

You are delicious. My delicious friend.

Delicious, Livia calls out again, before turning the corner.

It's hot, I decide to take a detour. Turn off the road, look left and right, and climb through the gap in the bushes leading to the slope. Crouched low, I move through the undergrowth. Shake the sandals off my feet, put them under the thick holm oak together with the jug. The face of an owl grows out of the trunk. Then, with my hands free, I slide down the slope to the Tigress's Stream.

A jay flies up, squawking, the water bubbles confidingly.

You're right, I say, I'll stay here for a while.

I put my feet in the cold water, let it lick my ankles, swollen from mosquito bites.

A wind suddenly rises. Sweeps through the grove, makes the silver leaves tremble. It blows strands of hair into my face, makes branches crack. Roaring treetops. Someone is waiting for me. I pull my feet out of the water, jump up and scramble up the ditch. The wind rushes down the slope, pushing itself against me. Dust rises, rearing up in front of me like a person, and settles on me menacingly. I rub my eyes, climb faster. My name flies up from behind and lands on my shoulder like a bird. I stop, turn my head.

High up in the branches, a cicada sits and laughs.

*

It's getting light outside, finally. The ghosts disappear in the dawn. I've been tossing and turning all night, grinding my teeth and sweating. Weird dreams that felt strangely real.

I woke up because something heavy was pressing down on my feet.

Sitting on the fireplace was the owl. It spread its wings and flew out of the window.

A figure was rocking backwards and forwards in the chair. I couldn't move a finger, couldn't make a sound.

The blanket was pulled off me. At the foot of the bed, a dark form dissolved.

A shadow in the bathroom doorway. I kept my eyelids pressed together as if I were sleeping, open just a crack. The shadow slowly approached the foot of the bed. I kicked my feet.

XI

The sound of an engine comes in through the window. Tyres crunch on the gravel, a car drives into the yard. The engine is turned off, doors slam, then I hear men's voices. I hold my breath. Try to make out Lorenzo's voice. I quietly pull back the covers and look out the window.

Next to the fountain is an SUV without a roof. Three men prowl across the yard. They look too young to be the Coach. The youngest is visibly excited, he is constantly turning his head and laughing. His blond curls reflect the sun, he's twenty at most. The stockiest struts wide-legged to the fountain, reaches his hand into it and then runs it through his hair, slicking it back. The third, tall with dark curls, exudes an elegant nonchalance. He leans on the bonnet while rolling a cigarette.

There's no one here.
    She's still taking a kip. He did say she sleeps forever.
    Pretty good life.
    Like you're working yourself to death!
    Shall we go and wake her up?

I make a gun with my fingers and point it out the window:

Stop! I'll shoot.

Is she nuts?

The laid-back one slowly raises his hands above his head and says: Take it easy, bimba, your cousin sent us.

My cousin?

Yeah, he had to go away for a few days. He asked us to look after you. He didn't want you to be here on your own.

Lorenzo? Where is he? When is he coming back?

He didn't say. He just said you should make yourself useful and come with us to harvest the grapes.

The laid-back one takes his hands off his head and points down the road towards the forest: There's lunch and we'll bring you back in the evening.

I lower the finger gun.

The blond boy stretches: I'm Angelo! This is my cousin Nicolò and our uncle Massimo. He's not much older than us, but all the uglier for it.

He rubs the back of his head, laughing. Uncle Massimo keeps his hand raised after delivering a slap. He's wearing a lot of camo and a shirt with cut-off sleeves. Impressive chest and arms, taut stomach. Black military boots on his feet.

How do you know Lorenzo?

Nicolò points at the forest again: We're from here, from the village.

The ghost village?

No, no, not up there. Down below, you know, where Lorenzo comes from.

I mumble to myself: Lorenzo didn't tell me anything about a living village.

Then I call out: Is there a train station there?

Angelo's eyes widen: You want to leave already?

Why not?

Well, because of the grape harvest! There's nothing more wonderful. We're not even farmers, but we can't say no to the grape harvest. Have you ever done it before?

I shake my head.

You see, the blond beams, you can go home tomorrow! Or do you have something better to do?

Do you promise to drive me to the station then?

Enthusiastic nods.

I've always been bad at saying no. Especially when it comes to company and drinking wine. Why shouldn't I have a bit of fun before I leave? And when Lorenzo finally comes back this evening, I can still give him a piece of my mind.

The horn tears me out of my thoughts.

Well, what's the hold-up, are you coming?

Bright faces of inexperienced, violent boys.

She's scared.

I'm not scared!

In the bathroom, I splash water on my face and gargle. The traces of blood in the basin have dried slightly, there have been no new ones. I undress, glance in the mirror, ruffle my hair. It's so stiff I can tie it up in a bun. I smell good, sleep is my favourite perfume. Then I slip back into my nightshirt and roll up the sleeves so that my shoulders are exposed, like Uncle Massimo. I watch the woman in the mirror as she points her finger at me. We smile.

*

A short time later, I'm sitting in the roofless Range Rover, squeezed between boys sweating cologne. They cheered when I came out of the house, I felt every step in my hips.

The physical proximity now makes them tactfully silent, arm muscles are tensing left and right.

We scrape the bollard – full speed in reverse out of the driveway, up the hill, off the road, through the olive grove, between the trees. I cling to the dashboard so I won't be thrown out of the car. My vision blurs from the juddering, and I have to duck as branches from the rushing trees whip at us.

Where are you going, shouts Nicolò, the vineyard is down that way!

In response, Massimo grunts like a pig.

Suddenly, he turns sharply and slams the brakes. We've stopped on a track in front of an entranceway. Massimo jumps out of the car and unlocks the rusty chain on the gate. Angelo and Nicolò stay in the car and talk in dialect, as if it were a secret language and I were an uncomprehending loaf of bread.

The bimba's cute.

Lorenzo's lucky. There's nothing more divine than sweeping one's cousin.

I clear my throat: I'm not a bimba.

It's fine, the little angel says, beaming like he's up on a cinema screen, that's just what we say here.

Not to me, I mutter, slamming the door behind me.

I follow their uncle through the open gate over dry mud to the enclosures.

Siena pigs, Massimo calls out proudly, look at how many piglets.

I count seven mighty sows and dozens of little piglets. When I approach them, they run in circles like they've been stung and squeal. They are black with a pink loop around their necks. The boar, a huge animal, is free to run around.

Don't be afraid of him, Massimo says, he's very stupid.

He spreads his arms and runs screaming towards the boar. The boar screeches in alarm and flees into his plot. The uncle closes the gate behind him.

You see, he says, he really is the dumbest thing.

The boar buries his nose in the ground.

He's like me, says Massimo, a horned beast, a cuckold.

He stands against the fence and spreads his arms: When the females are in heat, their scent flows through the whole valley. A male boar can smell it from miles away. They keep coming and tearing down the fences with their teeth. Look, here.

He points at a large hole in the wire mesh.

They've got tremendous force, their teeth. They tore my friend's femoral artery. We were out hunting together, there's nothing you can do about it. He bled to death in front of me.

Massimo touches his neck and pulls out a large, curved tooth on a leather tie from under his collar: I avenged him, killed him with my own hands.

He waits until I look suitably impressed, then he continues: When a wild boar like that comes in here, he impregnates everyone. I can hear the sows screaming all the way to my house. They make the cutest piglets. Do you see them? Half wild, half Siena. Look how beautiful their noses are. The others are ugly, with their short snouts. The mixed ones are much prettier than the purebred ones, I like them better. Oh, I like them all.

He sighs.

Do you eat them?

Me? No. I watch them grow up, they're very dear to me, just look at them! The gentlemen eat them though.

Who are the gentlemen?

Well, your cousin's bosses.

I wonder if he's one of them, the hunting society, as Lorenzo calls them. If he knows the Coach.

He looks at me sideways and says, as if he were reading my thoughts: I'm also employed by the gentlemen, I look after the land, the vegetable gardens. Maybe you've seen me before?

I shake my head. This area seemed deserted to me, empty and blurry, as if in a dream. One more day and I would have jumped off the edge of the cliff, convinced that I could fly—

Massimo turns back to the piglets. The garden outside my bedroom window pops into my mind: the well-tended flower beds and tied-up plants. That was him! What if he was watching me the whole time? Hadn't I felt like I was being watched in the villa and when wandering around in the whispering forest?

I live in the forest, Massimo announces, as if I had spoken out loud. In the old charcoal burner's house.

Where Sisina's brother-in-law lived – it bursts out of me.

He looks astonished: Sisina! You know about her?

I duck my head. I'm embarrassed; I don't want anyone to notice that I'm obsessed with a ghost.

Massimo strokes one of the sows: Sisina is real. She was here! She was very beautiful.

I've heard, I nod.

Beautiful as blood and milk, he repeats as if in contemplation.

He looks up: Come visit me at my house. If you don't have to leave.

Massimo, I say, how big are the estates?

Uh, he exhales, very big. When you stand at the highest point and look out over everything, it goes as far as the eye can see.

And it all belongs to the *gentlemen* who own the villa?

He looks at me with narrowed eyes and nods.

The village too?

No, of course not the village. Don't you know anything? If you stay longer, I can take you on a tour. Feed deer, guard truffles, mend fences. If the gentlemen agree.

What are they like? I ask.

Oh, Massimo says, I have no problems with them. They gave me the house when my wife – you know. Look here, another horny cuckold.

He pulls me over to a large deer antler hanging on the iron fence next to the boar enclosure.

I shot it with a spear. It was injured and suffering. Look.

Massimo kneels underneath the antler until it appears to be sticking out of his head.

If a woman cheats on you, you wear horns forever. So it's much better to . . .

He mimes stabbing a knife while laughing.

But what do I do? Pay her maintenance. Instead of shooting her and her lover, as is right and proper, I killed the deer. And then I boiled its head.

You must have needed a big pot for that, I say.

Brava, he says contentedly, as if he felt understood, very big in fact. But first I buried it in the ground for three weeks. Then I boiled water and vinegar in a very big pot and put the head in it. After a few days everything came off by itself: skin, fat, tendons.

And would you have done the same with your wife if you had shot her?

Sure.

He grins: Don't laugh like that, otherwise I'll fall in love with you.

From the gate Angelo calls that we shouldn't make out with each other.

I help Massimo feed the pigs, then we go back to the car.

A hill appears in front of us, Massimo puts his foot down on the accelerator. We howl up the steep slope, which ends abruptly. Then we fall into nothingness. As if by a miracle, we land on our wheels.

Shortcut, he grins.

In fact, we are now back on the road that leads to Sisina's memorial stone.

I breathe out deeply. Angelo puts his arm around my shoulders.

Brava, he says, smiling.

He's very young and beautiful, straight out of a Bertolucci film.

As we pass Sisina's stone, I know that she is insanely jealous.

*

A thin old man is waiting at the vineyard. His cheeks are gaunt; he complains: You're late, what have you brought, since when have we brought girls here, bah.

That's Lorenzo's cousin.

I smile involuntarily. They really think I have an Italian cousin.

The old man pulls a face: And what does she want here? To be Lorenzo's replacement? I can't stand him, hunchbacked servant of the *masters*, pah!

He spits, then hands out pruning shears to the boys and appraises them with a disparaging look: Is that the one who can't cook, ugh.

Massimo raises his hand as if to strike him: Shut up and get to work.

The old man walks away, grumbling: At least they left the snob at home today. Stupid boys, first they bring a lord, then a female—

Don't get too excited, Nicolò calls after him, the snob wants to come back, he told me so.

Did he? Massimo raises his eyebrows as the old man disappears into a row between the vines, cursing.

Nicolò shrugs and Angelo smiles at me: Don't listen to Igor, he's not in charge, he's just showing off.

Is he related to you too?

Massimo spits: Him? What makes you think that?

He puts a pair of shears in my hand and says: It's a shame. Usually there's a lot more people helping with the harvest. The grape harvest is actually a festival, a folk festival. When I was a child . . . Do you remember?

His nephews shrug.

You see, they didn't even get to experience it. Everything's going to the dogs, I'm glad I live in the forest – the village is full of old people and traitors.

Nicolò mutters: At least there's no safari cemetery.

Massimo snips at the ends of his hair with the shears and calls out: The forest belongs to the gentlemen, they can do whatever they want in it, we have no say in it.

He turns to me: But times have changed, you know. People aren't so dependent on them anymore. My grandfather's generation still lived on the leased farms around the villa and worked the landowners' fields. Nowadays, everyone lives in the village. Everyone who's still here. They have jobs and are paid by the Americans or the Chinese, not by the landowners.

And you?

We continue to work for them, it's a tradition in our family, we are loyal. Not Igor, he has no principles, he does it because he's poor. Look at him. How old do you think he is?

I don't know, seventy? Seventy-five?

Massimo yells over the vines: Did you hear that, Igor? The girl thinks you're half dead!

He's forty, says Nicolò.

Massimo pats me on the shoulder, crying from laughing, and puts a yellow plastic crate at my feet.

Just fill it up, he says. Any idiot can do that, as you can see. Do you know what a ripe grape is?

*

I cut down grapes eagerly. It's nice to hold a fat bunch of them. Their antennae, which I have to uncoil first, wind around the stalks like telephone cables. So satisfying when a vine is empty. I imagine myself as the young Lavinia, gossiping about Vito with Sisina. Then I remember that my grandmother grew up in the city, where her ambition was to work in an office. She had only been to a vineyard as an elderly woman, on one of her coach trips.

289

Angelo stays level with me, in the row opposite. Sometimes his face appears between the leaves. He winks and smiles and flicks his tongue like a lizard.

Why do you talk so strangely? he asks. You make these strange little mistakes, can you even speak Italian?

I'm not from here, I snap, but I speak pretty well.

Angelo shakes his head: Well, sometimes you sound a bit stupid.

I try to hit him through the hedge. He laughs and holds my hand tightly.

You're stupid, I shout, I'm from Switzerland!

Beautiful Switzerland, Massimo calls over, I have an uncle over there. I liked it, very clean. They make a huge song and dance about the coffee, with little milk jugs and sugar bowls and little chocolates. That was very nice. But expensive, porco dio.

Angelo doesn't respond to him: But why don't you speak like Lorenzo?

My grandmother emigrated to Switzerland. Her husband was Swiss and he didn't want her to speak Italian.

Lorenzo's grandmother? asks Massimo, while Angelo nods thoughtfully: You just have to adapt, integrate.

No, I say quickly, he was an idiot. And you're no better, the way you pester me. If my grandfather hadn't been a chauvinistic patriarch, I would verbally tear you apart today.

It's fine, Angelo says, it's fine. I just thought . . . Maybe you're an Albanian lover.

Me?

So you really are Lorenzo's cousin?

I shrug.

Massimo and Angelo wink at each other: There is nothing more divine . . .

You're all crazy.

A proverb! That's what we say here. It's part of our culture. You should learn from us if you're from here too.

I concentrate on plucking and filling the boxes. Old Igor is whining in the background, every few minutes he asks about lunch: Shall we go now? It's time now, surely. I have to starve because you got here late.

I feel sorry for him with his thin little arms, the cloth handkerchief under his hat against the burning sun.

Nicolò keeps turning his head towards the road as if he were waiting for someone. The snob? Angelo sings to himself a few rows away and throws me looks that are sometimes innocent, sometimes yearning, and are meant to placate me. Massimo has tied his shirt around his head and looks even more like a warrior. I can imagine him fighting his way through the forest with a machete. He lives in the old charcoal burner's house. I wonder if it's haunted there too?

I sneak up, slip through a hole in the row of vines and work next to him, a few metres away. Smiling, I say that I'm sorry about his wife: I mean, that she cheated on you.

He mumbles something about freedom.

After a polite pause, I ask innocently: What do you actually know about Sisina?

Massimo stops cutting and repeats: Sisina is real.

Then he points the shears at me: I know who didn't kill her. It wasn't her fiancé. Right up until his death he said it wasn't him. Even on his deathbed, he whispered: *My poor Sisina*. No murderer would do that; if you're dying, you can say, can't you?

He waits for me to agree and continues: It was the land-owners from back then. They were Swiss, like you. The son got Sisina pregnant and then hired an Albanian to kill her. So that the affair wouldn't come out, understand.

I wonder whether I should contradict him or whether this would insult him and blow my chances of getting more information.

I remember the woman in the newspaper who said she saw Sisina's murderer cycling past – she suspected him because of his 'ugliness': xenophobia mixed with superstition, the evil eye. The same old soup of resentment that gets boiled up during a crisis, while the perpetrators are sought among 'the others'.

Massimo turns away and calls across the rows: Get the tractor! After that we'll take a break. Igor lets out a sharp cry and hurls his pruning shears into his box.

Nicolò drives up in the tractor. Angelo climbs onto the loading bed and calls out: I love all women. Women are wonderful. Death to all men! May I be the only one.

I laugh, heaving the full boxes into his arms. Igor squats in the shade of a vine and nods at me: Brava, the girl is brava.

A strange warmth involuntarily spreads through me. It must come from childhood: they made me addicted to this patronising praise from an early age. Brava. It makes me angry, and yet – instead of standing up to them, asserting myself as an equal, I play along, letting myself fall back into this infantile behaviour: flattered giggles, sheepish blinks, shy squirms. It's just too easy to wrap them around my finger. But why do I even want to do that? Does it come from Magdalena, this ridiculous behaviour around men? Even if I don't like them, I want them to like me; I want them to find me desirable, to admire me, to compliment me. Maybe it's also intuition, a survival strategy: if he likes me, he won't kill me. Because in the rare moments when it doesn't work, when someone doesn't smile back, I immediately feel threatened.

Igor nods as if he had heard my thoughts: Just watch out for Lorenzo.

I frown. He says: You're interested in Sisina, aren't you?

I sit down next to him.

She wasn't married yet, he begins, looking me over: she was like you. Not very tall, but pretty, striking. You encourage men with your smile, and they tend to misinterpret it . . . Sisina's fiancé found it too much; he couldn't trap her, she was like the wind through his fingers. Not everyone can put up with it. It could have been him. But he was acquitted because he had the best lawyer in all of Italy.

Why?

Igor puts a grape in his mouth: Do you know what's funny? Vito then wanted to marry his sister-in-law, but she didn't want to. He moved away, found another woman and never came back. And his new wife, well, that's my uncle's cousin. Funny, isn't it? Do you know how they met? On the day of La Befana, he went from house to house with the male choir. A family invited him in, and inside he saw a shrine – it was for him, with photographs of him from the court! He was touched by it and made friends with the daughter, she became his wife. He's been dead for a few years now. Poor guy.

But what do you think, I ask impatiently, was it him? He shrugs his bony shoulders: The situation was very tense at the time. We basically had a civil war here after the war. Have you heard about the massacre where they killed an entire village to set an example for the partisans?

Igor, shouts Massimo, stop telling the girl communist lies right now.

The old man hisses a curse, gets up with a groan and drags himself up the slope, bracing himself against the sun.

After a while I mumble something about peeing and follow him into the forest. There is a rustling and hissing sound; a small footpath leads gently uphill through the undergrowth. Suddenly the path is blocked by a yellow tub full of grapes. I stop and see, concealed among trees, a hut made of branches and stones and camouflaged plastic sheeting.

Igor appears in the doorway. He strains to pull a hose behind him. He takes a quick look at me, then turns around without a word and is swallowed up by the darkness of the hut. I hear him panting, he rolls out a wooden wine barrel. He sets it upright and puts the end of the hose in a hole in the barrel.

What are you doing?

Why, going to squeal? The gentlemen let us do all the work and then drink the wine. If it was up to them, we wouldn't get a drop.

He reaches into the tub and passes me a handful of grapes.

Try, he orders. I start to eat the grapes. They are terribly sweet.

Now stop it, he grumbles, for God's sake, are you crazy, throw them away now.

He takes the grapes from my hand and throws them into the bushes.

I said try them, my God. Filling your belly with grapes, turista di merda.

I'm not a—

Yes, yes, says Igor, never mind.

With his sinewy arms he lifts the tub and empties the grapes into the barrel.

Is this your house? I ask.

He mumbles something and shakes the barrel.

Then he says: This is my hiding place to escape from my wife. Otherwise I would have killed her long ago.

I pick up a few grapes that have fallen to the ground and throw them into the barrel. What did you say before, I ask, when Massimo interrupted you?

Hmm, says Igor, why are you even hanging around with them?

It's not like I have much choice.

Igor nods: What brought you here?

Long story.

Then another way: What keeps you here?

I shrug: The secret of Sisina?

Ho-hum, he says, and I'm supposed to believe that.

Igor, I say, what was that about the civil war?

He sighs deeply and begins to tell his story: After the war, people were exhausted, hungry, tired. Strictly speaking it was peacetime, in reality, the fight continued to simmer between fascists and communists, partisans and allied forces. The north had been occupied, the partisans were in the south, but here was free land. Red zone. A few hills away, the Nazis had wiped out an entire village shortly before the end of the war. As a display of their determination against the partisans. Even after the war, a deep divide ran through communities. But alongside rampant suspicion, hope sprouted. Many started organising again in communist farmers' co-operatives, which of course did not please the large landowners. So they continued to support the fascists in the fight against the farmers' unions and the partisans. Maybe Sisina heard something—

A noise in the bushes makes him turn around, a cat jumps onto the path. She rubs against my legs, Igor shoos her away: Get out of here, you wretched spy!

I laugh, the cat dances off offended along the wall of the hut and rubs her head against it.

The old man takes a branch and lashes at her, the cat jumps and gallops up the path.

Cursing quietly, he turns his attention back to the wine barrel.

I clear my throat: Go on. What did Sisina hear?

Igor spits: Why do you even care? So you can go and tell the idiots, forget it.

No, I—

He stands up and points up the path, after the cat: Go on, ask her, she knows everything.

You mean . . . her ghost?

Ugh, ghost. The witch!

Witch, I mutter, that's what Lorenzo said too. To the woman in the car, who looked like an older Sisina. She sent us into the ditch!

Igor nods sombrely: She doesn't like guests.

Igor, I say breathlessly, are you saying that Sisina didn't die at all? That she's alive— He spits: The witch is alive, the murderess. She killed her husband and is hiding up in the ghost village.

He looks at me and laughs: That's not poor Sisina, she's just . . . she's obsessed with her.

For a moment I'm disappointed. Then excited again: Do you think she knows who killed Sisina?

Igor grabs my wrist hard: You stay away from her, do you hear? She's crazy, she's dangerous.

I nod. Names, faces, rockets swirl around my head. They slowly settle on the empty spaces, completing the picture. When I finally have it in front of me, they fly up like feathers in a gust of wind.

Massimo calls from the vineyard. I go back.

*

After more hours and harvested vines, Massimo announces that it's time to finish for the day. We load the boxes onto the tractor and drive off. Angelo and I sit on the bed of the trailer among the grapes. A shyness spreads between us; the engine is too loud for talk. The dirt road shakes us and makes our heads bang together. A storm of dust swirls around us: the particles shine in the evening sun when his lips touch my neck as if by accident.

A knocking drowns out the noise of the tractor. Nicolò is banging his fist against the cab window.

Hey, girl, he calls, muffled by the window. Have you ever been ghost hunting?

The tractor stops. Angelo pulls me up and jumps off the bed. We are at the fork where the dirt track meets the road. The roofless Range Rover is already waiting, Massimo honks: Change, Signora!

Nicolò has rolled down the window of the tractor cab and is talking quietly with his little cousin. They keep looking at me.

Are we going to the village now? I ask.

Oh, Massimo says, there's not much to see there. The grapes

still have to be taken to the press, Igor and Nicolò will do that, we're not needed. We promised that we would get you home on time.

But I don't want to go back, I say, I want a wine festival. Or to go to the train station.

Don't worry, Nicolò calls, we'll take good care of you. The boys will stay with you and I'll come for you on the motorbike as soon as I've taken Igor home.

Angelo snuggles up against me: You're interested in Sisina, aren't you? We know a lot about her case. That is to say, we're ghost hunters, we have equipment.

Massimo rolls his eyes. Nicolò adds: We've never had the chance to look for her in the villa. I'd bet she's there. Sisina worked in the villa—

I know, I say defiantly.

Well then, Angelo calls out, you want to know what happened to her too.

But I want to go to the village, I protest weakly, I want to go home.

Our grandfather knew her, Massimo says suddenly. He was a child then, but he remembers Sisina's father running around telling everyone that she was a loose girl and no longer his daughter, and that he wanted to take away her name.

I look from one to the other: they talk about Sisina as if they knew her. They grew up here, have a real connection to her: a grandfather who sat with her in church, bumped into her on the forest tracks. And I have a grandmother who told me everything about men and their power over names . . .

That tingling again, the deceptive feeling of belonging: it all has something to do with me too, with my story. I want to find out more!

What is one more night anyway? And ghost hunting – that sounds like something I must try at least once. Maybe we'll even meet Magdalena? She would enjoy teaching these boys to feel fear.

I can't help grinning. Angelo nods: I've got a really good feeling about this – I think Sisina will trust us more easily if we have a girl with us.

Nicolò gives an endearing smile: It would be an honour.

Angelo takes my hand: Or are you chicken?

Don't forget the equipment, he calls to Nicolò, pulling me towards the car.

I'll bring food, Nicolò promises.

Massimo pulls a face: But no snobs!

With that, he starts the engine and jolts up the road, the incline presses us into the upholstery.

*

As we pull crunchily into the driveway of the villa, the sun has not yet set. According to Angelo, we have to wait until late in the night to hunt ghosts – what am I supposed to do with them until then?

Massimo examines the pumpkin plants in the vegetable garden, and Angelo strides through the entrance hall and the drawing room, letting out approving whistles.

Not bad, madam. Swiss standards . . . Are you sure you're not related to the landowners of the past?

I find his awkward manner exhausting. In fact, their presence is making me nervous – what if Lorenzo comes back? I can't truly believe that he would like how they're conducting themselves here.

Massimo calls out: Don't worry about Lorenzo. He won't be back anytime soon.

What makes you think that?

Massimo makes a smug face: He's deserted, hasn't he? If the gentlemen find him here, he's a dead man.

I don't understand anything anymore. We tidied up the villa for these *gentlemen*. I thought the Coach was one of them, and the Coach was supposed to help Lorenzo.

I try not to let anything show and run outside, where Nicolò is turning off the engine. He's not alone. Also dismounting from the bike is the snob. No doubt about it: he moves as if through water, pure grace; coupled with an artificial flightiness that's possibly meant to come across as intellectual. Next to him, I immediately feel incredibly dirty. My hands are still sticky from the grape juice; my hair is stiff. Under the shapeless nightshirt, which seemed casually seductive to me that morning, my earthy knees are ashamed. On the road with Massimo and the cousins, I believed that I was a vibrant, natural country beauty. The tailored flannel suit, the silk scarf fluttering gently, the well-groomed fingernails and the exquisite whiff of cologne open my eyes: I'm scruffy. As elegant as that stupid, cuckold boar. Oh God, I probably even smell of the pig dung I enthusiastically climbed around in.

His head is large, his hair is thick, his mouth fleshy, his face red from sun and alcohol. His mouth tears open and twists when he speaks; he pretentiously grimaces while he articulates and gesticulates as if from a bygone era. When he speaks, heavy velvet armchairs fall out of his mouth, heirloom jewellery and wood polish, a signet ring—

I clumsily fend off his hand with an unnecessary reference to how disgusting I am.

We were out in *nature* all day, I say, rolling my eyes.

Nicolò smiles, I'm embarrassed.

The snob politely introduces himself as a neighbour. His great-aunt owns the next-door property, behind the hill with the ghost village.

She is of high nobility, he notes, and was friends with the previous owners of this property. But, he adds with a dismissive gesture, that was a different time.

I am from the city, he continues, I find this rural peace hostile, I cannot get used to it. But as we all know, life is not getting any cheaper, and so I thought to myself: time to make another appearance at my great-aunt's, the woman is not that young anymore and will certainly be happy to have a visit from a loving heir. Besides, I needed a break from all this *madness*.

I nod as if I know exactly what he's talking about.

I'm only here for a visit, I say apologetically, I'm also from the city.

Can he tell that I'm lying, that I left the city I studied in a long time ago? He doesn't let on and smiles: Then we'll behave like respectable guests.

He winks at Nicolò: I hear we have some adventurous plans tonight.

My name is Romeo, he continues, but Nicolò calls me Meo. He is my loyal friend here, isn't that right? We met in the village, on my first evening here. When was that, my dear? It seems like an eternity ago, time goes by more slowly here.

I nod inanel; he continues: I noticed Nicolò immediately. I like to surround myself with beauty, ugly as I am.

I protest, he plays it down: I have other qualities.

Is he making fun of me? Or is it possible that he hasn't noticed my embarrassing nightshirt, my matted hair and my shrill voice?

Please excuse me, I say, I urgently need to freshen up.

Ugh, he says, look at me! I need a *fucking* nap. Well, a drink would also do.

Angelo, I say, trying to sound regal: Go and break into the wine cellar.

Cheers go up, Massimo kisses the top of my head: Thank

you, girl. I've been harvesting this wine all my life, but we've never been allowed to drink it.

Meo looks at me amused: See you later, bambola.

*

We're sitting at the roughly hewn table in the garden. I smell of the kitchen soap that I used to scrub myself under the scalding water. I also used it to wash my city clothes. They were wet afterwards, so I stole a red velvet curtain cord from the drawing room, which is now serving as a belt for my nightshirt. It doesn't look that bad.

I silently watch Meo, the snob, as he blazes around making the cousins laugh. He is certainly seductive. I take quick, big gulps, try to combat my shyness. He had said bambola, doll, that must mean he likes me? Or did he just not catch my name?

I look back and forth between him and the country boys. Why do I always want to belong where I clearly cannot? First with the farmers, now with this dandy? I'm always pretending; trying to balance diffuse feelings of superiority and inferiority, as if I was yearning to be on an equal footing, as if I could be. In the city, at the university, it wasn't difficult for me, I played my role easily. But I didn't blend in. While Lavinia and Magdalena sold their bodies, their labour, I wrung out my brain. And the further I went, the further I moved away from them. Was that why I wanted to be so close to Sorella and Crocifissa, because I thought that maybe this was my real class?

How foolish. And now I want to be like a snob – a nobleman! It's as if I can hear Magdalena giggling: Make up your mind, this is getting embarrassing. What do you want, Fila: are you going up or down?

I got that from her: she talked, laughed, flirted with everyone; she didn't want any hierarchies. Whereas my grandmother constantly distanced herself from her class, from her dialect, from the other immigrants – I wasn't a foreign worker, she sometimes said, I came to get married.

As if that were any better.

*

It's grown dark, flickering candlelight leaps across our faces. The cicadas are quietening down. Meo pulls a cigarette out of the pack, then offers it around. I take one, look for Magdalena's lighter, which Crocifissa gave me. It's been so long since I thought about her. And where is Lorenzo? I light the cigarette from a candle.

Perhaps someone would like to enlighten me, Meo begins, about what we are planning to do tonight.

We're going to hunt ghosts, I giggle, and take a quick drag.

The girl from back then?

Or her murderer.

And if we find a ghost?

Then we'll talk to it!

Why would a ghost want to talk to us?

Nicolò frowns: Why not? Ghosts are happy when they find someone has contacted them. There's always something that they wanted to do in the world they left behind, so they long for someone living who can help them realise it.

I nod casually: Sisina wanted me to reconcile her with her fiancé.

The cousins' eyes pop out of their heads: You saw Sisina? What did she say? And what did you do?

I laugh: Nothing.

Massimo fixes me with a piercing look: She approached you.

I don't know, it was just a dream.

Massimo shakes his head, deep in thought: In all the years I've been here, Sisina has never shown herself to me. Others claim they have seen her, but I haven't. And yet every day I roam the woods, calling out to her. In winter, when no one else is here and I could use some company, I stand in front of the memorial stone in the fog, cross myself and say: Ciao, Sisina, how are you? The wolves howl, but she never comes.

So she doesn't exist?

Angelo jumps up: I think Sisina is just waiting to tell us her story. That way she can finally free herself from the in-between world.

*

We stumble around outside the house and cross the driveway. Nicolò stops by the car. Wait, the apparatus.

He lifts the sports bag out from the back seat and unzips it. He hands out torches to everyone and puts something resembling a walkie-talkie in Angelo's hand. He puts a second one in his jacket pocket and offers Meo a third one after Massimo declines, shaking his head.

What is that?

An original American K2 meter! Do you want to hold it?

Angelo holds it out to me. It looks like a cross between an old mobile phone and a metronome.

The K2 measures electromagnetic fields, Nicolò explains. He points to the little lights on the top which form a colour scale from green to yellow to red: It goes off when near sources of radiation, near the fuse box in a house, for example.

And I thought we were going ghost hunting.

With a technical source like an electrical socket, the device lights up until you move away from the source. But with a ghost, it lights up suddenly – and goes out again when the ghost moves away.

Hmm, I say, and it works?

He sets the machine up with a click, a green light comes on.

I drop it: It's lighting up!

Angelo laughs: That's green.

Nicolò picks up the measuring device and shines it around. His eyes sparkle: See? It's very simple. Green light means no ghosts present. It's only when it turns to orange that there are any nearby, but not in the immediate vicinity. The higher the scale, the closer the ghost, because of the magnetic field, get it? If it's a very strong field, all the diodes light up red.

And has that ever happened?

Angelo nods eagerly: Of course, there's always something

going on in the ghost village up there! And in the caves and places like that. We've seen it all.

Nicolò shoulders the bag: We'll show you the rest of the equipment when we get there. We'll go to Sisina's memorial stone first, what do you think? The crime scene, that's where she's most active.

Massimo pulls me aside: Are you sure you want to come with us? Making contact with ghosts is not without danger.

I thought you were professionals. Ghost hunters.

My nephews call themselves that. I'm only going to keep an eye on them. They're young and careless.

What do you mean?

They're from a different generation, they only see technology. American devices that have them duped. I don't believe in it, it's just a show. But you're a girl. You have too much compassion.

I hit his massive upper arm, he remains serious: Compassion, that's what ghosts want, they search for it desperately. And when they find it, they cling to you. Besides . . .

What?

He squirms: I don't want to accuse you of anything, but . . . Carnal love, it opens certain doors for girls, you know . . . within the boundaries of the physical world. Do you understand what I mean?

No.

Have you ever sleepwalked?

I don't think so.

Suddenly, I see him before me, in front of my door, putting flowers in the keyhole.

He grabs my wrist: I'm just saying that you should be careful. The forces that you're surrounding yourself with here are dark. If a real connection is made, we will learn things that no man should ever know in this life. You're easy prey for ghosts. They love slipping into someone like you.

XII

The forest has swallowed us up, it's full of noises. The beams of our torches tremble up and down the tree trunks. We are not alone, invisible creatures are moving in the darkness of the night. They creep and scurry and flutter around us.

I think of the first night after Sisina's death, when she lay lifeless on the forest floor. Cold and increasingly rigid, guarded by her father, her fiancé, her brothers-in-law – all of whom would soon be accused of her murder. The horror that sat in the men and dripped like sweat into the blackness of the forest. That caught in the trees that are now rustling around us.

In the light of the torch, details from the whale notebook flit around me like moths. The spatter of blood in the foliage. The pool in the hollow. The upside-down jug under the oak tree. Sisina's worn-down sandals. The drag marks; the leaves and branches on her earthy back, her new dress.

I wish I had never read the book. The thought that we should leave her in peace dances through my head. I hear my voice speaking this sentence, but my lips remain tightly closed. This sticky pitch blackness must stay outside my body.

We gather around the memorial stone in a semicircle. The torches are pointed downwards, small bright circles form at our feet. Like blood dripping from a knife. The photograph on the stone shimmers dully. My heart is pounding.

Such brutality, murmurs Nicolò, against such a beautiful young woman.

Not as beautiful as you, Angelo breathes on my neck, are you cold?

He tries to put his arm around my shoulder, I duck away, stepping next to Nicolò: The picture has cracked, can you see? As if someone had hit it with all their might.

I sigh, it feels good not to be alone in Sisina's universe anymore.

Nicolò shines a light on the picture, shaking his head: Who would do that? No, no, it must be from winter, it must have frozen.

Meo rubs his hands together and blows on them as if he were freezing: I don't know what everyone sees in her, she seems pretty basic to me.

Massimo exhales contemptuously: With all this friendliness, she'll definitely want to come and visit us.

Nicolò walks around the stone and shines a light on the inscription: I always wonder if that's a secret clue: *here* died *Sisina* of *Stefano*.

Yes, that's what I thought too!

Massimo shakes his head: That just means that she was his daughter. Back then they used to say: Sisina of Stefano . . .

Sure, I say, but I also read that her father was a suspect.

Massimo pulls a face: Her babbo? Absolutely not! He was a farmer like us.

I thought you weren't farmers.

Angelo shrugs: It was her boyfriend, Vito. He was jealous because she was messing around with everyone.

Massimo whispers in dismay: You can't talk about her like that here!

Nicolò looks around and says: Massimo's right. We're guests here, show a little respect. We have to ask her permission first.

Massimo turns off his torch and takes a step towards the memorial stone. He turns his palms to the sky and says loudly: Beautiful Sisina, don't be afraid. We don't mean you any harm. If you want to talk, we are here. We want to listen to you.

A brief silence, then Meo says in a low voice: I imagined this being funnier. Can we go back now?

Shh! Nicolò listens to the forest: What do you think?

Massimo tilts his head in concentration, Angelo nods: I don't think she has anything against it.

They pull out their magnetic measuring devices and point them towards the stone.

Sisina? Are you here?

The lights flash. The green flicker is reflected in the cousins' eyes. I clear my throat, try to control my breathing.

I don't believe in it either, I murmur, half to Meo and half to myself, but the way they do it might be interesting.

Meo shakes a cigarette out of the pack, lights it and noisily blows the smoke out: You don't believe in it? Then why are you shaking?

Nicolò holds his finger to his lips, a warning look. We stare at the devices, standard green flickering.

No ghosts present, I murmur.

Nicolò takes a step forward: Sisina, do you want to come closer to us? We won't do anything to you.

I hear myself breathing. The smoke from Meo's cigarette swirls in front of my face. Branches crack. Leaves rustle. Massimo jabs the air with his index finger, I flinch: Can you hear that?

Nicolò nods frantically: Where's it coming from?

Angelo shines a light into the forest behind the stone: the incline that leads down to the Tigress's Stream. That's where she lay, all night. I see her before me, the black blood, turn my gaze away from the bright circle that moves excitedly over the whispering leaves. Fear is in Angelo's voice: Sisina, please try to communicate with us via the instruments.

Meo gasps loudly, he stands stiffly and puts his hands on his thighs.

Nicolò tries again: Sisina, did you love Vito?

Meo breaks out of his trance: Well, I can't hear anything.

There! Angelo clings to my arm: A loud noise! Did you hear? An *ooh*! Like a wail.

I'm shaking; I croak: An owl?

Bird of the dead.

Nicolò undulates around the stone: Are you here with us, Sisina? Did you say something?

I try to concentrate on the bright green flickering of the measuring devices, try to melt my eyes into them to block out everything else. The dark has always frightened me, I expect the worst is hiding in it, ready to attack me from behind, to pull me into eternal darkness. So I stare into the glaring light of the torches and imagine that it is daytime, that I am Sisina, slipping into the opening in the bushes to finally be unobserved. I see her bare toes wiggling in the sun, the water jug, hear someone approaching. She wasn't afraid, it was broad daylight.

Bright green garlands dance on my retina, I squeeze my eyelids together a few times until I'm able to make things out again. Nicolò rummages in his bag and pulls out a kind of radio: Let's try the ghost box.

He puts the device on its base, next to the vase of dried flowers. Then he untangles two cables and connects the radio to a small round box. Straight away, choppy music comes out, as if the signal were jumping between different stations. The rhythmic noise flows into the darkness.

The cousins and uncle huddle in closer around the stone, Meo and I stand close together behind Nicolò.

I don't want to do this anymore, whispers Meo, come on, let's go.

It's a radio, I whisper, a broken radio. Look how much effort they're putting in. We can play along for a bit longer, then we'll go back.

Suddenly, the noise stops. Tension sucks us into a vacuum, we all hold our breath. Sisina, Nicolò calls, are you here?

The radio comes back on, scraps of words spat out among the broken music – Angelo shouts: She said yes!

You're all crazy, Meo shouts shrilly, it's newsreaders, radio operators, interference, I don't understand a word of it.

I want to nod, to agree with him, but instead my hand reaches out as if pulled by invisible fingers and presses against his mouth. In the music I see images, blurred and juddery, like a very old film: swinging skirts, braided hair, laughter.

Nicolò's voice brings me back: Remember, there are often several of them, so that their voices overlap when they speak.

Several . . . ghosts? Here?

We don't know.

Angelo screams against the noise: Sisina, who killed you?

Disco and piano music, shiny boots waltzing over the parquet, a woman's voice—

She said Vito! Did she say Vito?

No, I say sharply, be quiet, no one can understand anything when you're screaming like that.

As if the radio had heard me, the noise stops, and a man's voice comes out clearly: *Slit her.*

Angelo jumps out of the row and squeezes in behind me. Massimo turns around, his face wild: Did you hear that?

We nod quickly.

Angelo's voice trembles: He said it: I'll slit her open.

Nicolò tries to stay calm: I'm not sure. Sisina, can you tell us what happened? Incomprehensible voices are once again jumbled together in the radio, the chaos of devices; fluttering skirt hems, hurrying feet, whirling leaves.

Can you repeat that?

Thro—

Angelo jumps on my back like a little monkey: Throat! She said throat!

I wonder to myself if they're recordings, the voices from the box. But the fear in Angelo's body is real, I feel it creeping into mine.

The cold of the blade on my neck, a flash of heat—

Angelo gets off me, his lips are quivering, his eyelashes flutter; I'm boiling hot inside. He steps back in front of the memorial stone: Sisina, did they cut your throat?

My throat is throbbing, the clear male voice booms from the radio again: *Jealous.*

Fuck, whispers Angelo, I think Vito is here too.

I join the cousins in the line and hear my voice: Vito, were you jealous?

Meo pulls on my hand, I shake him off, Nicolò nods at me: Sisina, try to answer us. Two voices come out of the radio in quick succession, a man and a woman: *Everything is fine.* And: *I don't know.*

Sisina, Nicolò says urgently, we want to find out who did it. Tell us.

Forest.

Forest? You were killed in the forest?

The voice from the box is once more incomprehensibly choppy, an alien anger glows inside me, Angelo takes a step to the side, as if he were the one disrupting the reception: Sisina, were you afraid you were pregnant?

Fano.

Stefano? Your father?

Vito, says Nicolò, you and Sisina's father, did you get on well?
More or less.

More or less, we shout at each other, he said more or less!

Angelo's voice almost breaks with excitement: What's your name?

Si-sina.

She says it over and over again. Sisina. I imagined her voice to be so different.

The boys burst into euphoria, they grab each other by the shoulders, shake each other: Sisina! She said it! The ghost said it!

Nicolò asks in a carrying voice: Sisina, do you know us a bit better now? Do you trust us?

I roll my eyes, but the woman's voice can be heard clearly from the box:

Bravi.

I have to laugh, Massimo squeezes my hand, the excitement crashes over me, we jump around like children.

The radio rustles incomprehensibly, then suddenly there's the man's clear voice: *I'm behind you.*

Meo turns around abruptly, stares into the darkness with wide eyes. I close mine. *You're disturbing us.*

We hold our breath. Nicolò clears his throat: Sisina, is anyone else here with you?

My father shoots out of the box.

Can he show himself to us, on the instruments?

We look breathlessly at the lights. Nothing.

Nicolò mutters: He doesn't want to communicate.

A hissing sound comes from the radio: *Go!*

A blast of cold hits my face like a torrent of icy water.

What else do you need, calls Meo, he's telling us to piss off. Come on, let's get out of here.

Angelo shakes his head: Well, I heard *don't go*.

Crazy people – laughter comes from the box. The man.

Then the radio suddenly gets quieter, as if the volume had been turned down.

Angelo stands with his mouth open: Listen – nothing's coming from the ghost box anymore.

Truly. A ghostly silence surrounds us like a bubble threatening to burst at any moment. Massimo laughs: Mamma mia. I've got goosebumps.

I click on my torch, Nicolò knocks it out of my hand, he gasps: Sisina, are you here? Blink with the instrument of the person you want to talk to.

Massimo gestures wildly in my direction: Hers! Hers is glowing!

The device at my feet is blinking like mad. I pick it up. It's warm.

Nicolò is amazed: All her energy is here with you.

She is here, whispers Angelo, she is really here.

Meo cries out and presses his face against my shoulder, I shake him: What is it?

Something touched me!

Massimo hastily picks up the torch and shines it around. He laughs: It's just a moth. See?

The moth is dancing in the beam of light. Nicolò reaches out to it, completely enchanted.

It appeared right at this moment, he says, that's her! Her spirit has connected with the insect – harmless little bodies are easy for ghosts. Sisina, were you killed here?

Angelo calls out: Woah, look! Glowing, everyone's glowing!

Indeed: the devices all flicker red, Angelo thrusts his into the air like a sword and shouts: It's you! Isn't it? Sisina? She trusts us! Oh man, look, my K2, pure fireworks.

Massimo and Angelo fire questions into the night like bullets: Sisina, was it your fiancé who killed you? Was it Vito? Sisina, listen! Are you ashamed of something? Is there something you didn't want to do? You had many men, didn't you? You don't have to be embarrassed in front of us.

Come on, Nicolò starts again: Come to me. Can you make a noise?

He looks around, then turns to stone. Whispers: She kissed me.

What?

She kissed me! He puts his hand to his cheek.

Why?

How would I know why! She's happy.

Because she kissed you.

Yes, aren't you? Sisina, are you glad we're here?

We stand in a circle and look at the devices, their green-yellow sparkling in the night. The glow gets weaker; finally, it goes out completely.

Nicolò sighs: I think she's gone. But, if you ask me, she wasn't alone.

Incredible, shouts Angelo, switching on his torch, what a session! The things we all felt: Goosebumps. Melancholy. Physical contact!

He squeezes my fingers: She touched my hand, and an immense sadness came over me.

Nicolò smiles: She kissed me.

Massimo scratches his head: Now she's touching me! Here.

Angelo: Hey, me too! Mamma mia, the ghost of Sisina is a real sweetheart.

Nicolò gently strokes his own cheek: Poor girl, I think she's lonely. She knows she's dead, but for some reason neither she nor her boyfriend can move on.

Angelo gives a laugh: Or her murderer. What if he was the one that kissed you?

Meo retches. Nicolò pats him on the back: Let's go.

Ciao, Sisina.

Ciao.

XIII

We move away from the memorial stone, reversing faster and faster, until we start running. The boys howl and let out sharp cries, make owl noises. They laugh hysterically, pushing each other against trees. Only Meo trots along silently beside me, at some point we start holding hands, ice cold. Time and time again we jump, holding each other back abruptly: a branch cracks, a figure oscillates between the trees, a wind blows on the back of our necks.

We only stop when we have finally stepped out of the forest and the bright grove has opened up before us. The moon shines brightly on the silver leaves of the olive trees, which speak with bats in whirring whispers. The crickets chirp, they are laughing at us. We stand petrified and silent until we see the others climbing up the embankment, then we keep running.

When we arrive at the villa, I turn on all the lights while Meo staggers to the fridge and slams bottles on the table. He is a different person, high-spirited. The cousins calm down as soon as they enter the house. As if they were in awe of the stately drawing room, they sit down obediently at the table. Massimo unpacks a small bag of pills. He counts them, then us, and begins to crush the tablets with the handle of a knife. Meo rubs his hands together and smacks his lips: Cool, cool, cool, he says, and kisses my ear, stands behind Massimo and massages his shoulders. Massimo draws five blue lines from the powder and has us line up in a row. Meo excitedly pokes my side with his fingers while Massimo draws his nose once across the plate on the table. He cackles and bows to Meo to help himself: Your highness.

He invites Nicolò to go before him: After you, please.

They moisten the ends of their index fingers, run them through a line, put their fingertips in their mouths, rub their gums. Ahh, says Meo. I moisten a fingertip too, tap the blue and lick it. Bitter. Then we wait for something to happen.

Nicolò plays around with the K2, getting the green light to go on and off until Meo snatches the device from his hand.

No more guests, please.

Nicolò watches the fluttering of the candle flame; the sooty smoke is drawn up towards the ceiling in a swirling motion.

He frowns: I really think that we found ghosts who are aware of their own death this time. They were playing with us.

Angelo nods: Sisina was there and Vito. His answers were aggressive, he seems doomed to stay at the crime scene forever. Poor Sisina, she's still not rid of him.

Massimo shakes his head: Vito is not the murderer.

Angelo rolls his eyes, Massimo ignores him: Everyone knows who it was. The beautiful Sisina was killed by il Conte because she was expecting a child and wanted his name.

Lorenzo said that too.

Meo shakes his head: As a child of the nobility, I can assure you that such things were solved in other ways. How many servants do you think have become pregnant by their masters? They don't get their hands dirty with a common peasant's daughter.

Massimo shouts: No, it's even worse, they pay Albanians—

Meo interrupts him: For a rich man there are a thousand other ways to get around the problem. For poor peasants, on the other hand, the honour of their wives was the only treasure they had to protect at all costs.

What do you know, Massimo shouts angrily, who knows better, you or us? We do, of course we do, this is our land. That's the truth, we know the truth.

There were at least three ghosts, Nicolò interjects. Sisina and Vito and Stefano – he lured us away from the stone so that we wouldn't hear what Sisina was saying.

Massimo rolls his eyes: Are you starting that again?

Nicolò raises his hands: Me? She said it! You had to have heard it. Sisina said Stefano got her pregnant.

I beg your pardon?

Nicolò looks around excitedly: Everyone heard it?

I suddenly freeze and shake myself, as if I had to fend off ghostly icy hands.

Angelo lowers his voice: You mean her father . . . You think there was a sweet secret between father and daughter?

My tongue sticks out of my mouth involuntarily: Sweet?

Nicolò shrugs his shoulders: The family probably knew about it, but they kept quiet for fear of a scandal. The mother must have warned the father: 'Stop touching her, she's getting married soon. If I catch you together, I'll do something terrible.'

Angelo shakes his head in disbelief: You think the mother—

Nicolò interrupts him: But it was already too late, Sisina was pregnant. What would she have told Vito? No one would want to marry her anymore – the whole family would be dishonoured. And even if she could keep the pregnancy secret until the wedding, the risk that Sisina would tell her husband the secret was too great. Stefano had to make sure that didn't happen.

But Nicolò, Angelo shouts, the mother had nothing to do with it, did she?

Nicolò gives a shrug: She must have been jealous because her husband desired his daughter more than he did her. But he did it. Everything's become clear to me after tonight. He wanted Sisina to belong only to him.

Massimo roars: That's sick. A father who kills his daughter because of what might be said in the village?

Of course, Nicolò sputters, as Meo says: honour had to be preserved. And in any case it was a mortal sin. Unmarried pregnant women were often killed because it was said that giving birth would bring bad luck to the family.

Massimo waves it away: The nobleman wanted her. But she resisted, she didn't want to. He was humiliated, so he killed her.

That doesn't make sense, why would he have done that?

Back then, Massimo shouts, back then that's how it was! If he couldn't have her, no one could have her. A man of honour, what else could he do? She made him look ridiculous. After she'd put out for everyone else.

I straighten up from my stupor and ask: Would you kill me if I turned you down?

He looks at me for a long time, then says: Maybe.

I nod: We don't have to look far, the perpetrators are among us.

Meo sighs: Who wants more wine?

It's a shame we didn't find out more, Angelo starts up again. What do you think, maybe we would have better results with metaphonic instruments?

Absolutely, I murmur, the beautiful Sisina likes big devices.

They raise their eyebrows, I take a sip: What else do you want to find out? You're all unanimous: the culprit is Sisina.

You can't say that, protests Angelo.

Instead of thinking about what happened back then and drawing conclusions about your own behaviour, you're continuing the story. To distract from what's really going on, people just keep arguing about whether she was a whore or a saint.

Nicolò shakes his head: It's a good thing that after all these years there are still people who want to find out what happened to her.

She was killed, I say, and then dragged through the mud. And half a century later you geniuses come along and still want to know who she gave a blowjob to.

Angelo tries hard not to giggle. Massimo pulls a face: What's up with the little girl?

Meo toasts him: She's no little girl.

Nicolò calls out: We want to remember Sisina. Tell her story.

I laugh helplessly: What do you want to remember? That she

was too beautiful? That a woman could be killed for being too forthcoming? Or for resisting?

Nicolò waves me off: I don't know what your problem is. We talk about our unfortunate sister with sensitivity and respect. We politely communicated with her and with others who may have had something to do with her death.

You are stirring up ghosts for fun! Even if she shouted the truth in your face, you wouldn't hear anything. I had the chance to find out something, to solve the mystery, but you ruined the moment with your screaming about kisses. Sisina wanted to talk to me, have you forgotten that? Nicolò asked who she wanted to talk to and my device lit up. Mine! She wanted to contact me because, compared to you half-baked idiots, I can understand her. I am the only one who still cares about her. You don't care about Sisina; it's all about you and your narrow-minded fantasies of a forest nymph that you can wank off to.

Angelo laughs and then tries to look dejected.

Nicolò smiles: I'll never forget how she kissed me.

I scream out of sheer powerlessness: There you go! You just want to fuck her!

Angelo grins: Are you jealous?

Meo rolls his eyes: I am.

Then he clears his throat and clinks his glass with a fingernail: Let's forget about the dead and celebrate the living. My time here in the countryside is coming to an end and I want to thank you and say that it has been a very formative experience for me. You have changed my life. You are not significant and you are

326

not rich, and yet you are wonderful. I did not know this was possible. My life has become better because of you. You are like the brothers I never had.

Someone giggles in my ear. I turn around, but there's no one there. At that moment Meo tosses away his glass and starts scratching himself like mad.

What is that, he cries, ow, it itches terribly, bambola, look!

I pull up his shirt to reveal his back is covered in red pustules: Ouch. Nettles?

Meo rips off his shirt in horror.

Massimo rubs the powder residue on his gums and says: It is not without danger. I have heard of people who have approached black spirits. They have developed ulcers.

Help, shouts Meo, am I going to die?

Come off it, says Nicolò, go and take a shower.

Ice cold?

Why?

Don't I have to drive out the demon?

Nonsense, it's just a few mosquito bites.

Looks like more than a few. Thousands.

It itches so much!

Stop scratching and go and get under the shower.

Meo clings tightly to Nicolò's arm: Will you come with me? I'm scared.

You can go to my room, I offer.

Please, Nicolò.

Don't be like that.

I pat him on the cheek: We'll be waiting for you here.

Meo throws one last pleading look at Nicolò, then stomps dramatically out of the room.

We watch in silence as Massimo pours more blue powder onto the table. He makes four lines and then looks around nervously: Where's Angelo? With the snob?

Nicolò shakes his head.

Massimo stands up: What have I always told you? People like him don't stop at children.

Calm down, Uncle.

Angelo stands grinning in the doorway: Look what I found.

He holds up a gold-framed portrait. It shows an angry soldier with the face of a frog. Massimo salutes and starts singing, Nicolò hits him on the back of the head.

He takes the picture from Angelo's hand: Where did you get that?

Angelo beams: From the chapel. It's full of that stuff. Flags, badges, weapons, everything from that time. You have to see it!

*

Massimo and Angelo rummage through the boxes between the church pews. Nicolò and I stand in the broken-in doorway and watch them. Below the painted ceiling of the starry sky, the gaze of the suffering Jesus over the altar and the eternal smile of Sisina, they hoot and pull out old blackshirt uniforms and new machine guns.

Ah, calls Massimo, a dagger of honour!

Uh, a cross of merit!

What is that?

They unfurl a flag: Swastika, nice.

You can get a lot of money for that at the flea market. We can hawk it in the village, they'll snatch the stuff right out of our hands.

Are you crazy? Massimo puts on a steel helmet: I'm keeping it!

Do you think they'll notice if we take something?

Nicolò raises his voice: Put everything back exactly as you found it. They'll kill you if they notice you were in here.

Who? I ask.

Nobody answers.

Angelo opens another box and looks disappointed: Just paper.

I take a sheet of paper from his hand. A list of names, typed on a typewriter. *To be neutralised.*

Nicolò, I say quietly, what is this?

He glances at the papers and crouches down next to the box. He slowly combs through the documents with his long fingers, reads, shuffles. There are even more names, hundreds, *to neutralise.* Forms for death sentences. Yellowed leaflets announce Day X.

An indecipherable smile flashes across Nicolò's face: Boys, we've found the lodge's treasure!

Angelo cheers: Do you think there are gold bars buried in the garden?

Nicolò laughs: There could well be, very well in fact.

I become angry: You're happy to be in a Nazi weapons depot with old death lists? What is this, a nostalgic terrorist cell?

Nicolò shakes his head: You don't understand. These are remnants of the most famous secret lodge in Italy.

Angelo calls out excitedly: Nicolò knows everything about it!

Everything that can be known – he gives a dismissive wave of his hand – much is still in the dark.

Because it was secret, beams Angelo, right?

Nicolò begins his lecture: The lodge was founded after the Second World War. The most important men in the country were members: heads of the army, politics, the judiciary, the secret services. Generals, diplomats, bankers, industrialists, MPs, judges, prosecutors, Mafiosi . . . even the son of the last king. We still only know parts of the list of lodge members, there must have been hundreds. They met in secret locations, in villas in the countryside.

He puts his hand to his head and laughs in disbelief: In the village, there were always rumours that . . .

I pull a face: So all those parties that were held here after the war were actually secret fascist meetings?

Nicolò slowly shakes his head, pensively: Communism was very strong back then. Its rise had to be prevented—

Massimo interrupts: In order to rebuild fascism!

Nicolò clears his throat: The aim was to overthrow the system from within, a coup in several stages. The disappearance of all left-wing parties and the dissolution of the trade unions, as well as the undermining of the state media, while at the same time a private television system was being developed. Sounds familiar, doesn't it?

The former prime minister was one of them, calls out Angelo, his name was found on the list. Nicolò knows the membership number in his head—

1816. But above all of them was the venerable master, the powerful puppeteer who pulled the strings like a spider in his web. He was a genius. And a murderer: he had bombs planted, hundreds of people died. Years of terror—

Massimo interrupts him: Don't start all that again! Red propaganda – reading has melted your brain, repeating these lies.

Nicolò shakes his head: Nowadays we know that the puppet master and the lodge were behind the biggest terrorist attacks. The train station in Bologna—

Massimo groans: It was the Red Brigades, everyone knows that. It's proven and documented, what more do you want?

Nicolò waves a leaflet as if it were proof: He was a master at covering his tracks, at laying false trails! The public prosecutor took over the investigation and let it fizzle out. And the secret services had their fingers in it too, they were at his beck and call. They removed the real clues and laid false ones that pointed to the Red Brigades. To make them intolerable to society, how many times do I have to explain that to you?

Yes, yes, Massimo sing-songs, the Americans, right?

Yes, says Nicolò, them too. Secretly, everyone agreed that the communists must not prevail. After the strategy of tension and terror came the strategy of seizing power with the help of the mass media.

I raise my eyebrows: A conspiracy?

Nicolò beams: A real one. You can read about it.

I hold up a blank death warrant from the box: And what about this?

That was plan B, in case the communists won the elections despite everything. Then there would have been a military coup that would have set up a right-wing dictatorship. But it wasn't necessary. It all worked out.

Massimo lets out a whistle from the back of the room.

Mamma mia. Look at that.

Is that . . .

Explosives!

Angelo tries to reach into the box, but Massimo holds him back.

Careful. We'd better close it again. Very carefully. That's a proper amount. You could blow up ten train stations at once with that.

There's more here.

A piercing scream makes me jump. The cousins are busy with the boxes. The fact that Meo is screaming like mad doesn't seem to bother them.

*

Meo is lying naked on my bed, a pillow pressed over his face.

Disappointed, he lets it fall off: Oh, it's you.

332

Sorry, I say, insulted, and remain in the doorway, leaning my head against the frame. Meo turns to the side, groaning, pulls the blanket up to his stomach and grabs a bottle up from the floor. He takes a big swig and gargles. Then he holds the wine out to me, pats the mattress next to him and says: Come here, I've had a fright.

I put the bottle to my mouth, red wine. Now his spit is sticking to my lip.

Bambola, he says, look at that.

He pulls me onto the bed. We lie arm to arm, he is warm.

I was lying here, he says, daydreaming, when a sudden coldness trickled over me. I thought the draught was coming from the open door and that Nicolò had finally – But I was alone. And now look, up there . . .

He whispers: Bloody fingerprints.

Indeed. There are red spots above the headboard, fingertip-shaped, five in a semicircle. They weren't there before.

I take his hand and put it on my heart: Is it still beating?

I can't feel anything, he says, running his fingers over my chest.

Traces of blood, I whisper, again.

Meo taps my solar plexus with the palm of his hand: What do you mean, again?

I speak quickly: I was in the woods recently, in the enchanted one. And an owl grew out of a tree trunk. And a furious wind drove me home. And there was blood in the bathroom.

And you'd got your period – ow! No? Then you must have cut yourself shaving.

It wasn't my blood! I'm not even sure if it was really blood. It didn't taste like blood.

He snorts: You tried it?

Sure.

How?

I just dipped my finger in it.

He shakes his body: That's so you. When I think you can't be any more you, you say something like that.

I don't know whether I should laugh or not. Saying something like that seems somehow condescending; he doesn't even know me.

Meo brushes a strand of hair out of my face, I reach out towards the red spots on the wall and call out: Seriously! Don't you find that worrying? Red drops in the bathroom, then fingerprints on the wall?

He smiles crookedly: We should call the church and report this blood miracle.

What do you mean?

Images of saints crying blood; hosts with red mould; you know, blood miracles. My great-aunt would fall to her knees before these stains, she loves disgusting stuff like that. To her great annoyance, in today's church they are no longer in vogue. She claims she will not die until the priest reintroduces the feast of the bleeding Madonna.

Madonna del Sangue? The day Sisina died—

Meo acts the part of a screaming old woman: Our Madonnina

bled for us in the war, I saw it with my own eyes. It is not superstition; it is a miracle!

Blood miracle, I murmur, holy blood. Blood in the washbasin, blood on the wall. It must be a clue: Sisina is giving me a sign. That I am on the right track. Or is it a threat? I thought Sisina was a happy spirit. She jumps on beds and tickles people's feet. But bloodstains? And that's not all, strange things happen here all the time, there are flowers in the keyholes.

Someone wants to scare you.

Yes, but who? I have to sleep with the light on because someone chops wood at night, I'll soon go crazy.

Meo looks at me strangely: May I offend you?

No.

You already seem a little crazy.

No I don't!

You live in this run-down villa and seem to be more concerned with ghosts than with the living. You need to get out and about again. Look at yourself—

We look at ourselves in the mirror. A red-faced naked nobleman next to . . . me.

He nods with satisfaction: You are on the verge of neglect.

I quickly look away and squint my eyes so tightly that I can no longer see him. I lay my head on his shoulder and sulk. His skull is heavy and angular on mine, he rubs his ear against mine.

He giggles. And so am I.

He lights a cigarette and I see that he has Magdalena's lighter. I take it from his hand. Hey, he protests.

That's mine. I've been looking for it!

Yours?

He snatches it back from me and looks at it: I don't think so. I've had it for a while.

I get angry: Give it to me.

Don't make such a fuss, it's a cheap lighter.

He turns it to the highest setting and lets the flame flicker.

Dude, I say, stop wasting the gas. It's a memento, OK?

He looks at the picture of the stoned cat, then he gives me the middle finger, just like her.

I pounce on him.

It's mine, I scream, and before that it was my mother's! She's dead and has passed on her madness to me—

It feels so liberating to scream.

Meo shakes me as if I were an almost empty bottle of oil, and my words fall like droplets. My tongue feels strange, heavy like an ox tongue:

You can't tell anyone. My mother was murdered. Like Sisina. Because she wanted to be free and loudly proclaimed who she was. They resented her for that. I did too. She was unimpressed by what she was supposed to be; she wouldn't let herself be bent and belittled. She was fearless: we were all afraid of her. Her laughter stirred up storms and everything she touched went up in flames. I'm here to avenge her. To do that I have to become like her, at least a little. And I will free Sisina's spirit so that she no longer has to wear that ridiculous wedding dress, understand? They are the same, my mother and Sisina. Only they caught Sisina earlier, when she was still young and rosy.

Like putty in their hands, forever an object of desire, a childlike saint. That's why they love her, that's why she gets a monument. By killing Sisina, they saved her from becoming Magdalena. Nobody loves an old whore, understand? Even in death they feared her body, put it in the oven and burned the witch.

I get up and take the ashes out of my packed bag, hold them to my ear and listen solemnly: now she is quiet and fits inside a box.

Meo looks at me in shock.

Bambola, is all he can say.

I wave it off: She wasn't a particularly good mother. She was crazy.

But you know it's not true?

It is, it is.

I mean the thing with Sisina.

What are you talking about?

Well, the whole easy-girl story. It's just to pull the wool over everyone's eyes. It's old glue, and you stuck straight to it.

Me?

Do you want to hear the real story?

Meo looks at me meaningfully: She knew too much.

Sisina?

You know she worked here, don't you? As a maid, I think. And she probably went into the wrong room at the wrong time. She must have heard something that couldn't come out. So they silenced her.

I remember Igor hinted at something like that, but what exactly?

Meo swirls the rest of the wine in the bottle: The Italian aristocracy remained curiously rich after the war. They had the greatest interest in ensuring that communism did not take over. The rich always supported the blackshirts, especially in the countryside. And here, in mansions like this, they were planning the return of fascism: the great resurrection.

I grab his arm: The conspiracy! You know about it? Nicolò just told me. We found things, papers . . . You think Sisina burst in on the conspiracy?

Meo shrugs his shoulders meaningfully.

I imagine the scene: Sisina standing at the door to the drawing room with a serving tray, listening—

Then I shake my head: I've never heard that theory before. Where did you get it from?

Meo laughs: You know, my great-aunt is of noble birth. Her blood is as blue as an aquarium, and knowledge of the world's secrets flows through it. Especially those of her noble neighbours.

So you think the murder was for political reasons.

That's right.

But that would have nothing to do with all the talk about her being too beautiful and too promiscuous.

Of course not.

But everyone's still saying that to this day!

I jump up and get the whale notebook, leafing through it quickly.

Here, I call out, here it is: A guest from Villa C—— had to be driven in a mad rush to the train station in town on the day in question.

I wave the book in Meo's face in excitement: So it was someone from the villa after all! A small soldier in American military boots. Maybe it was even the officer Sisina was caught on the sofa with. Even if it was – that's not really the point. Except that she wouldn't have been afraid of him if he surprised her in the woods, because they knew each other. It could have happened that way!

Meo shrugs his shoulders. I slap the notebook against his forehead and say: But how can it be that there is absolutely nothing about your theory in here? I've studied the case, over sleepless nights – I don't know how many, I've lost track of time. How long have I been here? A few days? Weeks? Decades? You're right, I've gone crazy over Sisina! And now you come along with your inherited aquarium knowledge.

Meo raises his hands as if in apology: It's a dark chapter of history, still not properly dealt with. For falling into the orbit of plans for a coup like that, people fell out of windows by the dozen: alleged suicides, accidents, blatant murders. Drove into a tree, drowned in the bath, shot in the middle of the street. Never mind the victims of these attacks. How many of those deaths do you think were solved? It was all hushed up, erased and buried by the highest authorities.

I rub my face.

It all makes sense, I nod. Vito's lawyers – I always wondered where their interests lay. They were famous, political bigwigs, socialists – what did they care about a small farmer who was suspected of killing his fiancée? If, on the other hand, they suspected something political behind it . . . That everyone stayed silent also makes sense. The farmers were afraid – they lived by the favour of the landowner's family, their entire existence depended on them. And they showed what they were capable of – what happens when you stand in their way.

Meo wraps himself in the blanket, I pace back and forth: With a girl like Sisina, it was child's play. Say she was a slut – and the motive is there, a justified reason. Everyone is convinced, even the family; no one wants anything to do with the shame. Underwear gone, and it looks like a classic lust murder.

Sisina knew, I say slowly, that she had to die. She asked the fortune teller, who confirmed it. She must have been terribly afraid. She didn't want to go to the spring alone because she knew she was in danger. That's why she asked her friend if she would come with her. But she couldn't tell anyone anything, she swore to keep quiet. They slaughtered her anyway.

I suddenly have an epiphany. I shake Meo by the arm: Do you think she was a partisan?

He shakes me off, irritated: Who?

Sisina!

I see her before me: rifle slung over her shoulder, standing

340

on the road in the forest, over there, where her monument now stands, her fist raised. A group of peasant women surround her while she trumpets a fiery speech: To you, proletarian women!

Yes, I shout, perhaps she was a revolutionary, a trade unionist, an anti-fascist – and that is why she had to die. She wasn't just some housemaid who happened to be in the wrong place at the wrong time: she was a spy! She kissed the officer because she wanted to get information out of him. How did I not think of that earlier!

My right foot twitches involuntarily. It's as if the invisible cat is brushing up against my legs again. I sit completely frozen and whisper: Do you feel that too?

Meo bites into the pillow.

I think of the scene in the forest and shake him slightly: Earlier, when you heard the voices—

Meo takes the pillow off his face and looks at me. He's completely red.

There is no such thing as ghosts, he says, I just wanted to impress Nicolò.

Is that why you're naked in my bed?

What do you think?

That you're not stupid enough to want to seduce the handsome Nicolò.

Why else would I still be in this cursed backwater? I should have been back in the city ages ago. And you think it's hard to be obsessed with a ghost.

I shake my head: You really think he'll go with you? They're village fascists.

Exactly, Meo says, it couldn't be more homoerotic. You can see how he's tormenting me.

Poor rich nobleman.

He lays his head on my chest.

You have such silky hair, I say, why does everyone have silky hair except me?

Nicolò, he murmurs, Nicolò has silky hair.

I laugh. Then I press my fingertips on the red prints on the wall and say: There are a lot of explosives in the chapel.

Meo intertwines his fingers with mine: You're right, it's time to be sensible. My great-aunt is already so fed up with me that she's offered to transfer my inheritance early. Tomorrow morning I'm going back to town – and you're coming with me.

Me?

He sits up: Of course, what else are you going to do, stay here? I have an apartment with lots of spare rooms.

Relief spreads through me like a high, my head falls forward onto his chest.

He takes my face in his hands, kisses me between my eyebrows with pursed lips: Don't worry, tomorrow it will all be over. But first, let's have a few snacks, OK?

He jumps up and into his trousers. He smooths down his hair in front of the mirror, pinches his cheeks, pouts.

Does it really not bother you, I ask, that they are fascists?

Not in the slightest: I see this as an anti-fascist campaign.

When we're done with them, they hopefully won't be fascists anymore.

What are you going to do, tie him up and drive il Duce out of him?

We have one night to broaden their perspectives— Meo laughs: And if not, then at least I'll have fun while doing it.

What do you think, I ask, the little angel is too young, isn't he?

Angelo? – Meo puts his hand over his mouth – Can I watch?

He quickly kisses me on the lips. Then he rips open the door and shouts into the hallway: PANTS OFF!

*

We storm the drawing room.

Il Duce is sitting on the mantelpiece in front of the mirror, I turn him on his head. Then I drop onto the sofa next to Angelo and whisper: Sisina made out with a soldier here.

He bares his snow-white teeth: What have you been up to?

Getting hammered, I laugh, looking at Meo, who is pulling Nicolò towards him by his belt.

He breaks free and turns the picture the right way round.

Like a snake, shouts Meo, you are as agile as a snake!

Massimo snorts and chews his tongue, he wants to say something, but nothing comes out.

Nicolò raises his glass in the air: We wanted to celebrate the seance and that Sisina kissed me. Poor Sisina.

Meo pulls him close and kisses his cheek: Was it like this?

Nicolò giggles.

Or like this?

He bites his neck.

No, laughs Nicolò, not like that.

Then she doesn't know how to do it, says Meo, latching on.

Nicolò squirms away and licks his fingers, takes another blue line.

Meo raises a glass and exclaims: O faithful pelican, make me, the impure one, pure with your blood! A drop of it can heal the whole world of its crimes. Please make what I so thirst for happen.

Nicolò stumbles out into the garden, Meo follows him.

Leave him alone, Massimo calls after them.

Then he sizes us up over on the sofa of sin: And you? My nephew is underage, you know that.

That's not true, argues Angelo, I'm almost seventeen, I mean eighteen.

Massimo curses and runs his finger over the empty plate: My only problem is that we've run out.

He fills his glass to the brim and drinks it down, grabs the car keys from the table: I'll go and get more. Otherwise it'll be unbearable with you lot.

We stay lying there and hear the tyres spinning on the gravel. In my head, the car hits a tree, Massimo crashes through the windshield, flying in a high arc into the fountain. Angelo gasps in my ear. When I close my eyes, everything is spinning. Sisina and Magdalena spin between the boxes in the chapel, the armed women from the salami factory, Sorella – I hear my bones grinding, a rage scrabbles inside me. I grab Angelo by his tender neck and press his head between my legs.

XIV

Now everything is golden, and I'm ploughing through it. The morning sun drips onto the hills like liquid honey, the olive groves steam with dew. My steps rake through the steep gravel path, my thoughts fly a few metres ahead, get tangled in the branches, plunge into the depths, slash themselves open on the rocky outcrop – my head stays on, my body is pleasantly heavy from the sleepless night, the trembling of the angel still on my skin; the stellar constellation of his teeth fades with the waking of the cicadas.

One sentence sets the pace of my march: I'll show you I'll show you I'll – I don't know who or what, but I'll show you.

I'll show you, I say it out loud to myself, until I come to a stop: I've been here before.

The first few roofs of the abandoned village. I'm on the move again, I'll show you. The church comes into view, boarded up, opposite the small cemetery, a war memorial: faded banners, bleached plastic flowers, I'll show you. The cemetery gate is sealed with a rusty lock. Through the bars I can see the grass growing between the stone slabs, dry flowers wave at me, I'll show you. I'm looking for my grandmother's grave, what am I thinking? Dai Nonna, what a view you would have had here.

Look at the light on the hills, how can anyone stand it? And can you see the fig tree, so heavy with fruit, wrapped in barbed wire? Someone doesn't want to share. I'll show you! I stretch, pluck the little warm bodies, fig skin as soft as Angelo's, sticky milk, sickly sweet.

The tree giggles, a shimmer in the fig leaves. Owl, snicker, a tickle on my neck. I choke, cough. Sisina is sitting in the fig tree.

She swings her legs, translucent and fluorescent.
    Got you, she exclaims triumphantly.
    Sorry?
    Did you think I would forget-forgive?
    Me?
    You thought wrong!
    I look around to see if there are any other glowing figures behind me.
    I think you have me confused with someone else, Signora.

I don't know why I'm suddenly addressing Sisina formally. This whole time I thought I knew her, was close to her, as if she were a guardian angel who could see everything and is always with me, but no, she's a confused madwoman.

Her face darkens and she begins to scold me: Aren't you ashamed? Running through the morning all sticky-puffy. Chasing an engaged man? Well, did you have a good time getting lost together?

Who?

Oh, don't even try that! I know everyone is chasing after my poor Vito.

I have to laugh: Vito? You think I was with Vito? He's been dead a long time.

She looks at me carefully, her eyes narrowed.

Hmm, she says, strange! I seem to jump through time. One minute I'm at my funeral and someone's saying: *Shall we go grab a beer*? And then I'm standing by Vito's coffin and scaring people, icy hands around their neck and so on. He's grown old, Madonna, he's grown old. I'll never grow old, nobody can take that away from me. Have you seen his wife? A proper rag, always lukewarm, thin as gruel, doesn't suit my Vito at all, he needed a carpet beater. A little prison time and all the trollops were throwing themselves at him. Threw flowers at him like he was a racing driver. And what does he do? Brings the flowers from his admirers to his dead fiancée. Impious if you ask me. But nobody asked me.

Sisina tosses her hair and her head swings backwards, her neck opens, a gaping, gurgling cut. I stumble backwards.

Laughing, she flicks her head back in place.

If you only knew, she giggles. That hurt. Luckily, I'm in a good mood today. If you only knew what I'm capable of when I get worked up . . . You're on my turf here, girl, just be careful.

She rustles a branch until a fig bursts open on my head.

The plants, the stones, the animals in the forest, they all obey me. After I died, I couldn't talk to anyone, so I whispered to the trees. I told jokes to the cliffs, tickled them until they couldn't bear it anymore: they collapsed with laughter. The stupid bigots ran screaming out of their houses. They deserved nothing else, the poor things. What could I do, I was beside myself. Today I regret that they left – even in the cemetery, everyone either ascended and went or stayed lying down, no one is as restless as I am. At least no one I want to spend time with. Damned little souls, there's no helping them.

And you?

Me? I don't need anything.

Don't you think you could rest if you told me who it was?

Some poor wretch, what difference does it make? I can't sleep.

And why not?

Because my heart is racing. Because I can't breathe in this stuffy coffin.

You still want to breathe?

You are the meanest person I have ever met.

If you tell me who it was, I'll tell everyone.

And what good will that do?

What about justice?

Sisina throws herself backwards, dangles from the branch by her knees and falls to the ground laughing, where she crumples like a sheet.

I shout: The dead are wrong if no one defends them after their death!

Sisina stands up and floats radiantly before me: Look at me.

349

I'm famous. Young and beautiful, forever. What more could a girl want?

But that's not your story!

My story? What would that have been? Even more toil, having children? I wouldn't have a story without the cut across my throat. It is the only thing profound about my story.

That's not true, I say sadly. You still had your life ahead of you.

Sisina's eyes sparkle: My life! What do you know about it? What happened to me before the knife? I can't sleep because of my life, do you understand, not because of my death. The dying, the drama, the tears, the lies, it is all a joke! That is not my story.

Tell it to me.

Who are you talking to?

I turn around: Lorenzo!

He grabs my arm: What are you doing here?

I mumble: I've been looking for the murderer and I've found him everywhere.

I've been looking for you everywhere. Get in right now. The Coach is coming!

I drop the figs in shock, tear my hand open on the barbed wire. I pick up the fruit, suck on my bleeding hand and stick a fig between my lips. Good combination. I climb up the slope, look back: Sisina has dissolved.

*

Lorenzo is ranting at me and I don't care: Disappearing without a trace! He presses down on the accelerator so that the tyres spin on the loose soil of the dirt road. This is how we careen towards the villa, gravel spraying, Lorenzo sneering all the way. He saved me and this is how I thank him; the villa is a mess; I'm a good-for-nothing slut, etc, etc.

I don't listen to him at all. I watch a figure walk in front of the car, barefoot, with real black hair, a water jug on her head. She stumbles, sprains her ankle, continually looking around. Her face is tense, forehead furrowed, black in the bright light. She's wearing a necklace of red glass beads around her neck. She looks familiar somehow.

She is limping, I want to tell Lorenzo to brake, but he runs her over.

Now I see her in the rearview mirror, she wipes the dust off her shirt and walks more firmly, briskly, the jug stiffly on her head.

She comes closer, moves as if she were waving. She's walking next to us now, in front of my window, she turns her head and looks me straight in the face. I start: the picture next to my grandmother's bed – her mother! Died in childbirth, died while fetching water . . . She does not look away, her face is stern, and the line between her eyes deepens, a crack in a rock – don't worry, I want to say, nothing will happen to me.

She raises her eyebrows and the jug—

Yes, I call to her, the well! All my childhood I dreamed of a well, a well I fall into, I'm sitting in a bucket and falling

– why? What does it mean?

She looks worried now, looks behind her again, as if she were being followed. She hunches over, struggles to keep up with the car, she falls away. In the rearview mirror I see that she is pregnant, watermelon pregnant. She drops the jug in the dust and presses her hands to her back, red pearls burst from her neck and ping in all directions. She watches after us as we drive through the gate into the courtyard of the villa.

*

Lorenzo chases me into the house, the remains of last night in the drawing room. All of this has to go, he shouts, before the Coach arrives. How could you have caused so much chaos in such a short amount of time? He waves frantically, spills the full ashtray, knocks over a vase of wildflowers that Meo had picked for Nicolò. He collects a few empty bottles in a panic, trips over something that could be Angelo's underpants.

Calm down, I say, that's exactly how they left it. I've spent the last few days cleaning up their mess. Now it's their turn.

Please, says Lorenzo, pressing his hands together in despair, they'll be here any minute.

I take pity on him and run my palm over the table, sweeping crumbs onto the floor and wiping up the water from the vase using the hem of the nightshirt: Satisfied?

He opens his mouth, I speak over him: Do you even know what kind of pigs they are? I'm not going to clean this Nazi lair for another second.

I shake my head: What am I saying, of course you know. Are

you one of them? You carried boxes into the chapel too—

You were all in the chapel?

I look at him, his stunned face: I have no pity for you anymore. What on earth did I see in you? Ciao, Lorenzo.

He looks astonished: Where are you going?

Into town, with Meo. I'll get my things, then I'll be gone.

Mimma, he says almost with caution, there is no one here.

He must have gone to pack, then he'll come and get me. Don't try to stop me—

You don't understand, he says, it's too late.

His eyes widen; a car drives into the courtyard. Lorenzo shakes his head sadly: This wasn't the plan. You should have been here when I got home, I have to tell you—

Doors slam, footsteps can already be heard in the hallway. Lorenzo twists his head, rushes to the fireplace, where il Duce is sitting in the frame with a crown of penises: Meo's scribbles. In his haste, Lorenzo throws the picture to the floor – right at that moment a small man appears, his arm shoots forward and catches the falling picture. He strokes the glass before gently placing the frame on the table.

Had a little party, did we?

He smiles, but his eyes are like wells.

Coach, says Lorenzo, but the man doesn't pay any attention to him.

The Coach only has eyes for me. He comes slowly towards me,

I try to hold his gaze. Prepare myself for battle. The gun! I have to get the gun right now. My heart is pounding so hard it's as if I'm about to cough it up. The Coach stops right in front of me; I can smell his liquorice breath and his cologne. His skin shines with melting foundation. It's him, I know it. If he attacks me, I'll pounce at his throat like an animal. I'm strong. Stronger than him. Our eyes are level, his are filling with tears. He spreads his arms and in that moment I know what's going to happen. It's like a film that I've played over and over in my memory, like a nightmare, becoming unbearable—

He extends his fingers and grips each of my cheeks between his two claws. Pinches and twists the flesh as if he wanted to tear it off. My lip splits, I taste blood, his face comes closer. His lips smash against mine. He lets go of my cheeks, wraps his arms around me, I feel his belt buckle against my stomach, his nose on my neck . . . Can he smell Magdalena? She gave me her cells, I am made of her—

Sweet little Filuccia, he murmurs in my ear, finally we see each other again.

He grabs the back of my head, squeezes, digs his fingers into my hair. My ears start ringing. He strokes my cheek, I feel the long nail on his little finger without seeing it, and I hear my grandmother's voice: *Do you know what it means when a man has a long little fingernail? It means he's a pimp. And what do you do when a pimp speaks to you?* – I shout *aiuto*?

The Coach shoves me away from him as if I had spoken out loud. Then he laughs and calls out: Auguri! Babbo's here!

I open my mouth, nothing comes out. He's having a whale of a time, clapping his hands: Surprise!

I don't understand, Signore, I finally stammer, you think—

Stop being so formal, the Coach smiles, it's bad manners to be formal with a man, anyway, do I look like a Sir?

His smile freezes, he throws a hand out at the room: What kind of reception is this anyway? You were badly brought up, Lorenzo was right.

Lorenzo. He's standing with his back to the table, his head hanging. I feel dizzy. He betrayed me? The hands on my shoulders burn into my skin. I close my eyes. The Coach shakes me: Tired? Now is not the time to rest. You've got a lot of work ahead of you. The gentlemen are coming tomorrow, everything has to be gleaming. That goes for you too, looked in a mirror lately? Aren't you ashamed of facing your father like this? Get dressed and comb your hair. And Lorenzo – I have arranged a meeting with the officer. Before the official dinner, you will have soup with him. I've explained to him that you're not a deserter, that you were acting in my interest. He's not happy, expect consequences. But he knows that I need you. The soup will sort it out.

Thank you, Father.

Lorenzo puts his arms around him, the Coach kisses him on the mouth too.

They break away, Lorenzo lowers his eyes, the Coach says loudly: Now clean up this pigsty. I'm going to lie down for a while.

The Coach turns around and calls into the hallway: Sorella, go and see if my room is habitable at least. Lorenzo will show you the way, upstairs, in the tower.

Something stirs in the dark hallway. My breath stops. I blink. Sorella? She steps out of the shadows, her eyes lowered. It's her! She's alive! My ears start to burn, but she shakes her head imperceptibly.

The Coach follows our gazes: Of course, you already know each other. Sorella told me everything about your touching search. The Coach is not easy to reach, is he? But you did it, here I am! We're going to have a lot of fun together.

I stumble, he kisses me, his clean-shaven cheek brushes mine. He jerks his head at Lorenzo, who follows him like a dog. I hear Sorella whispering in the hallway. They close the door behind them. I sink to the floor. In the mirror, Sisina sits and laughs at me.

*

In my room, on the rumpled bed, there is a note from Meo.

Bambola, where are you? MISSION ACCOMPLISHED. Nicolò's driving me to the station. Take care <3

I crumple up the paper and fall onto the bed. I can still smell his strong perfume. Idiot. Where did he go? Why didn't he take me with him? Where was I when he left? I remember Angelo snoring softly; how I felt sick and went into the garden, the sun was coming up. And then suddenly I was in the car with Lorenzo. Between those points, everything is blank.

The gun! I jump up, shake the urn, a familiar rumble. I take the lid off, reach in. Ashes sail to the floor, to my feet. But all I have in my hand is a large stone. Damn Lorenzo. Exhausted sobs. My eyes remain dry. I sink to my knees. My naivety crashes over me and sweeps me away like a strong wave. I'm suffocating with shame. How could I have been so stupid? Lorenzo saw through me right from the start. He would have read Magdalena's name on the urn in the bar at the very least and put two and two together. In the car, while I was unconscious, he checked my identification. That's how it happened. He always knew who I was. He let me believe my fantasy, in the safety of his own gun. Maybe it was all part of the plan – whose plan? Maybe he followed me to the salami factory. Or it was a coincidence that we were both there, and Lorenzo took advantage of the moment to endear himself to the Coach. His voice booms in my ear: *I wanted to tell you . . . The Coach is like a father to me . . .*

I gag. Last night comes back to me all at once: the wine, the forest, the boys and the weapons; my panting. Blood-red bile. I can't even think about whether Sorella betrayed me too. I have to keep a clear mind, concentrate, but on what? I'm so close, I'm almost at the finish line. I just have to go through with it, but how? Mamma? Can you hear me? I'm doing it for you. For you!

With quivering fingers I scoop up the ashes from the floor, collect them in the palm of my hand.

Now would be the moment, I murmur, when you appear and say: Don't feel obligated, I haven't done anything for you after all. Or: Don't make a fool of yourself, you don't have to take revenge for me, I'll do it myself. I dance on his balls every night and breathe hell's breath into him.

But she doesn't come. The pieces of bone lie still and silent in my hand. He annihilated her. So I have to find a sword, seduce him, intoxicate him, cut off his head. I imagine it will be difficult. On account of the tendons. After that, I'll never be able to sleep again because he'll be rolling around and moaning next to me without a head.

I don't want this, I murmur, I'm getting out of here, straight through the forest, screw justice, it's not worth it.

Ashes trickle into the urn, a film of ash sticks to my skin, I brush it off. Maybe it will be easier than I think: sneak into his room and smother him with a pillow. But will that be enough? Doesn't revenge, the erasure of shame, also require danger? Won't I lose my pride otherwise? I could slit him open with a kitchen knife, like Sisina. I could run him over with the SUV, Lorenzo too. No, forget Lorenzo, miserable traitor, this is about the Coach.

I want to see him gasping for breath, I want him to whimper, and I want to watch the light in his eyes go out. The last thing he should hear is my voice: This is for Magdalena. She wasn't alone. And she will never belong to you—

Ah, I can't even give a speech. How am I supposed to kill someone? And won't I be like him then? He claims to be my father. Does that change things? What does he want from me? Am I in his trap or is he in mine?

Silly bambola, I hear my grandmother say, what do you do when the wolf comes? Run as fast as you can.

*

Brava, praises the Coach, toasting me: To my educated daughter! Beautiful and clever, you got all that from me, haha! Don't you believe me? Actually, you're right, knowing your mother, pretty much anyone could be your father, right? But believe me, she wasn't always like that. When I met her, she was a good girl.

We're sitting in the drawing room around the dining table. The Coach eats ham and melon with gusto like Tony Soprano. I have often been told that I eat like that. I watch him, fascinated. Stare at his hands. How they shine with fat, how juice drips off them, how he licks them. His fingers are smooth and rosy, they show no signs of combat. Shouldn't there be? If it was him. Or has too much time passed?

The hammy fingers pat my cheek: Ah, little Filuccia, you look like you did back then. Do you remember? You had barely learned to walk when you hit your chin.

I instinctively touch my chin, the scar.

His smile freezes: What were you then, a year old? Of course you can't remember. Your mother, *disgraziata*, tore us apart. She kept me away from you, hid you.

Memories burst open like clouds. The Coach's voice booms through the blazing emptiness: Her death is sad, but there's also an upside – we've found each other again. And I thought I had lost you forever. We have these two to thank for that.

The Coach opens his arms, Lorenzo lowers his gaze, and Sorella smiles past me. He pats her hand: The best horse in my stable, isn't she? She's taken over your mother's role, and she's doing a great job.

Sorella smiles, but she avoids my gaze.

Lorenzo told me you call yourself Mimma? That's what your grandmother called you, isn't it? Shame she's fertilising the potatoes now, I always liked her. She's taught you nice Italian, a bit old-fashioned, but good . . . You can communicate, that's the most important thing.

He wants me close to him, he says, he wants to catch up on everything. But he mostly speaks to Lorenzo, asks about the hunting equipment, the animal delivery, the meal plan for the coming days. Lots of people are coming. They talk quietly, the Coach asks questions, and Lorenzo confirms.

I notice Sorella listening, even if she's staring into space as if lost in thought. She's afraid of him, otherwise she wouldn't be behaving the way she is. Or would she? I'm silent, smiling, don't have a plan.

If it was him. If it really was him. Nobody has said directly that it was him. Like he says: it could have been pretty much anyone. Does he really look like a murderer? I imagine how he looked when he was young and kidnapped Magdalena in the convertible, her laughing. *Short and bald*, that's how she described him. What does a murderer look like?

He has a captivating manner. I don't like it, I want to please him. He claims to have known my grandmother, to have liked her. Why did he say that? When did they meet, where was I then? Why don't I know anything?

My head is buzzing, I'm dizzy. Maybe it's all wrong. Maybe Magdalena paid the doctor who called me to lie. So that I wouldn't judge her for drinking herself to death. So that I would pity her, in death. She's capable of anything.

She giggles in my ear: Maybe it was like that . . . maybe it was like this . . .

I get angry: When are you finally going to stop messing with me?

And when will you stop caring about what I thought? When will you stop feeling sorry for yourself? Boohoo, poor me, I never knew my mother.

I shake her off: Why am I trying to fool myself? Am I so

desperate that I'll even acknowledge this . . . this pimp as my father? Practise my Italian with him, elicit his 'brava'? As if we haven't all fallen on our chins at some point in our lives.

The Coach laughs. I have a blunt knife in my hand, but a fork could do it. Firmly in the eye, really deep, so that it goes into his brain. I would have to be quick, there's only one chance. Lorenzo would stop me, he's a soldier, trained in combat.

As the Coach cracks his knuckles and lights a cigarillo, I ask if I can clear the table. Lorenzo nods. He tries to hold my gaze, putting something like gratitude into his own. Sorella ignores me.

I tap her on the shoulder: Can you help me in the kitchen?

No, she says, without looking up.

The Coach reaches across the table and pinches her cheek: Come on now, don't be like that. Show your best side, future stepmother.

Sorella follows me into the kitchen. I grab her arm and whisper: Stepmother? Are you crazy?

She tears herself away: You can't say anything to me, traitor.

Me?

Her eyes flicker: I woke up alone after the battle. The rocket was gone, you were gone. They captured me, the Coach got me out.

I hiss: And now you want to marry him?

She leans forward and hisses: You stay out of it, Miss Normal

Life. You despised your mother for what she did, and naturally you despise me too. But let me tell you something – you're
wrong.

I laugh in disbelief: What is this, a game?

Sorella pulls me through the hallway to the back door and out
into the open. The moon peeks out from behind a cloud. The
crickets fall silent.

She pushes me hard against the wall: You ran away. With
a soldier! A fascist! We were right beating you up, we just
shouldn't have stopped.

Ow, I shout, are you nuts? I didn't run away, Lorenzo kidnapped me, I woke up unconscious in his car.

Then why are you still here? Do you have chains on your
ankles?

I don't say anything.

What can I say? That I was waiting for the Coach, that I want
to kill him? That I had a gun and now I don't? That I thought
about her every day and despised myself because she was right?
That I have no idea what I'm doing here, that for reasons that
are unclear to me I went with Lorenzo instead of going back
and looking for her? That I gave up on her like I gave up on my
mother – long before she was killed?

Sorella lets go of me: How could we have fallen for you?
What are you? Who do you work for?

I laugh, perplexed. Then I put my arms around her and smell
her neck. Tears come to my eyes: I thought you were dead!

She releases my hands and takes a step back: I am.

She doesn't look back and closes the door behind her. The crickets start back up, as if at the push of a button.

XV

I sleep badly that night. Faces float above and circle mine, slide over one another, merge together, drift past each other: Sorella, Lorenzo, the Coach . . . I try to hold on to them, to hold them in position: What do you want from me? – They laugh, they kiss, all together; Angelo, Meo, Nicolò, Massimo, voices; choppy, the noise of the ghost box. The owl at the window, eyes glowing red. It flaps its wings, shakes its head, taps on the windowpane, a scream—

I wake up with a jolt. I sit bolt upright in bed. My fingers roll and unroll the edge of the covers. Moonlight on the sheets, the fabric rough between my fingers. What am I doing? Lie down again. Silence, everyone is asleep. The owl calls outside the window. I'm already sitting up again and rolling back the covers, faster. The blanket slips off my feet, my legs jerk – Sisina giggles, she sits on the edge of the bed and tickles the soles of my feet.

Stop it!

She pulls a face: I'm so bored.

She's rocking the urn on her legs.

Give it here, I shout, what are you doing?

Sisina opens the container with a pop. She trickles Magdalena's bone pieces through her fingers with curiosity.

Stop that!

Offended, she drops the urn and crawls into the fireplace.

I get up and go into the bathroom. I pull on my tangled hair in front of the mirror. Meo was right, I say, and call: Sisina!

She's sitting on the toilet lid.

Can you cut hair?

Now I'm sitting on the toilet. Sisina pulls and tugs at my hair from all sides.

Twine witch, she complains, what kind of chaos is this?

I'm going through a weird time at the moment.

Do you know who you're talking to? Look: my hair is falling out, I have become so thin.

Because of Vito?

You think about him day and night, I suppose? I should leave this felt on your head, so at least you won't be competing with me.

Don't worry, I don't want him.

Everyone wants my Vito, he's a hero.

And I thought everyone wanted you.

Sisina bursts into loud laughter and snips at the air with her scissors: They followed me like flies!

She cuts, humming, locks of hair tumble down, I'm getting lighter and lighter.

Sisina, I ask, who were you with in the woods back then?

I don't want to talk about it, she says, it makes me sad.

She sings and the melody seems strangely familiar to me: *Praise, tongue, the secret of the glorified body and the precious blood.*

They found blood, I say, on Vito's trousers.

Sisina clamps my ear between the blades of the scissors and says threateningly: Maybe he cut himself and it was his blood.

I pull my head away: You just don't want it to be him, do you?

Bah, she says, blows a raspberry in my ear and disappears.

I've annoyed her.

The singing is now coming from the room. Sisina is sitting on the mantelpiece, dangling her legs: *What the eye cannot see, the mind cannot understand, firm faith sees.*

Ah, I call out, now I recognise the song: That's the toast that Meo sang.

Sisina snorts: Toast! These are highly religious songs. I sang this one when I was walking through the forest to lose myself.

Who did you want to . . . lose yourself with?

Sisina jumps down from the fireplace and whirls around me singing: *Whoever approaches him full of desire may receive him unharmed, undiminished, wonderful.*

What about the footprints, I say, size 40.

Vito had gigantic feet, she says and giggles: You know what that means.

Sisina is now lying on her stomach on the bed and leafing through the whale book. Look at my father, poor little shrunken head.

Yes, I say carefully, hard to believe that he—

My mother was strong.

With big feet?

Sisina nods meaningfully.

But it's your mother!

And? Was your mother a saint?

I shake my head: Parents are only that evil in fairy tales.

Ma va! Is my story not a fairy tale? The beautiful girl alone in the forest, the rich count, the poor parents . . . Have you ever thought about the evil stepsister? It's always the evil stepsister!

Your half-sister?

Sisina snorts: But my fairy tale doesn't end with *lived happily ever after*. Never mind, at least it is full of morals!

What morals?

Sisina yawns and rolls her eyes. Then she flashes the scissors across my forehead and a handful of hair falls onto the mattress.

Done!

And how do I look?

Sisina threatens me with the scissors: You *do* want to seduce my Vito!

Ma va! I'm only thinking of one man: Coach Holofernes.

She shrugs her shoulders: Fine by me, I don't know him.

Just watch, I say, I'm going to rip out his heart.

*

There is a long butcher's knife in the kitchen. It stabs melons and chops, cuts everything into little pieces. It's nice and sharp. I stuff sausage and cheese into myself, chew grapes and plums violently and with pleasure, like the Coach, and Sisina howls: *The poor and humble servant eats the master.*

I poke her with the knife to make her stop singing.

What's that about? she calls out indignantly.

Be quiet, I have to concentrate. Up in the tower, the man who killed my mother is sleeping.

Pig.

Finally! You're the first person to react that way.

The pig should be stabbed.

Right?

Absolutely.

Thank you! Will you come with me?

Of course. I want to see him squirt.

We giggle.

I look at myself in the reflective pane of the window.

Look at me, I am Judith, seductive and strong.

Who is Judith?

Well, Judith, I say, is a Jewish widow of considerable charm! She gets the murderous Holofernes drunk and takes his severed head for a walk.

Hmm, says Sisina, rubbing her neck.

I fidget with excitement: See, my hands are all warm. I'm going to – patiently and with a good amount of pressure – saw through his sinewy neck sausage.

Sisina shakes herself, then calls out: Yes, do it!

I feel so light, so happy. It's nice to finally be free of fear. In my dreams I can kill and die as I want.

Sisina opens her eyes wide: But this is not a dream.

Of course it is, otherwise you wouldn't be here.

What do you mean?

Well, you . . . You're dead, after all.

Sisina punches me in the arm: You're so rude! And stupid. And I thought we were friends.

Really?

Sisina sulks, I suppress a laugh: I'm sorry. Of course I'm your friend.

No, she gripes, you're a coward. Do you know how many people back then claimed that they would avenge my death? You're like them, big talk, nothing behind it.

No, I say, I really want to. I have to do it, for my mother. And for you, if you like.

What have I got to do with that pile of dust?

You were both murdered.

It's so nice, the way you've reduced us like that.

I'm sorry.

Sisina twists the corners of her mouth: So it's just about your mother, your guilt? I thought you were concerned about me. Then she tilts her head and smiles sweetly: But it's nice that you want to do it for me too. Will you really?

My heart is pounding, I can't let it show, I nod firmly: Yes. And you're going to help me. You've got to grab onto him and push him down, and I'll saw off his head.

She throws her hands in the air: Oh, if only I could! What I would give to stab a knife into a stomach.

She waves an imaginary sword: Take that! And that! Ah! Die!

Why can't you?

Sisina lets her arms fall: I have no strength. Don't you understand? The spirit world is here in the same place as the physical world. All of you who are alive are also in the spirit world but you don't feel it. And we don't have a body, we can't do anything. But sometimes we do find someone we can bond with. Someone like you!

Why me?

You're sleepwalking.

That's never happened to me before.

Are you sure?

I shrug my shoulders.

I can tell from all the empty bottles under your bed, you drink quite considerably. That makes it even stronger.

What are you talking about?

Your magnetic field is on fire.

That's what K2 said too.

Sisina purses her lips and lectures me, affectedly: If the light-body of the soul swells so much that it becomes more powerful than necessary, it can happen that the soul drifts into the spirit realm, where it comes into contact with those located there.

I laugh: What are you talking about so pompously?

Theory of spirit studies! Your soul has left your body with the will to find me. You feel light, because you no longer feel anything from the world of the senses.

I like it. Is this what it will be like when I die?

Sisina nods: I liked it too. And do you know what the best thing is? The celebrations in the realm of the dead! It's like every day's a wine festival. Do you want to come?

Sounds good, I say. Do I have to be dead for that?

She raises her hands as if in apology: Yes, you do. But I swear, it's worth it. You've got to see these guys – each one more delicious than the last.

Pomade guys?

Lots of them!

Tempting. But first I have to avenge my mother.

Sisina cheers: Let's do it! Up into the tower, assassinate the murderer. And then we'll jump straight into a party. They'll all lose their minds if I show up with you.

*

We sneak up the stairs to the tower. Sisina seems to be shivering. She approaches the door but recoils like a cat that has seen a ghost.

I flick her. What are you doing, I whisper, what's wrong with you?

Sisina presses her ear to the wood and puts her finger to her lips. Then she staggers back: the door opens. Sorella in her dressing gown.

Fila, she whispers, what are you doing here? What are you doing with that spoon?

What spoon, I laugh, it's a butcher's knife. Let me in, I'll seduce him and spoon out his eyes.

You're insane, hisses Sorella, do you want to get us all killed?

A voice sounds from the room: What's going on?

Nothing, calls Sorella in a low voice, it's just Filippa. She's lost.

Sorella waves her arms, trying to scare me away, but I keep her away from me with the knife: I'll free you.

Heavy steps, then the Coach is standing in the doorway. He looks at us in surprise. I immediately hide the knife behind my back and wrap my free arm around him. He's wearing a vest that accentuates his stomach. I press my forehead against his stubbled chest and rub myself against his boxer shorts.

Sorella pulls me away and shakes me. I can't focus on her face. The Coach looks amused: What's wrong with her?

Sorella waves her hands in front of my eyes: I think she's sleeping. Look, she's sleepwalking.

The Coach nods: She gets that from me. Take her back to bed. She needs to be tied down. So she doesn't hurt herself.

Lorenzo bumps into us on the stairs.

What happened in the kitchen? he whispers. I woke up from the noise, what's all this chaos?

My tongue is very heavy as I say: We treated ourselves to a little snack, me and my friend.

Lorenzo eyes me suspiciously: Why are you talking so strangely? What happened to your hair?

Sisina grimaces and snips through the air with her fingers. I snort.

373

Lorenzo grabs my arm: Are you drunk?

Sorella hisses: Don't touch her. She's sleepwalking.

Really? Lorenzo looks at me closely: It looks kind of creepy.

Sorella nods: The Coach thinks we should tie her up to be safe.

Are you crazy, says Lorenzo, what do you want us to do, handcuff her?

What else can we do? She doesn't know what she's doing.

I'll look after her.

You?

I let the traitors discuss things, pull Sisina into a corner and whisper: Damn! What are we going to do now?

Sisina keeps looking at Lorenzo, twirling her hair: What do you mean?

Well, about the Coach! That didn't work at all. He didn't even get a scratch.

Sisina shrugs: It was a stupid plan anyway.

And you're only saying that now?

She raises her shoulders innocently: We can still go to the party.

Maybe you're right, I mutter. Fuck the Coach, have you seen him? Being a guy like that is punishment enough. Let's go, nothing's keeping me here. I want to celebrate with my friend Sisina and some ghost pomade boys.

Sisina cheers and pulls me up: Come on, let's jump in. Straight into the fun!

Lorenzo seems to have won. Sorella stops on the stairs and looks after us worriedly – the bigot – while he manoeuvres me down the steps.

He keeps stopping in front of me: Now, stop staring, it doesn't suit you at all.

My vision's blurry, I mutter, I can't really see at all.

He sounds worried: Mimma, are you OK?

I can't see anything. Where's the balcony, boy, where's the balcony again?

What do you want to do on the balcony?

I'm going to the spirit world.

What?

There's a party, I'm going with Sisina. If you really want to, you can come with me, even if you're a boy and a soldier and a fascist and a miserable traitor. But only if you promise to change. Completely, from the ground up, understand? Character transplant. And you have to jump too.

All right, says Lorenzo, I'll accompany you to the balcony and I'll think about it on the way, OK? Come on, take my arm, this way, and don't fall now, we'll go really slowly.

Sisina sits on the edge of the bed as Lorenzo covers me up.

You stupid nut, she says, the boy has wrapped you up. You wanted to come with me.

You're here, I murmur, you're really here.

Yes, says Lorenzo, stroking the top of my head very lightly, I'm here.

I'm not talking to you, I whisper.

But Sisina has disappeared.

*

I walk through the forest and find her at the well, a man is next to her, I push him into the shaft. She watches him fall, jerking her head like a dove: Oh great. Thanks for nothing.

She disappears into the rustling of the trees. The man climbs out of the well, he is my father. He hugs me and stabs me. I die and cry: Promise you'll miss me.

He cries too and tries to shake me back to life.

The well spits me out, I open my eyes. Sorella takes her hands from my shoulders.

You saved me, I sigh, that means you still love me.

Sorella remains serious: Have you been sleepwalking for a long time?

I smile angelically: The legacy of my loving father.

I close my eyes, fall back into the dream: My father killed me.

Sorella grabs me hard by the chin: Wake up! Shit, Fila, we don't have time for your fantasies. What you did – you have to stop, Fila, otherwise you'll get us all killed.

She lets her eyes wander around the room, stopping at the empty wine bottles: Are you still drunk?

I laugh in her face: Who are you trying to be, my fucking mother?

Don't you understand, this isn't a game.

I know! He's a murderer, my mother's murderer, and I will avenge her—

The slap burns my face. I try to free myself from her grip, but her fingers are locked like iron around my wrists.

You don't know anything, hisses Sorella, her face twisted.

This is much bigger than Favorita. Fuck, why aren't you listening?

Because you're lying, you're all lying, lying to my face.

Desperately, I take her hands: Sorella, I'm afraid. That he'll kill us like he killed Magdalena, and that he'll bury us here.

I shake her lightly: Do you remember Otrere? I think she's here. Let's go to her, she'll help us, right? Sorella, you have to believe me, I haven't abandoned you. Crocifissa and you, you intercepted me. For the first time since my grandmother died, I no longer felt alone. I belong with the both of you, do you hear me? Let's get out of here together, we'll look for Croci, the rocket—

Sorella pulls her hands out of mine as if she had been burned.

Please, I say, don't give up.

Sorella is breathing heavily. Then she takes my face in her hands and squeezes.

Listen, she says, get out of here while you still can.

Where am I supposed to go? I shout.

She whispers: Be quiet! If you speak a word of any of this to anyone, if you even look at the Coach the wrong way, I'll kill you. Understand?

No!

Fila, I'm begging you. If you carry on like this, you'll ruin everything.

Everything is already ruined.

She looks at me, thinks for a while, opens her mouth, closes it again.

What?

The Society . . .

She stops and shakes her head: We don't have time. You just have to trust me.

Trust? How can I trust you?

A rectangle of light falls on the bed. Lorenzo is standing in the open door. Sorella exchanges a quick glance with him.

Is she OK?

Sorella nods.

Lorenzo mutters: That could have ended badly. The Coach says we should lock her in for the night.

I look from him to her and back. I have to laugh: What a set-up.

I throw back the covers and jump out of bed.

They try to stop me, but I'm a *cannone*.

XVI

I run through the night. My steps break the silence, I gasp, it's audible for miles, I'm a gigantic glow-worm, open season. The moon looks down at me with indifference from behind the curtain, the owl calls, bird of death, I'm running for my life.

Now the roofs of the deserted village, the church, the cemetery all come into sight. Bluish flames dance on the graves, stretched out gas creatures frolic in front of the barricaded church door, they ripple like shadows against the wall of the building. Bigots!

The village road is unlit, except for the moon covering everything with its mercury sheet. A wind blows through the deserted houses, their cold stoves, through chimneys full of blackberries and fig bushes, the cracks in the floors; they moan softly under its tender touch.

A small fluorescent haze wafts around my ankles. I stop and shake it off. The little flames ascend from the cemetery and scurry up the path. Like tufts of wool carried by the wind, they fly towards me and float around my body as if attracted by a magnet, swirling around themselves. They follow me as I walk down the street, float towards the houses, sit down on their own or in twos on an outdoor staircase, a collapsed balcony, in an exposed kitchen.

I walk to the end of the street, the light is on in the last house. Two cats are sitting at the window, eating symmetrically from a pot. When I knock on the Marian blue door, the light goes out. I run my fingers over the drawings of the moon rockets.

Signora, I call out quietly, my voice trembling, please let me in.

No sound from inside. I turn around – have I been followed? Is that Lorenzo panting or the wind? Sorella giggling or dry leaves?

I knock again and cry out as a cat rubs itself around my legs.

Otrere, I call, you have to help me, I'm in danger. Please, there's no one left.

I begin to shudder, my teeth chatter. A howl rises from my throat. The noise comes out of me from an organ I don't recognise. It sounds terrifying, like cats in the night, when you don't know if they're in agony or senseless from being in heat.

Bellissima Madonnina, it comes from me, bellissima Madonnina del dolore, Madonna del sangue, delle lacrime. Benedetta, Crocifissa, Genuflessa – ave Maria benedetta fra le donne – aiuto!

The Madonna above the door opens her left eye, winks, and a bloody tear rolls down her cheek. The door opens with a jolt.

Shut your mouth, a gruff voice says.

The cat slips between my legs and disappears into the darkness.

Are you alone? asks the voice.

Yes, I say tonelessly.

Come in.

I take a step, and the voice becomes hands pushing against my chest: Just leave the souls outside!

She begins to roughly brush the little blue flames off me with her hands. They sink to the ground and flee into the fig tree that has taken over the ruins opposite.

Quickly, she pulls me in and closes the door: They sting.

They didn't seem unfriendly to me, I mutter.

Bloodsuckers, she says, pests. They feel the warmth of a living body and attach themselves to it, trying to get under the skin.

She shoves me up the stairs. Then the light comes on.

You look like Sisina, I blurt out.

Her face contorts: Sit down.

I sit on a stool and a cat jumps into my lap. I don't dare push it off. The woman looks at me.

Sorella said you were coming.

I don't understand.

There's no need. The less you know, the better.

She goes to the kitchen cupboard, takes out a bottle, uncorks it and pours herself a glass. She downs it in one and sighs.

You drink?

She waits for me to nod, then pours. The wine is sweet. The woman closes her eyes. When she opens them again, she says: You shouldn't drink. It's in your blood.

How do you know that?

I'm Otrere, she says, I know everything.

The cat in my lap stands up, turns around and presses its paws into my thighs to find a more comfortable position. Then it lies down again with its front legs crossed. I can't move while Otrere walks around the kitchen, opening and closing cupboards. I follow her with my eyes; my gaze falls on a photo on the wall: the rocket, dozens of women in work clothes in front of it.

Otrere looks out of the window and says without turning around: Sorella told me that she didn't make it into the rocket because of you. That you're a traitor, maybe a spy.

I open my mouth to defend myself, but she says: I know that's not true. I've been watching you. You seem rather confused.

Otrere turns around and looks at me: You don't look anything like your mother.

My heart leaps: You knew her?

Otrere shakes her head.

She was like you. Came out of nowhere. She never said she was coming, she would just stand at the door expecting to be let in.

She was here?

The first time I almost ran her over. It was autumn, a rainy night. She was lying still on the road in the forest. In the light of the headlights she looked dead to me, like an animal that had been shot. But she was alive, and when I tried to help her up, she started throwing insults at me. She wanted to stay lying down and sleep.

Otrere snorts, playing with the cap of the bottle as if lost in her memories.

I hoisted her into the car, laid her here next to the stove. She wouldn't stop hurling abuse at me. The next morning she was gone.

But she came back?

Otrere nods.

What was she doing here?

The same as you. She was at the villa with the Coach.

The cat protests as I lean forward: When was this?

Otrere shakes her head. I grow impatient: I'm trying to reconstruct her life, you know. I always thought she left my father when she was pregnant with me. But now this Coach shows up, who she was with before she died, and he claims that he's my father! And that he saw me when I was a year old. So she went back to him? I don't understand. In my mind, she was always travelling around, to all these different cities, with different men. She wrote it in her letters: Seven husbands. A fairy-tale number.

Otrere pours herself another glass and drinks without offering me any more.

Then she stands up: It was a mistake to come here. You

shouldn't have come looking for her, she didn't want that. If you didn't know her when she was alive, you won't know her when she's dead.

Thank you, I hiss, and the cat jumps off my lap in annoyance, you're a great help!

I never offered help.

Otrere bends down to stroke the cat. Believe me, your mother didn't want help. I'm not a victim, she would say, I'm tough. I understand that, I was like that too. I could only tell her what I knew: people do to you what you let them do to you.

She sits up straight: I saw what he did to her. I experienced the same thing.

I don't say anything. Magdalena's bruises. My grandmother's fear, not saying my father's name. Was she really always going back to him?

Women stay with their violent men for various reasons, says Otrere, as if she had read my thoughts on my face: financial dependence, fear, shame—

My mother had no shame. And she had no fear either.

Sometimes out of love. Out of the hope that things will get better.

You think she loved him?

Otrere is silent.

My grandmother also said that women always hope things will get better. Suddenly I remember what Igor told me about Otrere: They say you killed your husband.

I fought back.

Why didn't you go to the police? Why didn't you get help?

She laughs contemptuously: You still think that someone will help us?

Otrere stands up and walks around the small room, she rummages through the cupboards and pulls out another bottle, uncorks it, gives me some, the stuff burns. She continues:

When a woman admits that she is a victim of violence, the same thing always happens: she is accused of lying. Or at least of having herself to blame: after all, she chose him. She's most likely not an easy person to be around either. She drove him to it.

She looks at me, shaking her head, and spits: Police! The police and the justice system are part of the problem. Women seeking help are not taken seriously. The police are reluctant to come before there's a body. We can't do anything about it, they say, when nothing's happened. But they often know for a long time that the man is violent. And then: embarrassed faces. What could we have done? Our hands are tied. But the neighbours must have noticed something? No, no one interferes in other people's private business. But there was excited murmuring behind closed doors: We thought he got a bit rough when he'd had one too many, but for him to be capable of that . . . She must have really got him worked up. It always takes two to have an argument, right?

Otrere looks out the window and turns back to me: This is how we silence one another. Even if someone dies, if she can no longer testify against him, they will continue to deny her

– while he brings tears to our eyes: He loved her so much. He can't recall any of it, what happened? We have to insist on the presumption of innocence. The poor man, he doesn't seem guilty. It's not uncommon for everything to be turned around and the perpetrator to be portrayed as the victim. And do you know what they say then? *There's a witch hunt against him.*

Otrere laughs, gesturing dangerously with the bottle: Do you understand how perfidious that is? Witch hunt! Of all things! Witches are women who don't submit quietly. Who don't cower and serve and are therefore dangerous, that's what we learned back then. Since the time of the witch hunts, we have been looking at each other with suspicion: Is she a witch, is she cursing me? Or is she denouncing me because she thinks I am a witch?

This is why we don't trust each other, that is why we are afraid of other women – because of the witch hunts. This is also why women who experience violence are not believed. In the ancient tradition of witch trials, a woman's bad reputation was considered proof of guilt. Accused women were raped to determine whether they were virgins: that is, innocent. As soon as a woman was accused of witchcraft, she could only lose. And that is still the case if a woman does not endure everything in silence, if she stands up and speaks out. A witch trial begins – but not against the person she accuses. The proceedings revolve around whether she should be believed. The trial is against her! She has to prove the impossible: that she is innocent.

I clear my throat: Do you mean like Sisina?

Otrere narrows her eyes and looks at me. Then she says: Of course, it was the event of the century. I grew up with the story. *The beautiful Sisina.* Tragic! Mysterious! But it wasn't that. It was a femicide. Simply the most extreme form of misogyny that is deep within all of us. It's not like things like that just happen. There's a reason that the most likely cause of death for young women is violence. All over the world, every day, in all countries, cultures and classes, women are killed by their men.

The cat jumps onto the table and listens to her speech with its tail flicking in interest: Violence is a decision. A demonstration of power. And it's tolerated, even needed, in our society, because it supports the ruling system. You want to know who killed her? It was all of us. We killed them. Sisina, your mother, all the women and people perceived as women who are killed by men every day. We did not prevent it. We accept it as if it were a law of nature that cannot be changed: men kill women. They have used all their force to make us accept the false belief as the definitive religion: there are two sexes, and one dominates the other. But the lie is obvious, and so men fight against what does not correspond to it, that which does not confirm their superiority. Because they fear us: our very existence makes them unravel. Because if we do not do what they want, they lose their power. That is why they kill us like flies.

And that is why, she says, lifting the cat from the table, we need revolution. We have to sweep everything off the table so that we can start again.

And then?

Revolutions need imagination. We have to invent them first.

The cat jumps onto my lap again.

Otrere takes a gulp of her drink and murmurs: My girl, nobody is going to help us. I helped myself and fled, to the only place where I knew I was safe. Here, on the blood-soaked ground that gave birth to my body. On this crumbling abyss, in the eye of the tigress, here I have peace.

People call you a witch.

Otrere laughs: That's good. It means they fear me.

And Magdalena? Why didn't she fight back?

She tried.

She didn't want to die.

Otrere takes a deep breath: What could I have done? She was a moth; I could only watch or turn off the light.

Otrere is silent and watches a moth circling the ceiling lamp.

I tried, I say, to solve Sisina's case. I saw my family history in her: my grandmother, Magdalena, me. Sisina was the key. And I thought, if I found her murderer, then I wouldn't have to avenge my mother. Because it's all the same.

What do you mean?

The oppression, the shame, the violence.

Otrere nods, her eyes half closed, I doubt she's listening.

But then she says: Sisina embodies and confirms the feeling all girls and women have of being under threat at all times. Everyone who deviates from the male ideal knows it. What happened to Sisina is the root of the fear, the nightmare. And her story, as it's told, is a warning: *Think of Sisina. That could be you.* The media, the court, the people, they fuel the narrative of the endangered girl, who always has to be careful, who can never feel safe alone. That's how they keep us small. They don't want us to be independent, to move around fearlessly and freely. After all, everyone has a hand in making that possible. But we have forgotten that it could be different.

I nod, but my thoughts have already moved on: Maybe Magdalena's thoughts were also occupied by Sisina. If she was here, she must have heard her story? She too could have felt a connection to Sisina, compared her to the women in our family. Maybe the story of her grandmother, my great-grandmother, dying while fetching water actually came from here, from Sisina. Maybe she made up the story, linked it to ours – like I did – to feel rooted.

Otrere opens her eyes and looks at me: You are not Sisina and you are not Magdalena. The violence that was done to them is not your story. You feel alone, you don't know where to go. I understand: there is a heavy secret, a family legacy that is dragging you down like lead. It's tempting, it feels safer than a fickle wind. I say to you: break free. Leave it all behind you.

I glare at her: Like you? Vegetating among cats, waiting impassively until the rock falls away beneath you? You're like Sorella, you've given up!

You're wrong. Now go home.

I remain sitting and pet the cat. Her fur is wet, she eagerly licks my tears.

My mother didn't want to be a possession. That's why she was killed.

Yes.

How can you be so calm! If you really allow these thoughts into your mind, they will burn through your insides. There's no relief except the idea of revenge, of ice-cold violence—

I know, she says, standing up.

Where are you going?

To bed, she says.

What about me?

Otrere remains standing in the doorway: Sorella told me what you're planning, but I don't think you'll go through with it.

There's no need, I say, mimicking her.

What do you hope to achieve? Would you feel better if he died too?

Yes.

Why?

I remain silent. Bite my lip and roll my eyes.

He's dangerous, I finally shout, a murderer. Someone who kills someone else doesn't hesitate—

She looks up: That's true. But that's not what you're after, not only that. The feeling you have is revenge.

I hiss like the cats: Revenge is all I have left.

Do you really think that you'll be at peace if you take revenge by committing a crime? That it will cancel out his crime?

She has pushed me into a corner. And I thought she was going to help me.

And what, she continues, if you're wrong? If it wasn't him? Then your fairness is unfair.

My voice rings out: Even if I'm wrong – shit, why don't you understand? I thought you were a murderer.

Otrere raises her eyebrows: That's different. I fought back. You want revenge, according to the rules of the Mafia: murder for murder.

So what if I do!

Either we all rise up together, or nothing happens at all, and definitely not personal revenge.

I jump up: I can do it in the name of the revolution too, just give me a weapon!

Otrere smiles: You want to join us?

I shout: I've wanted to for a long time! I couldn't help it if the rocket flew off without us!

Otrere stands up and brushes cat hair from her hands: Then go to Sorella and do what she says. She hasn't betrayed you.

Why should I trust you?

Because that's the only way it's going to happen.

What?

Otrere winks: The revolution.

She takes me to the door. The cat follows me for a while, then disappears into the bushes with a leap. A grey light is creeping in, I skid downhill, some little soul stings me in the neck, and

I scratch myself raw all the way to the villa. The lights are out. I slip inside.

XVII

Shh!

A shadow jumps out from behind the door and throws me onto the bed.

The springs groan, Sorella lies on me with all her weight, presses her hand over my mouth and listens. I bite, she lets go, raises her hand and murmurs: Now it's too late.

Then she rolls off me, props her head up on her hand and looks at me sideways: Otrere says she trusts you. But there's too much at stake. The less you know, the better for everyone.

But—

Be quiet, she whispers, standing up: We don't have time. They're already on their way.

Who?

Listen to me very carefully. Tonight the Coach is throwing a party for his influential friends. Some of the most powerful men in the country will gather here and plan what they're calling The Bright Future. The dinners at these meetings are held in the utmost secrecy. Even the staff have to be from the inner circle. It is considered a great honour to serve at one of these dinners. As the Coach's fiancée, I will be the hostess tonight and I have convinced him that you can help me. Your weird spoon attack has not made it any easier, but fortunately he seems to be no stranger to sleepwalking. It doesn't seem to have alarmed him. Listen! At a certain point in the evening I will have to disappear for a while and it will be your job to make sure that no one notices. If anyone asks, say I'm fetching the girls. But it would be best if no one noticed my absence. Can you do it?

What girls?

The most beautiful and capable girls you have ever seen. I chose them myself. They will be served to the gentlemen with grappa after dinner.

Sorella!

What? When they arrive, you're off the clock. Then you have to go up to the terrace on top of the tower immediately and wait for me there. No matter what happens, I want you to stay put, understand?

Sorella hands me a small pile of folded laundry: Here, your uniform.

What—

I can't explain anything right now.

Just one thing, please. Lorenzo. I don't understand, is he one of you?

Stay away from him. Don't talk to anyone, trust no one. Only me.

But—

We don't have time. You just have to follow my lead. Promise me, Fila, don't do anything else stupid. We're going to play hosts. Don't make a face, and keep your mouth shut. We'll meet tonight on the tower. Then I'll explain everything to you.

I look up at the ceiling, at the snake stretching out in the martini glass. It has a thick torso and a small head with a forked tongue flicking out of it.

*

Sorella orders me around all day. I wear a scratchy black dress covered in moth holes, a white lace apron and a maid's cap on my head. Sorella forced me to wear it when I tried to refuse: It's tradition.

I check the preparations in the drawing room one more time, following her curt instructions, while Lorenzo turns a pig on a spit over a fire in the garden. We close the door so that the grease-soaked smoke doesn't get into the house. I think of the Siena pigs, the half-wild piglets. The Coach is nowhere to be seen.

Out of the corner of my eye I see Lorenzo repeatedly looking in at us through the window. His lowly bent body expresses subservience. I cannot look at him. The shame of betrayal creeps out from my hairline in tremors. What did I want – to save him? Convert him? Cure his dark circles? I'm no better than Magdalena: unseeing and stupid with men. I made him a victim so that I wouldn't be one, convinced myself I was superior to him. I was so busy with my fantasy that I didn't notice him playing tricks on me the whole time.

Our eyes meet. He straightens up abruptly. The sound of

engines approaches from the road. His movements become panicked. They're too early! I quickly draw the curtain shut and open the door to the garden a crack so that I can listen without being seen.

Three figures are walking across the meadow.

Monsieur Deserteur, sneers Massimo, well then, are you preparing yourself a last meal?

Lorenzo narrows his eyes: What are you doing here?

Angelo stretches: Offering our services.

There's no work, says Lorenzo.

Nicolò clears his throat: There's a meeting. We want to join the Society.

Lorenzo laughs hoarsely: You don't know what you're talking about. Get lost, you've got no business being here.

Massimo approaches Lorenzo threateningly: We're not going anywhere. This is our land. We work it every day, making it fertile for the cause. That's my pig you're roasting. We have a right to be here. Besides, we know about the things in the chapel . . .

Lorenzo turns nervously towards the house: I've got no idea what you're talking about.

Angelo calls out: We're taking part in Day X!

Massimo salutes: Our honour is loyalty!

Lorenzo looks around quickly, then draws his gun – my gun! – and points it at Massimo: Get out of here, that's an order.

Massimo slowly raises his hands: You can't tell us what to do. Maybe you're fooling them, but we know what you've done.

You're a traitor, a deserter, they'll put you up against the wall.

Lorenzo brandishes the gun: Fuck off! And just keep your mouth shut. Talking nonsense will cost you dearly.

Is he trying to threaten us? I think he's trying to threaten us.

How rude, the Coach's oily voice rings out, excuse my over-zealous watchdog. Lorenzo, heel! The three of them lift their laughing heads to look up at the wall of the house, the Coach must be speaking from one of the windows on the top floor: Come in, boys, we'll find something for you to do.

XVIII

The gentlemen have arrived. Shiny racing and off-road vehicles and armoured limousines with single-digit licence plates are winding into the driveway. Hunting dogs are running around the grounds and sniffing around the garden, marking the walls with their thick piss. Lorenzo is wearing his military uniform again; the soup has taken care of everything. With slumped shoulders, he unloads trunks and carries boxes into the house, while Nicolò is turning the pig on a spit in the garden and Angelo scampers around him. The Coach is standing in the shade of the entrance porch talking loudly on the phone. Massimo is walking around by the gate with an important expression on his face, his chest puffed out, though no one is paying any attention to him. When a convoy of cars with trailers comes around the bend from the forest, he hurries out into the road and waves both arms, as if the villa could easily be missed. The cars stop, Massimo gesticulates. Then he climbs into his roofless Range Rover, sending up dust and the convoy follows him back into the forest. They are large trailers for animals. They will release them for hunting. Their roaring can be heard from here.

*

Day X is nearing. The collapse of the rotten, ailing West, the

breakdown of our culture, sucked dry by parasites, its complete
destruction through over-civilisation and the great replacement,
the extinction of our people . . .

Sisina gives a good long yawn. She's sitting on the mantelpiece
in the drawing room, swinging her legs. In front of her stands
a bespectacled boy with a little moustache, giving a speech that
is not actually all that fiery. The men at the table have given up
on sitting upright and keeping their faces looking determined.
The pig is in their stomachs, greased and weighed down by the
creamy desserts that Sorella and I served up a while ago. Since
then, she has disappeared without saying a word and I've been
standing next to the sideboard with its arsenal of bottles, sur-
veying the scene.

Sisina tugs at my apron: Where are your little friends? I haven't
seen them all evening. They're probably not trustworthy
enough to take part in this highly explosive meeting of
revolutionaries.

She giggles: Is that why you keep looking at the door, do you
miss your admirers?

Sisina, I murmur, they're fascists, I've got nothing to do with
them. I want to know what Sorella is up to.

She's getting the girls, that's what she said. That traitor has
taken your mother's place.

I don't believe that. She says there's a plan.

Are you really that stupid? She's stringing you along so that
you'll be quiet and well behaved. They'll never accept you into

their grand club. Waiting on political activists, these revolutionaries – that's just cowardly. You should have killed them all last night. I can't stand the sight of their faces any longer.

I'm going to do it, I really am. Didn't you make out with a soldier in here?

Sisina laughs: *She is a woman and never loves anyone but a warrior...*

Is that Nietzsche?

The soldier? He was from the Hunters of the Alps.

Which side?

What does that matter?

I once read that women who had flings with Nazis during the occupation were publicly humiliated after the war. Their heads were shaved, it was called a *purge*. They say that in the Witches' Forest they also *swept away* people, in other words, they purged them...

Pah.

What were you then, a communist?

Ts! You sound like Lorenzo.

Magdalena once claimed that she was a fascist.

You don't believe her?

I think she said it to annoy my grandmother.

And wasn't it her who said that Mussolini was a good man?

She was definitely not a fascist!

You mean fascism didn't even scratch her soul?

Pasolini?

Sisina dissolves into giggles, I stretch and straighten my little bonnet.

A dozen toupees, supposedly high-ranking signori, are lounging around the table. One is addressed as the police chief, another as your reverence. In fact, they look like limp hand puppets. One, probably a politician, looks familiar to me, he extends his arm in a Roman salute and announces with an important expression: The prime minister sends her greetings, unfortunately she cannot be here today.

It seems to be a joke, the men burst into whinnying laughter.

They don't look like they're excited about a coup. Instead, they're giving a smug and self-satisfied impression, as if they're attending a re-enactment, perhaps of the conspiracy in Sisina's time. Only the officer, a wiry man in uniform sitting opposite the Coach at the head of the table, keeps his back as straight as a rifle. His dead eyes stare into space and don't even twitch when the young speaker, who is standing directly behind him, accidentally touches his ear with his fingertip while gesticulating, whereupon the speaker falls into shock for a few seconds and turns as white as a sheet.

Everyone else's eyelids are heavy. The speech has already been quite long, it's sprawling and frequently uses repetition as a stylistic device. In addition, this young man, an intellectual and thought leader on the cause, fancies himself a bit of a poet, which is why he soon forgets the necessary tautness of his style and falls into an eurythmic pattern of waving, swaying and lurching, which he tries to pull himself out of by repeatedly crowing 'wake up!' at unexpected intervals.

Who is this wimp, a man with a tight facelift asks his neighbour, whose shirt is stretched over a considerable barrel. The man tears a wetly chewed cigar from his sticky lips: Austrian. I think. Bookworm from the youth movement, won the international competition for The Bright Future.

Hmm, says the other sullenly: I've never liked them. Weak boffins who talk so pompously you can't understand a word they're saying.

Me neither, the other nods, but they are needed. And the boy will go far. At his age he's already in great demand, he brings a breath of fresh air to the cause.

Hmm, says the other, as far as I'm concerned he could start striking the sail, I want to see the girls, not this spotty pseudo-philosopher.

The other man laughs and slaps him on the shoulder, then goes back to chewing on his cigar and listening to the boy's lecture, his ears glowing red with excitement and booze.

Affluent society is the cause of people's frustration ... The erosion of values through antisocial and hedonistic currents ... corrupted and worn down by the mixing of liberal, neo-Catholic and Marxist tendencies ...

Sisina stands in front of the dozing men, shaking her head: When I look at these heroes, they are the same idiots as back then, with their little secret society. How tedious that they never come up with anything new. Impaling communists, blowing up unions . . . The businessman claps his fat hands, praises the master race, and the girls serve dessert. Look at you, you are even wearing my old uniform, it is that revolutionary. What are you doing here? I will tell you something, it is not worth it. I once worked for these gentlemen too, wearing an apron because everything here was shiny and smelled of ham and shoe polish. And what did it do for me?

Sisina floats off to blow into the ear of a sleeping old man, who wakes up confused, puts his finger in his ear canal and wiggles it vigorously.

The young speaker, meanwhile, half-heartedly bangs on the table, immediately feels ashamed of the exaggerated gesture, and clears his throat: Today, politics is the breeding ground where the atrophy of all spiritual value and transcendence germinates—

And then a toupee booms: Listen, kid, that's enough now, atrophy won't germinate after all!

The boy stumbles and rustles his stack of paper, flicks through it hastily, coughs. Get to the end, calls the politician, and the others laugh loudly. The boy squirms, embarrassed, and finally waves his papers in despair: We must regain our old reputation, rejoin the ranks of the protagonists of history. We must restore the community of shared ideas between the dead and the living!

Bravo, shouts Sisina, clapping her white hands, whereupon the men at the table also begin to clap. The thunderous applause blocks any further awkward verses. Slaps on his shoulder force the poet to his knees, he's pushed into a chair and held down. When he opens his mouth, a bloated industrialist quickly stuffs a piece of cake into it.

Then it suddenly becomes quiet. Only two people in the hallway have missed the scene change, they laugh loudly until they become aware of their faux pas and fall silent in shock. A quiet smacking sound can still be heard, from the cigar chewer on the one hand, and on the other, the intellectual boy desperately trying to chew up and swallow the huge piece of cake.

The officer stands up. He brushes an invisible crumb from his lapel and looks around in silence. The gentlemen try not to give in to his numbing gaze. All the air seems to have been sucked out of the room. Sisina has disappeared.

Gentlemen. As our young friend from a friendly foreign country – the prize-winner chokes on his cake in shock – has correctly recognised, we live in a time of decline. I see it here too. The officer's voice is slightly creaky: What is this? Am I in a room full of worms?

A few uncertain laughs.

The officer has not blinked once: I am not joking. It is my duty to fight against the moral spirit of surrender. True warriors know that the fight has never stopped – and never will stop. War is the natural state of man. Peace makes him sluggish and weak, robs him of his masculinity.

The men try and sit up inconspicuously. The officer continues to stare fixedly over their heads and his voice saws through the silence.

There are men who remain standing to attention even in a hail of bullets. When I look around, I know that you do not belong to this group. Phlegmatic consumerist idiots. You are content to tread water while on the defensive. We have to be the ones who attack!

The men are now sitting up very straight and applauding eagerly. The officer raises his flat hand, where two fingers are missing. The stumps are still inflamed. The cigar chewer whispers: I heard it was a woman. A *female* shot them off while he was clearing out an occupied factory.

Amazed murmurs go around. The officer makes them evaporate with a blink. He stabs the commentator with his gaze and then crosses the room; the men duck involuntarily. The officer opens the double doors and whistles piercingly. He seems to be listening, then he turns around and continues: We must never lull ourselves into a false sense of security. The enemy is everywhere, and he is stronger than we would like to admit. We must stride onwards from words to actions. The violence – nowadays so restrained, inhibited, *well-tempered brutality* – must reach boiling point.

Uncomfortable, affected clearing of throats, restrained nods. A diffuse restlessness creeps through the room. Then a jolt goes through all of our bodies: a roar sounds from outside, which shoots into my chest, making my heart gallop like a gazelle. There is a tiger in the garden. It looks me straight in the eye.

*

Blood spurts as if from a water pistol, the cigar falls into a pool of it.

The tiger swipes a few bottles off the table with its tail and hisses. Its teeth are yellow and smeared with blood.

The officer makes a strange noise: he's laughing. Men rolling over each other in panic as they try to climb onto the table: so that's his kind of humour. And the screaming cigar chewer with his half-torn-off hand.

The officer slams his fist on the table and screams: Ride the tiger, come on! Rein him in, discipline him before he devours you, bring him under your control!

He snaps at the tiger with his remaining fingers. Then he slaps it on the flank, causing it to jump and then leap through the veranda door. I watch the tiger as it trots across the meadow towards the wood and disappears behind the curve of the hill.

The Coach closes the veranda door, trembling. His face contorted with anger, he yells: Sorella! Damn it, where are the bandages!

Sorella doesn't come. I run, fetch some kitchen towels, which I wrap around the bloody hand of the cigar guy who's wet with a cold sweat. Tighter, tighter! That's good, let it rot off.

The Coach pats the forehead of the wounded man, who is now lying on the divan, pale as wax, and announces: It's not half as bad as it looks!

The men slide back into their chairs, no one dares say a word.

The Coach steps up to the table and puts his hand on the officer's shoulder: We need a bit more practice at the tiger riding, eh?

A few uncertain laughs. The officer doesn't change his expression. The Coach shakes the uniformed shoulder slightly: I think we need a bit of a pick-me-up. Well, how about it, are you ready for the girls?

The men applaud with relief. The officer remains standing and raises his three-fingered hand: Not so fast. I haven't finished yet.

The men gulp and the Coach's smile is desperate: Of course, please.

The officer points to the wounded man delirious on the divan: Our friend mentioned women earlier. I would like to take up this point and remind you of what our great thinker said about women: They poison us and our environment.

The men murmur quietly: Hear, hear!

One of them grins: What would our prime minister say to that?

The officer silences him with a look and goes to the sideboard, where a few books stand in a row. He takes one and pulls a pair of reading glasses out of his breast pocket. The men don't dare breathe. The officer opens the book and lifts it up so that a tiger can be seen on the cover. The officer turns the pages noisily, almost whipping them, and hisses: I'm not concerned with petty morality. With the so-called honour a man has to restore when his wife cuckolds him. Or with the honour that a girl loses when she behaves indecently.

I look around for Sisina, but she's disappeared.

The officer continues to leaf through the book: I am concerned with the great morality.

A few men nod uncertainly.

The officer now speaks quietly, almost lisping: *A society that is doomed is typically marked by severe symptoms of poisoning. The witchcraft of oversexualisation spreads female rot and leads to rampant impotence. This is the foundation for so-called female domination, under which the male sex must shrivel.*

The officer pauses. Silent panic spreads, the men do not know how to react. The politician stretches a little and murmurs: That was always my opinion.

The young intellectual clears his throat. I cannot tell whether this is out of tactlessness or to actually express his disapproval. The officer focuses his attention on him like a spotlight. His voice cuts through the room: You think the great thinker is mistaken?

The boy shakes his head quickly and adjusts his glasses nervously.

You think times have changed? You think women should at least be given the opportunity to prove themselves? If they serve the cause, they should be accepted into our ranks, is that what you think?

The boy tries to sink into his chair, into himself. The man next to him pinches his cheek: He must have a little feminist at home, the weirdo.

The men laugh: His mother!

The officer laughs joylessly too, for a beat, then he falls silent, and everyone else with him.

No, he says. This young man is a child of his time. He embodies the decay of values. Look at him! His generation knows nothing but domestication. They no longer even recognise how skewed our relationships are. This young man is used to women telling him what to do. He thinks it's normal to have a woman as prime minister. In his own ranks! He thinks that's progress. And I think he's not alone in that.

A few of the men look at the table in shock, others throw up their hands and clap them over their heads. One shouts: My word! A woman can never be a brother!

The officer puts the book on the table and looks up.

In short, he says, women are a soul-destroying influence. A danger to the male community, to the cause, to the greater whole. There is a reason why we are among men. It is only within the community of men that the transcendental energy that makes our cause immortal can develop. Too much contact with girls and women, be it at home or in society, makes every man effeminate. Our great thinker uses the image of a deadly jellyfish that shimmers bewitchingly in the water: this is how the feminine penetrates the masculine armour. This is how women poison the radiant core with their slime, they wash it away, they undermine every foundation, they overpower—

But Comandante, the Coach interjects with a cautious smile, you don't mean to say that we all have to become abstinent? We wouldn't be able to stand that, would we, men?

A few murmur in agreement.

Besides, it would be bad for business.

The officer twists his face into a painful grimace and bends once more over the book:

What you allow yourself can be measured by what you are. The man at peace with himself is not afraid of the treachery of women: he can milk the female poison from the jellyfish and feed on it, grow stronger from it. The female body can, indeed must be used, if only as an exercise in not submitting under any circumstances.

Agreed, shouts the Coach. What was it again? You're off to see a woman? Do not forget the whip!

The men's cheer is a little subdued. A murderous jellyfish is dancing in my stomach. The Coach laughs heartily and applauds the officer: One final word, General?

The officer gives a toothy smile: If you're strong, a drop of poison won't harm you. And if you've got steel armour, you can bring a live viper into your house.

The Coach stands up, baring his teeth: Friends, the Comandante has spoken. Now for the fun part! Tomorrow's Day X for zebras, giraffes and apparently tigers—

I will avenge you, Ciccio, one of them calls out to the unconscious man on the divan and shoots his neighbour between the eyes with his fingers, I'll take care of the beast!

The Coach laughs: There's your fighting spirit, General. Tomorrow is Day X for the tiger – the day after tomorrow could be Day X for everything else. But let's enjoy ourselves today, one last time. Girls, bring in the champagne!

Sorella appears in the doorway and waves in a dozen *girls* amid applause and whistles. Their skin glitters in sea tones, their faces are covered by sparkling masks. They tiptoe and spin in circles, the men smack their lips violently.

Gentlemen, today is ladies' choice, calls Sorella, before clapping her hands. Sisters, choose one.

The masked newcomers sit down on the men, they make appreciative sounds and giggle obligingly. I watch closely how they move, how they splay their toes and scratch scabby bald heads with their fingernails.

The Coach puts his arm around Sorella's waist, she smiles. How calmly she serves these men all evening, applauding their embarrassing speeches. I try to imagine Magdalena in her place. I'm unable to. I can't believe she would have gone along with it. Never in her life would she have left the outpourings of these men unchallenged, silently accepting this behaviour, never. Even if she had actually harboured some kind of twisted sympathy for their prevailing ideology in her alcohol-corroded brain, she was still Magdalena, my mother. And she was first and foremost impertinent, loud and self-centred. She was only interested in herself and did not submit to any big ideas. She would have pulled the young speaker's ear, stuffed the cigar chewer's throat with his cheroot, and laughed shrilly at the officer with his little book. My mother, as I knew her, would have blared out her own speech in which she would have told everyone present to go to hell. There would have been a roar of laughter, a popping of corks and the clinking of glasses, and they would ultimately have eaten out of her hand – all of them except the officer. She would have put the men in their place, would have proved what a danger a woman could pose to a group of men. Probably without realising the danger she was putting herself in.

I look from the officer, who's shooing away a masked woman with his hand, to the Coach, who's whispering something in Sorella's ear. Sorella! She made big speeches at her telescope, *The Archive of Murdered Women*, after she must have watched close up how Magdalena stormed into the abyss with a roar. It would have become clear when she threatened the Coach with separation, though likely much sooner, that they wouldn't just let her go. She was like Sisina: she knew too much.

The Coach chimes his fork against his wine glass and begins: After all that hard work, we still have a merry performance to present to you. This is to show the officer that at least here on the land, the youth have not yet been corrupted. Boys!

Massimo, Nicolò and Angelo enter. They are wearing

tracksuits with an ironed-on emblem on the back. They line up in front of the fireplace and the angel begins to sing in a clear voice: *With the dagger and the bomb in the life of terror . . .*

The officer smiles sourly, the men sway, a few join in loudly. Massimo's knees shake slightly, Nicolò's expression doesn't alter and he stares fixedly at the ceiling. He avoids my gaze. The masked girls take the men's hands and clap them as if they were little children who hadn't yet learned how to: *youth, youth, spring of beauty . . .* Someone prods my back as they pass behind me; Sorella hisses: Go, get onto the roof of the tower!

When I turn around, she's already gone. I stand up and Angelo's eyes meet mine. He beams at me and sings of a black flame in a heart, of a dagger between teeth – *this is how we smile at death.*

The men join in and chant: *All ahead, all in the field; here you win or die!*

I see a masked woman walking towards the bathroom and follow her discreetly. She closes the door behind her, I knock softly. She doesn't answer. I hear the men shouting from the drawing room. I knock again and then try the door. It opens. The bathroom is empty. The window is open, she must have climbed out. Something glitters in the waste bin. I close the door behind me and undress. I throw the waitress uniform out the window, put on the dress and the mask from the bin. Just like that, I'm a glittering jellyfish. I have no plan, except that I want to sting a few faces with my tentacles. I sing along loudly: *I am young and I am strong, my heart does not tremble. When the howitzer is booming, my heart does not tremble.*

XIX

I serve champagne, let them touch my arse and scoff taralli. It doesn't take long before Sorella grabs my arm and hisses: What are you doing?

Working, I smile.

She pulls me into the kitchen, where I lie through my mask with my dog eyes: You know, I would really like to get to know my mother's world.

She looks at me suspiciously and her gaze lingers.

I grin. It feels good, this costume, the bare skin.

Fine, whispers Sorella, but make sure the Coach doesn't recognise you. And don't go off with anyone – you are only allowed to serve.

She looks at the clock: You have to be on the tower at midnight, understood?

I blow a kiss: Promise.

Spumante bubbles burst on the roof of my skull. Someone's chewing my ear off and blowing wet wine breath into my face. He wants to be the grandfather of my grandchildren. Get it, he puffs, bursting into a phlegm-coughing laugh. Shiny little pig eyes. I wriggle out of his embrace, murmuring: Ladies' choice. Release the suction cups, pull away all the tentacles and stumble to the garden. The booming laughter of the octopus, who didn't get up from his armchair, stuck in the sticky velvet, tickles my neck.

The sun has become tangled in the trees and is making raw egg yolk flow onto the lawn. A hunting dog stands against the wall of the house with its fur on end, growling into the void. I murmur: Sisina? The dog barks and runs away with its tail between its legs.

I sit down in the meadow and watch the sun bleed out over the pristine hills. They have released pheasants for hunting, and they're crowing out in the woods. I try to remember how many days I've been here. It seems as if a whole season has passed. Since it has become cooler, the cicadas have grown quieter. They sound tired, have slowed down, as if they are about to doze. Like children crying themselves to sleep.

There is nothing sadder than a sunset, a voice behind me says.

I turn around, it's Nicolò, he sits down next to me. I move away a little. Doesn't he recognise me? In his hand he's holding the neck of a bottle, the sun's rays are shining inside its stomach.

He stares at the horizon: It's as if it were pulling you down with it. As if it were taking all the light with it and leaving us in darkness.

That's how it is, I murmur.

Cruel, he says, and puts the bottle to his lips: I have to drink, otherwise I can't stand this beauty.

He gestures towards the nature humming all around us, the

rustling forest: Every morning when I wake up and it's light again, it seems like a miracle to me.

Mmm.

He squints his eyes, looking at the red, sinking disc: Do you know what the sun is? Ashes from dead stars.

The rays get caught in his curls. I want to ask him about Meo, whether he misses him. Why he didn't go with him, what's keeping him here. He doesn't seem enthused about what's going on. Or is he? Which side is he on? I'm desperate for an ally, take a breath—

Hey, wait for us! comes a shout. He's not much use anyway.

Nicolò sighs, his uncle drums the back of his neck; Angelo comes galloping up like a young giraffe. They have the young Austrian in tow, winner of the Bright Future competition. Massimo pinches my upper arm: And who is this?

Dolcetta, I murmur.

They sit down around us. Massimo moves closer to my body and puts his arm around me. No one wants to recognise me.

I remove his arm and mumble: Forget it.

Angelo snuggles his head against my bare leg and howls like a puppy. He lets his forehead fall on my knee and sighs: I just wanted to cheer you up a little. But I'm so tired.

Massimo pushes him away and slaps my thighs with both hands: Not me, I'm not tired at all.

Leave her alone, says Nicolò, why do you always have to be an arsehole.

Well, listen, his uncle crows, I'm only following the way of men.

Angelo laughs, Nicolò rolls his eyes.

I lie on my back, they bicker, my body is numb and my head is a rattling machine. What happened to them for them to become like this?

A hooting can be heard from the villa. A fluttering draught brushes my head, I open my eyes a crack: someone is running past us across the meadow, a rifle rattling over his shoulder. He stands a few metres away from us and fires randomly into the forest. Birds flutter up. The speech writer adjusts his glasses in irritation.

Such a depressing atmosphere, he states. I simply do not understand why there is no cultural awareness on the right.

Massimo offers him his joint: You think too much, kid.

Franz, he says, and takes a drag, holding it bravely in his lungs until a cough overcomes him. Massimo pats him on the shoulder: But you've got courage, have to give you that. Interrupting the officer during his speech? That takes balls – or stupidity.

Franz coughs, finally shaking his head, gasping: The right is buried under narrow-minded disinterest and chauvinism. It has nothing to offer the youth.

Yes, shouts Angelo, the more worked up we get, the more they tell us to keep quiet. As if they had anything to say! They are like cows, re-chewing old ideas—

Franz nods: That officer is the best example. What he

proclaimed may be philosophically interesting. But is it, in practical terms, the future? I do not think so.

Massimo slaps his palms against his chest: Look at us! We are the future, fascists of the present.

Fascists of the third millennium, Angelo crows. We are fighters, outside of the law and morality.

Franz calls out laughing: Away with nostalgia, bring on forward-looking ideas!

Ideas, ideas, Massimo mimics him, we want the squadrismo, we want action.

Angelo tugs on his uncle's sleeve: Tell him about how we destroyed the Communist Party office! Sometimes all you need is a few bicycle chains – and boxing training. In any case, you won't find a single plaque with anything about partisans on it in our village.

Massimo takes the joint from Franz's fingers: I don't know what you lot are doing, but we have concrete plans. A few bottles of liquid explosives are waiting in my garage. When I was little, my father took me to the fields and we used a metal detector to look for old bombs. I still have a few of those.

Franz shakes his head sadly: Terrorism? That is no longer necessary. The matter has been dealt with: the institutions have been infiltrated, we have control over the parties and the press. The decision-making centres are in our hands. The system does not need to be overthrown.

Massimo spits out: You're not a fascist if you don't fight against the state. Democracy is the grave of freedom. Didn't you hear the officer? We must attack before others do.

Better to live one day as a lion than a hundred years as a sheep.

For the first time, it's Nicolò's voice. I can't tell if he's being ironic.

Franz rubs his forehead: This is probably all normal. Naturally, this consumerist society, which lacks any higher meaning, is making us stupid and brutalised. We just deal with it in different ways. As the great thinker says: Some are driven to transcendence, others have the predisposition to be warriors.

Angelo and Massimo look at each other and shout as if on command: No purpose or place! We have no Great War! Our great war is a spiritual war!

Franz suppresses a laugh: What is that?

Angelo jumps up and waves his arms around: Don't you know *Fight Club*?

Maybe it would not be that bad, says Franz, if the likes of us got together. Perhaps this would create a turbo-dynamism within the movement: the fusion of politics and aesthetic violence—

I groan with my eyes closed: Why doesn't anyone make him stop talking?

The boys laugh and it sounds as if Massimo has put the Austrian in a headlock: The girl's right, friend, enjoy the silence for once.

Angelo giggles: You can't get any, can you? Only virgins talk like that. You just need to do a little lifting, here, build up some muscle – that's what they like, not your intellectual blabber!

He nudges me: Am I right or what?

Sure, I mutter, but he rides the tiger.

Massimo's hand sneaks up like a snake and grabs me: I'd rather ride you than a stinking tiger!

Franz looks at him with pity: You really are the opposite of stoic detachment! Anyone who wants to possess women is only showing their own deep insecurity: you need them for self-affirmation. You're not riding the tiger, you're sitting on the pig of your own animal instincts.

Massimo lets go of me and grumbles: Pigs are noble creatures.

Angelo asks: Do you really think you can ride a tiger?

Franz says seriously: Not us. But a very specific type of person can. A person who is different deep down inside.

What makes you think you know what I'm like inside?

Forget it, if there is no crystalline point, you can't have any expectations.

What's that supposed to mean?

Well, you would have to be inward-looking, build inner resilience. You need to be completely detached and turn away from everything.

That's a load of shit, Massimo complains. What are we supposed to do, sit around doing nothing? I can't stand it!

No, you loudmouth, says Franz, who has obviously gained some self-confidence, that is not what it means. It means being unmoved on the inside. It is about being completely impassive, understand?

I sit up straight. The boys are too engrossed in their conversation to pay any attention to me. I get up and stagger across the lawn to the house.

I can still hear Franz saying in a conciliatory tone: We also need people like you, who have enthusiasm and do not think too much about everything. You lot are making the tiger tired, weary.

Above all, I say, you're all making me tired, weary.

And then I see him.

*

He's standing in the garden in front of the veranda door talking to the Coach. It really is him: the doctor from the city. The doctor who let Magdalena die, who slandered and burned her. He's standing next to the Coach, they're laughing comfortably with one another. I hear him say: Sorry for the delay, my good man, an emergency held me up, you understand.

The bubbles make me burp 'Doctor!' He looks at me in surprise.

Do we know each other?

I'm furious that the pig doesn't recognise me. I'm tempted to take off the mask.

I wink, the Coach watches me carefully: An admirer?

I smile under the fish scale mask and grab a bottle of champagne from the ice bucket. I approach slowly, my toes splayed, the head of the champagne bottle pointed at them like the barrel of a gun.

Doctor, I whisper, you look thirsty. I tear the sharp metal foil from the neck of the bottle, grasp the cork and knead and twist it until I feel that it's about to come off. I look penetratingly into the doctor's eyes the whole time. He's embarrassed, he lowers his eyes. I whisper: But Doctor—

The cork pops, I almost let go of it, right in their eyes, there would have been spatter then. The thought makes me giggle; the men think it's because the foam is overflowing and champers is dripping onto the ground. I hold the glass to my lips, blow a little foam onto the doctor's nose, hand him the glass, and float up the stairs into the villa.

Crazy girl, I hear him say.
   The Coach laughs. Blood rushes in my ears.

I swim through the drawing room, filling glasses that greasy fingers hold out to me. I bare my teeth and curtsy, but all I feel is the doctor at my back and the magnetic field swinging between us. A little later his hand sneaks around my waist, creeps up my stomach, reluctantly comes to rest on my ribs, just under my breasts.

   I hold my breath. I would recognise that stench anywhere: the disgusting parasite oil that he rubbed on me.

   He breathes foully into my ear: I would love to find out where we know each other from.

   I grab his wrist, he strokes my fingers, I press harder, feel his pulse, want to stop the blood, want him to drop dead. I pull him through the double doors into the garden, past the Coach, who calls something after us, too *vulgar* for me to understand.

In my imagination his head explodes.

With the stinking lump of doctor in tow, I hurry towards the spring. When I enter the forest, I let go of him, slip between the trees, which immediately conceal me. I run a few trunks along and lean against cool bark, hear him struggling to squeeze between the trees, let him catch up a little, then run off again.

Sisina, I whisper, help me.

Then he grabs me, wraps his arms around me and licks my neck.

I gag – Wait, Signore, I call out, we're not there yet.

Yes, yes, he gasps, I can't wait any longer.

I talk myself into trouble: It's not far now, it'll be worth it. A secret place, you know, where young lovers used to meet, for free love, you know? It's very powerful, I want to show it to you.

He shows his teeth: There's a little romantic slumbering inside you, isn't there?

I tear myself away, run, hear him panting behind me.

Stop, you stupid little thing, he calls, I'm fed up with playing games.

Almost there, I call out, as the well finally appears in front of me, in the clearing, bathed by the moon. I sit on the edge, cross my legs and take a sip from the bottle.

The doctor appears between the trees, breathing heavily.

Well, I say, have I promised too much?

Full moon, he gasps, a real romantic.

He lunges at me, I wrap my arms around his neck like a constrictor and whisper: Well, would you like a show in the moonlight?

He takes a step back expectantly, I stand up and push him down by the shoulders until he's sitting on the edge of the well.

You look so very familiar to me.

Of course, I smile, we know each other.

From the city?

Mmm, I murmur, should I give you a clue?

He nods stupidly, I breathe: Shrunken liver.

I can see him thinking, he thinks very loudly and not very nimbly, it won't come to him, all his synapses are clogged up by the parasite oil. I keep smiling, let a little champagne trickle off my tongue, he grimaces as if he were having a stroke, gurgles, pants, the neck of the bottle is firmly in my hand. I step towards him, he grins eagerly, I swing—

With the first blow I miss his skull, only lightly grazing his neck. I freeze as he looks at me in amazement. Then all the power rises like magma from my depths, and I roar: I am the daughter of Favorita!

My voice is pleasantly amplified by the echo in the shaft. And this time I don't miss. An ugly sound as he lands deep below.

The moon burps approvingly.

XX

Restless wind. Electric sky. On the horizon, lightning that makes the night-black treetops dance. Twitching shadows on the rockface, surging thunder. Sorella is too late, the church clock on the tower of the villa has struck, struck, struck. Behind the forest the sky is breaking, a subdued crash. The cicadas quiver in the charged air. My skin crackles.

I climb onto the railings of the roof terrace and stretch out my arms. The storm is near, Hattifattener, I'm up high, high, strike me. The lightning darts its tongue out greedily, I twist my body, beckoning: Come on now, I'm offering myself up here.

The wind licks me lustfully, whispering lies: it would catch me and carry me away, swing me up to the moon; I don't believe a word it says. The wind is stiff and aggressive. Let me think, don't stress me out, I can do it without you.

My legs dangle over the courtyard, gravity is tugging pleasantly on my feet, so pleasantly. I would fall between the pomegranate trees, my face would become one with the gravel. At this thought, it runs warmly out of me. I look at the blood on my fingers and wait for the pain. It will make me undaunted by death, in 3, 2, 1—

The cramping starts like the lightning that illuminates everything, the thunder drowns out the footsteps. Hands cover my eyes.

Sorella?

No answer.

Lorenzo?

Breath.

Angelo?

Fingers press harder on the balls of my eyes.

Sisina?

A chuckle, the fingers release. I close my eyes, having recognised the smell. Hands rest heavily on my shoulders, rocking me gently back and forth.

Ninna Nanna oh ... What do you do when the wolf comes?

I slowly turn my head.

What do you do when the wolf has you in its teeth?

The Coach laughs: Now you remember, I can see it in your face. I sang that to you. Before your mother stole you away from me.

My mouth is dry, I'm rigid, only one thought in my head: The wolf, he's the wolf, it's him.

What is it, he says, do you want to jump?

I swing my legs over the railing, back towards the ground.

You really do look like me, laughs the Coach, you look like me more than I do.

I try to see my reflection in the drops of sweat on his forehead.

He shakes his head and smiles: You little girls are so

transparent. Did you think I wasn't watching you? The incident with the doctor – brava, I didn't think you had it in you.

Why didn't you stop me? I ask hoarsely.

Why would I do that, he calls out, you did me a favour. You can surely understand that, seeing how clever you are. But I hope you also know that you won't be able to get rid of me so easily.

He grabs my chin and holds it with iron fingers.

Dolce Filuccia, he murmurs, why are you doing this to me?

I try to free myself, he grips me tightly: It makes me sad that you prefer your mother to your father. It seems like hypocrisy to me. You and your mother, you never cared about each other. And now that it's too late—

I don't know anything, I whisper, I don't know anything.

The claws dig into my shoulders, the Coach snorts in my ear:

Amore del Papà, how I would like to believe you. Unfortunately, I can't trust you. You were never honest with me. And what's even worse: you got my best people to lie to me.

I whisper: What did you do to Sorella?

Don't worry, I'll deal with her later. It's father–daughter time right now. We have a lot of catching up to do.

He strokes my face gently and places his fingers around my neck: The death of a beautiful woman is, unquestionably, the most poetical topic in the world, isn't it? Unfortunately, no one gives a fuck about the death of an old whore.

I stare at his face, see my reflection in the well shafts of his eyes and have no more doubts.

Nobody will believe you, he hisses, and even if they do, nobody will want to hear it. Don't you see where we are, who my friends are? Go and tell the senators, the chief prosecutor, the police chief. You can't hurt me, little Filuccia, not you, and not your fucking mother, you are nothing, nobody, and nobody will miss you.

Flashes of lightning illuminate our little scene like strobes. The pain in my abdomen makes me groan. Irritated, he releases his grip, I knee him between the legs, much too weakly. His pupils dilate, he laughs and squeezes harder. I claw at his face, try to rip the bags under his eyes, stab my fingers through his eyes and into his brain. He wheezes, laughing at me; he's right, I can't, I can't kill him. I'm too weak. It's like in my dreams.

I'm lying in the well and dying. My father leans over me, sadness crushes me like lead, my senses dissolve, and I cry: Promise you'll miss me.

And as I slowly die, on this tower in a thunderstorm, a star rises over me. A ball of fire growing ever larger, racing towards me at roaring speed. So that's what it's like, I think, not at all a gentle light at the end of the tunnel. This comet will hit me and pulverise me. I can already feel its warmth, the vibrating roar. I close my eyes.

Deafening crash, the ground trembles beneath me. The heat melts me, so this is the end. I wait for the angel to arrive and pick me up – Sisina, where's the wine festival?

I hear shots below, then screams. There are hurried steps next to me, the Coach's cologne disappears – in fact, my throat is free. Then I start coughing: Fuck, I'm alive. Open my eyes. The moon opens its mouth, a cloud of dust swallows it up. We have a coughing competition.

A silhouette appears in the doorway.

Lorenzo, calls the Coach, what's going on down there?

He cowers behind me in the corner, I see fear flickering in his eyes.

A rocket, gasps Lorenzo, a rocket has fallen from the sky. It has demolished the bell tower. And the girls, they're armed – they're slaughtering everyone!

The Coach opens his eyes wide, his blazing fear is flooded with astonishment.

I laugh like mad, coughing. Lorenzo looks down at me curled up on the ground. What have you done to her?

The Coach straightens up: I just hugged my daughter a little too tightly, didn't I?

Lorenzo murmurs: Sorella was right. She was right all along.

He steps out of the dust, a gun in his hand.

How could I not have seen the fear in the Coach earlier? It licks his whole body, he writhes inside it like a worm, a maggot in purgatory. Burned eye sockets, fear has been eating him from the inside for a long time already. Lorenzo stands like a statue, wordless, not even the wind dares come near him.

The Coach raises an eyebrow and grins: What is this, a family reunion?

Lorenzo stands with both his arms stretched out in front of him, taking aim.

Ah, the Coach curls his lips in amusement, another ungrateful son. Haven't I done everything for you? What would you do without me? The officer will put you up against the wall, without me you are nothing—

I'm sorry, says Lorenzo.

I think he's saying it to me.

I see the bullet flying.

I see it spinning incredibly fast, feel it whizzing past me. Resolutely, not like my fingers, my nails, they didn't want to, not like that, they would never have been able to do it, even if I had bitten the dust in the process. But a bullet like that, you can't stop it. It doesn't care about the pitiful amazement in your eyes or the flames dancing in them. The bullet is reflected in the eye, vain and indifferent, before it tears it to pieces.

Warm rain on my face, a bang, and the statue falls.

Lorenzo!

A shadow: Sorry. A friend of yours?

There she is standing over me, Sisina with the rifle and a wildly determined face. Otrere, I stammer, what have you done?

She points the barrel at the prone Lorenzo: I only saw the

uniform. Believe me, you can't convert someone like that. You're better off without him.

Brother, I want to say, I think that's my brother.

But my voice has fled into the forest.

Otrere jumps down from the railing like a cat and puts a hand on my shoulder: Romantic love is always beautiful. And always sad when it ends.

Then she orders: You stay here, there's hell going on down below. It would be pointless for you to die in the crossfire.

She shoulders the lifeless Coach and looks over the railing into the garden: You don't need him anymore, do you?

Look out below, she calls out loudly, and lets him fall into the garden.

She rubs her hands on her trousers: We'll see each other later, sit tight.

I sit extremely tightly. Lorenzo is warm. The wind blows away and tears the clouds open as it flees. The moon is as indifferent as a circle.

*

What happened in the subsequent hours I experienced through an unconscious veil. I couldn't say what was a dream, what was reality, or delusion, or fantasy, or hallucination. Although they later assured me that everything happened exactly as it happened, I don't trust the images in my memory. It's as if I were spinning around in circles up there, on a swing carousel, the lights and events around me blurred—

I lie next to Lorenzo and sing him a lullaby, *Ninna Nanna oh* . . .
I weave my fingers through his, which are growing cold. I look
over the railing into the garden and see the smoking rocket. Its
nose is stuck in the grass. I see Amazons pruning men. I see the
Coach's twisted body lying next to the veranda steps. A woman
puts her foot on his back, as if it were a mountain peak she had
climbed. She looks up at me, she's wearing an eye patch. She
looks familiar to me, she waves.

Crocifissa!

Dolcetta, she calls, this is for Favorita!

I watch the officer being led out of the house by two women.
They hold his arms twisted behind his back. Crocifissa steps
out into the meadow, stretches her hands towards the forest
and lets out a long whistle. Then I see her.

The tigress appears between the trees and trots towards Crocifissa, who does not draw her hands back. A throaty snarl, the
tigress tosses her head to the side, Crocifissa scratches her neck.
The women pull the officer's arms closer together. The tigress
sniffs. The officer does not make a sound, but I can see him
trembling. The animal moves to stand in front of the officer
and growls in his face. Crocifissa mumbles something into her
fluffy ear. The women release the officer and step aside. He
spins around quickly. The tigress knocks him down with her
paw. The officer screams. The women run off. Only Crocifissa

stops and calls: Now show your worms how it's done: Ride! Ride the tigress!

I see a large cauldron on a fire, in it sit the mighty men crying. The women are dancing in circles around it. They sing: *Tremate, tremate, le streghe son' tornate* – tremble, tremble, the witches are back.

*

At dawn, four women and at least three ghosts walk up the road to the deserted village. The cicadas wake to their steps. The warriors stride stoically past the soldiers' monument, banner fluttering wearily on its wreath. They stop in front of the cemetery gate. They watch through the bars as the last moonstruck little souls disappear into the earth, into the cracks between the stone slabs, from which tender, tough weeds grow. Then one after the other, they climb over the fence.

Here lies Sisina. The same photograph is stuck to her grave as on the memorial stone in the forest. She is smiling, excited, full of anticipation for something that is coming soon. Sorella sits down next to the stone, draws up her knees and rests her forehead on them, closing her eyes. Crocifissa folds her hands and raises one eye to the sky. RIP RIP RIP RIP. Otrere puts her fingertips on Sisina's gravestone, leaving bloody spots. She slowly runs her fingers over the stone, white marble, on which now shines in red letters: FAVORITA.

I climb onto the cemetery wall, turn the lid of the urn. It pops open, the blast wave stretches out our hair. The villa explodes. Ghosts rush gabbling through the black smoke. Between my hands, ashes erupt into the four winds. They swirl, mixing with the ashes of the burning villa. A few flakes fall and settle gently on our heads. The sun rises and floods the wooded hills and the rocky precipices with golden honey. Magdalena in heaven. She flies and fades away.

AFTERWORD

Some time ago, I was a guest at the scene of a crime. Despite the murder of the young woman having taken place decades ago, people are still talking about it. The ideas and questions for this novel began to sprout from their stories. To what extent does this case from the late 1940s symbolise the countless murders of women and people perceived as women that are committed every day around the world – and how does it differ?

At the core of this novel is the confrontation between the reality of various cases of femicide and their portrayal in society. Some are covered up, similar to Favorita's case in the novel. Those that do become public are usually clichéd depictions that are quickly filed away and, paradoxically, forgotten as isolated cases. And then there are cases like this one, which became one of the biggest media events of the Italian post-war period and which still haunts people: the story of the fictional Sisina is based on this case.

The journalist Paolo Falconi documented the events of 1947 and beyond in his book *La Bella Elvira* (CLD Libri, 2002). This book also provides the source for the fictional newspaper articles in this novel.

Thanks go to L——, who brought this book to my attention and who, at my insistence, stole it from his mother's cupboard. I would also like to thank all the part-time wine growers in the area, the gamekeepers, truffle hunters, martial artists and beauticians who told me their versions of the story, and all my housemates in the haunted Villa who shared my obsession and made fun of it (and let me sleep in their bed on particularly spooky nights). Additionally, I'd like to thank the ghost hunters from TPE and their discussion-loving YouTube followers, as well as Johann Heinrich Jung-Stilling, who wrote the insightful *Theory of Pneumatology* over two hundred years ago.

Thank you Carlo Gori for the unforgettable insight into the world of Metropoliz, the ethical city in the old salami factory.

Thank you to Christina Clemm, Silvia Federici, Alessandro Silj, Giuseppe D'Alema and many others whose knowledge has been incorporated into this novel through their books.

Finally, a huge thank you to the readers of earlier drafts of *Favorita*, who helped it progress through their criticism and enthusiasm: Florian Illies, Laurin Buser, Sophie Steinbeck, Rebecca Gisler, Katharina Volckmer, Jen Calleja, and of course, Ricarda Saul.

*

The author and translator would also like to thank the Hotel Laudinella for providing a translation residency in St. Moritz. We circled the lake, talking, as it froze in the dazzling sun.